Some cause happiness wherever they go; others whenever they go.

Oscar Wilde

Works by Alex Willis

Fiction

The Penitent Heart
The Falcon. The Search for Horus.

DCI Buchanan series.

Buchanan 1. The Bodies in the Marina.
Buchanan 2. The Laminated Man.
Buchanan 3. The Mystery of Cabin 312
Buchanan 4. The Reluctant Jockey
Buchanan 5. Coming 2020

Non-Fiction

Step by Step Guitar Making
Step by Step Guitar Making (Revised and expanded)

The Reluctant Jockey

A DCI Buchanan Mystery

By

Alex Willis

First published in Great Britain by Mount Pleasant Press 2019

The story contained between the covers of this book is a work of fiction, sweat, and perseverance over several years. Characters, place names, locations, and incidents are either the product of the author's imagination or are used fictitiously. Any resemblance to actual persons, living or dead, or locals is entirely coincidental.

ISBN-13: 978 - 1723893742

Text set in Garamond 12 point.

Acknowledgement

I would like to extend my gratitude to the contributors and advertisers in Gallop and Horse and Hounds magazines for providing insight into the world of equine excellence.

This book is dedicated to those men and women who daily lay down their lives to serve their country.

1

Alone

For Julian Du Marchon it had been a defining moment in his career as an independent financial advisor. It wasn't every day one gets an email from the Financial Conduct Authority requesting details of a company's investment plans.

It had arrived just as he'd been packing to fly off to Sofia to take care of some pressing financial arrangements, and it had shaken him to the core. Who'd been talking? Had Sandra Harrison made good on her threat? If so, she needed to be dealt with. Or had one of the investors complained about a poor rate of return?

Had it not been for the email he might not have dreamed up his scheme for one last spin of life's roulette wheel.

♦

For Detective Chief Inspector Buchanan, today was a good day. He'd seen Karen, his wife, and Detective Sergeant Jill Hunter, their daughter, off on the early morning Newhaven ferry.

He was on administration leave and, to while away the time, had booked a week of horse riding, reading, relaxing, and sipping on his favourite malt at Castlewood Country Club. Come hell or high water, nothing was going to get in the way of that.

It was nice to be driving his own car for once he thought as he started the engine and wound down the windows. As he drove off, he pressed the play button on his phone and still marveled at modern technology as the bass thump of Tommy Emmanuel playing, *Deep River Blues* reverberated round the car's interior.

He exited the A22 at the Arlington turn-off and slowed as he approached the entrance to Castlewood Country Club. This was to be his home for the next eight days while the Independent

Office for Police Conduct in Glasgow reviewed the incident of just over a year ago when two men had died under a police car.

Castlewood wasn't difficult to find. A huge, green-painted, wrought-iron fence and gates with the name 'Castlewood' in an arch over the entrance made the club's presence obvious.

Buchanan slowed as he turned onto the gravelled driveway. On each side there were immaculate mowed verges lined with maturing plane trees, looking like soldiers on parade. Two hundred yards along, Buchanan came to a stop for a fox cub as it came out from under a bush. It looked at him, cocked its head, had second thoughts, then ducked back into the bushes and safety.

The grounds could have been laid out by Capability Brown thought Buchanan as he drove slowly up the long driveway past a huge oak tree. Just past the tree, the road meandered down a short hill and over a small humpbacked bridge, with a lake either side of it. Ahead was the Castlewood Country Club building.

His progress was further slowed by a large bright-red horsebox. The name, Branson Racing, was emblazoned in gold lettering across the back and down the length of the vehicle. Buchanan followed at a sedate space, wondering if there could be a connection between this horsebox and the airline owner.

The horsebox turned off at the entrance to the stable block while Buchanan drove on and came to a stop under the magnificent porte-cochere of Castlewood Country Club. As his car came to rest, a valet appeared at the driver's door and opened it.

'Good morning, Mr Buchanan. If you'll let me have the car keys, I'll take your luggage in and park the car for you.'

'You were expecting me?'

'Yes, sir. We were told to look out for you.'

'And how did you recognise me?'

'From your photo in the *Herald*, and your hat is quite distinctive.'

'I'm suitably impressed,' said Buchanan, thinking that Miasma, the *Herald's* crime reporter, had a lot to answer for. 'There's only one case in the boot.'

'Yes, sir.'

Buchanan followed the valet up the stairs, through the varnished mahogany doors and into the reception hall. Ahead and over to the right was a wide pilastered staircase with ancestral portraits of Sir Nathan Greyspear's antecedents adorning the walls. The valet stopped and waited for Buchanan to cross the carpeted floor to the reception desk.

'Jack Buchanan. I have a reservation,' he said to the receptionist, while noticing the painting of Sir Nathan in full military uniform, seated on Moonbeam, still hung on the wall.

'Ah, yes, Sir Nathan said you'd be checking in today. If you'll sign here, Mr Buchanan. Have you stayed with us before?'

'No, I've been here on business a couple of times, but never as a guest.'

'Well, I hope your visit is a pleasant and restful one.'

Buchanan ignored the pen on the desk and reached into his jacket for his Conway Stewart 388. He unscrewed the cap and signed the register in black ink. He smiled to himself, it was strange to hear himself not being referred to as Detective Chief Inspector Buchanan. Was this how he'd feel if he was retired? Did he need a title to feel complete?

'We've put you in room number six, Mr Buchanan,' said the receptionist, as she coded his room key. 'It's a corner room with views out over the western lawns and the stable block. I understand you are here for the riding?'

He nodded. 'Yes, really looking forward to getting out on the cross-country trail.'

'You'll not be lonely.'

'Why is that?'

'It's race week, the first ever Castlewood Cup.'

'I'm not sure I understand you.'

'Sir Nathan has instigated what he hopes to be an annual event. It's a cross-country horse race to raise money for the charity Macmillan Cancer Support UK.'

'How does it work?'

'Those who are invited, pay a fee to enter. Part of the fee goes to cover the prize money and a substantial donation to a charity, plus the winning jockey and trainer get their names on the cup.'

'Does the winner get to keep the cup?'

'No. It will be on perpetual display in the members' bar.'

'How much is the entry fee?' Buchanan asked, thinking he might try to get himself invited. After all it was going to a very worthy cause.

'Twenty thousand pounds per horse entered. But that donation does include full board for the owner and two other guests.'

Oops, thought Buchanan, a bit out of my league. 'Sounds interesting. How many horses are taking part?'

The receptionist looked under the counter and took out a clipboard. 'Now let me see, as I explained, it's by invitation only,' she said, running her well-manicured nail down the list, 'I count twenty competitors all together, but I don't see your name on the list?'

'I'm pleased about that.'

'But I thought you were here to ride?'

'Ride yes, race no. I'm here for a relaxing eight days. I've no intention of competing with anyone,' Buchanan said, grinning.

Up to now his only experience of horses had been at the local stables as a lad, and a mad ride on Mercury here at the club just over a year ago. Now, footloose and fancy free, he could choose to ride every day, or just sit in the library and read, and of course sip on his favourite single malt.

'In that case I wish you a quiet and restful stay, Mr Buchanan,' said the receptionist. 'Your room key works in the members' bar as well. If you go with Max, he will show you to your room.'

'If you'll follow me, Mr Buchanan, we'll use the lift,' said Max, as he picked up Buchanan's room key and suitcase.

'How many bedrooms does the club have?' Buchanan asked, as they rode the lift to the first floor.

'The main building has twenty bedrooms, two of which are sometimes used for other functions.'

Buchanan nodded at the memory of Sir Nathan's wedding and himself being escorted into what was on that day called the morning room.

'There are also rooms in the attics that are used by the live-in staff. Guests never stay in any of those.'

'Where will the jockeys be staying?' Buchanan asked, thinking jockey wages probably didn't extend to staying in the plush surroundings of the country club.

'I understand some will be staying in their horseboxes. A couple have been given rooms in the staff quarters. I had a look at one of the horseboxes that's just arrived. Not like any

motorhome I've ever been in. Room to sleep six, plus stalls for transporting five horses – quite a horsebox.'

'The large red one with Branson Racing on the side?'

'That's the one.'

'Do you think there's any relationship to the airline owner?'

Max shook his head. 'I'm sorry, Mr Buchanan, club rules, staff are not permitted to talk about guests.'

'My fault,' said Buchanan, 'habit of a lifetime, I should know better than to ask. Does the lift go up into the attic?'

'Yes, and also into the basement. It's quite small, only holds six at a time. The kitchen is located in the basement with its own service lift up to the ground floor. Staff are told not to use the guests' lift if guests are waiting for it.' Max stopped in front of the door to room six. 'This is your room,' he said, as he inserted Buchanan's key-card into the lock.

Buchanan walked into the bright and cheerful room, stopped in the middle, looked around and nodded. 'This will do fine.'

'Your bathroom is in here,' said Max, opening a door to the right. 'There's free wi-fi in your room and there is a USB charging socket beside the writing desk. Lights, TV and air-conditioning are controlled by *Alexa*, just ask. Room service is available twenty-four hours a day, just ask *Alexa* for reception.'

'Thanks, Max,' said Buchanan, passing him a two-pound coin. 'I think I'm going like being here very much.'

'Enjoy your stay,' said Max, as he placed Buchanan's room key on the side table and closed the door behind him.

This was a very different situation for Buchanan. Usually when he was away on business it would be for only a couple of nights at the most and then he would just have an overnight bag with a simple change of clothes. On the other occasions when he and Karen travelled, she would take care of the emptying of their suitcases and putting everything away in the drawers and cupboards. He looked at his suitcase sitting on the bed-runner at the foot of his bed, shrugged, and set to emptying its contents.

Suitcase emptied, he hung his jacket in the cupboard, slid on his yellow cardigan and stopped to admire his reflection in the full-length mirror. He briefly turned sideways and realised he might be spending a bit too much time in Starbucks.

Undaunted, he closed the bedroom door behind him and headed for the lift and the members' bar. He pressed the call bell and waited for the lift. It dutifully arrived full with a service trolley overflowing with bed linen and an apologetic young maid. Buchanan put up his hand and said, 'Don't worry, I'll take the stairs.'

Starting down the stairs, he marvelled at the shine on the varnished mahogany handrail and panelling. At the bottom he looked at the reception area, busier than when he'd arrived. He could see through the front doors an airport minibus being emptied of suitcases – probably those of the assembled guests.

A very insistent female voice was talking over the protestations of another guest. 'If you don't mind, we were here before you.'

Buchanan stopped in front of a glass-fronted noticeboard displaying before and after pictures of the main house of the country club. He refocused at the reflection of the group checking in and the growing spectacle. They all looked like they could afford the twenty-thousand-pound entry fee twice over.

At the sound of the raised voices, a smartly-dressed female, the duty manager, thought Buchanan, emerged from a door behind the desk. He continued to watch and listen as the hubbub descended into a murmur of peaceful acquiescence on the part of the complainant. He smiled as the duty manager and the other receptionist checked-in the aggrieved guests.

What sort of holiday was this going to be he wondered, as he recalled the adventure he and Karen had on their recent Dutch canal trip? The memory of his chief suspect and the investigating officer came to mind. Would there be a happy coming together between them, he hoped so, they were perfectly suited to each other.

At least there wouldn't be any crimes for him to investigate here at Castlewood. DI Hanbury was Duty SIO for the duration. PC Hunter was available to help Hanbury if needed, and PC Dexter was taking a couple of weeks off to be with his wife and their latest child. Buchanan could relax and just enjoy the enforced time off.

He refocused on the pictures of the club and decided to ask Sir Nathan when they next met about the transformation of the building. It was clear everyone had gone off to their rooms. He liked that sort of efficiency and turned left into the long corridor. Though not as opulent as rooms in the Portrait Gallery in London, this corridor also had its walls festooned with pictures, mostly of horses going through their paces. He stopped in front of one: it was of Sir Nathan on horseback jumping over a fence at some event. He looked closer and saw by the plaque it was at Badminton.

On his left he thought he recognised two pictures of riders on horseback. Looking closer, he was proved correct. They were of

Aisha Bashir and Deborah Silverstein going through their paces in a dressage competition. The engraved brass plaque underneath said this was taken at last year's Horse of the Year Show at Olympia. He looked away from the pictures and wondered where Karen would put the photo of Jill and Stephen's wedding in the new house; probably in the hallway.

He continued down the corridor and turned right into the area of the members' bar. He was met by a waiter dressed in black and sporting a perfectly tied bowtie.

'Good afternoon, Mr Buchanan.'

'You recognise me?'

'Yes, sir, I have a penchant for remembering faces.'

'You should be a policeman, Lewis,' said Buchanan, reading the waiter's name tag. 'B Lewis, what's the B stand for?'

'Bob. With a surname of Lewis, and being a former policeman, I get called Lewis by most everyone. I was a policeman till I had a leg smashed with a scaffold pole during a bungled robbery in Hackney.'

'When was this?'

'Just going on for five years ago now. Though the bones in my leg mended, I decided maybe frontline policing wasn't for me. I applied for a transfer to CID but was turned down.'

'You got caught in the staffing freeze?'

'Yes,' he said, nodding.

'How did you manage to end up here?'

'After I left the force, I grabbed the first job that was offered. Bit of a strange transition going from a ten-year policeman to that of being a wine waiter.'

'How did you get to be working at Castlewood?'

'The first event I worked at was at a large garden party in a winery in Sussex. That was followed by a posh wedding in Chelsea, then up to Scotland and a boat launch in Greenock. And I thought I was done being a policeman!'

'Why, what happened?'

'The security company had a problem with some of their team missing a train, so I volunteered to do a stint till they got there.'

'What were your duties?'

'All I had to do was to stand beside the gangway looking smart and check invitations.'

'So how did you end up working for Sir Nathan?'

'A couple of guests had a bit too much to drink and started bothering Sir Nathan's wife. Without thinking I stepped in and resolved the situation. When the atmosphere calmed down Sir Nathan came over and thanked me. We had a short discussion about my past occupation and when he found out I had been a policeman, he offered me this job.'

'As a wine waiter, Lewis?' asked Buchanan.

'My main responsibilities are for the club security, and that of the guests when visiting the club.'

'Even serving at the bar?'

'Here at Castlewood we work as a team. I don't mind working behind the bar.'

'And I suppose you can eavesdrop on conversations?'

'I suppose if this was a detective novel, you could say I sometimes work under cover. No, the real reason is Sir Nathan said to keep an eye out for you; he said things happen when you're around.'

'Is that really what he said?'

'Yes, sir.'

'Interesting comment.'

'We're also a bit short on staff. We don't normally have so many guests booking in at one time.'

'That makes sense.'

'Can I get you something to drink?'

'Yes, please, could I have a whisky and water?'

'Do you have a preference for a particular distillery?'

'Do you have Lagavulin?'

'I'm sure we do. Where would you like to sit?'

'The library looks quiet; I'll sit in there.'

'If you go through, I'll have Karl bring you your drink. Can I have your room number?'

'Six.'

'Thank you, Mr Buchanan.'

There it was again, *Mr Buchanan* thought Buchanan. No matter how often he rolled the name round his mind like his anticipated whisky, he couldn't bring himself to be just called Mr Buchanan; Detective Chief Inspector Buchanan was who he was, though he did realise he would have to retire someday – but not just yet.

There were several well-read newspapers on a table to his left as he entered the room. He paused and glanced through the selection. On the top of the pile was *The Guardian*. He looked at the front page and grinned when he saw the article about teachers going on strike again. In the end he picked up copies of the *Eastbourne Herald* and *The Telegraph*.

He chose a leather Chesterfield chair in the corner of the room beside the window overlooking the driveway and waited for his whisky. The *Eastbourne Herald* was first, and he saw with great interest that the sheik had purchased Hastings pier. Good for him thought Buchanan, if anyone could turn round the fortunes of the pier, the sheik could.

'Mr Buchanan, your drink,' said the waiter, placing a glass with a small jug of water on the table beside the chair.

'Thanks, Karl.'

'Can I get you anything else?'

Buchanan thought for a moment, then realised he'd missed lunch. 'Is there such a thing as a bar menu?'

'Yes, there is, shall I get you one?'

'Please.'

'I'll be right back.'

Buchanan ordered a cheese and pickle sandwich and a packet of plain crisps.

He was halfway through an article on policing in *The Telegraph* when the sound of the insistent female voice interrupted his reading of the newspaper.

'Really, Margo, he actually said that to Penny – oops, sorry, didn't realise anyone was in here,' said the owner of the voice. '*She's a bit hard of hearing, need to talk loud on the phone,*' she mouthed. 'Look. Margo, something's come up, I'll call you later,' she said, pressing the hang-up button on her phone. 'Sorry to disturb you. Cynthia Mountjoy.'

'That's all right, Cynthia, my name is Jack Buchanan,' he said, putting down his paper. 'I was about to order another drink; can I get you something from the bar?'

Cynthia's reply was pre-empted by the arrival of the waiter. 'You wish something, Mrs Mountjoy?'

'Yes. Do you make cocktails?'

'I don't, but Daniel, our barman, can.'

'In that case can I have a martini?'

'Mr Buchanan?'

'I'll have the same again, please.'

'Are you here for the racing, Jack?' asked Cynthia.

He shook his head and smiled. 'Not quite. I'm taking time off work. I will be riding, but not racing.'

'On holiday?'

'No, just taking time off.'

'Been unwell?'

'I was involved in a bad car accident a few months ago.'

'Your drinks,' said the waiter. 'Where shall I put them?'

'Over here,' said Cynthia, as she moved a selection of *Horse and Hound* magazines to the side of the coffee table. 'Let's sit by the fireside, so nice to have a fire on these late spring days,' she said, as she went to sit on the settee. Buchanan chose the single armchair to her right.

As she sat, she crossed her legs, not embarrassed by the fact that her short skirt showed off quite a bit of her long shapely legs.

She took a sip of her drink and smiled at Buchanan. 'You said you were involved in a car accident a few months ago, and you're still not back at work. It must have been a very bad accident.'

'Oh, I've been back to work since the accident.'

'Then if it's not the accident, and you're not on holiday, have you been a naughty boy?'

A quick thinker thought Buchanan. 'There was an incident at work a couple of years ago that was supposed to be closed, but someone who wanted to create trouble for me had it reopened.'

'So, you *have* been a naughty boy! What did you do?'

'It's not what I did – two men died because of their own foolishness.'

She took a large gulp of her cocktail, leaned forward, showing off her ample bosom and asked, 'Did you kill them?'

'No, I was in a bar having a drink and watching football when they tried to pick a fight with me. Someone called the police and, when they heard the siren, they ran out of the pub and got run over by the police car responding to the call.'

'Were you hurt?'

'I woke up in Glasgow Infirmary.'

'Not a very lucky boy, are you, Jack?'

'Life has its moments. What about you, are you here for the race?'

'Sort of. My husband has brought three of our horses with us.'

'Why three horses? He can't ride all three at once.'

'Two of them are for racing, the third is my horse, Doxy. Our jockey will try the two racehorses and ride the fastest of the two in the race, my husband will ride the second fastest. I get left out, as usual.'

'But you said it was your own horse?'

She shrugged. 'Yes, so I did. Still feels like a case of leftovers, though.'

'You employ a jockey?'

'Yes, Pat McCall. Heard of him?'

Buchanan shook his head. 'I don't know much about horse racing. Other than a mad ride here last year it has been many years since I last rode. Will you be riding in the race?'

She nodded, 'Yes, but not competing, I prefer a different kind of sport. Look, since you aren't racing, we must get you back in the saddle and out for a quiet ride, I understand there are many quiet bridleways through the forest we can try. My husband won't have any time for me while he is involved with the race preparations, and I don't intend to spend the week on my own.'

'We'll see,' said Buchanan, wondering how he was going to extract himself from an increasingly uncomfortable situation.

His rescuer was in the form of Cynthia's husband, Colonel Mountjoy.

'Ah, there you are, thought I'd find you in the bar.'

'How's Turpin?'

'Fine. Pat said all three of them had travelled well. Pat's looking after them till the lads get here. He's giving them a good brushing down before putting them into their stalls.'

'Good. Victor,' said Cynthia, motioning to Buchanan, 'this is Jack, he's going to take care of me while you and the boys are busy with the horses.'

Buchanan raised his hands, smiled, and said, 'Jack Buchanan. Mrs Mountjoy has misunderstood me. I'm here on a rest break. I will be riding, but I'm not involved in the racing. In fact, I didn't even know there was a race till I heard from the reception desk when I checked in.'

'That's just like Cynthia, picking up the strays,' said the colonel, guffawing, while staring at his wife.

In all his years as a policeman, Buchanan had become quite good at reading facial expressions and, although the colonel's words to his wife were that of endearment, his face carried an expression Buchanan had only ever seen in faces of men one step away from a desperate, irreversible, act of violence. Not a good omen for the week's upcoming events.

'Dear,' said the colonel, 'I'll be wearing my tux to dinner this evening, make sure my shirt is properly ironed, must make a good impression. Can't have Jackson showing me up – again, can we? Good day, Jack, maybe see you at dinner.'

Buchanan glanced at Cynthia. The colour in her face was slowly changing from the red of an angry sunrise to the grey of an approaching storm.

She did her best to smile at Buchanan then said, 'That's my husband, ever on parade.'

'Who's this Jackson he was referring to?'

'The Jackson my husband was referring to is Major Andrew Jackson; you may have noticed him, he's the only male black face at the event.'

'I'm sorry, Cynthia, I'm colour blind.'

She looked at Buchanan, then nodded, 'I see. Wish my husband was. He can be a real embarrassment when we go to functions. I keep telling him that one day someone will really take offence at what he says.'

'Other than the issue of Major Jackson's colour, is there is anything else between Victor and him?'

'Andrew is an army lawyer, just like Victor. Though Victor is senior in age, Andrew is senior by rank, and a far better advocate.'

'And that's why Victor is so angry with Major Jackson?'

She shook her head gently while sipping on her drink. 'No, not quite. About four years ago, in Bielefeld, Germany, Victor was defending a black soldier who had been accused of raping a local girl. Andrew was Victor's junior in the case. Despite Andrew's excellent advocacy, Victor believed the soldier was guilty and made sure the case was lost.'

'That must have been a blow to Major Jackson.'

'It was more than that, the soldier hung himself the first night in cells.'

'What did Victor have to say about that?'

'Just shrugged and said the suicide was an admission of guilt, he'd got what he deserved.'

'How about Major Jackson?'

'He was furious, not just because it was a stain on his career, he really believed the soldier was innocent. But the real reason for Andrew's anger was the young soldier was his nephew. In fact, so sure was he about the soldier's innocence, he instigated a reopening of the trial and, when new evidence was presented, the soldier was found not guilty.'

'What evidence was that?'

'A guilty confession from the girl's former boyfriend.'

'So that's why your husband dislikes Andrew so much.'

'Not as much as Andrew dislikes Victor. Excuse me, will you, Jack? I've got a shirt to iron, catch you later.'

Buchanan returned to his chair with his drink to think. Just what was going on between Victor Mountjoy and his wife, and Victor Mountjoy and Andrew Jackson? Whatever it was, he didn't want any part of it. He was at Castlewood to be inconspicuous, go riding alone, and to read. He didn't want any part of whatever Cynthia Mountjoy had in mind. Or the animosity between the colonel and the major.

He glanced at the coffee table and saw, under the pile of *Horse and Hound* magazines, a copy of *Gallop,* a horse owners' magazine he wasn't familiar with. He picked it up then returned to his chair. Looking through the magazine he saw it was a world he knew nothing about. He flicked through the pages and saw through a window onto a world of equine profligacy.

The waiter returned to tidy the tables and asked Buchanan, 'All well, Mr Buchanan? Can I get you something from the bar?'

'Er, yes please, Karl. I'll have another whisky.'

He returned a few minutes later with Buchanan's drink.

'Thanks,' said Buchanan. 'Do you know what time dinner is served this evening?'

'Normally the restaurant opens for dinner at six. This week times have changed to enable guests to take care of their horses. The main dining room has been booked for race contestants and their guests for the duration of the race event. This evening Sir Nathan will be welcoming all the contestants. Dinner will be served starting at seven.'

'Where will those guests that are not here for the event be eating?'

'Tables will be set in the bar.'

'Oh, I suppose that's where I'll be eating.'

Karl shook his head. 'You are to be Sir Nathan's guest at his table. Lewis had us all look over the guest list this morning, so we would know who was who.'

'Smart man.'

Buchanan returned to his magazine. Being this close to real thoroughbred horses, their trainers and jockeys gave him a whole new appreciation of the equine world. He never realised that some horse owners didn't just own horses and stables, they also owned the tracks that they raced their horses on. He looked at the houses for sale section and at houses with stables and riding rings. Prices in the multiple millions had him shaking his head in disbelief. Who could afford such prices? Some of the American horse ranches had stables for twenty horses.

Then a thought struck him, here he was at Castlewood Country Club, one of the most prestigious privately-owned country clubs in the UK. The main building had a members' library, guest bar, restaurant and a ballroom, plus at least four meeting rooms. Guest accommodation consisted of twenty double bedrooms, all with en-suites. The main stable block had stalls for at least twenty horses, and that didn't count the stalls in the adjacent indoor exercise ring; all owned by one man: Sir Nathan Greyspear.

Buchanan liked Greyspear. Whereas Buchanan was a career policeman, Greyspear had spent many years in the British army, and now ran one of the world's most prestigious yacht-building companies. Though they had both served their country in their respective organisations, and Greyspear outranked Buchanan, a genuine and lasting friendship had grown between them.

2

The Cast

Buchanan spent the rest of the afternoon reading through *Gallop* and saw, to his surprise, the upcoming Castlewood Cup referred to in one of the articles. It went on to say several American owners had entered horses.

At six o'clock Buchanan left the library to go up to his room to change for dinner. As he walked across the entrance hall, he saw three people waiting for the lift. The most noticeable was a tall, salt-and-pepper-haired man talking to a very attractive, tall, blonde woman who had a shorter version standing beside her – the daughter, thought Buchanan.

To Buchanan, the man's voice sounded like that of a television announcer, then he heard the accent and changed his mind to thinking he could be a politician, or even be one of those American preachers that Karen used to like watching on the internet.

'Good evening,' said Buchanan, to no one in particular.

'Oh, hi,' said the woman. 'Oh my, you have such a cute accent! Where's it from?'

'It's not from anywhere, thank you. I was born with it,' replied Buchanan.

'And where might that be?'

> *'My heart's in the highlands*
> *But my body stands here*
> *Missing your arms*
> *Wishing you were here.'*

'Oh, you're a poet!'

Buchanan smiled. 'Actually, it's Glasgow, Scotland,' he replied.

'Do you wear a kilt?' she asked, with a huge smile on her face.

'Not recently, and before you ask, yes I do.'

The conversation was cut short by the arrival of the lift. Buchanan stood to the side as the three guests entered. The man, with shoulders as wide as a barn door and hands big enough to pick up a melon one-handed, being about six foot-four, had to duck under the lift door opening. Buchanan stepped in and stood with his back to the door, still wondering about the man's occupation. Was he a professional wrestler or, since he had an American accent, an American football player?'

'Travis Grant,' said the man, smiling and extending his hand to shake Buchanan's. 'This is my wife, Shelly, and our daughter, Poppy. Please excuse my wife. She's seen all the Downton Abbey films and is nuts about anything to do with England.'

Another husband with an unguided wife, thought Buchanan. 'Glasgow is actually in Scotland, Mrs Grant, and my name is Jack Buchanan.'

'Gee, how about that, and both of us with Scotch surnames.'

'Are you here for the race, Jack?' asked Travis.

Here we go again thought Buchanan, wondering how many times he would have to answer the same question this week. 'No, I'm here for a week's relaxation, it's been a tough year. How about you?'

'Our church just reached the twenty-thousand membership target I set three years ago, and the elders, in gratitude, said I deserved a month off for all my hard work. So, I packed up a couple of my best mares and headed over the pond. You go to church, Jack?'

'No, but my wife sometimes does.'

'You should try it, get to know the man upstairs.'

'You're a minister?' asked Buchanan.

'Pastor, shepherd the flock.'

'And you have twenty-thousand members in your church?'

'At the last count, twenty thousand and growing.'

'Must be a large building to hold that many.'

'Five services on Sunday morning. Sunday school in the afternoon, then a traditional service in the evening.'

'And you run the church?'

'Absolutely. But I do have ten assistant pastors to help out.'

'You must have studied hard at seminary to get qualified to run a church that big.'

Travis shook his head. 'Seminary was fine. I also got my degree in business administration from Stanford.'

'But –'

'It's like this, Jack. When the Lord calls, he equips.'

The 'doors opening' announcement saved Buchanan from further questioning.

'See you at dinner, Jack,' said Travis, as Buchanan exited the lift, turned to his right and started down the corridor to his room. He managed two steps before he realised the Grant family were going in the same direction.

'I usually ride quarter horses,' began Travis, 'but when I saw the competition advertised in *Gallop,* I said to myself it was God's blessing for all my hard work. So, I thought, why not give it a try? I've got nothing to lose by entering.'

Best mares, thought Buchanan as he listened to the chatter between mother and daughter as they walked together one step behind.

Travis Grant stopped outside room eight. 'Eight. This is your room, Poppy; your mom and I are next door in room seven.' He was quiet for a moment then smiled and declared in his best preacher's voice, 'The Lord is surely good to me, another omen, we're in room seven, the perfect number.'

Buchanan shook his head and continued to his own room. He was about to close the door when he heard a familiar voice, that of Cynthia Mountjoy.

'Hurry up, Victor. I need a bath before dinner.'

20

Buchanan peeked through the gap in his almost closed bedroom door and saw Colonel Mountjoy, following Cynthia, enter room five. He was bracketed by the Grants in room seven, and the Mountjoys in room five. He felt the peace of the week ahead disappearing like the setting sun.

♦

18:30

Buchanan showered, shaved and dressed for dinner. He wasn't sure quite what to wear but assumed since there would be Americans at dinner he could dress quite casually, but not too casual. He chose grey slacks, white shirt, a plain blue tie and his blazer with his name tag clipped neatly to his right lapel. It felt a bit odd to be wearing a name tag to dinner, but he assumed whoever was organising the event wanted to make sure everyone knew each other. His only acquiescence to anonymity was to wear his Glasgow Rangers supporters' cufflinks.

♦

18:50

He closed his door and sauntered along the corridor towards the lift. He'd gone five steps when a hand grabbed his elbow. It was Cynthia Mountjoy.

'On your own, Jack?'

'I thought you'd be ironing a shirt?'

'Nah. His shirt was pressed before we got here. All he had to do was hang it up when he took it out of the suitcase. His comment about having his shirt pressed was his way of trying to put me in my place.'

'And do you need to be put in your place?'

'Frequently, would you like to apply for the position?'

'If you don't mind me asking, where is your husband?'

'Probably still standing before the mirror asking, *mirror, mirror, on the wall, who's the smartest of them all? And why am I?*'

To Buchanan's relief as they reached the lift, they were joined by two other guests, Shelly and Poppy Grant.

'You guys go ahead,' said Buchanan. 'I'll take the stairs.'

He saw a fleeting glint of sadness in Cynthia Mountjoy's eyes, before she recovered and said, 'See you at dinner, Jack.'

As he slowly descended the stairs, in his mind he listened again to the sound of Cynthia Mountjoy's voice and saw the look in her face. It made him realise she was a very lonely and vulnerable woman.

Buchanan turned right at the bottom of the staircase and followed a couple across the reception floor towards the dining room. He was greeted at the door by Lewis.

'Good evening, Mr Buchanan. If you'll follow me, I'll show you to your table.'

As Buchanan followed Lewis past the tables, he began to get an idea of just how big this event was going to be. Not only were the horse owners dining, but the grooms, jockeys and trainers were also in attendance. There was quite an excited buzz coming from the tables as he passed:

'The stalls are so clean, and the staff are so friendly …'

'The M1 was a nightmare, it took us two hours to go five miles, we stopped at Toddington and waited till the jam cleared …'

'Arthur said he'd leave me in the dust, I bet him twenty quid he'd never get past the water …'

'The damn horse got colic last week, it was touch and go whether she would be ready to race this week …'

'I caught him in the act, told him I'd castrate him if he ever did that again …'

Most of the guests were already seated though there were a few stragglers still in the bar. Debbie Silverstein saw him and waved, he waved back. She was seated at one of the large round tables with her parents, as was her friend, Aisha Bashir, and her parents. The number was made up with the airline owners, the Carstairs.

As he worked his way towards the head table Buchanan saw that although most tables were set for eight, this one was set for ten. To his dismay he found the Mountjoys had been seated there and, interestingly, he'd been placed between Cynthia Mountjoy and Susan Greyspear. Beside Nathan Greyspear and his wife, Buchanan recognised Travis and Shelly Grant and their daughter Poppy.

As he sat, he smiled and introduced himself to Dean and Shelly Branson, the other couple at the table. 'Jack Buchanan, here for a rest.'

Cynthia was busy looking at the menu but looked up as Buchanan sat down. Her face lit up with a huge smile when she saw who had just joined her.

'Jack, how nice to see you again.'

Buchanan glanced at her husband. His face was not pleased.

'Good evening, Mrs Mountjoy, Colonel,' said Buchanan, as he noticed how smart the colonel looked in his Tuxedo. Cynthia had indeed done an excellent job on her husband's shirt.

'Good evening, Jack,' said Susan. 'How are Karen and Jill?'

'They're fine, gone to see Karen's mother. They should be back in a couple of days.'

'Where does your mother-in-law live?' asked Cynthia.

'In France, just outside Dieppe.'

'Good evening, Mr Buchanan. I don't recall seeing your name on the list of entrants?' said Colonel Mountjoy, looking up from his menu to see who his wife was talking to.

'It's Jack, Colonel, and your observation is quite correct. I'm not here for the event.'

'Jack's just out of hospital, Victor,' said Cynthia. 'He's recovering from a very bad accident. Two men died.'

It never failed to interest Buchanan how witnesses to a situation often got the events muddled when retelling what they remembered. A situation often exploited by barristers.

Mountjoy glanced back at Buchanan, assessing what he was seeing. 'Two men died?'

Buchanan looked round at the faces at the table; they were all staring at him. He smiled and took a deep breath.

'I had nothing to do with the deaths of the two men. I was minding my own business when they assaulted me. They left me for dead, ran off out of the pub and stepped out into the street, where they were run over by a police car. My recent visit to hospital was because I swerved to avoid an oncoming car causing me to hit a tree. See, nothing sinister about it.'

'Oh,' said Cynthia, as the rest of the diners returned to looking at their menus.

'You're a bit accident-prone,' said Mountjoy.

'That's life. You play with the cards life deals you.'

'Then why are you at this table?' asked Mountjoy.

'Because he's my guest,' said Greyspear.

'Oops, sorry, Jack. Do you ride?'

'Yes, Colonel, I do, but not good enough to race. I'll leave that to those much more experienced than me. I'm only here to unwind and get the cobwebs out of my head, it's been a very busy year'

'Wise man, Jack. Leave the racing to the professionals, that's what I always say.'

'What do you do, Jack?' asked one of the guests opposite.

Buchanan smiled as he read the name tag and once again wondered if there was any relationship between them and the Branson of the airline fame. 'Good evening, Angela. I'm afraid it's nothing as glamorous as what the colonel does, I'm just a civil servant.'

'So, what brought you down here to Sussex?' said Mountjoy. 'Could it have anything to do with the two men who died under a police car?'

'Victor,' said Cynthia, 'you're not prosecuting tonight, give it a rest.'

'That's all right, Cynthia. Don't fret over it,' said Buchanan.

'I'm sorry, Jack,' said Cynthia. 'Victor's job in the army is that of a lawyer; he sometimes forgets when he's not on base.'

'No offence taken, Colonel. I'm used to it, it's all part of the job,' said Buchanan, winking at Greyspear.

'Will Karen be joining you at Castlewood when she returns from seeing her mother, Jack?' asked Susan.

'She hasn't decided. She may go over to our new house to get the measurements for curtains and decide where everything will be going.'

'What do you do, Dean?' asked Cynthia.

'I'm a doctor.'

'What of?'

'I'm an orthopaedic surgeon.'

'What does that entail?' asked Cynthia.

'I perform a lot of operations on hips and knees, plus soft tissue repairs.'

'Ever work on horses?' asked Mountjoy.

'No, Colonel, I haven't. Though there are some similarities in structure and articulation.'

Mountjoy nodded then turned and looked at Travis. 'I take it you're here for the race?'

Travis nodded and took a sip from his glass. 'Been a long time since I was in the UK, it's great to be back.'

'When were you last here?' asked Greyspear.

'Quite a few years ago. I was passing through on my final deployment in Afghanistan.'

'You were in the armed forces?' said Mountjoy.

'I was a colonel in the US Marines.'

'Oh.'

'Victor,' said Greyspear, 'how are your horses, travel okay?'

'Ah – oh, the horses, yes, they're fine. Checked them an hour ago; Pat, our jockey, will keep an eye on them during the night.'

'Are we ready to order?' asked the waiter, who'd been hovering in the background.

'I believe we are, André,' said Greyspear.

'I'll have the soup, followed by the rib-eye steak,' said Mountjoy, ignoring the normal etiquette of letting the ladies order first.

Buchanan smiled to himself, thankful he was no longer of any interest to the others at the table. He patiently waited for them to order.

♦

The food was served and eaten without incident, though more than once during the meal Buchanan felt Cynthia's hand brush against his leg and give his knee a squeeze.

Finally, with desserts eaten and coffee and brandy served, Greyspear stood and tapped his teaspoon against an empty wine glass. As he did so, a large projector screen descended from the ceiling.

When the general hubbub of after-dinner conversation descended to a quiet chatter, Greyspear began his address.

'Ladies and gentlemen – if I could have your attention for a few moments? I won't keep you long. Firstly, I would like to welcome you all to Castlewood Country Club and the inaugural Castlewood Cup. As I'm sure you are all aware, the race is to take place on Saturday afternoon. Should give you all time to familiarise yourselves with the jumps. The course will be closed to horses on Monday morning, this will enable those of you who wish to walk the course to do so without having to watch for riders.

'If I can draw your attention to the map of the course shown here on the screen. You will notice that the cross-country course passes right round the perimeter of the golf course. Of course, those of you who arrived by private plane will already have had a glance of the course, and I hope you paid attention to the information on how short the landing strip is.

'The golf course will be open to golfers during the event. It is highly unlikely that you will have any issues with the golfers as the golf course is designed to keep the play within the bounds of the golf course. For those of you who wish to use the golf course, access is from the clubhouse and the public bar.

'Starting tomorrow morning there will be a notice board set up in the reception. On the board you will find the times that the course will be open for practise rides; during those times, only competitors' horses will be permitted on the course. Also, on the board will be a complete list of owners, riders and horses' names. You'll also see details of any changes to the week's programme.

'For those of you who wish a quieter ride, there are many bridleways through Arlington Forest. There is a map of the bridleways in your programme. You'll see they are all named after trees; that should help to orientate yourselves. On Saturday evening there will be the prize-giving ball and I have the honour to announce that we will be entertained by the Dave Bennett Swing Band. I will be in the bar after dinner if anyone has questions,' said Greyspear, before sitting down.

'Sir Nathan,' said Shelly, 'I've been dying to ask, how old is Castlewood?'

'In its original form Castlewood is reputed to have had its foundations laid sometime between 1745 and 1750. The Jacobite rebellion had just been crushed and peace and security had returned to the countryside. It was the historic seat of the Hamsworth family,' explained Greyspear, nodding to the waiter that they needed more brandy. 'They lived in the house for several generations.'

'Are any of the family still alive?' asked Buchanan.

'No. During the 18th century,' continued Greyspear, 'the Hamsworth family had been successful farmers supplying produce to the London and local Sussex markets. Their produce was so well appreciated that it frequently graced the dinner table at Windsor Castle. As a sign of appreciation, James Hamsworth was created the 1st Earl of Arlington. He took his title from a now extinct line of the family on his grandmother's side.

'Arlington? So that's where the town got its name from,' said Dean. 'I thought it was named after the racetrack.'

'Not quite, said Greyspear.

'What's that?' said Mountjoy, looking like he'd just woken up. 'Another racetrack? Is it available to ride on?'

Greyspear smiled. 'Sorry, Colonel, it's not that kind of racetrack. This one is used for car racing, mostly what's called destruction derbies.'

'Wrong kind of horsepower, dear,' said Cynthia, patting the back of the colonel's hand. 'Why don't you go back to your port and leave the conversation to those of us who are listening?'

Buchanan looked at Greyspear's face then at Cynthia. Greyspear grinned while Cynthia made a face at her husband then said, 'Please continue, Sir Nathan, some of us are interested in what you have to say.'

'The first Earl had been quite content with the family home, but his eldest son, Edward, the second Earl, had grander ideas. Returning from a visit to Hampton Court Palace, Edward decided that the existing family home was not in keeping with his now perceived elevated position in society. The local family firm of Baldocks was engaged to design and construct Edward's idea of a suitable edifice. Originally it was to have been a simple alteration and enlargement of the existing house but, by the time Edward had finished pondering and changing his mind, the original building had been incorporated into a small section at the rear of the new stately house.'

'What about the grounds? Who designed them?' asked Angela.

'At one time, this part of England was heavily wooded, mostly with oak, and other hardwoods such as ash, beech and birch. Over time, the oak was commandeered by the
government for shipbuilding. This left many acres of land to be turned into either farmland, or country estates.'

'Is that what happened here?' asked Angela.

'More or less. Hunting became a passion for the wealthy landowner and this estate was no exception. If you choose to ride in the forest you will find several bridleways through what remains of the forest. These bridleways are separate from the cross-country trail. They are very secluded, and one can experience a great deal of excitement when riding through them at speed.'

'I might have a go at one of them tomorrow,' said Angela.

'Would you like company?' asked Cynthia.

'Yes, certainly, the more the merrier.'

'How about you, Jack? Fancy a fast ride through the forest?' asked Cynthia.

Buchanan shook his head. 'No thanks, Cynthia. I plan to sleep late, then have a leisurely breakfast while reading the newspaper.'

'When did the estate become a club?' asked Mountjoy, motioning to the waiter to refill his glass.

'Sometime in the late forties, just after the war. The estate had been used to billet troops prior to their departure for the front. It was also used as a hospital. But sadly, the owner was killed in the D-day landings and there were no heirs to take over the running of the estate. It lay idle till a few wealthy businessmen got together and purchased the estate and turned it into a not very successful club.'

'Is that how you found it?' asked Travis.

'Yes. In the early days the club had a very exclusive membership; they had at one time half the British cabinet as members. Most visitors would arrive by train at Hailsham station with a short taxi ride to the club. Unfortunately, due to the short-sightedness of Dr Beeching, the Hailsham station came under his axe and was permanently closed.

'The club continued to operate till the late fifties when the cost of maintaining the buildings and grounds started to escalate beyond its financial abilities. So, unfortunately for the members, the club closed, and the building and grounds were put up for sale.'

'Is that when you bought it?' asked Shelly.

'No. The estate went through several owners before I purchased it. It was quite run down and took the best part of two years to bring it up to the standard you see today.'

'Well, I think it's lovely,' said Angela. 'I'm so looking forward to my stay.'

'Are you riding in the race, Angela?' asked Colonel Mountjoy.

'Yes. I can't wait to get out on Stargazer.'

'Please excuse the question, Dean,' said Cynthia, 'but are you related to Richard Branson?'

'If I had a pound for every time I'm asked that question! No, sorry, there's no relationship,' replied Dean Branson, standing. 'I'm just a doctor. See you all at breakfast, we've had a long drive today and I want to be up early in the morning.

Buchanan glanced round the restaurant and saw most of the diners had already left. 'If you'll excuse me, I think I'll have a drink in the bar before I turn in for the night.'

'An excellent idea,' said Mountjoy, as he rolled his shoulders. 'Cynthia, will you be joining me?'

She looked round the near-empty restaurant and shook her head. 'No, I think I'll go and check on the horses first, don't wake me when you come up.'

Buchanan rose from the table and followed Mountjoy and one of the other diners through to the bar. He watched as Mountjoy hustled his way to the front and ordered his and his friend's drinks. As the crowd at the bar left with their drinks, Buchanan ordered his and retired to his chair in the corner of the library.

Reclining in his chair, he took a sip of his whisky. As he did so he could hear the unmistakable sound of Mountjoy's voice talking to the other diner.

'So far so good, Julian,' said Mountjoy.

'I'm glad to hear that. With what we've got invested you can't afford to fail.'

'Oh, I won't, don't you worry about that.'

'Remember, you're not the only one relying on this deal. I'll catch up with you shortly, I'm going outside for a cigarette.'

Buchanan downed his drink and headed for bed. To his discomfort, when he arrived at the lift, Cynthia Mountjoy was also waiting.

'Lovely dinner,' she said to Buchanan.

'Yes, I enjoyed it very much.'

The lift arrived and Buchanan ushered Cynthia into it, then followed her in and leaned back against the lift door. As the lift started upwards, Cynthia lost her balance and fell forward against Buchanan.

'You smell nice,' she said, looking up at him as he gently pushed her away.

'It's my cologne, a Christmas present from my wife.'

'You said she was still in France?' said Cynthia, as she leaned against the far wall of the lift.

'She's visiting with her mother; she's not been well.'

'Why didn't you go with her?'

'I had to be here for the furniture movers. They are delivering our furniture to our new house on Thursday.'

'So, you're all alone for the week?'

'Looks that way.'

'I know what it's like to be lonely,' she said, smiling at Buchanan while running the tip of her tongue round her lips. 'Being married to Victor does that to one. You know there are some days when we hardly say a word to each other? We're just simply poles apart.'

Buchanan smiled and said

> *'Like North and South*
> *That cling together*
> *North to North and*
> *South to South*
> *Oft grow asunder'*

31

'Nice analogy' said Cynthia. 'We don't even come close. At home we sleep in separate rooms. He says I snore and keep him awake.'

The lift came to a halt and the door opened. Buchanan stepped aside and ushered Cynthia out onto the landing.

'Do you fancy a nightcap?' she asked, as they walked down the corridor to their respective rooms.

Buchanan stopped in front of his room, took out his key and unlocked his door. He turned to her and said, 'I'm sorry, Cynthia, but I need a full night's sleep. Good night.'

She stood looking at him, shrugged and said, 'Maybe another time? Sleep well.'

Buchanan shut his door and walked into the middle of the moonlit bedroom. The room was too warm to sleep in so, instead of turning on the air conditioning, he opened the window and stepped out onto the small balcony looking out onto the grounds of Castlewood. In the distance he could see the flag of the eighteenth hole flapping gently in the moonlight. Just beyond that and to the right he could see the marquee that had been set up in front of the start-finish line of the race.

The sound of footsteps and voices caught his attention. He leaned over the balcony and looked below. He was able to make out the form of Colonel Mountjoy and one other person. Buchanan leaned further to hear what was being said.

'I want *you* to stay with Turpin and Rambler tonight. I don't want anyone bothering them.'

'What, you mean you want me to –'

'Sleep with the damn horses if necessary. I don't want anyone going near them, especially tonight. You know how funny they can be after a long drive.'

'But why would anyone want to go near them?'

'Never mind, just keep an eye on them, sleep in the stable if you have to. Just make sure no one goes near them, you hear?'

'What about tomorrow, who's going to keep an eye on them then?'

'Don't worry about tomorrow, George and Lenny will be here then.'

'Where will you be if I need you?'

'In bed, where do you think I'll be?'

'Just wondered – you know?'

'That's none of your business, now get to work or I'll find another jockey.'

Well, well, what do we have here, wondered Buchanan, as Mountjoy turned and went back into the bar. The one referred to as the jockey stepped out of the shadows and walked round the corner of the building. His curiosity aroused; Buchanan went over to the other window on his right. He opened it and watched as Colonel Mountjoy's jockey descended the veranda steps and carefully made his way along the covered walkway towards the stable block.

Buchanan was about to turn away when he saw the figure of another person, someone he thought he recognised, following the jockey. It was Cynthia Mountjoy! Did she also want to make sure no one went near their horses? Or was she looking for company since Buchanan wouldn't play ball?

Just as Buchanan was about to leave the window, two other figures came out from the bar. One was Colonel Mountjoy; Buchanan didn't recognise the other. The newcomer said in a low voice, 'I've been waiting for you, we have things to discuss. Let's go for a walk.'

Buchanan watched as they walked away from the building, out of the light of the ground's floodlights and into the shadows of the hedges that bounded the tennis courts.

Buchanan undressed, climbed into bed and pulled the blankets over his shoulders, wondering how Cynthia would go about helping the jockey watch the horses.

3

Act 1

06:55

Buchanan woke just before seven and dozed until eight, realising he hadn't slept this late in a long time. He asked *Alexa* to turn on the television for the news and weather and at eight-twenty he rolled out of bed, put his dressing gown on and went to the door. He opened it slowly and saw that the night porter had delivered his newspaper. As he stood with the newspaper under his arm, he saw a rather dishevelled Cynthia Mountjoy walking towards him. She grinned and put her index finger up to her lips. Buchanan nodded sagely and returned to his room.

He shaved, dressed, picked up his newspaper from the dressing table and went down to his much-anticipated breakfast. Most weekdays, breakfast would consist of either a bowl of porridge washed down with a cup of reheated coffee, or a sticky bun and coffee from Starbucks.

Today it was going to be different. From the moment he'd been put on administrative leave, he'd planned this week to himself. His breakfast menu had been meticulously planned. Today he would start with a small bowl of grapefruit segments, complete with a sprinkling of white sugar, next he would have the full English, consisting of, two fried eggs with soft yolks, beans, two sausages, two rashers of bacon, black pudding as a substitute for haggis, and fried bread. Then he'd finish with a pot of tea and toast and marmalade, all this while slowly working his way through the newspaper.

As he closed his door, he sensed a presence behind him and saw his quiet breakfast float away from him.

'Thanks,' said a voice, from behind him.

He didn't have to look back, he knew who belonged to the voice.

He turned to Cynthia and said,

'Your affairs are your affairs
My affairs are mine
Let's keep them that way
So, they don't entwine.'

'Oh, poetry first thing in the morning – I like that. Do you do anything else?' she said, as they walked along the corridor towards the lift.

'Have you robbed any banks lately?'

'No.'

'Kidnapped anyone?'

'No.'

'How about a juicy murder?'

'Do you have anyone particular in mind?'

'You tell me.'

'How about that oaf of a husband of mine?'

'If you were to have done something like that, then it would be my job to investigate. If I found out, as a result of my investigations, that you had indeed killed your husband then, as a public-minded citizen, I would report it to the appropriate authorities.'

'But you're just a civil servant, you said as much at dinner last night.'

'I'm not just a civil servant. You could say I sometimes investigate things.'

'You're a spy, a James Bond! Oh, do you carry a gun? Are you licensed to kill?'

Buchanan was spared any further conversation as the lift arrived.

'So, if I do something naughty, will you come and investigate me?' said Cynthia, leaning on the back wall of the lift. Thankfully for Buchanan, two other guests entered after him.

Moments later the door opened, and Buchanan, still ignoring her question, stepped out amongst the crowd of guests waiting to use the lift. By now, due to the persistence of Cynthia Mountjoy, he'd resigned himself to missing his first breakfast of the week. He momentarily managed to escape from her presence when her husband pushed his way through the waiting throng.

'Where have you been? I had to have breakfast on my own.'

'I might just ask you the same question. I assumed you and Julian would be sharing a breakfast, you spend enough time together. And for your information I went to check on Turpin, and it's just as well I did. His rug had slipped, he was in danger of tripping on it.'

'Oh – well – good show. I'm off upstairs to make a couple of phone calls, then I'm going to walk the course with Pat, that's if I can find him. Will you join us?'

'Not just now, I need something to eat, then I'm going riding with Angela. You go ahead, I'll have a look at it later. Oh, I think you'll find Pat in the stables, if I remember correctly you told him to sleep with the horses last night.'

The muscles on Mountjoy's face tightened, he clenched his jaw, thought for a moment, then turned and walked away.

Although tables had been assigned for guests at dinner, breakfast was a much more casual affair, and it had been suggested that guests might like to mingle. Buchanan made good his escape from Cynthia and selected an empty table in the middle of the room close to one of the windows. He'd barely had time to sit when Cynthia joined him.

'Thought you'd like some company. Have you ordered yet?'

'Excuse me, Mr Buchanan,' interrupted a porter.

'Yes, what is it?'

'A message from the assistant stable manager. He wants to know if you will be riding Mercury today.'

'Ah, yes, thank you. Please tell him I will.'

'What time would you be down to the stables? And would you like him to get Mercury ready for you?'

Buchanan looked at his phone. 'Bit late for a morning ride. How about you say to him I'll be down about two o'clock and thank him for the offer of helping to get Mercury ready.'

'That will be fine, I will let him know. Sorry to have interrupted your breakfast.'

Before he could pick up the menu, another interruption in the form of a stable lad appeared. This time the question was directed at Cynthia.

'Excuse me, Mrs Mountjoy, Pat McCall asked if you'd come to see him in the stable.'

'Why? I'm just about to order breakfast.'

'He said to say he was concerned about Doxy. He said to say that Doxy was sweating heavily.'

'Sorry, Jack,' she said, standing up, 'I'll catch you up later. And when we do, I'll expect an answer to my question.'

What was her question? wondered Buchanan, as he watched her walk through to the bar and the exit for the stables. He pondered on it for a moment then remembered. He hoped he wouldn't have to do any investigations on her. He was here for a rest, and besides, he was sure Mr McCall would be doing all the investigations Cynthia Mountjoy required. He nodded to the waiter that he was ready to order breakfast.

'What can I get you, Mr Buchanan?'

'Could I have a full English breakfast?'

'With black pudding or haggis?'

'Haggis, this far south of the border?'

'Yes, it's one of Sir Nathan's favourites. How would you like your eggs?'

'Could I have soft yolks, please?'

'Brown or white toast?'

'White, please.'

'Tea or coffee?'

'Tea, please, I drink enough coffee as it is.'

'Thank you, Mr Buchanan. I'll go place your order.'

♦

10:30

After his leisurely breakfast Buchanan retired to the library and the rest of his newspaper.

'Can I get you something from the bar?' asked the waiter, as Buchanan relaxed into one of the Chesterfield armchairs.

'I'll just have a coffee, please. But not in one of those dainty little cups.'

'I understand,' the waiter said, nodding. 'When we have American guests staying with us, they also want their coffee in mugs, along with their doughnuts.'

'You have doughnuts?'

'Yes, sir. One of the chefs spent a few years working in the USA and he likes to make them for the early risers. If there are any left, would you like one with your coffee?'

'Why not? One doughnut isn't going to burst my belt.'

'Quite right. I'll be right back.'

Buchanan glanced round the library and realised he'd done it again. He'd chosen a seat in the library with a view not only of both doors, but most of the other seats as well. Old habits die hard he thought, when he saw he not only had a perfect surveillance position for the room but could also see out the window on his right to the road that led up to the club. To his left he could see out the windows on either side of the fireplace across to the covered walkway that led to the stables.

The waiter returned a few minutes later with his coffee and to Buchanan's delight, a fresh jam-filled sugar-coated doughnut.

'Thanks, oh, I don't need the milk or the sugar.'

'Certainly,' said the waiter, putting the milk and sugar back on his tray. 'Can I get you anything else?'

'No thanks, this will be fine.

'Then, in that case, I'll leave you to your paper.'

Buchanan picked up his paper, but something through the window on the left caught his attention. It was Cynthia Mountjoy and, Buchanan assumed, Pat McCall walking hand-in- hand away from the stable block. Now why would they be doing that? Then he remembered Mountjoy had said he was going to walk round the point-to-point course after he made some phone calls, looks like Pat was hard to find. But why be so brazen about what was going on? He watched till his view was blocked by the fireplace wall. When he next caught sight of Cynthia and Pat, they had let go of each other's hands and were walking over to one of the tables in the bar. Buchanan watched to see what they'd do next.

He was surprised to see them enter the library and take a couple of chairs in the far corner, just four feet from him. They were apparently so intent on each other's company that they didn't see him. He tried to overhear their conversation, but they spoke too quietly for him to hear.

They stayed for one drink then stood to leave. That was when Cynthia saw Buchanan sitting in the far corner of the room. The smile that had been on her face as she stood vanished like the summer sunshine when obscured by a passing cloud. He could almost hear her think: *have I said something he could have overheard?*

He raised his hand, waved and smiled, then returned to his paper.

♦

11:15

Coffee and doughnut consumed, paper read, Buchanan left the library; he needed fresh air. He rode the lift to the first floor and returned to his room. He found a pair of jodhpurs laid out on the bed and a pair of correct-sized boots on the floor beside it.

He thought about getting changed but decided to wait until the afternoon. For now, a visit to the stables was all he wanted. He collected his jacket from the wardrobe, closed his bedroom room door behind him and started along the hall to the lift. As he passed the Grants' partially-open door, he could hear the raised voice of Travis Grant.

'How could you do this to your mother and me? Do you realise what this could do to her reputation with the Mothers' League back home if news of this – this stupid affectation – gets out?'

Buchanan strained to hear the answer to his question, but it was too muffled to make out.

'Do you realise, Poppy,' Travis continued, 'he has a criminal record and is currently out of prison on probation? Just think for a minute, what will the elders think when they hear their senior pastor's daughter is cavorting with a known criminal?'

Once again, the reply was lost, but the words, *love him*, and *give him a chance*, rose above the muffled reply.

Buchanan smiled as he realised that the Grants' daughter had found someone to share her heart with, be it only temporarily. walked along the corridor he wondered who the mystery man was in Poppy Grant's life. It wasn't likely to be any of the guests, as he hadn't seen any suitable young men at the dinner tables the previous evening. Then could it be one of the stable lads? Yes, that was probably the likely answer. He remembered a previous conversation with Sir Nathan about working with the youth offenders' department; this must be what he had been talking about.

He rode the empty lift to the ground floor and recognised the familiar profile of someone standing at the reception desk. He wandered over to say hello.

'Good morning. Hope you're not looking for me?' said Buchanan.

'I'm certainly not,' said Helen, the Assistant Chief Constable, as she turned and smiled at Buchanan. 'I just popped in for a couple of days in the spa.'

'Didn't realise there was a spa at Castlewood,' said Buchanan.

'One of the best in the area.'

'I've been here several times; I've never seen one.'

'It's in the old walled garden.'

'Ah, that explains it.'

'How are you enjoying yourself? Been riding yet?'

'No, not yet. I was thinking about going out for a ride this afternoon.'

'Excuse me, Mrs Markham,' said the receptionist.

'Yes?'

'Your receipt and room key. When you are ready, Alice will show you to your room.'

'Thank you.'

'I'll catch up with you later,' said Buchanan.

'Oh, I'll only be a moment. Why don't we meet in the bar for a coffee? You can tell me all about your holiday. The part about what you and Karen saw and did. I already know the bit where you and Karen played Holmes and Watson.'

'Fine, see you when you're ready. I'll be in the library, much quieter in there,' said Buchanan.

♦

12:30

Buchanan returned to his armchair in the far corner of the library.

'Can I get you something from the bar, Mr Buchanan?' asked the waiter.

'In a minute, I'm waiting for someone.'

'Certainly.'

Buchanan picked up another copy of *Gallop* to read while he waited and was once more amazed at how much money was involved in horse racing. He was deep in an article about horse

41

breeding and realised that when it came to horse racing, horses were held in high regard.

'Interesting read?'

Buchanan put down the magazine and said, 'A life beyond anything I could aspire to. Must be nice to be able to afford owning a racehorse.'

Helen sat across from Buchanan in the other Chesterfield. 'Have you ordered?'

'No, I was waiting for you.'

As if on cue, the waiter appeared to take their order.

'Can I have a Cappuccino, please?' said Helen. 'Jack, my treat.'

'Thanks, I'll have an Americano, no milk.'

As the waiter left to get the coffees, Helen leaned forward and asked, 'Do they know who you are?'

He smiled. 'No. Well, Sir Nathan does, everyone else thinks I'm just Jack Buchanan, a civil servant.' He smiled at a memory.

'What's funny?' asked Helen.

'One of the guests thinks I work for MI5.'

'How did they come to that misunderstanding?'

'An unhappy marriage and too much wine. It's not that important.'

'Interesting. How do you feel about that?'

'It would have been even better if they thought I was just plain Jack Buchanan. And you? Do they know you are the assistant chief constable for Sussex?'

'No, and don't you dare tell them.'

'Ok, I won't.'

'How about we just use our civilian names? I'll be plain Helen Markham, and you can be plain Jack Buchanan.'

'That's fine by me,' replied Buchanan, as the waiter delivered their coffees.

'So,' said Helen, 'tell me about your holiday. What stood out the most for you?'

Buchanan took a sip of his coffee before replying. 'Probably the peace and quiet at night. There were a couple of nights when I woke at about three in the morning. I lay on my side and looked out the veranda window and just watched the passing night-time scenery.'

'Such as?'

'When we were sailing through the outskirts of Amsterdam, we passed alongside a busy road all lit up with streetlights. Then there was the railway line, oh, and one of the more interesting moments was when we entered one of the locks. These were the type where the lock gate rises to let the ships and barges pass under.'

'Why would that be so interesting?'

'The first indication was the sound of canal water dripping from the lock gate as we passed under. Once or twice I would get up and watch from on deck. Simply amazing how large the locks were.'

'How about Karen? What were her memories?'

'I'd say the highlight for her were the Keukenhof Gardens and the tulip and lily display.'

Buchanan was lost in his thoughts reminiscing about his holiday on the Dutch and Belgian canals and didn't notice the hurried approach of Cynthia Mountjoy.

'Jack, why didn't you tell me you were going for a drink? Oh, sorry didn't see you there,' she said, as she realised Buchanan wasn't alone.

Buchanan stood and said, 'Cynthia, this is Helen Markham. Helen, this is Cynthia Mountjoy. She and her husband are here for the cross-country race.'

'Hello, Cynthia,' said Helen, trying not to smile at Cynthia's momentary confusion.

'Ae you going to be riding in the race?' Cynthia asked Helen.

'No. I'm only here for a couple of days pampering in the spa.'

'Oh, I wasn't aware there was a spa.'

'Yes. It's in the old walled garden.'

'So, you're just here for the spa, you're not going riding?'

'No, I'm not going riding. I come here partially because it has all the grandeur of a country house with all the amenities of a modern hotel. And at the same time, it is quiet and peaceful. In the colder evenings, when the days grow short, there's always a crackling log fire in the library. I sometimes go for long lazy afternoon walks in the forest. It's a great place to be pampered. Then at the end of the day, when you've worked up an appetite, there's the Michelin-starred food and wine.'

'You sound like an advert for the place. Do you come here that often?'

'Not as much as I'd like to. I usually manage a weekend away after the summer holidays are over and the children aren't around.'

'How many children do you have?'

'Two, both girls. One's at university, the other has just started work. Do you have children?'

Cynthia shook her head. 'We tried, but well, you know, some women are not meant to have children. At least that's what my husband tells me.'

'I find autumn is the perfect time for a grown-up getaway,' said Helen, when she saw Cynthia's eyes start to tear. 'Some days, when the leaves in the trees begin to change colour, I go for long walks in the forest. I love it when there's been a frost and the leaves crunch under your feet. Did you know Castlewood forest is famed for its glorious autumn colours?'

'No, I didn't. This is my first time here. What treatments do they have in the spa? Maybe I'll book in for one or two.'

'Mostly Thai-inspired treatments. There is a large swimming pool, a hydrotherapy pool with massaging jets, body massages and facials. Upstairs they have a full gym. The facilities are mostly what you'd expect from a top-line spa. And of course, the best night's sleep you've had in ages. Makes me feel relaxed just thinking about it.'

'You and Jack are friends?'

'Not quite, we both work for the same company.'

'Helen is my boss,' interrupted Buchanan. 'I do what she tells me to.'

'That will be the day,' said Helen. 'You know, Cynthia, Jack's the most disobedient employee I've ever had to manage. If I didn't keep a firm grip on him, he would just simply do as he wished.'

'You never complain about the results,' said Buchanan.

'That's because we know each other so well, don't we, Jack?' said Helen, winking at Buchanan.

'Well, if you two are busy, I'll just go and – I'll just go and check on my horse. Angela and I are going for a ride.'

Buchanan watched as Cynthia walked purposefully out of the library, hips swinging like a Hollywood star. He continued to watch as she walked through the members' bar to the door that led to the exit for the stables.

'What have you been up to, Jack?' asked Helen. 'Have you been dallying with her?'

'Of course not, I've done absolutely nothing to encourage her.'

'You do realise, while you are on administration leave, you are not supposed to be doing any investigating? Or fraternising with other police officers, or going on to any police property?'

Buchanan looked at her, trying to see where this conversation was going. 'I'm not sure what you are driving at.'

'You must have done something to create the reaction in Cynthia – she looked extremely annoyed that we were having coffee together.'

'I think she is a very lonely woman.'

'You said she's married.'

'Yes, but I don't think there's much love in the relationship.'

'Well, whatever's going on in their relationship, don't lead her on, and remember what I've just said.'

'I won't, and besides I think she's already involved with someone.'

'You think?'

'Just a couple of incidents I've witnessed.'

'Be careful, Jack. Remember you're supposed to be keeping a low profile. Now, if you'll excuse me,' she said, standing, 'I'm off for my first treatment. Maybe we could have dinner before I leave?'

Buchanan nodded. 'That sounds fine to me.'

'Ok, I'll catch up with you later.'

'Will the lady be returning?' asked the waiter, as he picked up the empty coffee cups.

'No, she's gone off to the spa.'

'Can I get you anything else?'

'A large Lagavulin, with a splash of water.'

'Certainly, anything to eat?'

Buchanan picked up the bar menu and looked down the list of food available. 'Could I have a tuna sandwich, please?'

Sandwich eaten, he returned to his room to change for a walk round the course prior to his afternoon ride.

♦

13:15

Buchanan stepped off the bottom step in reception and caught sight of his reflection in the door to the porter's room. He quickly looked round to see if anyone was watching, and, content no one was, pulled himself erect, put on his riding hat and stared again at his reflection. A scene from the movie *Patton* came to mind. It was the scene at the beginning where George Scott, playing the part of General George Patton, comes into view as he prepares to give his momentous speech.

'I've seen the movie; you'd look great in the part.'

Startled by the voice, Buchanan turned to see who'd spoken.

'Sorry to interrupt,' said Travis. 'You were thinking of the opening scene in *Patton,* weren't you?'

'Ah, my vanity exposed.'

'What a man Patton was! Knew exactly who he was and what he was placed on the earth for. Pity we don't have leaders like him around today. All we have are jackasses like the one in The White House.'

'You refer to your present president?'

'Who else would I be talking about?'

'I thought all you religious types say it is God who appoints leaders – provides the people with just the leader they deserve?'

'He certainly does – and what an indictment of our present depraved and hedonistic way of life we Americans lead. What a shame it is for us Americans to have someone like that as our commander in chief. At least you Brits have someone who you can respect. Someone who is dignified in all situations at home and abroad.'

'You are referring to our Queen. Yes, she is a paradigm of decorum and etiquette,' said Buchanan, seeing a look of puzzlement grow on Travis's face. 'She's a well-mannered lady who knows when to speak and when to just smile and say nothing.'

'You guys are so lucky. I take it you're going riding?'

'I was going to have a walk round the course first, then go for a ride, probably go for a wander through the forest.'

'Have a great day, maybe see you down there.'

Buchanan nodded and walked off towards the stable block. He wondered about the recent revelation. Was the ACC really a regular at the spa? Could she be checking up on him? But if she was, why?

As he walked his boots made a clicking sound on the pathway. Momentarily, he was back on the police college parade-ground. He pulled his shoulders back, stomach in, pushed his chest out and marched ahead, his riding crop tapping the side of his boot as he went.

As he approached the stables, he saw a large horsebox disgorging its contents of three fine-looking Arabian horses. Once again, he wondered about how much money was involved in owning fine racehorses. He walked between the stable block and the indoor riding ring and stopped under the archway to admire the view. On either side of the arch were tack rooms for resident horses.

He remembered a conversation he'd had with Sir Nathan when they'd first met and how he had said the stable block pre-dated the present house. It was laid out around a large open square with a fountain in the middle. The stable wings, in opposing blocks, contained indoor stalls for eleven horses each. A wide internal walkway connected the wings. Facing the entrance was the administration wing containing the stable manager's office, separate toilets, tack shop, feed and bedding storage.

He stood for a moment and took in the scene before him. Several horses were being groomed; others saddled. Over in the left-hand corner he could see Cynthia and Angela saddling up their horses. The Bransons' were fussing over the foot of one of their horses, and Poppy Grant was holding on to the reins of her horse while deep in conversation with one of the stable lads.

'Do you have daughters, Jack?'

Buchanan turned to see he'd been joined by Travis Grant.

'No, Travis, I don't.' Then he thought about his work partner, Jill. She'd become as close a daughter you could ever have.

'They're nothing but trouble. You start off with a cute cuddly bundle in your arms and, before you know it, they are twisting your heartstrings chasing after boys.'

Buchanan smiled. 'I'm sure it's nothing but a summer holiday infatuation. She'll forget him as soon as she gets back home.'

As Travis made to enter the stable yard, Poppy leaned forward and kissed the stable lad on the cheek

'That does it,' said Travis, 'I'll soon put an end to this!'

Before he could take a step, Poppy mounted her horse, blew a kiss to the stable lad and urged her horse on. Travis walked briskly to intercept her, but she just smiled at him and kept going.

'See what I mean, Jack?' said Travis, as Buchanan caught up with him. 'There was a time when I was the centre of her life, now

I'm just the guy who pays the bills and provides a roof over her head.'

'I'm sorry, Travis, but getting angry with her will only drive her away from you and further into his arms.'

'But he's a con.'

'By that comment, do you mean he's a convicted criminal?'

'Absolutely.'

'What did he do? Do you know?'

'All I know is he's out on parole.'

'And you don't know what for?'

'What does it matter what he did? He's still a con in my book.'

'Which book would that be, the Bible? I thought Jesus said to forgive those who sin against us.'

'Are you preaching at me, Mr Buchanan?'

'No, not at all. Just wondered which book you are quoting from.'

'If you must know, it's the book of life. I recognise a bad apple when I see one.'

'Travis, I think you are more worried about your reputation than your daughter's happiness.'

'You on her side?'

'I'm not on anyone's side. Have you tried talking to this lad?'

'No, why should I?'

'Sometimes it's best to ask the defendant for their side of the story before you pronounce them guilty.'

'But, he's a con. Poppy said as much.'

'Would you like me to see if I can find out about him for you?'

'How would you do that?'

'I know someone who may be able to find out what he was in trouble for.'

'Great, go ahead. That should put an end to this relationship once and for all.'

'Are you going for a ride?' Buchanan asked, trying to steer the conversation away from Poppy and her young man.

'I was, but I need to talk to my wife first, tell her that you are on the case.'

'Sorry, I'm not quite as you say, *on the case*. I will have a word with the lad for you if that helps to put your mind at rest.'

'Fine, do that, and do it quick before I need to take the matter into my own hands.'

Buchanan thought about the size of Travis's hands and the possible damage they could do.

'I'll get on it this afternoon. In the meantime, might I suggest you keep calm.'

Buchanan watched as Travis strode off back to the club. The clattering of horse hooves brought Buchanan back to the purpose of his visit to the stables.

He resumed his walk across the yard and saw the origin of the noise of horse hooves. Cynthia Mountjoy was half on the saddle of her horse, her foot having slipped from the stirrup while she tried to mount Doxy. Angela's horse stood demurely waiting to be off. Buchanan remembered a story told by the stable owner in Busby, Jock Laidlaw. He said horses were very sensitive and would quite often bond with their rider. When the rider was having a bad day the horse sometimes would pick up on this emotion and either act up, or work with the rider. Cynthia's horse had obviously decided to act up.

He waved at Cynthia and Angela as he walked past and into the stable block.

As he stepped out of the bright sunshine and into the gloom of the stables, the sweet-sour smell of horses assailed his senses. He remembered when as a lad he'd gone to stay on his grandparents' farm and they'd been cutting and storing fresh grass for the winter silage. It had taken him a couple of days to get used to that smell. Now, here in the Castlewood stables, he recognised a kindred aroma.

As his eyes adjusted to the change in light, he saw the interior was illuminated by the sun shining through dusty skylights, the dust dancing in the shafts of sunlight. Oak beams from former men of war supported the roof. Greyspear had told Buchanan some of the timbers had come from one of Nelson's fleet when the vessels were no longer financially feasible to continue in service. As a result, they were broken up and the timbers sold off. Greyspear had also said that many of the barns in Kent, Sussex and Hampshire owed their frames to former ships of the line.

Buchanan looked up at the dust-covered beams and noticed, ensconced at the end of one of the beams, a huge grey cat. As he looked at it, the cat turned and stared at him for a moment, then deciding he wasn't any threat, went back to looking at the ground for any movement that might signify a tasty treat.

He continued past an empty stall and saw a scrawny ginger cat surrounded by a group of fluffy grey kittens. No guessing who the father was, thought Buchanan. Beside the cats lay an old dog; it looked up at Buchanan with its one good eye, wagged its tail then returned to guarding its charges. A few chickens clucked contentedly as they pecked at the straw-covered ground in another empty stall.

As he walked past the stalls, some of them empty, he observed the one on the end was being cleaned by the young man Poppy had been talking with.

The lad looked up as Buchanan approached; he looked puzzled for a moment, then relaxed.

'Oh, it's you, Inspector.'

'You know me?'

'Not directly, I remember seeing you in court when you gave evidence in Danny's appeal.'

'Danny?'

'Yes, Danny. He'd been wrongly convicted for breaking into a shop and stealing booze and cigarettes.'

'Ah yes, now I remember. But that was months ago now. What were you doing in court?'

'I was up for a case of taking without consent.'

'Not a smart thing to do, especially if you get caught.'

'I actually didn't take the car, that was Sam and the other guys. I'd just been let go from my job as a landscape gardener and was feeling a bit down, so I went to the pub for a drink. That's where I met Sam and the others. They invited me to go along with them. They said they were going clubbing in Brighton. I didn't know the car I was given a lift in had been stolen. The police stopped us on the A27 just past the Drusillas' roundabout; I got arrested along with all of them.'

'What happened when you went to court?'

'The judge said that, since our prisons were so full, and it was my first offence, he was going to be lenient and not give me a custodial sentence.'

'I take it you were given probation?'

'Yes. I had to get a job and not reoffend during the next twelve months.'

'How did you come to be working here?'

'My former boss heard about my situation, I guess he felt bad that he'd had to let me go. Since we'd done some work here at Castlewood, he had a word with the owner and here I am.'

'A bit of a change for you, from gardening to working with horses?'

'Sort of, but then I'm not really a gardener. I'm ok cutting the grass, trimming bushes, that sort of thing, but ask me to tell the difference between a pansy and a geranium,' he said shaking his head. 'I can't tell one from the other. Now horses, they're a completely different matter. They don't discriminate, they don't care who you are or anything about you. Just treat them right and they're your friends for life.'

'How much longer do you have on your probation?'

'Three weeks.'

'You're quite friendly with Poppy Grant.'

'Her dad doesn't like me, calls me a con.'

'To your face?'

'No, behind my back to Poppy. He keeps telling her to not talk to me. That's a laugh, how's she supposed to do that? I work here, I feed and look after the horses, it's my job.'

'I wonder if you could do me a favour?'

'What's that?' he said, a look of concern crossing his face.

'I'm here at the club for a few days' rest; no one knows I'm a policeman and I'd like it to stay that way.'

'No problem, I know what it's like to not want to be known for something.'

'Excellent. Can you tell me which stall Mercury is in?'

'Stall six. I'll show you, follow me.'

'What do they call you?'

'Harry.'

'How many days do you work here?' asked.

'As many as I want, I live here.'

'I don't quite understand?'

'I'm employed to work forty hours a week but, since I live here, I get paid for the forty, plus a few hours overtime if I do them.'

'You live in the clubhouse?'

'No, I could never afford to do that. There's a couple of flats upstairs here in the stables. Me and some other lads live-in. Sir Nathan likes it that way, always someone here if a horse gets in trouble.'

'That makes sense.'

'Here's Mercury.'

At the sound of his name, Mercury turned away from his haynet and looked to see who had just walked down the corridor.

'Hello boy,' said Buchanan, 'remember me?'

Mercury snorted and leaned further over the door of his stall and stared at Buchanan.

Buchanan leaned forward and gently breathed into Mercury's face and scratched his forehead. Mercury sniffed and bent down and nudged Buchanan's jacket pocket.

'Ah, you do remember me,' said Buchanan, as he reached into his pocket and removed the sugar lumps he'd purloined from the breakfast table sugar bowl. 'Here you are, my friend.'

'He likes you,' said Harry. 'You can always tell by the way a horse responds when he likes someone. Shall I get him ready for you?'

'Thank you. Although I'm fine riding horses, I get a bit muddled when putting the bridle on them.'

'No problem,' said Harry, as he collected the rope halter from the doorpost, slid the bolt back, and stepped in. Buchanan watched as Harry talked quietly talked to Mercury as he slipped the rope halter onto his head while rubbing his neck. Halter secured, Harry led Mercury out of the stall and tied him to a hitching post

'Shall I brush him for you?'

'No, thanks. If you don't mind, I'd like to do that.'

'Fine, I'll get the tack ready. Do you have your own brushes?'

'No. Not the sort of kit a policeman carries with him.'

Harry shook his head and said, 'I guess you're more likely to carry mace and handcuffs.'

'Not anymore. These days I spend too much time behind a desk doing paperwork.'

'You should try sitting exams, now there's a lot of paperwork I was glad to see the back of.'

'What subjects did you take?'

'Maths, English, you know, the usual stuff.'

'Thanks,' said Buchanan, as Harry passed him a bucket with a collection of brushes. 'How did you do?'

'I got all As, three of them at A plus.'

'I bet your parents were pleased?'

'My mum was. My dad was away at sea at the time. He's an engineer in the merchant navy.'

'University – did you consider it?' asked Buchanan, as he started to brush the dust off from Mercury's shoulders.

'Yes. I was in my second year when Mum got ill. Dad was in the Far East and couldn't get home for three weeks, so I left university to look after her. I sort of never went back.'

'What subject were you reading at university?'

'I have a good head for figures, so I was studying for a BSc in accounting and finance.'

'Will you miss out by not going back?'

Harry shrugged. 'Too early to tell. Right now, I'm enjoying myself working here with the horses. I'll go get Mercury's bridle, be back in a minute.'

Buchanan held Mercury by the rope halter till Harry returned with the bridle.

'Thanks for your help, Harry,' said Buchanan, as he mounted Mercury.

'You know the cross-country course is closed today?'

Buchanan nodded. 'Yes, thanks. I walked the course before I came down here. For now, I'm going to try the bridleways through the forest, should be nice and quiet at this time of the afternoon.'

As Buchanan rode across the stable yard, he saw Travis Grant walking purposefully towards the stable block. He changed direction when he saw Buchanan and walked towards him. Buchanan stopped Mercury and waited.

'Did you find out anything?' demanded Travis.

'A little. I'd go easy on the lad for now, he's had a rough time of it.'

'Maybe. But if he harms my Poppy, I might just forget I'm a senior pastor of the largest church in our state.'

15:30

Buchanan turned right out of the stable yard and followed a group of riders, while reminiscing about the last time he'd ridden this way. It was just over a year ago when he had come out to the club to interview Sir Nathan Greyspear about the death of a young woman whose body had been found floating in the Marina. After a leisurely lunch, Greyspear had suggested a ride in the country – and what a ride it had been! Buchanan almost ended up going headfirst down into the disused quarry when he ignored a shouted warning from Greyspear.

Now he was alone and after the pestering of Cynthia Mountjoy he was glad to be away from her unwanted attention. Though he reminded himself he wasn't really alone; he was out in the open-air riding Mercury. As he passed the end of the stable block, he saw that the Branson horsebox had been joined by two others, all with their sides extended.

Next to the Branson bright-red Oakley horsebox was a silver and blue Alexander with a large image of a horse and rider jumping over a five-bar gate. On the far right was an olive-green KM horsebox with the words *Ride-On* in gold leaf. An interesting display of equine profligacy thought Buchanan.

He continued along the broad, grassy boulevard at a walking pace towards the distant trees of Arlington Forest. As they turned the corner at the end of the path, Mercury recognised one of his stable companions in the distance. His ears went forward, and Buchanan felt Mercury's shoulder muscles tense.

'Ok boy, let's go say hello to your friends,' said Buchanan, as he leaned forward and gently squeezed Mercury's sides. Mercury snorted, then set off at a trot. By the time they'd got to the start-finish line, Mercury's stable-mates had begun walking back. Buchanan was surprised to see Angela as part of the group, but not Cynthia. She smiled as they approached each other.

'Hello, Angela,' said Buchanan, 'I thought you and Cynthia were going for a ride together?'

'We did, but she said she'd forgotten something and turned back just as we entered the forest.'

'That's odd, I've just come out of the yard and I didn't meet her on the way.'

'Maybe she met Victor. I saw him inspecting the jump at the end of the start-finish straight earlier.'

'Ah, that explains it. Going in for the day?'

'Yes. I've got a bit of a headache and the fresh air isn't doing anything to help improve it.'

'Hope it gets better, see you at dinner.'

'Thanks. 'Bye.'

Buchanan continued to make his way past the start-finish line and on to the end of the straight. At the end, the track turned to the left, over a five-bar gate and across the field towards the hill leading up to the quarry.

'Ok, boy,' said Buchanan to Mercury, 'Plenty of time to ride the course another day. Just now, I think we'll try the bridleways in the forest.'

He reached into his inside jacket pocket and took out the map of the Arlington Forest bridleways. He saw, looking at the map, that each bridleway had a name. Most of them were named after trees. The main one was called Oak and started at the end of the start-finish line and curved away to the right all the way down to the narrow road that led to Greyspear's sister-in-law's house. Leading off Oak was a track named Millpond Way. Buchanan's curiosity had him wondering. An idea was forming in his mind and he decided to follow a hunch.

Buchanan had Mercury trot along Oak till Millpond Way appeared. He almost missed the track due to a low-hanging branch from a nearby tree. He carefully pushed it aside and urged Mercury on into the overgrown track. As they made their way along the lane, Buchanan thought he could hear voices in the distance. Looking down at the track, he noticed that he wasn't the only one who'd been along it recently. Together with a set of tractor tyre marks, two sets of hoof prints could be clearly seen imprinted in the soft soil at the edges of puddles. As the track continued round to the right, the sound of subdued voices became clearer.

He'd expected at least one of the voices to be that of Cynthia, but was surprised to hear the other was male. For a moment Buchanan was back in the Scouts playing a game: he'd been sent out to reconnoitre the enemy camp and report back. Gently he slid off Mercury's back and tied the reins to a low tree branch. 'Shush, Mercury,' he said, patting his neck, 'I'll be back in a minute.'

Instead of continuing along the track, he set off into the brush in the direction of the voices. It was a short path and he soon came to a pond. On the far side, a building stood in a clearing – the old mill, thought Buchanan. Sitting on a bench were Pat and Cynthia, their horses tied to an old wooden wagon. Although they were on the other side of the pond, and speaking quietly, their conversation travelled quite clearly across the still water of the pond.

'Are you sure this is what we should do?' said Cynthia.

Pat shrugged. 'We don't really have any other option. I'm sick and tired of him treating you like one of his horses.'

'If only he did,' she said, laughing.

'It'll be risky, we can't have him know what we're planning.'

'It won't matter when it's all over, he'll be out of our lives forever. Then we can be together all the time. Just think, Pat, with him out of the way it will all be ours.'

'Including the debt if we're not careful how we go about it.'

'Don't worry, Andrew said he'll take care of that.'

'Are you sure Andrew doesn't want anything?'

'Absolutely. All he talks about is getting even with Victor for how he treated him in that court case when they were stationed in Germany. I smile inside when I see Andrew and Victor talking and joking in the bar, and all the time Andrew is plotting his revenge on Victor.'

Interesting, thought Buchanan. Pat and Cynthia were planning to ace Victor Mountjoy out of his assets, leaving him with nothing but his debts. Or he hoped that was all they were planning. A scene from the movie *The List of Adrian Messenger* came to Buchanan's mind. It was the fox hunt scene where the character played by Kirk Douglas was supposed to jump a wall and get impaled on a farmer's grass spinner. At least Cynthia and Pat weren't planning anything nefarious like that – or were they? Just what had Cynthia meant by her statement, *It won't matter, when it's all over, he'll be out of our lives forever.*

Still, hopefully it was to be nothing more than a messy divorce and financial settlement with a twist of revenge, mused Buchanan, as he made his way back to Mercury.

Buchanan mounted Mercury and they made their way from the millpond and onto Oak. He wondered what sort of revenge Andrew Jackson was planning. Being a major in the army he outranked Victor Mountjoy.

During a time of war, a colonel could be expected to be with his men on the front line where bullets gave no consideration to rank. Was that how Andrew was going to take his revenge on Victor? Get him sent to a dangerous situation where an accident could be engineered? But that wasn't really likely. Especially since they were both lawyers and, in all likelihood, neither of them would ever see a battlefield.

It was quite possible that helping Cynthia through a complicated divorce case was all that Andrew Jackson required to see permanent ruin to Victor.

Buchanan continued halfway down Oak then stopped and consulted the map of the bridleways and saw, if he backed up fifty feet, he could join Elm, which would take him back to the stables.

Not exactly a wild ride, but a very pleasant and relaxing one, thought Buchanan as they turned the corner back into the stable yard. He slowed to a gentle walk when he saw Mountjoy, not looking very happy, talking with two people. Buchanan wondered who they were. Then he realised they must be the lads who were going to look after Mountjoy's horses.

Buchanan stopped by the entrance to the stable block and dismounted. As he did so, Harry came out.

'Nice ride?'

'Yes, thanks. It was indeed very interesting. Tell me, Harry, those two men talking to Colonel Mountjoy, when did they show up?'

'About an hour ago. Why?'

'Nothing special, just wondered.'

'They don't know much about horses, at least the skinny one on the right doesn't,' said Harry, picking up a bucket of fresh water for Mercury.

'Oh, really? Why do you say that?' asked Buchanan, as he ran up the stirrups.

'The one on the right, the tall one with the limp, he's called Lenny. The colonel asked him to get the halter for his horse, he had to ask the other one what a halter was.'

'Do you know the name of the other one?'

'George. I think he knows something about horses.'

'George and Lenny. Sounds like a comedy duo.'

Harry offered Mercury a second bucket of water.

Buchanan scratched Mercury's forehead. 'Ready to go in, boy?' Mercury shook his head and flecks of sweat flew in the air.

'I think he's ready for his rubdown,' said Harry. 'Would you like help?'

'Please,' said Buchanan, as he gathered the reins and began to lead Mercury into the stables.

'Did you notice anything else about George and Lenny?' asked Buchanan, as they walked towards Mercury's stall.

'Why? Are you on a case?'

'Me? No, of course not. I'm just curious,'

'Once a policeman, always a policeman?'

'You could say that. But, no. I'm not on any case. I'm just here for a quiet week's resting, riding and reading.'

'Do you need help taking the bridle off?' asked Harry, as Buchanan reached for the rope halter.

'Yes, please.'

Buchanan watched as Harry removed Mercury's bridle and tied him to the hitching post with the rope halter.

'Are you all right with the saddle?' asked Harry.

'I'm fine,' said Buchanan, reaching over to undo the girth strap.

'I'll get the brushes for you.'

Harry returned a few minutes later with the brushes and asked, 'Would you like me to keep an eye on those two for you?'

Buchanan smiled. 'Don't make it obvious. It may all be quite innocent.'

Harry smiled. 'Bit of an odd situation, me on probation working as an undercover policeman.'

'Now hold on a minute,' said Buchanan, as he picked at Mercury's hoof. 'I admire your desire to do your civic duty, but you're not working undercover for the police. All I suggested is to just keep an eye on them, Ok?'

'Sure.'

'What do you think of Colonel Mountjoy's horses?'

Harry shrugged. 'They look fine to me, but then I'm not an expert on horses.'

'Where are their stalls?'

'One and two, down at the far end, close to the stairs that go up into the loft.'

'Are they the same stairs you use to go up to your flat?'

'Yes.'

'George and Lenny up there as well?'

'No, they're in the Old Coachman's Lodge directly opposite stalls one and two. I'm in flat one upstairs with one of the other lads. I saw George and Lenny moving in when I came down a short while ago. Not sure why they're in there, the colonel's horses arrived in a horsebox with room to sleep six.'

Buchanan knew the reason for them not sleeping in the horsebox; he reckoned that was where Pat took care of Cynthia.

When Buchanan was finished brushing Mercury, Harry led him into his stall, removed the halter, left and bolted the door.

'Do you know the names of Colonel Mountjoy's horses?'

'Turpin and Rambler. Turpin is in stall one, and Rambler is in stall two.'

'What about Mrs Mountjoy's horse?'

'Doxy? She's in stall five, it's next to Mercury's stall.'

'Is Doxy in her stall?'

'She wasn't a few minutes ago when I walked past. Do you want me to go check for you?'

Buchanan shook his head. 'I'll look as I leave. Thanks for your help, Harry.'

'No problem. See you tomorrow. Oh, how will I get in touch with you if I hear anything?'

'Don't worry about that. I'll be here every afternoon, except Thursday, when I have business elsewhere.'

'Ok, I'll see you tomorrow after lunch.'

Buchanan would have patted Mercury goodbye, except for the fact the horse had his head down and was busy licking at his salt block.

He walked slowly towards stalls one and two and could see as he approached that both horses were in residence. Buchanan stopped in front of the stalls and stared at Mountjoy's horses. Above each of the doors to the stalls were solid-looking webbing strap nets, which prevented either horse from putting their heads out of the stall. Regardless of this restriction, Buchanan could see they certainly were fine animals. He also noted the one on the left looked nervous, its eyes wide open; it was scared of something.

'You looking for something?' said a gruff voice behind Buchanan.

He turned to see who was speaking. It was George, one half of the George and Lenny duo.

'You must be George,' said Buchanan, taking a step forward and extending his hand in friendship. 'Jack Buchanan. Just admiring Victor's horses. Glad I'm not racing against them, they look extremely fit.'

'You know the colonel?'

'Of course I do. Had dinner with him and Cynthia last night.'

'Oh, if that's the case – just don't get to close to them, don't want them being spooked.'

'I won't. You look after the colonel's horses?'

'Yeah, me and Lenny.'

'What about Mrs Mountjoy's horse? Who looks after Doxy?'

George shrugged. 'I suppose she does.'

'How about your partner, Lenny?'

'No way. He and I only look after the colonel's horses, no one else's.'

'Where is Lenny?'

'Somewhere, why?'

'Just wondered.'

'Maybe you should go do your wondering somewhere else, you're bothering the horses.'

Buchanan recognised the warning tone in George's voice, just like a dog when it rolls its lips back and starts to growl.

'Fine, wouldn't want to spook Victor's horses. Be seeing you,' said Buchanan, tapping his temple with his finger and walking off towards the far end of the stables. As he passed the entrance, he saw Lenny approaching.

It was going to be useful to have Harry keeping an eye on things, thought Buchanan as he continued walking. He stopped at the end of the stalls and looked back at the far end and stalls one and two. Lenny was talking to George and they were both looking at him. Buchanan felt the hair on the back of his neck bristle.

Buchanan turned the corner and walked towards the row of stalls on the far side of the stable block. As he passed the office, he saw Harry, phone to his ear while sitting at the desk typing on the computer keyboard. Harry turned and waved Buchanan into the office.

Buchanan waited as Harry completed his business and hung up from the call. Harry saw the look of curiosity on Buchanan's face. 'Part of my responsibilities are to order feed, bedding and supplies for the tack-shop as and when needed.'

'So, you're a bit more than a stable lad?'

'That was what I was hired on to do. But when Olivia, she's the stable manager, saw what I was capable of, she just let me get on with managing basic jobs around the stable.'

'I hope you get compensated for your responsibilities.'

He smiled. 'I do, I only pay a quarter of the rent on my flat.'

'Harry, I've had second thoughts about getting you involved. I don't want you to get hurt.'

'Why, what's up?'

Buchanan shook his head. 'Nothing is up, least I don't think anything is going on. My concern is that George and Lenny are a rough pair and would think nothing of doing you harm if they felt threatened.'

'I wouldn't threaten them. The first sign of bother, all I need to do is mention it to Lewis and they'd be barred from the club. Not to worry, I can take care of myself.'

'I do believe you could, Harry. But characters like George and Lenny don't play by the rules.'

'They'll have to behave themselves while they're here at Castlewood. By the way what do I call you, since I can't say Inspector?'

'I call you by your first name, just call me Jack.'

'Ok. So, Jack, what's going on?'

'As far as I can tell, nothing's going on. But – after being a policeman for over thirty years, I can sense when something's not right.'

'I could always sense when things weren't right at home,' said Harry, 'especially when my dad was getting ready to go back to sea. My mum would slam doors and huff around the house.'

'I wonder if that is it?' said Buchanan.

'What?'

'The Mountjoys. They' re not a very happy couple, maybe I'm picking up on their emotions.'

'Then why have you warned me to watch out for George and Lenny?'

'I really don't know, Harry.'

Further conversation was prevented by Harry's phone ringing.

'I'll catch you later,' said Buchanan, as he stood to leave. Harry waved and reached for a pen.

Buchanan stopped at the male toilets and, when he came out, he could hear Cynthia's voice.

'I told you Victor; Doxy went lame. I told Angie to go ahead and I'd walk Doxy back. There's nothing sinister in that, is there?'

'All the same, you should have waited for help.'

'That's just like you. Just stand around flapping your mouth and let someone else take care of things.'

Buchanan decided to let them sort out their own problems. He quietly retraced his steps and left the stables by the door opposite the manager's office.

As he made his way back to the house he thought about the situation. There was a great deal of money invested in the event. At twenty thousand pounds a horse entry fee, with up to twenty runners, that came to four-hundred thousand pounds. Subtracting the prize money would leave three-hundred thousand pounds. Of course, there was the cost of food and accommodation for the competitors and hangers-on to be paid for. Then there was also the cost of stabling twenty horses and a substantial gift to Sir Nathan's charity to deduct from the pot.

But even if that was as much as a hundred thousand, there remained a substantial profit for Sir Nathan. Buchanan shrugged and continued with his walk and thoughts. All of that seemed fair enough, Sir Nathan was entitled to make a profit, so what was it that niggled him? He could have rationalised everything had it not been for the arrival of George and Lenny on the scene. They just didn't fit into the equation.

So, if a crime was brewing, where and what was it? It was unlikely to be the cash involved in the race, Sir Nathan would have all that tucked away in his bank. What else could it be?

It wasn't till he was standing in the shower with the hot soapy water streaming over his body that his reason returned. His thinking had been affected by the amorous approaches of Cynthia, the angry frustration of her husband, and the anger of Travis Grant against his daughter's infatuation with Harry. That was all it was. It was time to go on holiday and let everyone else sort out their own problems.

Buchanan looked in the bedroom mirror and smiled as he recalled Cynthia's remark about Victor. *Mirror, mirror on the wall ...*

Pulling his door closed, Buchanan proceeded down the corridor to the lift. There was something different about the atmosphere this evening. Although the club heating was maintaining a twenty-two-degree temperature, he felt a chill about his shoulders as he stood in front of the lift. Yesterday there had been the sounds of guests going back and forth, there had been happy banter from some of the open rooms, but now an eerie stillness pervaded the corridor. At least there was a glimpse of normality in the lift, the sound of soothing piano music still emanated from the speaker.

He exited the lift and walked through the ballroom to the restaurant. Although this was only Monday evening there were signs of preparation for the upcoming celebration evening on Saturday. A huge empty net was hanging from the ceiling – probably for balloons he thought –, and he could see several stacks of chairs nestled in the far corner by the stage.

Dinner this evening, as it would be the rest of the week till the gala awards dinner on Saturday evening, was informal. He entered the restaurant behind a couple of young men dressed in what he would have once described as smart casual. He stood for a moment and watched as they were greeted by two excited young girls who immediately led them off to their table. A memory from many years ago flooded back. It was the time when he was a young constable in Glasgow. He and Karen had just started dating and he'd saved up to take her out to the cinema then on to dinner at

Dino's. Ah, such fond memories. It made him sniff when he thought of Karen in France with her mother, when here he was on his own fending off the amorous advances of Cynthia Mountjoy.

As he approached his table, he noticed that it had been reset for eight and Greyspear's seat had been taken by Poppy Grant. Buchanan took his place, smiling at those already seated and wondering where Greyspear was. He glanced at Cynthia on his left, she looked at him, gave him a wry smile, then without saying anything returned to chatting across the table with Angela Branson. On his right, Poppy Grant, her eyes red, was busy muttering to herself about the injustices of the world. Shelly, seated opposite, was trying to get Travis's attention, her jaw muscles flexing as she ground her teeth. Travis sat between Poppy and his wife ignoring her while drawing patterns in the tablecloth with his table knife. Buchanan picked up his copy of the menu and glanced round the table. Seated next to Cynthia was her husband, his face red – from what, wondered Buchanan? Probably from arguing with Cynthia. Impervious to the seated gloom was Angela Branson. She was busy nattering to Cynthia.

Buchanan noticed that almost everyone had cocktail glasses in front of them. He decided to wait and just have wine with his dinner, he could always have a nightcap in the bar later. An exciting evening ahead he mused? Not very likely.

The waiter duly arrived to take their orders.

'I'll start with the soup,' began Victor, 'followed by the fillet steak, rare.'

'Victor,' said Cynthia, 'there are ladies present.'

'What – what did I say?'

Cynthia shook her head. 'It's not what you said, it's your manners. What ever happened to ladies first?'

Buchanan watched Victor's face getting redder by the moment.

'Then they should pay more attention to the menu than spending time talking.'

'Why can't you be more considerate of others for once in your life?' she said, turning to Buchanan and smiling at him.

'André,' said Buchanan, when it came to his turn to make his selection from the menu, 'where are Sir Nathan and his wife this evening?'

'He had a meeting in Southampton with a customer. I understand they will be back sometime tomorrow afternoon.'

'Thanks.'

The waiter left with the dinner orders and conversation returned to the table.

'Wine anyone?' asked Dean Branson, holding up an open bottle of red wine.

'Yes, please,' said Travis, reaching across the table for the bottle. 'Do this, whenever you drink of it, in remembrance of me,' he intoned, as he filled his glass.

Glass full, he offered the bottle up. 'Anyone else for the red?'

There were no takers, so he put the bottle down and returned to drawing patterns in the tablecloth with his knife, ignoring his wife.

Poppy looked up from her plate, looked around the table then picked up the wine bottle that her father had just placed on the table. Unnoticed by either of her parents, she poured herself a large measure of wine, lifted the glass and took a long sip. Before she had the chance to take a second, her father reached over and grabbed her hand containing the glass.

'No, you don't young lady! You're not old enough to drink.'

'Yes, I am,' she replied. 'In this country you can drink at eighteen. At least they treat teenagers like adults here – not like children.'

Travis took the glass from her hand and firmly put it on the table out of Poppy's reach. She pushed her chair back, threw her napkin on the table and stood up.

'I can see children are not welcome at this table,' she said, then stormed out of the restaurant.

Travis went to stand, but his wife put her hand on his and said something quietly to him. He relaxed back into his chair as she got up and walked after Poppy.

'Children! What can you do?' said Travis.

It wasn't till the desert stage that Poppy and Shelly returned, Poppy looking sullen and her mother still grinding her teeth.

That evening, the library bar was empty, so Buchanan ordered his nightcap and went up to his room. He undressed, showered and climbed into bed.

Although it was ten-fifteen in England, it was an hour later in France. He dialled Karen's mobile then pressed the speaker button and waited while the sound of France rang out.

'Hi, you still up?'

'I've been waiting for a call from my boyfriend, but he hasn't called yet.'

'Can I apply for the position?'

'I was wondering when you'd call. How are you?'

'I'm fine, how is your mother?'

'She's fine, as usual. She and Jill are playing cards and trying her latest taste in brandy. How is your room?'

'It's fine, the bed is fine and the room quiet.

In the still of the night
When my mind is at rest
I'll sing of the joys of sleeping
In my warm and comfortable bed.'

'Yes, your bed might be fine, but are you getting much riding done?'

'I went out for a short ride this afternoon. Went on the bridleway tracks through the woods. The course was closed this morning so competitors could walk the course and not get trampled under horses' hooves.'

'What do you mean by the course?'

'I found out when I checked in that Sir Nathan has instigated an annual cross-country race. The club is full of people who have horses entered in the race. I'm one of the few who are just here for the relaxation.'

'So, what have you been doing?'

'Just relaxing in the library and taking with the guests, speaking of which, guess who's here?'

'The queen?'

'No, Helen, the assistant chief constable'

'She's there?'

'Yes. I met her in reception yesterday.'

'Is she in the race?'

'No. She said she was here for a couple of days of pampering in the spa.

'Lucky her. What else has been happening? Any murders for you to investigate?'

'No. No murders, though things are turning out to be a bit of a melodrama here.'

'Really? Tell me more.'

'Well, to start with, there's Cynthia Mountjoy, she's married to Colonel Victor Mountjoy, though that's as close as they get. He prefers male company and she makes up for the deficit by chasing after other men, single or married.'

'Does that include you?'

'She did make it obvious that she was looking for company, but I think I have made myself clear that I'm not interested, and besides I already have someone in my life.'

'I'm very glad to hear that. What else is going on?'

'Well, Cynthia Mountjoy and Pat, he's their jockey, are having an affair. Pat rides their horses at events like the one here at Castlewood. They are planning some sort of divorce from Cynthia's husband Victor. I overheard one of their conversations where they are planning to clean him out financially and leave him ruined.'

'I almost feel sorry for him.'

'Victor is an army lawyer and so is one other of the competitors. His name is Major Andrew Jackson. Andrew Jackson is going to assist Cynthia get a divorce from Victor.'

'That sounds reasonable enough. Is there an issue with both men being army lawyers?'

'I don't think so. But I don't mind telling you, there are more twists in this story than there are in a yard of three-strand manila rope. Several years ago, Victor and Andrew worked together in defending a young soldier who had been charged with raping a young girl. Victor was the lead barrister and Andrew his junior. The problem occurred when Victor refused to let Andrew cross-examine one of the witnesses and the young soldier was found guilty.'

'Was he guilty?'

'No – and what really got Andrew Jackson angry was the young soldier was black and one of his nephews.'

'What did Andrew do about it?'

'He immediately set about getting a retrial and was able to get the conviction quashed.'

'Good for him, justice was served.'

'Unfortunately, it wasn't. The first night in jail the young soldier hung himself, leaving a young wife and twins.'

'How awful.'

'Yes, I believe when the divorce case gets underway, Andrew Jackson will do all he can to take his revenge on Victor.'

'My, you have been busy keeping up with what has been going on.'

'That's not all of it.'

'Hang on, let me refill my glass, back in a moment,' said Karen.

'Fine, I need the loo.'

'Mother says hello, so does Jill. Ok, I'm ready for you to spill the dirt.'

'There's an American family here, they're called the Grants. He's someone big in his church. He' accompanied by his wife and daughter.'

'What's his first name?'

'Travis, why?'

'I've seen him on the God channel.'

'Is he any good?'

'He seems to have a high opinion of himself and his preaching.'

'That sounds typical of those prosperity preachers.'

'It's not about how good you are as a preacher, it's about the message.'

'Well, as far as messages go, I'd say he's a bit of a blowhard. He goes on about how important he is and how big his church is. Not only that, he's a bit of a tyrant towards his daughter, Poppy.'

'Why do you say that?'

'She's fallen in love with one of the lads who doubles as the assistant stable manager.'

'What's wrong with that?'

'He has a criminal record. Travis is worried if news of it gets back to his church, he and his wife could have an awkward time explaining why their daughter is spending time with a known criminal. They have banned her from seeing Harry.'

'You're right it does sound a bit of a melodrama.'

4

Monday AM

06:42

Buchanan woke and turned on to his side to look at the time on the bedside phone display: six-forty-two. Still a bit early for breakfast. He rolled onto his back and pulled the blankets up round his face. What a luxury this week is turning out to be he thought, as he lay there listening to the gentle drizzle falling on the bushes below his window. Not that he didn't miss Karen, it was just being on his own and not having anyone to report to that gave him the freedom to do as he wished when he wished. He momentarily toyed with the idea of ordering breakfast in bed but dismissed it as just a bit too decadent.

As he lay there his mind drifted to the events of yesterday. As hard as he might try, he couldn't dismiss the idea that something was up. As Holmes would often remark to Watson, *the game's up*, but just what was the game?

Not for the first time he wished that Jill was back from France. He could get her to check up on George and Lenny. At least that would put his mind at rest, especially if nothing was known on them. Then he thought about Stephen; he was working with Hanbury this week, he could run a check for him. Now all he had to do was somehow get a decent photo of George and Lenny and send them to Stephen.

Situation resolved, Buchanan threw back the bedclothes and headed for the bathroom to shave then get dressed before going down for breakfast.

He walked into the restaurant and saw Andrew Jackson sitting by himself. Though not in uniform and wearing a sleeveless sweater over a crisp white shirt, Buchanan could see a man dedicated to looking after himself. An upright posture, broad shoulders and muscular arms that wouldn't look out of place in a boxing ring.

'Mind if I join you?' asked Buchanan.

Jackson looked up from his breakfast, smiled and gestured with his hands. 'Not at all, take a seat.'

Buchanan pulled his chair in to the table and smiled. 'Thanks. Here for the race?'

'Yes, and you?'

Buchanan shook his head. 'No, just taking a few days off work and doing some casual riding. My life's a bit too sedentary to do any kind of competitive riding. Besides, I don't even own a horse, do you?'

Before Jackson could reply the waiter appeared to take Buchanan's order.

'Could I have a bowl of grapefruit segments followed by scrambled eggs on toast, with tea, please?'

'Certainly.'

'You were about to say something,' said Buchanan to Jackson.

'Yes, you asked if I had a horse. I have two, but I've only brought one with me.'

Buchanan's next question had to wait as the waiter returned with his grapefruit. 'Your eggs will be ready in a few minutes, Mr Buchanan. Would you like your tea now, or shall I bring it with your eggs?'

'I'll wait till you bring my eggs.'

'Very good.'

'You're in the army?'

Andrew smiled. 'Yes. I'm a lawyer.'

'Just like Victor Mountjoy?'

'Not quite, I outrank him. He's a colonel, I'm a major.'

'Kindred spirits nonetheless.'

'You might say that.'

'But you beg to differ?'

Andrew smiled. 'I see you are perceptive man, Mr Buchanan.'

'Some might say it's my job to be perceptive,' Buchanan said, as he picked up his knife and fork. 'And it's Jack.'

'Andrew. And just what line of work requires you to be inquisitive, Jack?'

'I'm a civil servant.'

'I see,' said Andrew smiling. 'Might one ask which department of civil service you work in?'

Buchanan smiled back. 'If I told you I'd have to kill you afterwards.'

'Interesting answer, Jack. With that type of answer, I'm assuming you neither work for MI5 or MI6.'

Buchanan nodded as he put a mouthful of scrambled eggs and toast in his mouth.

'You're definitely not military, so I presume some sort of civilian duties. A job with responsibilities, authority, a certain amount of seniority.'

Buchanan continued to smile and nodded.

'I see you wear a wedding ring, one that shows signs of age. Is your wife here this week?'

'No, she's in France visiting her mother.'

'A married man on holiday, must be a good marriage.'

'Thirty-five years this year.'

'I think I'll guess at Inland Revenue. How's that for a guess?'

'Close.'

'But no cigar?'

Buchanan shook his head and put down his knife and fork, 'No cigar. Tell me something, Andrew. What does a lawyer do in the army?'

'Just about anything that requires a legal opinion. Everything from defending a soldier for being AWOL to invading a foreign country.'

'Not quite like civil court?'

'You're wrong there. To get to where I am in the ALS as an army lawyer, you need to be fully versed in the law of the land, plus possess a knowledge of military law and be a good advocate. Do you ever attend court in your line of work?'

'A couple of times, I was just giving evidence, nothing special.'

'Ever get a grilling from the barristers?'

'You know something, Andrew? You're quite good at what you do.'

'Thanks, Jack. That's my advocacy training showing through.'

'What's involved in being an advocate?'

'There's a bit of showmanship involved. You need to know your audience, mostly the jury. Although there are times when you want to make sure the judge is on your side, especially when it comes to the summing-up stage. Plus, you definitely need to know the facts you are presenting. Then there are some instances, especially if you feel the judge is against you, you need to be fearless and stand up against them. Finally, the most important fact, you must know the law.'

'You certainly are very passionate about your work.'

'All part of my training as an army lawyer.'

'Do you prosecute or defend?'

'I take whatever I'm given, I show no partiality to either defending or prosecuting a case.'

'Do you and Colonel Mountjoy ever work together on a case?'

'Once, but that was a few years ago. I was his junior in that case.'

'Junior? What is a junior?'

'A junior barrister is a lawyer who's either not experienced or senior enough to handle a complex case. They are usually led by a more senior barrister, often a QC. In a big case which would be too much work for one barrister alone, the more senior barrister will usually conduct the advocacy.'

'Bet that was interesting for you.'

'Yes, it was. I learned a great deal in that case.'

'You seem troubled. Did something go wrong?'

'Jack, it was a travesty, the wrong man was found guilty and I was blamed, and it was all Colonel Mountjoy's fault.'

'I don't understand.'

'Mountjoy, excuse me, I should say Colonel Mountjoy, wouldn't allow me to cross-examine one of the witnesses. He insisted on doing that himself. If I'd been allowed to do the cross-examination, I firmly believe the defendant would have been found not guilty.'

'What was the soldier accused of?'

'Raping a young girl in a nightclub in Hamburg.'

'You didn't think he was guilty?'

'It wasn't whether I thought he was guilty or innocent that was the problem. It was how he was defended that was the shame of the matter.'

'And this happened while you and Colonel Mountjoy were defending?'

'You might call it that,' Andrew said through pursed lips, then leaned forward and lowered his voice. 'The defendant was a young black soldier, one of my cousin's kids, sort of a nephew. If I'd known just how prejudiced the colonel was, I'd have asked for an adjournment.'

'How would that have helped?'

'I would have suggested to the young soldier that he asked for different counsel.'

'You say he was found guilty – what sentence did he get?'

'Demoted to private, five years imprisonment, a dishonourable discharge and his name added to the sexual offenders register.'

'That was a tough sentence. How old was he?'

Buchanan looked at Jackson's hands: they were balled in fists, the knuckles slowly turning white as the fork in his left hand slowly bent.

'He was only twenty-one, married two years and his wife had just given birth to twins. I was so sure of his innocence that I immediately pressed for a retrial. Unfortunately, it came too late.'

'Why was that?' asked Buchanan, already knowing the answer.

'The soldier hung himself in his cell.'

'And you think you could have got him found not guilty?'

'Absolutely.'

'Did you get a retrial?'

'Yes, but by then it was too late, the soldier was dead, his wife a widow and his children condemned to never to knowing their father. At least at the re-trial the real culprit was found and confessed.'

'And the young soldier died for nothing?'

'Yes.'

'What did Colonel Mountjoy say to the news of the lad's innocence?'

'He laughed and just said, *you can't win them all.*'

'What did you think about his remark?'

Jackson shrugged, thought for a moment, then said, 'What I thought should not be shared with a stranger. But I will tell you this, I decided I'd never to work with him again and vowed to go out of my way and expose him for being the racist prig that he is.'

'Yet, here you are at the same event. Did you know when you booked that he'd be here?'

'Jack, I definitely get the feeling that you are not quite what you seem to be. Let me tell you something. I've been practising law for quite a few years and during those years I've developed a sixth sense for telling when people are either being evasive with their answers or simply outright lying. For a civil servant, you certainly do ask a lot of questions.'

'Sorry, bit of a habit with me. My parents always said I was a nosey kid. But Andrew, I can assure you, I'm neither being evasive nor lying.'

'Hmm, they certainly were right about you being nosey.'

Buchanan shrugged and smiled.

'You asked if I knew Victor Mountjoy would be here this week. Well, I did know. When it comes to horses, this event isn't the only time our paths have crossed. We recently competed at the Badminton horse trials.'

'How did Victor Mountjoy do?'

'He made a complete arse of himself.'

'What happened?'

'He charged at one of the jumps when his horse wasn't ready. At least his horse had better sense. It stopped dead and Mountjoy sailed over the jump on his own and landed in the mud on the other side.'

'Was he hurt?'

'Only his pride. He did get a standing ovation from those manning the jump for managing a full summersault before landing on his backside in the mud. There's a video of it somewhere on YouTube. When I want to get up his nose, I repost it on the company Facebook page.'

'A man with a sense of humour. So, you think you can beat him in the race?'

'The horse he will be riding is fast, but so is my horse, Warrior. I've competed against the colonel's horse before and I know its weaknesses.'

'Which are?'

'Well, it's not the really the horse that is the issue. The issue is Victor. You said you only ride occasionally?'

'Yes.'

'Well, let me tell you something. To be competitive in cross-country, you not only need a good horse, you also need to be a good jockey, and you need to be fit. Do you have any idea what sort of training jockeys use to get and remain fit?'

'No, Andrew, I don't.'

'Well, first you need to have a strong body. Somewhere between that of a gymnast and a ballet dancer: strength and agility, that's what's needed. To gain a licence you need to pass a fitness test.'

'What does that entail?' said Buchanan, picking up his cup and leaning back in his chair to get a good look at Jackson. He indeed was fit.

'You need to be totally fit, both physically and mentally,' continued Jackson. 'I spend at least four evenings a week in the gym doing sit-ups, pull-ups and use the rowing machine. The toughest exercising is to get on the mechanical horse and crouch on the stirrups as though you were galloping down the final straight. That tests your ability to remain crouched and balanced while the horse gallops, a real test of strength in the lower limbs. Can you imagine what stresses your body is subjected to while the horse is galloping at speeds of up to forty miles an hour?'

'Not quite. The closest I've ever come to that was last year here at the club when the horse I was riding decided to have some sport with me and shot off galloping towards the quarry. What does Victor do to keep fit?'

'He trains at the bar, exercising his elbow raising a glass of his favourite tipple. I tell you, Jack, the days of jockeys sitting in hot tubs drinking champagne are long gone.'

'Does he play any kind of sport?'

Jackson smirked. 'When he plays his kind of sport, it's always with the other side.'

Buchanan was puzzled for a moment with Jackson's answer, then nodded. Mountjoy's relationship with his wife now made sense. He preferred the company of men to that of women.

'Victor used to be a damn good horseman. There was a time when I would have been confident betting my pay on him winning at a horse event. But not any more, the years and his propensity to spend time at the bar have robbed him of the ability to be competitive. Though if you were to ask him what he thought his chances of winning the race were, he would just laugh and say something like, *just watch me thrash the lot of them.*

'I thought drinking was encouraged in the officers' mess?' said Buchanan. 'And getting drunk was seen as a badge of honour?'

'Unfortunately, there still is a reluctance by some senior officers to dissuade those under them from drinking to excess. Some condone it and see it as you said, a badge of honour. I've seen some officers smile when they see soldiers on parade hardly able to stand up to attention.'

'And Victor Mountjoy is one of those?'

'That and more.'

'I see.'

'Jack, whatever department in the civil service you work in, I think your line managers must think of you as an asset.'

'I wish they were here to hear your comments. I understand from talking with his wife, Cynthia, that he has entered two horses. Have you met Cynthia?'

'Yes, a couple of times at army functions. Though it won't matter which horse he rides.'

'Why do you say that?'

'Simply because Victor will probably insist on riding the faster of the two horses, and, well, you've seen him, and after what I have just said, does he strike you as the fittest rider you've seen?'

'No, he doesn't. But I thought they have a good jockey, someone called Pat?'

'Ah yes, Pat McCall,' Jackson said, nodding. 'Now there is a good jockey, pity his career was interrupted. Given the right horse he could beat all of us. But as I just said, Mountjoy will take the fastest of his mounts and leave Pat to make the best of a bad deal.'

'You know Pat McCall personally?'

Jackson looked at Buchanan and thought for a moment before replying, 'Not personally.'

'Pity, I was going to ask you if you would ask him for a tip on which horse to back in the race?'

'We've only said hello in passing in the stables, that's all. I was getting ready to go out for a ride on my horse. He held the horse for me while I mounted. As far as asking him for a tip on who's going to win, I suggest you ask him yourself.'

'I heard a rumour about money being bet on the race?'

'I haven't heard that, but it doesn't surprise me. I imagine some of the owners will have a friendly bet with each other as to whose horse is the best.'

'Have you met Mrs Mountjoy since you arrived? I understand she's entered her own horse in the race?'

'I did notice her name on the list of entrants.'

'When I talked with her, she seemed to think she has a chance of being successful,' said Buchanan, while looking for a reaction on Jackson's face.

'Jack, I do believe you are fishing.'

'What do you mean?'

'I'm still not quite sure what you do for a living. But I just can't see you as an ordinary civil servant,' he said, shaking his head. 'I think it more likely you are a private investigator trying to dig up some sort of dirt on Mrs Mountjoy. Are you working for Colonel Mountjoy?'

'Whatever gave you that idea?'

'Jack, if that is your real name, ever since you sat down, you've been asking leading questions. What are you really looking for?'

'Andrew, I can assure you, I'm neither looking for dirt on Mrs Mountjoy, working for Colonel Mountjoy, or am a private investigator. I'm simply here for a few days' rest.'

'Then why all the questions?'

Buchanan leaned forward and, in a lowered tone, said, 'Cynthia Mountjoy keeps coming on to me, I don't quite know what to do. What would you advise?'

Jackson leaned back in his chair, clasped his hands behind his head and studied Buchanan. 'Are you asking me if it's all right to have an affair with Cynthia Mountjoy? Because if you are, I must warn you I am not in any way obliged to keeping this conversation confidential.'

'What's to keep confidential? I've no intention of having any type of relationship with Cynthia Mountjoy. I just assumed that you and Victor, being in the same branch of the army, that you would know Cynthia well enough to be able to have a quiet word in her ear and say I'm already taken and am not about to jump ship.'

'We may have met at army functions, Jack, but I'm afraid you'll just have to man up and fend for yourself. Now if you'll excuse me, I have a horse that needs exercising.'

'Ok, see you around.'

♦

08:45

Nicely done, Jack, muttered Buchanan as he walked through the restaurant into the bar and his first cup of coffee of the morning. He realised it was becoming a bit of a game to keep his occupation a secret, and he was enjoying it. So far, he'd been described as a civil servant, a tax inspector, a secret agent, and now a private investigator.

The thought of the latter intrigued him; could he really work undercover as a private investigator?

'Your usual coffee, Mr Buchanan?' asked the waiter, as Buchanan walked past the bar.

'Yes please, but could I have it with milk this morning?'

He relaxed into what was becoming his regular armchair, sipped on his coffee, and thought about the life of a private investigator. A scene from a movie floated into his mind. It was from *Farewell, My Lovely* with Robert Mitchum as PI Philip Marlowe. Buchanan closed his eyes and thought about the opening scene from the movie. PI Marlowe, dressed in his best and probably only blue double-breasted suit, wearing the unmistakable fedora, stood looking down out of a hotel window. His sardonic voice-over described how he'd gone out on a job to find a runaway teenager who just liked to dance. The opening music, *Marlowe's Theme,* with the sound of a piano accompanied by a muted trumpet drifted over the scene. Buchanan was in LA standing looking up at a dancehall sign, the outline of Moose Malloy hovering nearby.

'Oh Jack, on your own again?'

It was Cynthia. All things considered, at that moment Buchanan would rather have been in LA.

He dragged himself away from his daydream.

'Good morning, Cynthia.'

'I saw you sitting there looking a bit forlorn and I said to myself, Cynthia, go cheer Jack up.'

'That was nice of you.'

'What's the matter? Aren't you glad to see me?'

Buchanan smiled. 'Of course, I am. I was just thinking.'

'About something nice, I hope?'

'Yes, I was.'

'Well, in that case I won't interrupt your nice thoughts. I'm off for a ride, see you around.'

Buchanan closed his eyes as the whirlwind called Cynthia departed. He re-joined Marlowe and not for the first time thought that a good night's sleep did one wonders.

He was in Florian's bar with Moose Malloy. Malloy was looking for his Velma. She'd not written to him these last six years while he was in prison doing an eight-year stretch for a bank robbery.

Malloy was looking for his Velma, while Buchanan was looking for a crime not yet committed. No matter how hard he tried to ignore his thoughts, he just knew something was up, but what? He finished his coffee and left the bar to go visit the stables and have a chat with Harry.

09:45

There was an appreciable difference to the atmosphere in the stables this morning. Gone was the casualness of yesterday. Today the stables buzzed with excited voices, the clatter of horses' hooves and the sound of whinnying. The chickens were clucking noisily as they pecked at the straw and the grey cat was stalking something at the back of the feed store.

Buchanan made a beeline for the office and Harry. He wanted to know if Harry had any news about George and Lenny.

The office was empty. Buchanan was about to leave when he saw a partially-drunk cup of tea sitting on the desk. He reached down and felt the cup – still piping hot; he decided to wait for Harry.

On the office wall, behind the desk, was a feeding schedule for the horses. Buchanan looked down the list and saw that each horse, including Cynthia's mare, Doxy, were being catered for as though they were guests staying in the clubhouse. All that is, he saw, except for Victor Mountjoy's two horses Turpin and Rambler. Now why would that be – especially since their stabling costs were included in the entry fee?

'Morning, Jack,' said Harry, entering the office and picking up his cup. 'Can I get you a cup of tea?'

Never refuse a friendly cup of tea, Buchanan remembered his old Glasgow sergeant saying. 'Yes, please, just a splash of milk, no sugar.'

Harry clicked on the kettle and dropped a teabag into an empty mug

'How are things today?' asked Buchanan.

'A lot different from yesterday. Just about everyone is either out on the course or getting ready to go out.'

'Even Victor Mountjoy?'

'Yes. He went out on Rambler and Pat McCall was on Turpin.'

'How about Major Jackson?'

'Yep,' said Harry, turning to look at the board, 'he's on Warrior. Now there's a really fine horse. I'd say that one stands a good chance of winning. Your tea.'

'Thanks,' said Buchanan, taking the offered mug. 'I was under the impression that either one of the Mountjoy horses were the favourites?'

'That's the story being put about.'

'By whom?'

'The Mountjoy crowd, mainly George and Lenny.'

'Talking of George and Lenny, are they about?'

'I just saw them down at the feed station filling hay nets.'

'Harry, I wonder if you'd do me a favour?'

'Sure, what is it?'

'I need photos of George and Lenny and I was thinking, if I handed you my phone, you could take their photo without them realising what you were doing.'

'I can do one better than that.'

'How?'

'One of the security measures we have here in the stables is CCTV. There are cameras everywhere. Let's see what I can find.'

Buchanan helped himself to a gingersnap biscuit and sipped his tea while Harry scanned the CCTV looking for George and Lenny.

'Got the lazy sods,' said Harry. 'Now, how about a close-up of Lenny first,' he said, adjusting the image size on the screen before saving a copy of George and Lenny's faces. 'Shall I email them to you?'

'That would be fine,' said Buchanan, handing his business card to Harry. 'The address is on the bottom of the card.'

'They're on their way.'

'Thanks. Have George and Lenny been behaving themselves?'

'Mostly. The only awkward thing is the stairs to the flats are just past the horse stalls where Colonel Mountjoy's horses are stabled, and the Old Coachman's Lodge is. Any time we want to go up to our flat we have to walk past George or Lenny; one of them is always there.'

'What do you mean, one of them is always there?'

'Sunday, when the horses arrived, Colonel Mountjoy and his jockey spent most of the day fussing around the horses, which you'd expect after such a long journey. Then Sunday night, the jockey stayed in the Old Coachman's Lodge. He left Monday morning when George and Lenny showed up.'

'Why is that an issue?'

'It's sort of odd. Yesterday, when they arrived, they stood around the stalls all day. Then last night there was always one of them standing outside. They just give me the creeps.'

'Was the jockey alone on Sunday night?'

Harry smiled and shook his head. 'My job is a six day a week one, and one of my duties is to do the rounds of the stables between eleven and midnight. Sunday evening when I came down the stairs, I heard a female voice coming from the Old Coachman's Lodge.'

'Did you recognise the voice?'

'Are you asking as a policeman?'

'Not particularly.'

'It was Mrs Mountjoy; there's no mistaking her laugh.'

'That's interesting. I had a walk round the stables this morning and I noticed that the Mountjoy horse stalls were the only ones with webbing nets over the doors. Why would that be?'

'Colonel Mountjoy asked for them to be installed. He said it was to keep his horses from being disturbed by what was going on in the stables.'

'Does that make sense to you?'

Harry shrugged. 'Not to me it doesn't. I would have thought the horses would be more at ease if they could see what was going on around them. Besides, here at Castlewood we hang the hay nets on the outsides of the stable doors.'

'Why do you do that?'

'Stops the horses dropping expensive hay into their bedding and making a mess. There's also the possibility that they could get tangled in their hay net. Same reason we have the feeding bowls down low. It's healthier and more natural for the horse that way.'

'That makes sense. Can you think of any logical reason for the netting on the Mountjoy stalls?'

'Maybe it's to stop the horses from sticking their heads out of the stall and biting Lenny or George when they stand guard?'

'That's one possibility,' said Buchanan, chuckling as he imagined a horse mistaking Lenny's bald head for an apple. 'Do you know what George and Lenny's surnames are?'

'Hang on a minute,' said Harry, as he reached up for a clipboard hanging on the office wall. 'I've got a list of all names of everyone concerned. Now let's see… yes, here we are, George's surname is Reilly, and Lenny's surname is Crandall.'

'Thanks, Harry,' said Buchanan, taking a note of the names on his mobile.

'Are you going riding this morning? Just about everyone is out on the course?' Harry asked.

'No, I think I'll stay out of the way of the racers. I'll go out this afternoon, there's still some of the bridleways I'd like to explore. Thanks for the photos and the tea.'

Buchanan looked at the time on the office clock and saw he still had plenty of time before lunch to do a bit of snooping. The CCTV screen showed George and Lenny still stuffing hay nets at the feed store.

♦

10:15

Buchanan turned left out of the office and walked to the corner of the stables. He looked back towards the feed store and saw no sign of George or Lenny. He continued past the rows of empty horse stalls till he came to stall two. The thick webbing net hung limply to the side above the open doorway. He saw the holes in the netting were too small for a horse to even stick its nose through; poor horse, he thought.

The bedding had been pulled up to one side of the stall, showing a clean and dry concrete floor. In the far corner, a green, self-filling water bowl stuck out from the wall, a salt lick lay underneath to the side. Nothing unusual here either, thought Buchanan, as he checked stall number one. He exited the stall and looked back along the corridor; still no sign of George or Lenny. Then he tried the door to the Old Coachman's Lodge; it wasn't locked.

Buchanan took another quick glance down the corridor then opened the door. He had no idea what he was looking for or what he might discover. Whatever George and Lenny might be, tidy they weren't. The room had never been designed to have two people live in it, even less spend a week camping. On the right, under a dusty, partially-curtained window, was a divan with a rumpled blue sleeping bag. Behind the door on the left was an armchair and a large wooden crate with two pillows on top making a rudimentary bed, complete with a ripped orange sleeping bag.

On the floor sat two weather-beaten suitcases. A cursory rummage in the left-hand one revealed tee-shirts, underwear, socks, jeans, a flat-cap and pullovers. In the top section of the case he found a large padded envelope containing two aerosol spray cans: one was of white hair paint, the other brown. Additionally, there was a small bottle of baby shampoo, some rags and several pairs of black latex gloves.

The other suitcase had a similar collection of shirts and underwear plus something Buchanan did not expect. In the top of the suitcase there was a long sleeveless evening dress, fishnet tights, black high-heeled shoes and a long black wig. Which one was the cross-dresser, wondered Buchanan? The hairy arms and unshaved face of George precluded him being the owner of the clothes, which left Lenny. Buchanan lifted the wig and was surprised when he saw the wig even had a streak of white. An image of the Disney character Cruella De Vil came to mind.

A quick glance in what passed as a bathroom revealed two washbags. Buchanan had a quick look inside them. One had a scrunched-up tube of toothpaste and a toothbrush that looked like it had been used to scrub the floor. Next item was an almost empty pack of antacid tablets plus a pack of ibuprofen tablets. The other washbag contained a tube of tooth-whitening toothpaste, rolled neatly from the end, and a toothbrush in its own plastic brush holder. This washbag also contained a partial pack of ibuprofen tablets, plus a pack of omeprazole tablets. Buchanan looked at the pharmacy label and saw they were prescribed for George.

Not knowing what the medication was used for, Buchanan removed the information leaflet. He read that omeprazole was prescribed for people suffering from reflux, and the recommended dose was one tablet a day, taken in the morning, with or without food. So, he thought disappointedly, not an opiate medication. He read down the information on the ailment and saw some of the well-known side effects of the medication were headaches, gut pain and diarrhoea.

As he turned to leave, he saw a pair of women's underwear lying on the floor. He looked at them, hesitated for a moment, shook his head and turned to leave the bathroom – and almost walked right into Cynthia.

'I saw you go into the room and just for a moment wondered if you were looking for me,' she said

Cynthia was dressed in tan-coloured jodhpurs, black hunting jacket, black riding boots, and a well-brushed riding cap. She had a huge grin on her face as she gently tapped her left hand with her riding crop.

'Buchanan looked at her, searching for a plausible reason for being where he shouldn't be. He was caught in the act of searching premises without reason or a warrant. *Think fast, Jack,* he said, to himself. 'No, sorry, I was looking for the colonel's grooms. Have you seen them?'

'They've just gone into town. Victor told them they could have a couple of hours off while he tried out the horses over the course.'

'Has your jockey gone with him?'

Cynthia smiled and took a step closer. 'Yes, he has. Why would you want to know that, unless... unless... do you have something in mind? We are all alone.'

Buchanan smiled. 'Er – I wasn't actually looking for the grooms.'

'You weren't looking for me?'

'Sorry, no. I was really looking for a toilet. I ate something at breakfast this morning that didn't agree with my tummy. I did knock, but when no one answered, and the door was unlocked, I came in. But after seeing the state of the one in there,' he said, pointing to the partially-open toilet door, 'I think I'll just scoot up to my room. 'Bye for now.'

♦

11:40

Buchanan sat on his bed and composed an email to Stephen, attaching the photos of George and Lenny.

> Hi Stephen, hope Hanbury isn't working you too hard. Would you run these photos through the police computer for me and see if anything shows in the police records? The tall bald one is called Leonard (Lenny) Crandall, and the short curly-haired one is called George Reilly, sorry that's all I have just now. Please email me your reply when you have time.
> Thanks, Jack.

As he sent off the email, he looked at the phone display. There was time for a whisky before lunch.

♦

12:15

He settled back into his now favourite armchair, picked up a newspaper and waited for his pre-lunch whisky. With most people out riding, the library was quiet. He'd reached an article on farming post-Brexit when his phone dinged to tell him he'd received an email. That was quick work, thought Buchanan, as he opened the reply to his earlier enquiry.

> Hi Jack. I had a look on the PNC for the names you supplied. Here's the details.
> Lenard Crandall, one case of GBH, six-months custodial sentence suspended, three cases of credit card fraud, one case of driving off without paying, one count of DUI, and one case of driving with no insurance and driving while banned. Never served any jail time. Struck off as a High Court Enforcement Agent for trying to extort money from the debtor. Suspected of being involved in extortion and racketeering.
> George Reilly, two cases of GBH while working as a club doorman. One term of eighteen months and another of six months, the six-month term suspended. He served nine months of the eighteen-month sentence. Three convictions for forging cheques, two convictions for credit card fraud, no prison time for either crimes. Struck off as a High Court Enforcement Agent for extorting cash from the debtor.

Very interesting, thought Buchanan, just what you'd expect from a couple like George and Lenny. But why would Mountjoy employ them? Surely, he'd see them for what they were, two chancers, although if Mountjoy did know about their past then he must be up to something – but what? The obvious thing would certainly be something to do with the race and the huge amount of money involved.

Something smelled rotten in the State of Denmark, thought Buchanan. What were two chancers like George and Lenny doing working as stable hands for an army lawyer? Neither of them had any real experience of working with horses.

As he was wondering about the suitability of George and Lenny to be looking after horses, he wondered about Pat McCall. Did he have form?

Back onto his phone and an email to Stephen about Pat McCall. While he waited for a reply, he googled the name of Pat McCall. The results of his google search were quite interesting. An article in the *Racing Post* caught his eye.

> A blast from the past
> Jockey Pat McCall comes out of obscurity to ride in the Castlewood Cup. Once tipped to be the next Tony McCall, Pat McCall (no relation to Tony McCall), at nineteen gave up a promising career in jump racing to look after his ailing parents. At twenty-seven, and single, he returned to the horse world working for various stables, riding out on the more difficult mounts. Word on the turf has it that the intervening years he was away from the track weren't spent idly watching the grass grow. He will be riding Victor Mountjoy's horse, Turpin, in the event. Although the Castlewood Cup is a private race, McCall is becoming the bookies odds-on favourite to win.

No pressure, thought Buchanan, glad he wasn't in Pat McCall's shoes. The reply to his email to Stephen came back blank: **Nothing known.**

Pat McCall was emerging, in Buchanan's mind, as a completely different character from the one he'd first imagined when he'd overheard him talking with Cynthia Mountjoy. Although he had been fooled once before – there was the case of Archie Hemmings, the award-winning, caring, nurse poisoner at the Langstonview Nursing Home. He'd poisoned five of the occupants before he was caught. Could Pat McCall be another Archie Hemmings? A wolf in sheep's clothing? Buchanan hoped not.

He put his phone away and left the library for an early lunch. He found the restaurant almost empty. There were three occupied tables, two of which had groups of women busy in conversation. The third table had three men, two of which were George and Lenny. Buchanan felt mischievous and decided to invite himself.

'Good afternoon,' he said, sitting down. 'No point in messing up another table. Jack Buchanan, here as a guest, not racing, though. Ah, we've already met,' he said, in the direction of George and Lenny. 'Yesterday, down in the stables, I was admiring Victor's horses.'

Three startled faces stared at him.

'You're a friend of Victor's?' asked the third occupant at the table.

'Well, I couldn't quite describe us as friends, more like acquaintances really. Cynthia and I sit together at the dinner table, Victor sits the other side.'

Lenny turned to look at George and tried not to smile at Buchanan's remark.

The third occupant at the table introduced himself. 'Julian Du Marchon, Julian to my friends. You say you're not racing?'

Buchanan shook his head. 'Been a bad year for me, spent a few weeks in hospital after a very bad car accident. I'm just here to relax and not overdo the exercise. And you, Julian, are you racing?'

Buchanan watched Julian Du Marchon's eyes. They looked off to the side, then down at the floor and back up again. He nodded. 'Hope to. I've entered my horse, but she's not in the same league as some of the others. I'll give it a go, but really I'm just here for the atmosphere.'

'You been involved with horses long?'

Julian's answer was interrupted by the arrival of the waiter. 'Are you having lunch, Mr Buchanan?'

'Yes please,' said Buchanan, looking at the menu. 'I'll just have the cream of celery soup and the roll please, I'm not very hungry today.'

'Certainly, I'll be right over with your soup.'

'As a child mostly,' replied Julian. 'My parents had horses, and I used to tag along to the events. Now I go riding when I get time. I find it is a good way to meet people. You do know all meals are included?' he said, when he saw the waiter bring Buchanan's soup.

'It's the accident,' said Buchanan. 'I have these moments when my appetite just deserts me. Besides I'm going for a ride this afternoon and don't fancy bouncing up and down with a full stomach. How about you two? Will you be able to get out on the course? I'm sure Victor wouldn't mind you borrowing his horses.'

Lenny shook his head. 'No way will I get on a horse! They're dangerous animals. The one in stall two tried to kick me this morning. All I was doing was cleaning out its stall, ungrateful beast.'

'How about you?' Buchanan asked George.

He laughed. 'I'd fall off, no sense of balance. Besides, I don't really like horses.'

'So how did you two come to get jobs working with horses if neither of you like them?'

'It's a job,' said George, as Lenny chewed on his fingernails. 'I needed the money.'

Lenny nodded as he continued to chew on his nails.

'Do you think one of Victor's horses will win the race, Julian? I hear some of the owners have a bet going on who will win.'

'I've heard whispers to that effect. Why – do you fancy putting a wager on?'

'I was thinking about it.'

'How much were you thinking of wagering?'

'Oh, not too much. I recently sold a piece of property and made a nice profit from the deal. I was thinking, maybe five hundred. Do you think that would be enough?'

Julian shrugged. 'I don't really know, but it sounds like it should be. Would you like me to ask? I did hear the same story about the owners putting bets on.'

'Please, I don't know much about betting,' said Buchanan, thinking the name Julian Du Marchon needed investigating. 'What do you do, Julian?'

Julian smiled and leaned back into his chair as the waiter collected Buchanan's soup plate.

'Would you like anything else, Mr Buchanan?' asked the waiter.

'No thanks, I'll have my coffee in the library.'

'I'm what is called an independent financial advisor,' continued Du Marchon.

'You advise on pensions and mortgages, that sort of thing?'

'I do advise individuals on investments and pension matters. I also work with companies. I mainly look after their pension plans for them.'

'All a bit over my head.'

'Do you have a pension, Jack?'

'Yes, it's only what the government offers. If I hadn't sold my piece of property, I doubt I'd be able to afford a holiday here at Castlewood. Or be able to dream of retiring in the next five years. At least the cash from the sale is sitting in the bank, collecting interest.'

Du Marchon grimaced. 'Not the best place to put your cash if you wish it to work for you. What do you do, if you don't mind me asking?'

Buchanan looked at George and Lenny, they were waiting for him to answer. 'Not much, I'm just a mid-level civil servant. Do you think you could help me with a safe investment for my cash?'

'I'm sure I could do something for you. But without doing a full risk assessment of your finances, I can't say how much I could help. Do you live locally?'

'I'm staying at the Marina at the moment, but we will be moving into our new house next week.'

'Where is that?' said Julian, as George and Lenny got up and left.

'The village of Westham. Do you know it?'

'Is that the village with the pond with dead fish lying on top the *Herald* newspaper has been talking about?'

'Afraid so. Apparently, the issue of pond maintenance has been going on for many months and the council seem incapable of resolving the issue.'

'I'm sure they'll get it fixed before long. They need to, I hear the village is a much sought-after place to live. If I give you my card with my phone number,' he said, reaching into his pocket to get to his wallet, 'you could give me a call when you get home. That way you won't be bothered by phone calls from me. These days with so many telephone scams going around, I find that customers like to feel they're in control, besides I'm in between offices at the moment, I'm renting a temporary office in town – just till I find somewhere more suitable.'

'I'll give you a call when I get home,' said Buchanan, looking at Du Marchon's business card. which read, in neat Edwardian script, Sovereign Secure Investments.

'Please do.'

'Ah, before I go. Do you know the Mountjoys?'

'We've met at social occasions. At the office I handle some of their financial affairs, that's all.'

'Well, that's a good recommendation for your services if ever there was one, especially since Victor is an army lawyer.'

'Good, I'll be hearing from you then?'

'Oh yes, you certainly will be hearing from me,' said Buchanan, wondering just how secure his investment would be with Julian Du Marchon.

5
Tuesday PM

13:45

Buchanan sauntered into the library and went over and sat in his regular seat. As he waited for his coffee, he googled the name of Julian Du Marchon. He found three Julian Du Marchons. One was an Australian opera singer, the second was an environmental control officer for the State of California, and the third was Julian Du Marchon, Independent Financial Advisor, Gildredge Place, Eastbourne.

Buchanan looked at Du Marchon's business card and saw the phone number checked, but the address was different. The address on the card said 37 Mark Lane. That didn't make sense. From memory, Buchanan knew Mark Lane was short and probably didn't have addresses that went up to number thirty-seven. Now why would Du Marchon put that on a business card? Could it be Julian Du Marchon's investments were not as successful as they once were?

Buchanan sent Stephen another email and asked him to check out Julian Du Marchon, then went up to his room to change into his riding clothes.

♦

14:30

Buchanan entered the stables by the door next to the Old Coachman's Lodge expecting to see either George or Lenny on guard. When he saw stalls one and two empty, he realised that they were probably taking advantage of their charges being out on the course and were skiving somewhere out of sight.

Instead of going straight to Mercury's stall, he walked up to the office.

'Hi Jack, need any help getting Mercury ready?' asked Harry.

'No thanks, I think I'll manage. Just wondering if you've seen our boys?'

'I last saw them heading into town to the betting office, right after they finished cleaning out the stalls. Did you find out anything about them?'

'Yes, and I'd advise you to avoid them if you can. They both have convictions for GBH amongst other nefarious crimes.'

'Thanks for the warning. I for one can't wait for them to be gone from here.'

'Has Poppy been in to see you today?'

'She said hello this morning, but she didn't hang around. I think her dad has told her in no uncertain terms to stay away from me.'

'You sorry about that?'

His head dropped, and he shuffled his feet. 'She's nice,' he said, lifting his head and smiling. 'She brought me a sandwich for my lunch this morning because I said I wouldn't get time off for lunch today, on account of the stables being so busy.'

'You like her?'

His smile grew. 'What do you think?'

'I'd watch out for Dad. He may be a church pastor, but she's still his little princess.'

'I can take care of myself.'

'I'm sure you can when it comes to horses, but little girls' fathers are a whole other matter.'

'Thanks, I'll keep an eye out for him. Are you going out?'

'Yes. But first I was going to see who's in and who's still out on the course.'

'I'll get your tack ready while you do that.'

'Thanks, be right back.'

Buchanan turned left out of the stable office and wandered along to stall five where Cynthia Mountjoy had her horse stabled. No sign of her or her horse. He walked back to Mercury's stall and saw that Harry had hung Mercury's tack on a harness hook for him.

As Buchanan put on Mercury's saddle, he saw George and Lenny enter through the door at the end of the corridor. That must mean Victor Mountjoy was not far away, thought Buchanan. He led Mercury outside into the yard, climbed onto the saddle and set off.

He stopped at the start-finish line and watched as a string of riders returned from the first day's practise on the course. He looked for but did not see Cynthia Mountjoy or Pat McCall, but he did see Victor Mountjoy on his own and not looking very happy.

Buchanan set off to explore the remaining forest boulevards. He was curious to see if Cynthia and Pat were having another one of their conferences by the old mill. As the last horse trotted past, Buchanan entered the peace of the woods. He recalled from looking at the map of the woods that Ash led directly to Oak, the main thoroughfare, with Douglas leading off to the right halfway along.

At the end of Ash, he turned left on to Oak and made his way at a sedate walk along to Holly, the turning that would take him to the old mill building. He turned on to Holly, walked a few paces then stopped. He dismounted and walked further along while listening for the sound of voices. By the time the mill building came into view he saw no sign of Cynthia or Pat. He remounted Mercury and walked round the mill pond till he got to the front of the old mill building. He dismounted and tied Mercury's reins to the wooden cart. Mercury snorted and bent down to munch on the long grass of the verge.

The building looked like a typical Sussex barn, the walls constructed from flint, and with red clay tiles on the roof. There were double barn doors on the left and a small single cottage-type door in the middle. To the right of this was a single four-pane window. Above the door were two more four-pane windows, giving the impression of living accommodation.

As he got closer, he could see several sets of footprints leading up to a bench situated on the left of the double barn doors. The bench was where he'd seen Cynthia and Pat chatting. The building looked in good condition, with no broken windows or peeling paint on the doors. Although there was a large hasp and padlock on the barn doors, the padlock hadn't been locked. He pulled the hasp back and the doors swung open on well-oiled hinges revealing a fairly new, dust-covered, red Massey Fergusson tractor with a grass cutting device hanging off the back. Probably used to cut the grass on the estate, thought Buchanan. Further in and to the left of the barn was an old blacksmith's forge.

To Buchanan's eye, the old mill barn was the Castlewood groundsman's maintenance base. He returned to the entrance and after a few minutes of fumbling in the gloom found a pull string for the light switch. Night became day as four fluorescent light-strips lit up the workshop.

On his immediate right there was a small door. He tried the handle and found this was also unlocked. He opened it and went through into a small hallway. There was a flight of stairs on the left, with a passageway beside it leading to the kitchen. In front of him was a door to a front room, which was bare.

He'd seen enough; there wasn't anything sinister in the barn or the small attached cottage. He turned off the barn light, closed the doors and returned to Mercury who by now was looking decidedly bored.

He retraced their steps out to Oak, turned left and trotted back to the main boulevard. He came out of the trees in time to see Cynthia and Pat about forty feet in front of him, – he was too far back to hear their conversation. He looked at his watch and decided since the course was now closed to racing, he'd go for a swift canter up to the quarry. As Mercury set off, Buchanan's mind drifted back to the previous occasion when he'd ridden this route.

As Mercury approached the corner before the quarry, Buchanan pulled in the reins and slowed him to a steady walk. As they turned the corner, Buchanan saw a riderless horse standing above the prostrate form of a rider.

'C'mon boy, let's see what's happened,' said Buchanan, urging Mercury on.

He stopped and dismounted beside the other horse, and while holding on to Mercury's reins, bent down to find out the state of the rider lying on the ground. It was Poppy Grant. She was lying on her back, her eyes open, and breathing slowly.'

'Are you all right?' he asked.

She blinked and looked up at him. 'Yes, I'm absolutely fine. Why?'

'You scared me, I thought you'd fallen and hurt yourself.'

She smiled at him then sat up. 'It's so beautiful and peaceful up here. No one to tell you what to do or what to think.' As she spoke, her horse leaned over and mouthed at her hair. 'I love you too, Pepper.'

'Your horse is called Pepper?' said Buchanan, sitting down beside her.

She nodded. 'Poppy and Pepper. Where I go, he follows.'

'Care for a fruit gum?' he said, opening a tube.

'No thanks.'

'What were you doing?'

'I was watching some sort of large bird; I think it might have been a buzzard. It was going in circles, getting higher and higher. I wished I could do what they do, just climb up into the sky and disappear.'

'You like Harry?'

'Who told you?'

'Nobody, I was in the yard yesterday when your father tried to talk to you.'

'Oh.'

'And today, Harry said you made him a sandwich for his lunch.'

'He said no one's ever done that for him before. My dad calls him a con.'

'I know, he told me. Do you know what Harry was in trouble for?'

'Yes, he told me everything.' She fell silent, then said, 'It wasn't his fault, he didn't know the car was stolen.'

'That's what he told me.'

'You know him?'

'We've chatted. Did he tell you he wants to work in some form of business management or as an accountant?'

'He said he would like to work here at Castlewood.'

'Doing what?'

'He wasn't sure. He really likes working with the horses but finds the stable management a bit chaotic.'

'That's probably because they don't have anyone to run it full time.'

'How do you know that?'

'I live locally and stop in from time to time.'

'Harry has so many ideas of how he'd run this place.'

'I take it you and Harry are more than just good friends?'

'Sounds silly, love at first sight, but when we met, I was sure he was the man for me.'

'How about Harry, is he in love with you?'

She smiled again, blushing as little dimples appeared in her cheeks.

'I'll take that as a yes.'

'It's absolutely crazy. My dad, well you know what he thinks, while my mom wants me to marry Chuck.'

'Who's Chuck?'

'He's the college football running-back.'

'Do you like him?'

'Chuck's all right, but all he thinks about is football and his pickup truck.'

'Don't American football players make a lot of money?'

'As long as they are playing, they do. Get injured and they end up selling insurance for a living.'

'When do you go back home?'

'Dad's on a month's vacation, we go home next Thursday. He says he's on a pilgrimage. He wants to go to Oxford.'

'To university?'

'No, he said there's a cross in the street marking where two martyrs were burned at the stake for their beliefs. Then he wants to go to Lewis.'

'Lewes? That's not far from here. I sometimes have to go there to see my boss.'

She shook her head. 'No, not that one. He wants to go to the Hebrides and visit Lewis, the island where the great Hebrides revival took place.'

'How about you, do you want to visit there?'

'Not particularly, that's my dad's thing.'

'You'd prefer to stay here with Harry?'

She nodded. 'I just don't know what to do. I know I should respect my parents, but – it's my life, surely I should be allowed to make up my own mind?'

'If you don't mind me asking, how old are you?'

'I'll be nineteen at my next birthday.'

'I see,' Buchanan said, nodding.

'See what?'

'Why you were angry at the dinner table last night.'

'You were there?'

'I was sitting beside you.'

'Oh, how embarrassing.'

'Your dad really loves you; he only wants what he sees as the best for you.'

'He thinks I should join the marines like he did.'

'Your dad said he was in the marines at dinner. It still seems a bit odd to me, especially him being the pastor of a church.'

'He had a tough time in Afghanistan. He saw one of his team blown up in front of him; he suffers from PTSD.'

'Badly?'

She nodded. 'Sometimes he gets very angry. Our kitchen wall back home had so many holes from him punching it, we had to call in a repairman to fill them up. Mom says it's not so bad now he's running the church, it sort of keeps his mind occupied.'

'Is he ever violent towards you or your mother?'

'No, never. Are you married, have children?'

'Married yes, children not quite.'

'What do you mean?'

'A young lady I work with has sort of become our family. Her parents died when she was a young girl. I gave her away when she got married.'

'Do you think I'm wrong to want to marry Harry?'

'It's not wrong to want to do something. Marriage is special. To my mind it's something you do forever.'

'You're sounding like my dad.'

'Are you an only child?'

'Yes. My parents tried to have more children, but it didn't work out for them. It was something that happened to my dad when he was in the marines.'

'My wife and I tried to have children, but it didn't work out for us either.'

'What's your wife's name?'

'Karen, and our adopted daughter is called Jill.'

'What did you think when she said she wanted to get married?'

'She was already engaged when we met.'

'Oh. What did your wife say when she heard the news?'

'She cried. But she said Jill was old enough to make up her own mind.'

'That's what I told my parents, but they don't listen.'

'I need to get back,' said Buchanan, standing up. 'Will you be all right?'

'Yes, I'll be fine. Thanks for stopping and talking with me.'

'You're most welcome.'

'If you're going back to the stables,' said Poppy, 'I'll ride along with you.'

As they entered the yard Buchanan could see the Grants. Travis was having a heated discussion with Harry and kept pointing at him while shaking his head. When Shelly Grant saw Poppy riding towards them, she said something to her husband who turned to look. Harry took the opportunity while Travis was distracted to take his leave and disappeared into the stable block.

Travis Grant stood with his hands in his jacket pockets and waited for Poppy to dismount. Before he could say anything, Buchanan said, 'Travis, Shelly, good afternoon, what a lovely day for a ride. Poppy and I have just been up at the old quarry admiring the view. Have you had time to get up there yet?'

Travis's shoulders slumped, he breathed out a long and slow breath and shook his head. 'No, Jack, I don't believe I have.'

Poppy walked up to her father and asked, 'What were you saying to Harry just now?'

Before Travis could say anything, Shelly Grant stepped in between father and daughter, 'Your father was just explaining how important your studies were and how you needed to concentrate on them. Getting involved romantically is not what you need just at this moment in your life.'

'Stop trying to live my life for me, I'm a grown woman,' Poppy said, taking the reins of her horse and walking off into the stable.

Travis went to follow but Shelly put her hand on his arm and said, 'Travis, she is right, she is old enough to make up her own mind. You go get ready for dinner and I'll have a word with her.'

'If he hurts my little girl, I'll cut him in pieces, and make his house a dunghill,' said Travis, as he walked off in the direction of the club.

18:30

Buchanan stepped out of the shower as the phone dinged to say he had an email. It was from Stephen.

> I checked the name Julian Du Marchon on the PNC. He has one entry for DYI five years ago and one SP50 for doing ninety-five on the M25. While in town I went to his office, are you sure the address you gave me was correct? There is no number 37 Mark Lane. I stopped into the community hub and asked there, no one there has heard of Julian Du Marchon.
> When I saw he was an IFA I checked with the FSA. IFA's are not permitted to use client money in the course of their own business activities. The group Julian Du Marchon was with were using client funds for a high-risk investment. They were lucky that the investment paid off. But the syndicate was fined, and all the client funds returned. The syndicate was forced to disband. That's all I could find out about your man.

This case that wasn't yet a case, was starting to look like a case, thought Buchanan, as he towelled his hair dry.

The sound in the restaurant was of excited chatter about the upcoming race. As he walked past the tables on the way to his seat, he heard phrases such as:

'The quarry corner, that fence caught me by surprise …'
'The long gallop behind the golf course, I nearly fell at the ditch …'
'Twice round, I don't know how I managed to stay on …'

He saw that Greyspear had returned and was seated between his wife, Susan, and Poppy. Buchanan smiled when he saw the remaining spare seat was his, between Poppy and Cynthia. This evening Cynthia was smiling.

She looked at Buchanan as he sat and said, 'Wonderful day, did you go out riding, Jack?'

'Yes, I did, thanks.'

'On the course?'

'Not at first, although I did go for a short gallop after everyone was off. I didn't want to get mixed up with the competitors, I'm not that good a rider.'

'Oh, I'm sure you'd be fine,' said Cynthia.

'What did you think of the wall with the ditch behind, Jack?' asked Shelly.

'I didn't get that far. I only went up to the old quarry, then turned back,'

'Jack is a very good rider,' said Poppy. 'I rode back with him, I think if he was entered for the race, he'd stand a good chance of winning.'

'Thanks for the vote of confidence, Poppy. But I think there are a lot of better riders here than me.'

'Quite right,' said Victor. 'Our jockey Pat McCall, now there's a top-class rider. If I were a betting man, I'd put my money on him.'

'Officially there is no betting on this race,' said Greyspear. 'But, if the owners want to put on a small wager, well then, that's their decision.'

'I'd put my money on Harry if he were allowed to race,' said Poppy.

Buchanan glanced at Poppy. She was grinning defiantly at her father.

'Well, he's not, so you can put that idea right out of your head,' said Travis.

'It's people like you who –'

'Poppy, dear,' interrupted Shelly, 'you know Harry is an employee and is probably not eligible to race.'

'What your mother says is correct, Poppy,' said Travis. 'Now, please. Let's not hear any more about the matter.'

'You're just saying that because Harry isn't one of your people.'

'Poppy, I've said that's enough, subject closed.'

'It's not fair! You just don't want me to have any fun, I wish I'd stayed home,' she said, biting her lower lip, then twisting her napkin into shreds and throwing them on the table.

'Poppy Grant!' said Travis. 'I said that's enough, you're embarrassing your mother.'

'It's you who are embarrassing me,' she said, standing and walking out of the restaurant.

Buchanan glanced round the table, everyone except the Grants were studying the dessert menus.

Travis murmured something to Shelly, she nodded then got up and presumably went after Poppy.

'Children!' said Travis, shaking his head. 'She'll be fine when she calms down, just a bit of jetlag.'

Poppy's outburst broke the mood of excitement round the table and set the mood for the remainder of the meal.

♦

21:30

'If you'll excuse me,' said Greyspear, pushing his chair back. 'I have a busy day tomorrow.'

Victor and Cynthia followed, leaving Buchanan and Travis alone at the table.

The waiter came over to the table. 'Would you like something from the bar?'

Travis looked at Buchanan, then shook his head. 'I think I'll go through to the bar. How about you, Jack?'

'Sounds like a plan.'

'Thank you,' said the waiter.

'Shall we go?' said Travis.

'You lead, I'll follow,' said Buchanan.

Travis went into the library and sat beside the fire. 'This reminds me of home,' he said, relaxing back into the armchair and crossing his outstretched legs.

'Can I get you anything from the bar?' asked the waiter.

'I'll have a Jack Daniels on ice, make it a double, will you?' said Travis.

'Mr Buchanan?'

'I'll have a Lagavulin, with a splash of water, please.'

Buchanan sat across from Travis and watched him as he sat quietly staring at the fire.

'You know something, Jack?' said Travis, looking up as the waiter returned with their drinks.

'I know lots of things, Travis. Anything in particular?'

'Very good, Jack. What I was going to say was – do you have children?'

Buchanan thought for a moment and decided it was time to be decisive on the issue. 'Yes, our daughter, Jill, adopted us. Her birth parents died when she was a young girl.'

'I think you need to explain that?' he said, taking a large sip of his drink.

'Just over a year ago I was transferred from Glasgow to work in our Eastbourne office. Working there was a young lady called Jill. We worked well together and became friends as well as co-workers. One night I received a phone call to say she was sitting on the edge of Beachy Head cliffs.'

'I've heard of them,' said Travis. 'It has the sad reputation of having one of the highest suicide rates in the world.'

'The gaping mouth of hell, I call it,' said Buchanan, as he threw back the dregs of his whisky. Travis raised his hand to the waiter, signifying they wanted another round of drinks.

'Although we had only arrived in Eastbourne recently, I was well aware of the reputation of Beachy Head. I probably broke every traffic rule driving up there. When I arrived, the Beachy Head chaplaincy and police were already there. I don't know what would have happened had I not got there, but thankfully she listened to me and stepped back from the edge. I took her home and my wife put her to bed. It was a strange sensation from never having had children, to suddenly being responsible for someone so fragile, albeit for a brief moment in her life. From then on, we just grew together as a family. I gave Jill away in marriage to her husband, Stephen, just a few months ago.'

'And I thought I had problems,' said Travis. 'Shelly and I have a real issue with Poppy. You've seen how she behaves around that con, Harry. I tell you something, Jack. If word of this infatuation gets back to the elders of my church, well, I don't want to think about the consequences.'

'I thought you Christians preached forgiveness of sins?'

'That's an odd statement from someone who I presume isn't one?'

'Why do you say that?

'What, that you aren't a Christian?'

'Yes. It's not my fault I don't get to go to church. I'm just too busy during the week and Sunday is the only day I get to relax.'

'Going to church doesn't make you a Christian, Jack. Neither does arranging flowers.'

'So, what does?'

Travis sat up and looked straight at Buchanan. 'By admitting you're a sinner, Jack. Believing in your heart that Jesus died and rose again shedding his blood to pay for your sins.'

'So, what am I supposed to do then?'

'Then simply like a child, accept Christ into your heart as your saviour.'

Buchanan looked at Travis. 'My wife has said that more than once.'

'What did you do about it?'

'Listened, then got on with life. I suppose if there's some sort of divine being, when it's my time to go, I will be judged on how I lead my life.'

Travis smiled. 'For by grace you have been saved through faith. And this is not your own doing; it is the gift of God, not a result of works, so that no one may boast. Ephesians, chapter 2 verses eight and nine.'

'You put your faith in your Bible and an unseen God. I put my faith in my ability to stay alive and keep my wits about me.'

'Sometimes I feel I don't know the Bible well enough.'

'You must be doing something right, especially if you have a church of twenty thousand.'

'Yes, but twenty thousand what? A few months ago, I had the group leaders ask their groups how many of them read their Bible regularly. You know what the result was?'

'No, Travis, I don't, what was it?'

'Only twenty percent. Just think, Jack. All those smiling faces that sit in the pews each Sunday, listening to my voice and all the time thinking about anything other than what I was preaching. Twenty thousand professing Christians and probably less than a third really born again. What hope does our country have when the barbarians come knocking at our doors?'

'That's beyond my remit, Travis.'

'I suppose it is. We are also warned to watch out for the wiles of the Devil who seeks to steal, kill and destroy.'

'And you think Harry is the Devil?'

'Not quite. We read in the Bible that we shouldn't be unequally yoked. Poppy has been brought up in a Christian home, been going to church from when she was two weeks old. She helps in Sunday School and sings in the youth choir. So, you see she can't have a relationship with someone who hasn't made a confession of faith.'

Buchanan nodded to the waiter for another round.

'Suppose they love each other, isn't that enough?' asked Buchanan.

'In some churches it might be, but it's not encouraged in ours. And since I am the senior pastor, my family has to set an example.'

'Surely Poppy is old enough to make up her own mind?'

'Not while she lives under my roof. I will not countenance any disobedience from her.'

'Suppose she disobeys you. In the UK, at nineteen you are seen as an adult and can make your own decisions.'

'As I said, while she lives under my roof, she will obey the house rules, and do as I say. No one will be permitted to change that.'

'You were in the army?' asked Buchanan.

'Marines.'

'Serve overseas?'

'Poppy's been talking, hasn't she?'

Buchanan nodded.

'Three tours in Afghanistan.'

'Poppy said you saw some serious fighting.'

Travis nodded.

'Were you injured?'

'Only slightly, worse luck,' replied Travis, as he threw back the remainder of his drink.

'Why do you say, worse luck?'

Travis let out his breath and waved at the waiter for another round. 'You ask why I say worse luck? Well, my friend, when I think about what those men of my platoon suffered under my command, and I realise I only suffered from a bit of shrapnel in my arm, it makes me sad to have let them down.'

'Do you suffer from flashbacks?'

Travis nodded, leaned forward and placed two logs on the smouldering fire. 'The worst is at night. I go to bed about one, fall asleep immediately only to wake a couple of hours later. My heart is racing, my body tensed, ready for anything. In my mind I'm back in Kandahar. I can't lie there; the fear drives me out of bed and downstairs. I always go down silently in the dark. I realise this may sound strange to someone who's never been confronted by death, but that's what happens when fear grabs the mind. I go into the lounge and take the cushions off the settee and lay them on the floor behind it for a bed. That way I feel protected – out of sight.'

'Do you wake before Shelly comes down in the morning?'

He shook his head. 'Shelly lets me sleep till I wake myself. Why not wake me in the night and get me to return to bed, you might ask? I'll tell you why. She'd heard a story about one soldier who suffered from PTSD. His wife tried to wake him from a nightmare and if it hadn't been for his son hearing the ruckus, the soldier would have strangled her.'

'Do you have these incidents often?'

Travis shook his head slowly. 'Not too many now. They usually happen after a stressful day, or if I'm in a crowd. I sometimes turn when I hear my name called and, as I turn, I see Joe smiling, just like he did the moment the IED exploded – I suppose Poppy told you about what happened on my last tour of duty?'

'She mentioned something about an IED.'

'It was during my third and final tour in Afghanistan. Patrolling day and night in life-threatening conditions we were never far away from being shot at or blown up. Some of the soldiers I served with were severely traumatised by what they saw and experienced; death knocked on our door daily.'

'I've heard some of these stories from friends who served in Afghanistan.'

'Each time we went out on patrol and walked the back streets of Kandahar, you could feel the hair stand on the back of your neck. We all knew that at any moment we could turn a corner or enter a building and come face to face with the Taliban. When that happened, that was when our intensive training took over, especially if they shot first.'

'Did that happen very often?'

'More often than I'd wished. Typically, when it happened the combatant would let off a couple of bursts of his AK47, those bursts were usually only for a couple of seconds and due to the raghead's inability in preventing the natural lift as they fired their weapon, they would end up spraying the ceiling. At the first moment of him firing, we'd drop and aim. As they took their finger off the trigger to see what they'd shot, I'd fire three shots, two in the mouth and a third between the eyes as they fell. End of argument.'

'You were going to tell me what happened the night of the IED explosion.'

'It was an evening just like many that had gone before. As per usual, we'd sort out our finances, make sure our wills were up to date; then sit down and write letters to our loved ones back home explaining why we went and letting them know we would always love them. When we went out on patrol, we always did all we could to make sure no one had to read those damn letters. We fought to stay alive, and we also fought to make sure our brothers made it back to base to rip up those letters.'

'As a Christian, how do you rationalise the taking of a life?'

'There's nothing in the Bible that says you shouldn't act in self-defence.'

'I've only ever read little bits of the Bible, and that was at Sunday school.'

'You should read it, it's life's instruction manual.'

'You were going to tell me what happened on the night you were injured.'

'On the night it happened, before we left the base we checked everything from the radio to the rifles. Our assignment was to check out one of the back alleys in Kandahar. There were four of us. We stopped beside a wadi, next to a poppy field. I can remember thinking my daughter's name was Poppy.

'We'd stopped to check our location. While I checked the map, the others kept a look out for trouble. I heard a noise and looked up. Joe thought he'd seen someone hiding in the wadi and had taken a couple of steps away from us to get a better look. The sound I'd heard was his boots scraping the dirt as he turned to walk back. That was when it happened. His right boot caught the tripwire and the IED exploded. One-minute Joe was there, smiling at all of us; the next I was wearing him.'

Travis shook his head at the memory and threw back the remainder of his drink. 'You know, I'm not supposed to drink this stuff,' he said holding up his empty glass and waving it at the waiter.

'I can't imagine what you must have gone through,' said Buchanan. 'Do you have a support group, people you can talk with?'

'There's the Veterans Administration, and of course there's private agencies, such as Real Warriors, who do so much for the veterans.'

'What about your church?'

'I have a group of friends, mostly ex-servicemen who support me in prayer.'

'What about your doctor? Can he prescribe something?'

Travis smiled at Buchanan. 'My doctor is one of the members of the prayer group. She says prayer is the best medicine. But I can have medication any time my symptoms require it.'

6
Wednesday Early

06:43

Although Castlewood Country Club was situated in the Sussex countryside, it wasn't far enough away from the A22 to shield it from the sound of a police or ambulance siren. So, on Wednesday morning at six forty-three, Buchanan woke from a peaceful night's sleep to the wails of an ambulance and police car arriving in the stable block carpark directly under his bedroom window.

Now wide awake and thoroughly curious, he rolled out of bed and walked over to the far window. There was a police car stopped behind the ambulance. Two yellow-coated paramedics were carrying a first aid kit, a resuscitator, plus an oxygen cylinder. Buchanan realised this ambulance wasn't for any horse, it was for a human patient.

After thirty-five years in the police force, he knew when something was up. He dressed quickly and, not waiting for the lift, dashed down the stairs and through the building out to the stables. He stopped at the door to the stables and watched as a police constable tried to wipe vomit from the sole of his boots.

'Sorry, sir, you can't come in through this door. The ambulance crew are taking care of an incident. Would you mind going round to the other entrance?'

Buchanan was about to introduce himself when he thought it might be good to stay incommunicado. 'Certainly, I'll go around to the main entrance. Er, do you know what's happened?'

'I think one of the people who work here has been injured by a horse.'

'Which stall are they in?'

'I believe it is stall number six.'

117

Mercury's stall thought Buchanan. He saw Lenny leaning out of the door to the coachman's lodge, he was grinning. Seeing Lenny, Buchanan figured it was unlikely to be George who was in the stall. He fervently hoped it wasn't Harry.

If it was, what on earth had happened? Had he seen something and decided to investigate? Or worse still, had Travis, after drinking late into the evening, caught up with Harry as he was checking on Mercury and decided to take matters in hand? Had there had been an argument, a struggle, with Harry ended up being badly injured? Maybe Travis had come to his senses and left Harry on the floor of Mercury's stall.

Buchanan stepped back and walked the long way round to the main entrance. The double barn doors were shut but not locked. He pulled the right-hand door open enough to enter and sauntered down the corridor towards the end stalls. The policeman who had previously prevented him from entering was now outside dealing with one of the anxious horse owners. Trying not to attract attention to himself, he walked down the corridor and stood outside stall six, Mercury's stall and watched while one of the paramedics worked on the unconscious blooded body of Harry.

It was awkward for the paramedics; the horse was still in the stall and kept whinnying and shuffling about as the other paramedic tried to keep it still while holding up a saline bottle. He must have had some experience in handling horses thought Buchanan because he had managed to get the rope halter on Mercury.

'Here, let me help,' said Buchanan, stepping into the stall. 'Pass me the halter and I'll lead the horse out of your way.'

Grateful to be able to concentrate on his patient the paramedic passed the halter rope to Buchanan who gently lead the now jittery Mercury out of the stall and tied him to a hitching post.'

Now free of his charge, Buchanan re-entered the stall and stood beside the paramedic who was still holding the saline bottle.

'How is he?' asked Buchanan.

'Do you work here?'

'No, I'm a friend of Harry. He doesn't have any family round here.'

'He's alive, but unresponsive. He's lucky, much longer and that horse would have trampled the life out of him.'

'Where will you take him?'

'We're not. The air ambulance is on its way, it will take him to the DGH. We're concerned the ambulance ride could be too much for him in his state.'

♦

07:30

Something just wasn't right, thought Buchanan as he watched the air ambulance lift off from the lawn. He took his phone out of his pocket and looked at the time. Good, Doctor Mansell should be up by now. He pressed the call button and waited.

'Don't tell me, you got a dead body for me to look at?'

'Ok, I won't.'

'Good. I thought you were on leave?'

'I am.'

'Then to what do I owe this early morning call?'

'There's been a bad accident here at Castlewood. The assistant stable manager has been severely trampled by a horse.'

'Have you run out of dead bodies that now you want to get in on them before they die?'

'Listen, there is something bothering me about this accident. The lad is on his way in to the DGH by air ambulance. His name is Harry Janski. Could you have a look at his injuries and tell me if they are commensurate with that of a horse trampling on him?'

There was a pause, then Mansell replied, 'I'll just finish my breakfast. That should give the trauma team time to stabilise him. I'll call you as soon as I've been to see him.'

'Thanks, breakfast sounds good. All this fresh air has given me an appetite, I'll talk to you later.'

◆
08:00

Buchanan walked briskly back to the clubhouse, the whereabouts of Travis Grant high on his mind. He entered the restaurant and went over to one of the waiters.

'Good morning, Mr Buchanan, you can sit at any table. Would you like me to bring you a coffee?'

'In a minute. I was wondering if the Grant family have been in for breakfast yet?'

'I don't think so. Would you like me to ask the other waiter for you?'

'Yes please, I'll wait here.'

The waiter was back in four minutes, 'I asked David, he was on before me and he said he hadn't seen them yet.'

'Thanks.'

Buchanan stood for a minute deciding what to do next, when all three of the Grants came in and sat at one of the empty tables. He poured himself a coffee then walked over to them.

'Good morning, may I join you?'

Travis Grant looked up from his phone; Shelly and Poppy stopped talking.

'Oh, hello,' said Poppy. 'Please, there's plenty of room, we've just sat down.'

'Thanks,' said Buchanan, sitting down beside her. He looked across at Travis and was aware of how what he was about to say would affect Poppy. He said, 'did you hear about the accident in the stables last night?'

Travis shook his head. 'No – should we have?'

'I just found out the assistant stable manager was injured by a horse during the night.'

'Is he all right?' asked Poppy.

'I don't know. He was still unconscious when the air ambulance took him off to the hospital.'

'Oh, no!' said Poppy. 'Mom, we have to go see him. Where is the hospital, Jack?'

'It's in town, about a twenty-minute drive from here.'

'Mom, we have to go,' said Poppy, standing up.

Buchanan looked back at Travis; he was massaging his right fist and looking at the table.

'If it helps, I could drive you?' said Buchanan.

'Mom, please, we're wasting time. Dad?'

'If Jack wants to drive you and your mom, it's fine with me. I'd just get lost,' said Travis.

'Let's go, come on,' said Poppy, starting for the door.

♦

08:45

Buchanan pulled up across from the emergency entrance.

'You two go on in and I'll park the car.'

Buchanan joined them in the emergency waiting room. 'How is he?'

'They won't talk to us. They say we're not family,' said Poppy.

'Hang on a minute. Maybe I can get an answer, I'll be right back.'

Buchanan went over to the reception desk. 'Good morning, DCI Buchanan. I'm enquiring about the young man just brought in, Harry Janski. He was injured in a horse stall.'

'Is it a police matter?' asked the receptionist.

'Do you need to see my warrant card?'

'No, I remember you from before. I'll go and ask the doctor.'

She was back in five minutes. 'Inspector, there's a Doctor Mansell with the patient, he asked if you'd join him. I'll show you through.'

♦

09:15

'Hello Doctor, finish your breakfast?'

'Yes, I did, thank you.'

'Find anything?'

'Just what you thought I'd find. You suspected something, that's why you called me.'

'Well, what did you find?'

'A nice big bruise on the back of the head, just where you'd expect to find one when someone gets coshed from behind. I'd say he was beaten unconscious then dumped in the horse stall hoping the horse would complete the job; leaving everyone to think the horse killed him.'

'He's not dead, is he?'

'No, thankfully. But do you notice anything odd?' said Mansell, as he lifted Harry's hand and pulled back the gown from his arm.

Buchanan shook his head. 'No, what is it I'm supposed to notice?'

'His wrists, look at them.'

'Aren't they just bruises caused by a horse when it stood on him?'

'I'd say they were more like the marks left when someone has their wrists tied together, then their body is suspended from a height."

'Oh, hell, a punishment beating.'

'Exactly, Jack. Someone was either giving him a message or trying to teach him a lesson and it went very badly wrong.'

'It reminds me of the reports of IRA beatings we used to see when I worked in Glasgow.'

'I've seen the actual results. Did you know that kneecapping still goes on today?'

'I had heard stories to that effect. So, whoever did this to him chucked him in the stall hoping the horse would trample him to death and cover their tracks?'

'That's what it looks like. Do you think there could be a paramilitary connection?'

'I sure as hell hope not.'

'How about suspects, anybody in mind?'

'There are two stable-hands looking after a couple of horses for an army colonel. Both have form, and then there is the father of the lad's girlfriend. He'd told his daughter to stay away from him.'

'Aren't you on administrative leave?'

'Supposed to be. I'll see if Hanbury is free and bring him up to date. It will be up to him to figure out if it was related to the lad's past, or something to do with the race this coming Saturday.'

'The neurologist is going to do a CT scan,' said Mansell. 'He wants to see if there is any bleeding in the brain.'

'Has he regained consciousness?'

'Not yet. What do you want me to do?'

'There's a young lady and her mother waiting to hear how he is doing – what do you suggest I tell them?'

'Are they related to him?'

'Not yet. The young lady has a crush on him. They've only known each other for a couple of days.'

'Young love, eh?'

'You said it. What are his chances of recovery?'

'I'd say that barring a negative result on the CT scan, he should make a full recovery.'

'Thanks, can you keep me posted?'

'Will do. Would you like me to talk to the girl's family?'

Buchanan nodded, 'Yes please, that should reassure them, but please don't mention I'm a policeman and that you are a police surgeon. They think I'm just plain Jack Buchanan, a civil servant.'

'Working undercover – I thought you just said you were on administrative leave?'

'You're right, I am on administrative leave, and to a certain extent I suppose you could say I am working undercover, but not officially, yet. I'll let Hanbury do the preliminary investigation.'

'Yet?'

'Well, it's you who pointed out the injuries to the wrists."

Mansell nodded. 'Mum's the word.'

Buchanan and Mansell walked back to the waiting room and a very anxious Poppy.

'How is he?' she asked.

'He's still sleeping. The neurologists would like to do a CT scan,' said Mansell.

'Oh no!' said Poppy, putting her hand over her mouth.

'It's just a precaution, you needn't worry.'

'Can we see him?'

'Not just at the moment.'

'Has he said anything?'

'No, he's still unconscious.'

'Oh, Mom,' said Poppy, turning to look at her mother. 'I have to see him, he needs to know I'm here.'

'But we can't stay here indefinitely,' said Shelly. 'Jack needs to get back to the club.

'That's all right,' said Buchanan. 'I tell you what, I need to run a couple of errands in town, so why don't I leave you two here with Dr Mansell? He can keep you updated on Harry's condition. When I'm done, I'll return here and collect you.'

'Please, Mom,' said Poppy, looking anxiously at her mother.

'Are you sure that's all right, Dr Mansell?'

Mansell looked at Buchanan and shrugged. 'Sure, no problem, I've got work to do here at the hospital this morning.'

'Great, thanks.'

'I shouldn't be long,' said Buchanan.

♦

10:00

The stage was set, the actors in place, it was time for curtain up, thought Buchanan, as he drove into Hammonds Drive.

'Good morning, sir,' said the desk sergeant, as Buchanan entered the police station. 'Back from your holiday?'

'Not quite. Is DI Hanbury in?'

'I saw him with PC Hunter about twenty minutes ago – they were going upstairs.'

'Thanks.'

Buchanan turned left at the top of the stairs and walked down the corridor to Hanbury's office.

'Oh, you're back,' said Hanbury, as Buchanan entered.

'Not really. I'm here to ask a favour.'

'You're enjoying yourself so much you want to take more time off?' said Hanbury.

'No, it's nothing like that. Last night, the assistant stable manager was severely injured. It was made to look like he's been injured by a horse trampling him. In fact, it looks more like a punishment beating that went very badly wrong. It's possible he might have seen something he wasn't supposed to see, or something from his past caught up with him. Either way, it was made to look like he was trampled by a horse while in the stall. Doctor Mansell thinks that the lad was tied up by the wrists then hung while he was beaten. I'm not sure what evidence an SCI team would find, but you might want to have a look around the stall yourself while you're there.'

'Do you have any suspects in mind?'

'Yes. Two cons called George and Lenny, they are the prime suspects. Stephen has the details of their criminal records. There is one other suspect, but I would like to pursue that one on my own just for now. Could you also check further into the background of the jockey, Pat McCall? He seems to be clean, but he could be hiding a shady past.'

'What do you want me to do about George and Lenny?'

'Can you go and see Dr Mansell, he's at the DGH this morning, and find out how the injured lad is doing? The girlfriend and her mother should be there waiting for news. Then could you pay a visit to Castlewood Country Club and interview George and Lenny? They're staying in the Old Coachman's Lodge in the stable block. The door to the lodge is just down the corridor from stall six, where the stable manager was found this morning. George and

Lenny are supposed to be keeping an eye on the horses in stalls one and two.'

'What am I to say I am investigating?'

'You could say the doctor at the hospital says the injuries to the lad look quite serious and he might not make it.'

'Couldn't you question them yourself?'

'The reason I would like you to question George and Lenny for me is I want to stay undercover for a little while longer. There's something brewing and I'm only guessing about the who and the what of the case.'

7
Wednesday Midday

11:00

Buchanan left the police station and drove up Rodmill Drive towards Willingdon and the office of Achmed Bashir, IFA.

'Inspector Buchanan, 'said Aakifah Bashir, as she opened the door. 'What a lovely surprise, please come in. Are you looking for Achmed?'

'Thanks, yes. I was wondering if he is available?'

'Did you have an appointment?'

'No, but I shouldn't keep him long.'

'Please come through,' she said, as she led Buchanan through to the lounge. 'Take a seat and I'll let Achmed know you are here.'

He relaxed back into an armchair and marvelled at the decor and the painting hanging over the fireplace – it looked just like a Monet.

Aakifah Bashir returned a few minutes later. 'Achmed will be with you shortly. Can I get you something to drink while you wait?'

Buchanan thought back to the last time he was here. 'Tea will be fine.'

'I shan't be a moment,' she said, turning and walking off, her hair flowing behind her.

This case is puzzling, thought Buchanan as he waited for his tea and Achmed Bashir to be available. Firstly, there was Cynthia Mountjoy. She was in an unhappy marriage to someone who *played for the other team*, according to what Buchanan was able to pick up. She was also having an affair with their jockey, Pat McCall, and working on getting a divorce. The idea of Harry suffering a paramilitary beating and Pat McCall being Irish crossed Buchanan's mind. Was there a connection? Cynthia's divorce from

127

her husband, Victor, was being handled by her husband's army cohort, Andrew Jackson. Now there was a conflict of interests. Of course, Andrew Jackson had reason to dislike Victor Mountjoy, Jackson held him responsible for the death of his nephew. Adding to the case was Julian Du Marchon, an IFA whose business seemed to be on the move between addresses and probably profits. He in turn seemed to have a working acquaintance with George and Lenny who in turn were looking after Victor Mountjoy's horses. And last but not least was Harry, the assistant stable manager and ex-con, as described by Travis Grant, the father of Poppy, who was now Harry's girlfriend.

Aakifah Bashir returned carrying a gilt tray with glass cups held in little gold-plated holders. But unlike the last time he visited the Bashirs, she had brought a small milk jug.

'I remember you prefer milk with your tea, Inspector.'

'You should work for us, the last time I had tea here was last year. Thanks.'

'Achmed will be with you soon. Did I see you at Castlewood?'

'Yes. I'm staying there for a few days rest, relaxation and riding. I'm not racing, though.'

'Aisha and her friend Deborah are entered in the cross-country race.'

'I thought that might be the case. There's quite a few riders entered; some are professional.'

'We know that, but the girls are doing it for the fun,' said Achmed, entering the room. 'Now surely you didn't come here to talk about the girls riding in the race, did you?'

'No. I have been approached by someone seeking to invest the profit from the sale of my house in Glasgow.'

'Is it a substantial sum?'

'There is no cash, I just said that to see where he would go with the information. I have one of my feelings that this chap isn't on the level.'

'Let's go through to my office, I'll see what the internet can tell us.'

♦

11:30

'What's his name?' asked Bashir, as he relaxed into his office chair.

'Julian Du Marchon.'

'Let's have a look,' said Bashir, as he started typing on his keyboard.

'Where are you looking?' asked Buchanan.

'The Financial Conduct Authority. They are the regulators of all financial services firms, including individuals. Hmm, it looks like Mr Du Marchon is being a bad boy, offering investment advice. The record says that his firm can no longer provide regulated products and services. Previously he was authorised by the PRA and or FCA. His firm has requirements or restrictions placed on the financial services activities that it can operate. Requirements or restrictions can include suspensions.'

'He said he was in between offices.'

'He may be between offices, but the record says he is no longer authorised to provide regulated products and services, even though they were previously authorised, and also, he is no longer a tied agent.'

'What is a tied agent?'

'A tied agent can act on behalf of another firm or individual regulated in another country in the European Economic Area. Additionally, he is unable to undertake insurance distribution. If I were you, I'd stay well away from him and his advice.'

'Don't worry, I have no intention of letting him get anywhere near our money.'

'Is there anything else?'

Buchanan shook his head. 'No, that should do for now, thanks.'

'I'll see you out.'

♦

12:00

As Buchanan drove back to the hospital he thought about the day's developments. Travis being an ex-marine, suffering with PTSD, and massaging his right fist at breakfast, made Buchanan wonder if there were any holes in the Grants' bedroom walls. Could he have been responsible for Harry's injuries? How much had Travis had to drink last night? At least three double Jack Daniels, he remembered.

'Jack,' said Poppy, as he entered the waiting room, 'we were wondering if you were coming back.'

'I'm here, how is Harry?'

'The doctor says there's no brain damage, but he's still unconscious.'

'Is the doctor still here?'

'Yes, he said he was waiting for you.'

'Do you know where he is?'

'He said to ask the receptionist.'

'Thanks.'

Buchanan went back to the reception area to ask for Dr Mansell.

'I'll take you to him,' said the nurse.

Buchanan followed her through into the emergency suite and the room where Harry was lying.

'How is he, Doctor?' asked Buchanan.

'See for yourself,' he said, gesturing with his hand.

Harry turned his head and looked up at Buchanan.

'Good to see you're awake. How do you feel?'

'Like shit.'

'Do you remember what happened?'

'No. All I remember is doing the rounds and hearing a noise. Next thing, I wake up here in hospital.'

'That's all?' said Buchanan.

'Sorry.'

'His scans are all normal,' said Mansell. 'There are a couple of broken ribs and the rest are just bruises.'

'What can you remember?' asked Buchanan. 'For instance, what time did you do your rounds?'

'The last rounds are done about eleven.'

'And was that the time you started last night?'

'Yes. I watched the end of the news on BBC, then went down to do my rounds.'

'Do you remember seeing anyone?'

Harry thought for a moment and went to shake his head, winced and squeezed his eyes as the pain went down his neck. 'Whew, won't do that again in a hurry. To answer your question, I don't remember seeing anyone.'

'Where did you start your rounds?'

'I usually go to the far end of the stables then work my way back checking the horses and locking the doors as I go. That's my favourite time of the day. By then some of the horses have gone to sleep, others are nibbling at their hay nets. I usually get a snort or whinny of recognition as I pass their stalls.'

'That would be stall twenty-two where you started?'

'Yes. I look into every stall and room as I go along to make sure there's nothing amiss.'

'Does that include the feed and bedding stores?'

'Yes, and my office and the tack room.'

'How about the doors?'

'The doors to the outside at the end of the corridors are locked from the inside, as is the one opposite my office. The main stable doors are shut and locked, but they have panic bars on the inside in case of emergencies and we need to get the horses out in a hurry. There are small doors built into them for people to enter and leave after hours.'

'Do they get locked?'

'Supposed to be locked. But some of the regular horse owners have their own keys, and there's also a copy at the main reception desk.'

'Could someone go out through one of the doors at the end of the corridors and leave it on the latch?'

'They're not supposed to, but I suppose they could.'

'And you don't remember what happened to you?'

Harry remembered not to shake his head. 'No, absolutely nothing.'

'Do you remember the names of the others in the car the night you got arrested?'

'That was a while ago. Sorry, my mind's a bit hazy.'

'Never mind, I'll check the court records.'

'Do you think it could have been them?'

'I don't know, Harry.'

'Oh shit,' he said laying back onto his pillow, 'why can't I remember what happened? Every time I try to think, the pain in my head gets worse.'

'Can I offer you some advice?' said Buchanan.

'Yeah, sure.'

'The neurologists assured Dr Mansell that it is quite likely your memory will recover. When it does, and until we know what happened to you and by whom, tell no one till you've spoken to me or Dr Mansell, understand?'

'Yes.'

'You will be staying here for the rest of the day,' said Mansell. 'Then, as long as nothing untoward shows up, you will be free to go home Friday.'

'In the meantime,' said Buchanan, 'there's someone waiting to see you.'

'Poppy?'

Buchanan nodded. 'And her mother, so be on your best behaviour.'

'I'll show them through,' said Mansell.

'Oh, Harry!' said Poppy, as she looked at his face and the bruises on his chest. 'What did they do to you?'

'I think I'll leave you three to talk,' said Buchanan. 'I'll be waiting in the cafeteria with the doctor.'

♦

12:30

'What will you do now?' asked Mansell, as he poured milk into his cup.

'It's beginning to look like my holiday is disappearing over a fence. I think I'll ask Hanbury to check up on Harry's conviction and the whereabouts of those convicted with him. In the meantime, I suppose I'm providing a taxi service.'

'You know Hanbury has been to see the lad?'

'I expected that. How did it go?'

'He asked the basic questions like you did, then he went and talked with the lad's girlfriend and mother.'

'Did you listen in on the questions?'

'I was in the room. I don't think Hanbury recognised me in my hospital coat. Stephen did, but he kept quiet while Hanbury talked.'

'What sort of questions did he ask the mother and daughter?'

'I got the distinct impression Hanbury is gunning for the father.'

'Why?'

'The mother said something about the dad not being in favour of the daughter dating the lad, on account of the fact he had a record.'

'That I already knew.'

'How about the father being an ex-marine suffering from PTSD?"

'I also knew that.'

'What you may not know is, I think Hanbury has already made up his mind that the father is the guilty party.'

'That I didn't know, and it isn't good news. I'll need to have a chat with Hanbury and see what he's basing his thoughts on.'

'In that case, I'll catch up with you at the next body.'

'Very funny, see you later.'

Buchanan relaxed into one of the plastic chairs in the waiting room and thought about the unfolding tragedy. If it had in fact been Travis who was responsible for Harry's beating, how could the family and the church reconcile themselves to the fact that he was a violent man?

◆

13:15

Buchanan had time to drink two cups of coffee before Shelly and Poppy reappeared.

'How is he?'

'He doesn't remember what happened,' said Poppy. 'It's so cruel. Why aren't the police doing something about it? That policeman who was here earlier, all he did was just to ask a whole lot of questions. Why isn't he out looking for whoever hurt Harry?'

'I'm sure Detective Inspector Hanbury is working on the case right now,' said Buchanan. 'The police are very busy these days, especially now since there are a lot less of them.'

'Would you mind driving us back to the club?' asked Shelly.

'Certainly, my car is just outside.'

Shelly and Poppy followed Buchanan out through the main entrance and along to his car.

'Aren't you worried about getting a ticket for parking in a restricted area?' asked Shelly, as she looked at where Buchanan had parked.

'I had a word with them and said it was an emergency.'

'Oh. You must have talked to the right person. Back home you'd have been towed away for less.'

Shelly and Poppy sat in the back of the car as Buchanan drove. Poppy cried, while Shelly tried to console her.

Buchanan pulled up in front of the main entrance to the club. Shelly and Poppy got out while the valet took Buchanan's car keys.

'Will you require your car again today, Mr Buchanan?'

He shook his head. 'No, not today, thanks.'

Buchanan stood at the foot of the entrance steps and looked out across the lawns to the lakes as three geese charged across the water. He continued to watch them as they climbed into the sky and flew off, honking excitedly, over the trees.

He climbed the steps and entered the club reception. He was going to go up to his room but saw Shelly and Poppy having an agitated conversation with the club manager. Poppy saw him come in and waved him over.

'What is it, Poppy?'

'It's Dad, he's been arrested for assaulting Harry.'

Things had moved faster than Buchanan thought they would. 'Tell me exactly what happened, Shelly?'

'According to the manager, two policemen came here, went to the stables then asked to talk to Travis. I mentioned before that Travis suffers from PTSD, well, one of the things that sets him off is to be put on the spot and be questioned about what he has or hasn't done. He's fine when he's in charge, but not the other way round.'

'When did this happen?'

'About half an hour ago. What should we do?'

This was getting awkward, thought Buchanan. The easy way to resolve the issue would be to reveal who he was and take over the investigation. On the other hand, if he did that, he would probably lose the thread of what was behind Harry's assault. He had given consideration to the possibility that Travis assaulted Harry but was leaning more to the idea that either George or Lenny, or both, were responsible. Travis could fit in with what information he had, but not in the greater scope of the events. He made his mind up

'Would you like me to call my friend and find out what's happening?'

Shelly looked at him. 'Just what kind of civil servant are you? Back home I'd assume you work for the DA's office?'

'DA?'

'District attorney,' replied Shelly.

'Ah, in this country that would be the CPS, Crown Prosecution Service.'

'Is that who you work for?'

'Not directly, but our paths do cross from time to time.'

'You certainly are an enigma. Yes, please call your friend and ask.'

Buchanan stepped away from the group at the reception desk, took out his phone and called Hanbury; he got his voicemail. 'Hi, it's Jack, can you call me when you get this message?'

Next he called Stephen. As he waited for the call to be answered he walked further away from the group towards the porter's desk.

'Stephen, it's Jack – yes, I just found out. Where is he being held? Is Hanbury around? Ok, when he's done, ask him to meet me at Starbucks in half an hour – yes, our usual one at Pevensey. Thanks, see you shortly.'

Buchanan walked back to Shelly and Poppy. Their faces showed their grief.

'Well, what did your friend have to say?' asked Shelly.

'He didn't want to talk over the phone. We've arranged to meet at our local Starbucks. In the meantime, you could call the police station and ask how Travis is doing. I doubt they'll be able to tell you much, though.'

'Can I come with you?' asked Poppy.

Shelly rummaged in her handbag for her phone, 'I'm going to call the US Embassy. This whole thing is ridiculous. Just because Travis suffers from PTSD, he's being blamed for assaulting someone he hardly knows. It just doesn't make any sense at all.'

Buchanan looked at Poppy's face and nodded.

'Ok, let's go,' she said. ''Bye Mom see you when we get back. C'mon Jack, we're wasting time.'

'My keys, we won't get far without them.'

Buchanan walked over to the reception desk and asked for his car to be brought round.

Five minutes later they were flying down the A22 towards the Cophall roundabout and the A27 to the Pevensey Starbucks.

As they followed an Alsford's timber lorry along the A27, Buchanan looked across at Poppy's face, and had the feeling of déjà vu. Just over a year ago, driving from Lewes to Polegate on the A27, he'd looked at another young female face. That of his present partner, and now daughter, Jill. What should he say to Poppy? Should he tell her who he was? Could she keep a secret?

'Poppy,' he said, breaking into her thoughts, 'I have a confession to make.'

She looked at him with an expression of apprehension.

'I'm not what you or your mother think I am. To be perfectly frank with you, I'm not just a civil servant, I am a policeman. I'm taking a break while some matters at the office are sorted out. The persons who we are going to meet are a Detective Inspector Hanbury and Police constable Stephen Hunter, also my son-in-law.'

'So, who are you, what do you really do?'

'I'm Detective Chief Inspector Buchanan, of the Sussex CID.'

'CID? Is that like the FBI?'

'Sort of.'

'Are you working undercover?'

That question again, thought Buchanan. 'No. I really am on leave.'

'Well, you certainly fooled all of us.'

'This thing about Harry bothers me. I believe there is more going on than just what happened to him.'

'Do you think my dad hurt Harry?'

'Do you think you can keep my identity a secret – just till I figure out what is happening?'

'As long as it doesn't cause unnecessary suffering for my dad or Harry.'

Buchanan shook his head. 'I'll do my best, and to answer your earlier question, did I think your dad is responsible for Harry's injuries, I'm sorry, but until I have all the facts I can't say.'

He slowed at the roundabout, turned off the A27 and into the Starbuck's carpark. Hanbury and Stephen were sitting in the far corner. Stephen waved as they entered.

Buchanan waved back and led Poppy over to their table.

'Thanks for meeting at such short notice. This is Poppy Grant; you arrested her father earlier today for the assault on Harry Janski. He's Poppy's boyfriend.'

'DI Hanbury and this is PC Hunter,' said Hanbury.

'Hi,' she said, smiling.

'I've told Poppy who I am, so you needn't keep anything back from her,' said Buchanan. What would you like to drink, Poppy?'

She looked at the menu on the wall and said, 'Could I have a venti caramel coffee Frappuccino?'

'Large?'

She nodded.

'You two want anything?'

Hanbury shook his head. 'I just got ours,' he said, pointing to the two coffees on the table.

Buchanan ordered drinks for Poppy and himself. Poppy stuck a straw in hers and waited for Buchanan to ask the questions.

'Right, let's have the full story,' he said. .

'After you left the station,' began Hanbury, 'Stephen and I went to the hospital and met up with Dr Mansell. He told us about the condition of the injured lad –'

'His name is Harry,' said Poppy.

'Dr Mansell brought us up to date on Harry's condition, and how, in his opinion, Harry's injuries weren't caused by any horse. I looked at the bruises and to me they seemed like what happens when someone is given a severe beating. It reminded me of some of the results of beatings I saw when I worked in Derry.'

'But my dad would never do that to anyone.'

'We left the hospital,' continued Hanbury, 'and drove up to Castlewood. We talked to the two stable hands that you mentioned. Both gave alibis for each other. When asked if they saw anything, the tall one said he'd seen the assistant manager doing his rounds and the American caught up with him. That's when they started arguing.'

'Did he hear what the argument was about?'

'He thought it was about a girl.'

'That's all he heard?'

'That was all he said?'

'Did he say if he tried to break up the argument?'

'He said it was none of his business and went back into the lodge and let them get on with it.'

'And that was your reason for arresting Travis Grant?'

'I had no other suspects.'

'Did Stephen tell you about the stable lads' records?'

'Yes, but we weren't able to find anything to incriminate them. I thought with Travis Grant in custody it would be easier to get to the truth of the situation.'

'But my dad would never do anything to hurt Harry!' exclaimed Poppy.

'We interviewed your dad in his hotel room, Poppy. There were fist-sized holes in the bathroom walls,' said Stephen.

'It's his illness. He suffers from flashbacks; he was a marine and saw horrible things in Afghanistan. He – he sometimes sees something reminding him of what happened there and he either gets angry, or just breaks down and cries. Mom says there are some nights she wakes and goes downstairs and finds him sitting in his armchair sobbing.'

'PTSD does that,' said Hanbury. 'I have a friend who was in the army, he said he shares his life with his memories.'

'My dad almost died when he was in the marines,' said Poppy. 'He was out on a patrol when his best friend stepped in front of him and was blown to pieces by an IED. Dad had bits of his best friend plastered all over him. He says it should have happened to him, not his friend. All the squad suffered injuries, one of the other soldiers lost his leg and Dad carried him on his shoulders for two miles till they got back to base.'

'Quite a hero, your dad,' said Stephen.

'That's why I cannot believe he would have hurt Harry.'

'Bombs and bullets show no favouritism,' said Hanbury.

'I realise that,' said Poppy. 'But it still doesn't change what I believe about my dad.'

'And that's all you have found out so far?' said Buchanan. 'What about Julian Du Marchon?'

'He's next on the list.'

'Ok, while you're checking on him, I'll take Poppy to see her dad.'

'Aren't we going to get some flack about this from the boss?' asked Hanbury.

'Don't worry about her. I'll have a word when we have dinner this evening. She's staying at the club while she gets pampered in the spa.'

'You're joking,' said Hanbury.

'No-one was more surprised than me to meet her at Castlewood. She said she was due back at work tomorrow. Don't worry, I'll bring her up to date on the investigation.'

'Thanks,' said Hanbury. 'With all that's going on and our low numbers it's getting harder to do our job. Especially since we have to watch out for those hardened criminals that wolf-whistle at women.'

'Don't worry about that. Did you catch the news item this morning from Sara Thornton about how it's time for the police to refocus on what they should be investigating? Even Cressida Dick backs her on that.'

'I was too busy working,' said Hanbury.

'There's one more thing I would like you to check on. Harry Janski was involved in a case of taking without permission a few months ago. Could you check up on those who were arrested with him?'

'Do you think one of them could be responsible?' asked Poppy.

Buchanan shrugged. 'Who knows? Even if they're not involved, it would be good to eliminate them from the investigation.'

'I'll get on to that,' said Stephen.

'Now about Travis Grant,' said Buchanan, 'I suggest we let him go. I don't think he had a hand in Harry's beating. He may have been there in the stable and argued with Harry. But it is my feeling that an argument was all that took place.'

'Fine by me,' said Hanbury. 'You're the SIO in this case.'

'Can we go, please?' said Poppy.

'Anything else before I take Poppy to see her father?' asked Buchanan.

Hanbury shook his head.

'I talked to Jill last night,' said Stephen. 'She and Karen are enjoying themselves. They visited the market yesterday and Karen has bought something special for the new house. Oh, and there's a message for you.'

'Yes, what's that?'

'Something about making sure the foot of the bed doesn't face the front door – what's that mean?'

'An old superstition about when you die, the undertaker takes you out feet first.'

'Do you believe that?'

'Who knows? When you're dead it doesn't matter.'

'What's an SIO?' asked Poppy, when they got in the car.

'It stands for Senior Investigating Officer.'

'Thanks,' she said, before falling silent. As they turned on to Lottbridge Drove Poppy said. 'I've decided to keep your secret. Do you really have the authority to release my dad?'

'Yep.'

'And you don't think he hurt Harry?'

Buchanan shook his head as the gate to Hammonds Drive Police Station slid back. He parked in front of the station. Poppy followed him inside to the reception desk.

'Back again, Inspector?'

'I just don't seem to be able to stay away. Can you have someone bring Travis Grant here to one of the interview rooms, please? I'm releasing him.'

'I thought Hanbury was looking after that case?'

'He is, I'm assisting him.'

'Ok. Stan, can you bring cell number four through? Interview room two is available,' the desk sergeant said, to one of the other officers.

'Sure thing.'

'Interview room two?' said Buchanan.

'Yes,' said the desk sergeant. 'Would you like something to drink?'

'Make it three coffees.'

Poppy drummed her fingers on the interview-room desk as they waited for Travis to be brought through from the cells.

The sound of a door being closed announced his arrival. Buchanan was shocked at the change in Travis's countenance. The last time they'd met, Travis stood tall and straight, a look of confidence in his face, a glint of cheekiness in his eyes. Now Buchanan saw a broken man, an empty face with tears in his eyes. The policeman left and shut the door, Travis stood and stared straight ahead.

'Dad, what have they done to you?' said Poppy.

'Travis, come and sit down,' said Buchanan.

Travis breathed out slowly, walked forward and sat facing Buchanan.

'I'm sorry you have had to go through this, Travis,' said Buchanan. 'Inspector Hanbury was only doing his job.'

Travis stared past Buchanan at the wall.

'We're here to take you back to the club, Dad.'

Travis turned to look at Poppy. 'Where's your mom?'

'She's calling the Embassy.'

'Why?'

'To get you out of jail,' said Poppy, with tears running down her cheeks.

'Travis,' said Buchanan, 'can you tell me what happened last night, after I left you in the library?'

He looked at Buchanan then down at his coffee cup. 'I had another drink or two while I thought about things.'

'What sort of things?'

'How I'm a fraud as a leader and parent.'

'You're not a fraud,' said Poppy.

'Really? Is that all you've learned from going to Sunday school? One Timothy, chapter three, verses two through seven says: *Therefore, a leader must be above reproach, the husband of one wife, sober-minded, self-controlled, respectable, hospitable, able to teach, not a drunkard, not violent but gentle, not quarrelsome, not a lover of money. He must manage his own household well, with all dignity, keeping his children submissive, for if someone does not know how to manage his own household, how will he care for God's church? He must not be a recent convert, or he may become puffed up with conceit and fall into the condemnation of the devil. Moreover, he must be well thought of by outsiders, so that he may not fall into disgrace, into a snare of the devil.*

'I'm none of those, my own daughter disgraces me in front of all to see. She goes against my wishes when told not to see someone. Then last night, I fell into the arms of the demon alcohol. Now I'm a criminal. It's all over. When we get home, I'll have to resign as pastor. Maybe the church will find a job for me somewhere, maybe they'll have a Potiphar's prison where I can start again.'

Poppy got up from her chair and went round to the other side of the table, bent over and wrapped her arms round her father. 'I'm so sorry, I didn't mean to hurt you.'

'Whatever you may think about yourself,' said Buchanan, 'you are certainly not a failure.'

Travis looked up at Buchanan. 'I – I don't understand.'

'Can we go back to what happened after I left you in the library last night?'

Travis took in a deep breath, patted Poppy's hand and sat up straight. She returned to her chair and coffee.

'I had two, maybe three more double Jack Daniels,' said Travis. 'I shouldn't have. As the senior pastor, I'm supposed to set an example to the congregation – some example, me.'

'Did you go up to your room afterwards?'

'No, I went outside to think.'

'What time was that?'

'About eleven-thirty.'

'Was it raining?'

'No, it was dry and quite warm.'

'What did you do next?'

'Why are you asking me all these questions?'

'I'm just trying to understand what happened to Poppy's friend, Harry.'

Travis laughed.

'Dad, there's nothing to laugh about,' said Poppy.

'Isn't there? Yesterday I was telling you to stay away from him because of his record, and now here I am, a criminal myself.'

'But you're not a criminal, the police are not going to charge you with anything.'

'They're not?'

'No,' said Poppy, looking straight at Buchanan. 'Detective Inspector Hanbury has withdrawn the charges against you. We're here to take you back to the club.'

Buchanan smiled and thought how smart Poppy was to keep his identity quiet.

Travis sat in silence contemplating the situation; Poppy and Buchanan drank their coffees while waiting for the news to sink in.

'You were so right, Jack. I shouldn't have judged Harry. *Judge not that ye be not judged:* Matthew seven verse one, King James version. I think maybe I should go back to seminary. Poppy, I am so sorry not to have trusted you and your maturity. How is Harry?'

'He's going to be fine. He doesn't remember anything of what happened to him. The doctor at the hospital said he should be able to come home tomorrow.'

'I'm pleased to hear that.

'Travis,' said Buchanan, 'can you remember what happened after you went outside?'

'I'm sorry to say I was full of anger towards Harry. I decided I'd go down to the stables and have it out with him. I was going to lay down the law and make him understand he wasn't to bother Poppy anymore.'

'What time was that?'

'I think it was close to midnight.'

'Did you expect him to be up and waiting for you to chat?'

'I was in no mood to be rational. The alcohol and my anger were driving me. I stumbled across to the stables. I tried the barn doors, but they were locked. Then I remembered there was a door at the end of the block. That door wasn't locked. I pulled it open, went in and just stood there, unable to think of where to go next.'

'Were there any lights on?'

'Yes. But it wasn't bright like it would be during the day.'

'Did you see anyone?'

Travis thought for a moment. 'Yes, a tall bald-headed man. He was sitting on a stool just inside the door. I didn't see him at first, he was in shadow. He had headphones on listening to something on his phone, he had a beer can in his hand.'

'Did he say anything?'

'No. He looked at me then back at his phone.'

'Did you say anything to him?'

'I must have asked him if he'd seen the assistant stable manager. He just laughed and said, *Yes, but he's gone to bed for the night.*'

'What did you do when you heard that?'

'Since I couldn't see the stable manager, and my head was swimming from the drink, I went outside. The cold air of the outside was too much after the warm, muggy air inside. As soon as I stepped out of the stable, I threw-up.'

'Did you see Harry at any time when you were there?'

'No. When I'd finished emptying my stomach I wandered back to the club and went to bed.'

'What happened to your right hand?'

'I suffer from PTSD and. one of the side effects is I sometimes get angry. When I get angry, I've been known to take out my frustration on the kitchen wall.'

'And hotel bedroom walls,' said Poppy, smiling for the first time that day.

'I think it's time we left,' said Buchanan. 'Shelly will be getting the US Cavalry out to recue you if we don't show up.'

'I can go?'

'Of course, you can,' said Poppy. 'You've nothing to answer for.'

15:23

Buchanan stopped in front of the main entrance to Castlewood.

'I'll see you inside,' he said, to Travis and Poppy, as he handed his car keys to the valet. The mists were clearing thought Buchanan as he entered the reception. Travis was in the clear about the attack on Harry, which pointed the blame back at George and Lenny – unless Harry's former partners in crime could be implicated.

'Thanks for going to get Travis,' said Shelly. 'He's gone upstairs for a shower and a nap.'

'Yes, thanks for all you've done for Dad,' said Poppy.

Buchanan caught a look of curiosity on Shelly's face.

'Yes, thanks,' she said, 'but we were sure of his innocence right from the start.'

'No cavalry on the move then, Mom?' said Poppy. 'Jack said you'd have the cavalry out to rescue Dad.'

'Fat chance of that. All I got was a recording saying, *If you know the extension you want, dial it now.* I ask you, just what do we pay taxes for?'

'Nothing new in that,' said Buchanan. 'I have to go. See you at lunch, oops, bit late for that now. I'll catch up with you later, I have some thinking to do. Thanks for your help, Poppy.'

'My pleasure, thanks for bringing Dad home.'

Buchanan smiled, the net was closing on the catch, but just what was he fishing for? Was it just a couple of little sprats like George and Lenny, or was there a Moby Dick out there somewhere?

8

Wednesday Afternoon

15:35

As Buchanan closed his bedroom door his phone dinged to say he had a message from Stephen,

> Checked the names in the case that involved Harry Janski. Two of the three are incarcerated, the third was killed in an RTA two months ago.

So, if it wasn't Travis, and it wasn't any of Harry's previous associates, it had to be either Lenny or George, or more likely both of them, thought Buchanan. One to cosh Harry unconscious, the other to quickly tie up his wrists and possibly put a hood over his head so he couldn't identify either of his assailants. Next, Lenny, because he was the taller of the two, would have lifted Harry up on to a harness hook to be used as a punch-bag. But why?

What must Harry have thought as he regained consciousness? To wake in darkness, wrists tied tightly, and his arms above his head. Then the sting as fist after fist hammered into his body before he mercifully succumbed to unconsciousness.

What could Harry have seen that made George and Lenny set out to kill him? Or were they only supposed to teach him a lesson because he needed to be kept quiet? Had there been a third or fourth party to the beating, someone who had orchestrated it and had a lot to lose if Harry wouldn't keep quiet about what he'd seen? Was it more than a beating that went wrong? Was it in fact a sadistic execution? If so, just who could be behind it and why?

Buchanan wished he was back in his office where he had all his regular tools to aid in putting together a logical scenario, but first things first, it was time for a drink. He collected his notebook and pen from the bedside table and left for the bar thinking he could never retire. Just what would he do with his time? He did realise the day would eventually come, but in the meantime a policeman was what he was.

'Your usual, Mr Buchanan?' asked the waiter, as Buchanan sank back into the armchair in the library.

'Yes, please.'

The waiter returned a few minutes later with Buchanan's whisky and water.

'Is there anything else you require?' he asked, setting Buchanan's drink down on the side table.

He looked at the clock. 'Any chance of a salad? I missed lunch.'

'Certainly, what would you like?'

'Something with shrimp.'

The waiter left with his order. Buchanan took a sip of his whisky then opened his notebook. In the centre of a clean page he wrote 'Harry'. To the left of Harry's name, he wrote 'George and Lenny'. Above their names he wrote 'Du Marchon' and below he wrote 'Mountjoy'. To the right of Colonel Mountjoy he wrote 'Cynthia and Pat'. In the middle on the right-hand side he wrote 'Travis', and below he wrote 'Poppy'. Finally, he added the name of 'Jackson' below Cynthia and Pat.

He drew lines between Harry and the duo of George and Lenny. Then a line between Du Marchon to George and Lenny, and a line between George and Lenny to Colonel Mountjoy. He drew lines between the colonel and Cynthia and Pat, and Cynthia and Pat to Major Jackson, then a line between Major Jackson and Colonel Mountjoy. The relationships between the names became clear when he drew lines between Travis and Poppy and Harry and Poppy.

George and Lenny were the leg men for Du Marchon and Mountjoy and were quite clearly in Buchanan's mind the culprits responsible for Harry's beating. One question remained, what were Du Marchon and Mountjoy working together on?

The lines between Travis, Poppy and Harry were self-explanatory. Cynthia and Pat had links to Jackson and Mountjoy. The line between Jackson and Mountjoy was an obvious one. And as yet, he had no information to suspect what the link was, other than friendship between Victor Mountjoy and Julian Du Marchon.

His thoughts were interrupted by the arrival of Helen. 'You mentioned dinner?'

'Yes, I did', replied Buchanan, looking at the time on the library wall clock, 'but it's a bit early yet.'

'That's ok. I still have to pack for tomorrow. How about we say we seven?'

'That's fine for me. We will probably be in the bar as the main dining room is reserved for the competitors. Though I seem to be flavour of the month with Sir Nathan, as he's seated me at the head table.'

'It always helps to have friends in high places.'

'If you say so.'

'See you at seven.'

♦

17:12

Buchanan watched her walk off then returned to his musings in his notebook. He needed more information on Du Marchon and his business dealings, and since Mountjoy was possibly connected, a background check on him would also be useful.

Buchanan looked back at the clock and saw he still had an hour and a half before dinner. A walk to the stables and back would do his appetite no harm. He swallowed the last dregs of his whisky and left the library for a leisurely walk there. He went into the restaurant and selected an apple from the fruit bowl, a late afternoon treat for Mercury.

As he entered the stable block, he wondered who was looking after the horses while Harry was in hospital. He didn't have to wonder long. He opened the stable door and saw a young female seated at the desk in the stable office.

He knocked on the door frame and leaned in. 'Hello.'

'Can I help?'

'Not particularly. Just wondered who was looking after the horses while Harry was away?'

'Is there a problem?'

'No. No problem.'

'Are you one of the competitors?'

Buchanan shook his head. 'No, just a guest at the club for the week. I was here when the paramedics attended to Harry.'

'Are you a friend of his?'

'More of an acquaintance. I took his girlfriend and her mother in to see Harry earlier.'

'How is he? Any news about his condition?'

'You are the stable manager?'

She nodded, 'Olivia De Olivero, and you are?'

'Jack Buchanan. When I left Harry, he was awake and talking, but he doesn't remember anything about what happened to him.'

'Ah, we finally get to meet. Sir Nathan mentioned you'd be riding Mercury while you were here.'

Buchanan chuckled. 'I've only managed a couple of short rides.'

'They are better than none. Are you going out now?' she asked, looking at what Buchanan was wearing.'

'Oh, no. Not now, it's a bit late. I will try to find time tomorrow afternoon. I just thought I'd pop down and see how Mercury is doing and give him a consolation treat,' he replied, showing Olivia the apple.

'You do realise you shouldn't give a horse a whole apple?'

Buchanan nodded. 'I was going to borrow a knife and cut it in slices.'

'Here, let me,' she said, reaching for the apple.

Buchanan watched as she held the apple in both hands and wrenched it in two. As she broke the halves into smaller bits she said, 'It would be a pity to loose Harry, he is so good with the horses and I've never seen the stable accounts so tidy.'

'He mentioned he might like to do accounting.'

'Well, he would be a real asset if he decided to put down roots here at Castlewood,' she said, handing him the apple pieces.

'Thanks. I'm quite impressed by how well you and your staff are managing the influx of guests and horses.'

'Thanks, it hasn't been easy. And now with Harry away in hospital, I really have my hands full.'

'The doctor said, barring any surprise changes in Harry's condition, he should be able to come home tomorrow.'

'That's the best news I've heard all day, especially since we have three new horses joining us tomorrow.'

'I got the impression, with the contestants here for the race, there aren't any spare stalls?'

'We've managed to board-out most of our regulars. These new horses won't need stalls for a few days, they are going out into the pasture till the race is over.'

'I don't understand.'

'Sir Nathan doesn't like it when old horses have to be put down. So, when we have space, he buys ex-racehorses from the auctions and allows them to live out the remainder of their lives in peace.'

'Isn't that a bit expensive? Racehorses aren't cheap.'

'If you had time, I could tell you what happens to ex-racehorses and their ilk when they are no longer of any use to the owner.'

'I have time,' said Buchanan, looking at the office clock.

'Well, if you are sure,' said Olivia. 'It is estimated that in each year in the UK, six to ten-thousand horses and ponies are slaughtered for human consumption in Europe.'

'Every year?'

Olivia nodded.

'That sounds like big business. It must employ a great deal of people and be very profitable.'

Olivia shook her head. 'Not as much as you might think. There was an article in the *Guardian* a few years ago about a famous racehorse purchased for seventeen thousand pounds as a one-year-old, then four years later it was sold at auction to be turned into horsemeat.'

'Not sure whether to be sorry for the owner or the horse.'

'Never be sorry for the owners. But that isn't the worst of it. One breeder paid five-hundred thousand dollars as a mating fee between two famous horses. Later, the one-year-old horse was sold for nine-hundred thousand dollars.'

'Now that's good business.'

'Not when you hear that six years later the horse was sold for five-hundred guineas. I tell you Jack, there's no sympathy given to horses in racing. The horse either performs or ends up on someone's dinner table.'

'I didn't realise people ate horsemeat.'

Olivia's face tensed, 'In 2012 the UK exported four thousand tons of butchered horsemeat, a large part of it to France. I ask you, horse meat sold as a delicacy?'

'I'll stick to my beef steak, thank you.'

'Do you realise that's the equivalent of at least eight thousand horses, ponies and donkeys that are no longer thought to be worthy of looking after? Could you imagine going to a car dealer and paying thousands for a brand-new, top-of-the-line model, then three years later selling it for pennies? Of course, not – sorry, it just disgusts me how some people, supposedly horse lovers, can be so callous when it comes to their animals. Exporting horses, unlike sheep, isn't worth the newspapers reporting on.'

'I had no idea,' said Buchanan.

'That's a big part of the problem, people just don't know,' she said, putting her empty coffee cup onto the desk. She shook her head. 'Sorry, you didn't come here to listen to my rants. How do you know Harry, are you a relative?'

'No, we only met a couple of days ago. Harry recognised me from somewhere he'd seen me before.'

'Lewes court?'

'Ye-es.'

'Don't worry, your secret is safe with me. You probably don't remember me, but I remember you from last year when you were here investigating the death of that young girl in Abbotts Wood. Did you ever find out who killed her?'

'Yes, we did. You have a good memory.'

'I remember people who treat their horses properly.'

'I'm glad you think that of me.'

'Monday afternoon, I walked past the office when you and Harry were having your chat. I left you alone and kept going. I thought you were his probation officer.'

'You know about his past life?'

'Yes. Sir Nathan and I discussed Harry's initial suitability as a stable hand before we accepted him to work here, and boy are we glad we did. I can just let him get on with the job of running the stables. It frees me to spend time in the training ring.'

'You teach riding?'

'We have two young ladies that are working towards the Prix St George level of dressage.'

'That wouldn't be Deborah and Aisha, would it?'

'You know them?'

'I know their fathers from work. How are they doing?'

'They have a friendly rivalry to see who can out-dressage the other. Of course, it's not just the riders that have to know what they are doing, the horses are just as important.'

'How are the four of them doing?'

'To my mind there isn't much to differentiate between any of them.'

'What do you think about the occupants of stalls one and two?'

'Harry's been keeping an eye on them. I suppose it was you who asked him to do that?'

'I feel bad about it. I just hope there isn't any permanent damage.'

'You and me both. You asked about the occupants of stalls one and two. I don't quite know what it is, but my sixth sense says there's something odd about those horses.'

'In what way?'

She shook her head. 'I'm not quite sure. They both look healthy while standing in their stalls and when they walk across the yard, their gait is ok – oh, I just realised something.'

'What's that?'

'I've never seen them together, outside.' Olivia saw a look of confusion on Buchanan's face. 'What I mean is, I've never seen them walk, trot or canter side by side. If I didn't know that there are two of them, I'd say there was only one horse. But that's silly of course. We could walk down the corridor to their stalls right now and see there are definitely two of them.'

'That's an odd remark.'

'Odd or even, there's definitely something not quite right about those horses.'

'What about their handlers?'

'I've seen their type before. They're typical of the hangers-on you see at most events. Always looking for a way to pick up some casual money doing someone's dirty work.'

'Is that what you think of George and Lenny?'

'I think I've seen them somewhere before. It might have been at an event where Sir Nathan had one of his horses entered. Yes, that was it, last year at Plumpton racecourse. There was a controversy about a steward's decision when they asked a competitor to withdraw an entry.'

'Why was that?'

'The horse was distressed. I heard it had been allowed to become dehydrated, then given too much water to drink. It's a simple way to nobble a horse, especially a good one; when you want the horse to underperform.'

'Do you think it was a deliberate act, or an accident?'

'The post-race news said it was an oversight. Both lads thought they were the only ones to give the horse a drink.'

'If it wasn't an accident, why would someone do something like that to a horse?'

'I'm not sure. It made no sense to me at the time, and especially since it was the favourite.'

'And you think George and Lenny were looking after the horse in question?'

'Yep. Their horsebox was next to ours.'

'Do you happen to know who owned the horse in question?'

'Sorry, I don't remember.'

'Do you remember the date when this happened?'

'Not off hand. I'll need to have a look at last year's diary.'

'Would you, please?'

'I can't do it just now. I have the rounds to do. Come back later, after dinner and I should have dug up the information then.'

'Ok, I can do that. I'm having an early dinner this evening. Nine o'clock all right?'

'Nine it will be. Oh, if you hear anything about Harry, would you let me know?'

'Will do.'

♦

18:35

Buchanan showered, dressed for dinner then went downstairs to meet with Helen. He saw by the reception clock he was early and decided to let his fellow diners know he would not be joining them this evening. As he made his way through the tables, he listened to snippets of conversations:

'She was quite indignant when she was told she was too big for her horse, and of course, Harry's remark about her being broader in the beam than her horse didn't help…'

'I tell you, I didn't realise Margery knew such language …'

'They said they were planning on instigating reverse qualifications as an interim rule to force riders that weren't up to the grade to step down a level ...'

'... said she'd spent over four-thousand getting the horse delivered, only to find she'd have to spend that much again in lawyers' fees to challenge the decision. She should have listened to the advice the society gave her about purchasing a horse from abroad ....'

'Riding in the evenings as the sun is setting can be quite romantic, but I wouldn't do it again, not after my horse misread a jump and put me in the hospital with a fractured pelvis ....'

'... the vet had such delicate hands; the sutures were almost invisible.'

'Hello everyone,' said Buchanan, as he stood behind an empty chair. 'Sorry I won't be dining with you this evening. I have a previous engagement.'

Cynthia looked up and frowned at Buchanan. 'You're dining alone?'

He shook his head. 'No, I am dining in the bar with a friend, just for this evening. I will rejoin you tomorrow.'

'Promise?'

'Yes, I promise.'

As he turned to walk away he saw that look in Cynthia's eyes again that he'd first seen on Sunday evening. He realised he'd not quite understood the look when they'd first met. But now, it was not just a look of fear, it was more than that, it was definitely the look of fear mixed with a look of longing for freedom. But not as he he'd first imagined it.

He remembered the look on Tommy Findlay's face the night he'd been chased up on to the roof of the McSween pub in Glasgow by the Busby gang. Buchanan and two of his team had gone up to the roof of the building next door to cut off his escape. Tommy, realising he was trapped between a certain fatal beating and that of being arrested by Buchanan, decided the only way of escape was to leap across to the adjoining building and the safety of a fire escape to the street below. The sound of Tommy's scream as he fell five floors to his death still haunted Buchanan's dreams.

That was what he'd seen in Cynthia's face. It was the look of, '*Should I stay and be beaten. or jump and hope for a safe landing?*'

Helen was already seated at the table. 'Hello, I was wondering if you'd forgotten our date.'

'Definitely not,' he said, sitting down across from her. 'I was just letting the others at the table know I wouldn't be with them this evening.'

'Good,' she replied, picking up her menu. 'What do you recommend?'

'It's all good. If you like fish, I hear the lobster is very good, the salmon is line caught and brought down from Inverness twice a week, and the beef is from a private herd of Angus cattle.'

'Thanks.'

'Good evening,' said the waiter. 'Can I get you something from the bar?'

'Could I see the wine list please?' sad Helen.

'Certainly, I'll be right back.'

'Dinner is on me this evening, Jack.'

'Thanks.'

The waiter returned with the wine list and placed it in front of Helen.

'White or red, Jack?' she asked, as she opened it.

'If I'm drinking wine, I prefer red, and you?'

'White. But I usually like to start with a cocktail, you?'

'Whisky.'

Helen waved at the waiter to say they were ready to order.

'Yes, madam?'

'Could I have a Manhattan?'

'Certainly. Sir?'

'Lagavulin, with a splash of water.'

The waiter left with their order.

'I think I'll have the fillet steak,' said Helen.

The waiter returned with their drinks and left with their dinner order.

'How was your visit to the spa?' asked Buchanan.

'Refreshing, as it should be. What about you, are you managing to relax?'

Buchanan smiled. 'It depends on how you define relax.'

'I take it by that statement you are working on something?'

'Last night, the assistant stable manager was severely beaten and left for dead in one of the horse stalls. The dumping of the body in the stall was a deliberate act to make the beating look like he'd been trampled by a horse. To my mind, whoever was responsible for the act, hoped the horse would finish what the miscreant had started.'

'Do you have any evidence, suspects?'

'Two suspects, but unfortunately very little evidence to go on.'

'Bit unusual for you,' she said, smiling and taking a sip of wine.

'Crime doesn't play by rules.'

'That's not what I mean. How do you think Mr Miasma of the *Herald* will be able chronicle your current investigations without the drama of a dead body? That's been your modus operandi so far since you joined the Sussex force.'

Buchanan smiled. 'Is that how you see me?'

'It's an historical fact. Did you know that some people are calling the town Midsummer Eastbourne?'

'Really? I had no idea. It must be the sea air that brings out the best in me.'

'I had a chat with one of your former bosses in Glasgow. From what he said I got the impression you didn't operate any differently up there.'

'I just did my job – why were you talking to him?'

'I called him to find out what was happening about the enquiry into the two men under the police car incident.'

Buchanan put down his glass and took a deep breath. 'What did he say?'

'He said that you had nothing to answer for and the matter was now officially closed.'

Buchanan exhaled, smiled and slowly shook his head. 'Finally – it's about time.'

'So, what about retiring, have you thought about that?'

'I don't get much chance not to. I know the force would like me to go, and I presume that includes you. Please,' he said, raising his hand, 'let me finish. I realise my rank is seen as an anachronism in today's ranks of university-degreed constables and sergeants. But how do you teach what thirty-five years of field experience have taught me? What I know can only come from doing the job.'

She smiled at his fervent outburst. 'Jack, I'm not one of those who want you to go. Bottom line is, you make me look good. I understand where you are coming from and as long as we have crime on our patch, you are a very valuable resource I cannot afford to lose. I do realise there are areas of policing where you are short on experience, but that doesn't appear to slow you down one bit. You have created a very excellent team that demonstrates the old adage that the total is greater than the sum of the parts.'

The conversation was interrupted by the return of the waiter to collect their dinner plates. 'Would you like to see the dessert menu?'

Helen shook her head 'I'll just have a coffee.'

Buchanan nodded 'Same for me.'

'Should I be expecting dead bodies to show up this week?' asked Helen.

'I hope not. The young lad found badly beaten in the stall was bad enough.'

'Could it just be a bit of horsing around that went wrong?'

'I wish it was that simple, but I suspect there is more to what's going on than that.'

'Your suspicions are?'

160

'I believe the injured lad saw something he shouldn't have. He was confronted and given the choice to keep his mouth shut or else. He must have said something about telling what he saw and suffered the consequences.'

'Do you think he was supposed to have died?'

Buchanan shook his head. 'Difficult to tell at this point. Although he has recovered and will be back tomorrow, he says he can't remember anything about what happened.'

'So, what do you think it's all about?'

'Money. Get to the bottom of most crimes and you'll find money is involved somewhere.'

'All crimes?'

'No, not quite all,' answered Buchanan, about to take a sip of his coffee. 'But in my experience money is usually the common denominator. Criminals in all forms, from shoplifting schoolchildren to company executives robbing company pension plans, they're all in it for the money. What they use the money for, well that's another issue.'

'What about domestic violence?'

'That is an exception, though lack of finances is quite often a contributing factor as are unemployment, drugs and alcohol.'

'Well, make sure you keep me posted,' she said, putting down her empty cup. 'I don't want to find out what's going on in the *Herald*.'

'I'll do my best.'

'Good. Now if you'll excuse me, I have an early start in the morning. Good night.'

Buchanan watched her go then got up from the table and wandered out of the bar towards the stables for his meeting with Olivia. He had an idea forming in his mind, though as yet there were a few holes in it. Determining the name of the horse that was forced to withdraw from the race at Hickstead was crucial to his forming idea.

♦
20:55

In the stables, he listened for the sound of late evening activity. The only sound he heard was Lenny leaning back in a chair humming along to a tune he was listening to through his headphones. Three empty beer cans lay on the floor.

The sound of a metal pail being dropped caught Buchanan's attention. He shook his head at the scene of Lenny supposedly being on guard and walked off in the direction of the errant pail. As he walked, he listened to the sounds of the stables. One horse had his head out of the stall tugging at the haynet, another looked at him and snorted. The remainder of the stalls' occupants were sleeping. As he passed them, he realised horses snored.

He caught up with Olivia as she came out of one of the top stalls.

'I was beginning to wonder if I'd see you back here this evening,' she said, as she bolted the stall door.

He shrugged. 'It was a very interesting dinner. Not often do the senior management hand out compliments.'

'Much deserved, I'm sure. If you'll follow me to my office, I have the information you asked for.'

She unlocked the office and beckoned Buchanan to enter and take a seat.

'You feel it necessary to lock to the office door?' asked Buchanan.

'We keep certain equine medications in the safe. Locking the door is just a precaution. Here are the names you wanted.' She passed Buchanan a photocopied sheet of A4 paper.

Buchanan wasn't surprised when he read: *Horse owner, Lt Colonel Victor Mountjoy, horse names, Turpin and Rambler.*

'Is that what you were looking for? You don't seem to be surprised.'

'How about the lads who looked after the horses?'

She shook her head. 'There's no mention of their names. But doing my rounds earlier today, I ran into both of them. I don't know why I should have been surprised, but I was. Do you suspect those two of hurting Harry?'

'Let's say they're high on my list of suspects.'

'The shits. I'll have to tell Sir Nathan. Can't have two thugs like them living in the stables with all the beautiful horses. A tent in the yard is all they deserve.'

'Might be better if I have a word with Sir Nathan. There's some other related matters I wish to discuss with him.'

'Ok.'

'In the meantime, I recommend you don't go near stalls one or two at night without someone being with you.'

'You think they're that dangerous?'

'Not as long as you don't make them feel nervous. If you feel threatened, I can have someone stay here till Harry is well enough to return.'

'That won't be necessary. I'll have a word with Myrtle, she'll come and stay till Harry gets back.'

'Who's Myrtle?'

'She breaks in new horses and is studying at Plumpton for a degree in equine science and coaching. She's also a black belt in judo. She won't stand for any nonsense from those two, no one messes with Myrtle. As soon as you leave, I'll give her a call, she's always looking for opportunities to stay here at the stables.'

'Ok. I'll have a word with Sir Nathan first thing in the morning. But before I turn in for the night, I was wondering if you knew anyone who could explain betting odds for me?'

'That's an odd question at bedtime. I'm sure you're aware Eastbourne has many betting shops and most of them could answer your questions for you?'

'Yes, but I'd prefer an introduction.'

'Tell you what, after I've called Myrtle, I'll call a couple of my friends and ask for you, they might also be able to fill you in on what happened when Colonel Mountjoy's horses were withdrawn. As it's late and you are probably off to bed, I'll leave a message for you at reception.'

'Thanks for your help.'

9

Thursday Morning

07:00

Buchanan was out of bed and dressed by seven, today was going to be a busy one. First on the list was a stop at the reception desk to see if Olivia had been successful in finding someone to answer his questions about betting. Next was a chat with Sir Nathan, followed by a visit to the new house to be present when the furniture was delivered; and finally, a trip into town and hopefully a visit to a betting shop if Olivia had been successful. As he opened his room door he noticed a folded note on the floor. He picked it up and read it:

> Mr Buchanan, your wife called to say the French dock workers have gone on strike and she might not be able to sail today. She will call you later.

That was a relief, thought Buchanan, as he descended in the lift. He'd forgotten Karen might be back today.

'Good morning, Mr Buchanan, how can we help?' asked the receptionist.

'I was wondering if Sir Nathan was available? I need to have a quick chat with him.'

'He's with the stable manager at the moment, can I take a message?'

'It's about the stables I wish to talk with him.'

'Oh, just a minute'.

While he waited, Buchanan watched the antics of one of the guests. It was a very active beagle puppy. No matter how hard it tried, it just couldn't catch its tail.

'Mr Buchanan, Sir Nathan asks if you would come through,' said the receptionist, lifting the counter flap.

Buchanan followed her into the manager's office.

'Good morning, Jack,' said Sir Nathan. 'Just been listening to a rather disturbing report from Olivia.'

'Yes, that's why I wanted to have a quick word with you.'

'How is young Harry?'

'The doctor says he'll make a full recovery, all bar his memory of the event.'

Greyspear shook his head, 'I want you to get to the bottom of this, Jack. I can't have my staff treated this way. You say he's lost his memory?'

'Just the memory of what happened that evening. I've told him when his memory does return to say nothing to anyone, except me.'

'You think he's still in danger? Surely not from one of my staff?'

'No, I don't think it's any of the staff,' Said Buchanan.

'Do you have any suspects?'

'Yes, but without Harry's testimony, my hands are tied.'

'Jack, just what the hell is going on? We've never had anything like this happen before.'

'You've never run a cross-country race before. To my mind, when we get this sorted, we'll find that money is behind whatever is going on.'

'Do you think any of my guests are involved in this?'

'I've got some more investigating to do before I can answer that question.'

'Is anyone in danger?'

'No, I think we've closed that door.'

'But you do suspect someone?'

'Yes, but I'd rather not say who at this time.'

'Well, if you are sure no one is in danger. But what about the race? I can't have any scandal associated with the inaugural race.'

'I'm afraid that's out of my control, but you know me well enough by now. I will be as discrete as I can be in my investigations.'

'Thanks, Jack, I know you will. What's next?'

'Olivia has said she would see if she can find someone to help me understand betting odds.'

'Yes,' she said, 'I've had a chat with Myrtle, and she said to try Campsiebet. They are an independent betting shop on North Street in Eastbourne. The manager's name is Danny Tomasso.'

'Thanks. I'll go and see them later.'

'Who's officially in charge of the investigation?' asked Greyspear.

'DI Hanbury, but he liaises with me on all matters.'

'Good. I'm up in Glasgow today and back tomorrow afternoon, please keep me posted. You have my mobile?'

'Yes.'

'See you later, then,' said Greyspear.

'I've got morning rounds,' said Olivia. 'Let me know how you get on with the betting shop.'

'Will do.'

♦

08:30

According to a prearranged plan, Buchanan was supposed to be picking up Karen and Jill from the ferry at Newhaven, but the message about the French dock workers going on strike had made him change his plans. No wonder so many people had voted to leave the European Union, he thought. At least Britain was no longer the sick man of Europe.

He was early for meeting the movers, so instead of driving down the A22 he turned into Diplocks industrial estate and drove slowly along Diplocks Way. He passed the factory where the National Crime Agency had recently discovered an illegal firearms factory. He negotiated the mini-roundabout and left Hailsham behind him on Ersham Road. As he drove, he lowered his window and let the damp freshness of the morning swirl around his face. He took the left fork just past the garden centre and slowed for two horses being ridden by yellow-jacketed riders. They waved their appreciation for slowing and continued chatting. A mile ahead he had the choice of turning to the left and going through Rickney and along the marsh road, or to the right and through Hankham. He chose the road to Hankham. He turned left at the school and passed the house where the IRA had assassinated the MP Ian Gow by placing a bomb under his car.

The road led out of Hankham, over the A27 and down the Hankham Hall Road to Peelings Lane. Buchanan wondered about the history behind the local street names as he crossed Peelings Lane on to Gallows Lane, then on to Rattle Road at the bottom.

He was in plenty of time for the movers and remembered Karen's edict to make sure the foot of their bed didn't point towards the front door. By the time the furniture was installed in the new house, it was lunchtime. But before he left, he went from room to room and took photos of the furniture in order to email them to Karen. In honour of the task being completed, he decided to try lunch from the Swan fish and chip shop.

♦

13:00

He parked outside the betting shop and went in. The racing for the day had just begun and the shop was almost empty. A man sat in front of a fixed-odds betting terminal. He tapped the screen buttons with his right hand while chewing the nails on his left; he looked worried. Buchanan recognised the two customers who were engrossed in looking at the list of runners on a wall display – they were George and Lenny. One of the widescreen TVs was showing a floodlit race from Hong Kong. He walked, unobserved by George and Lenny, over to the betting desk and asked to speak with the manager.

'He's busy, come back later.'

Buchanan smiled and said, 'Olivia at Castlewood phoned and made the appointment for me. Please go tell Mr Tomasso I need to have a word with him, I won't keep him very long.'

'All right, no need to get shirty. I'll go and see if he's got time to talk to you, he's a very busy man.'

Buchanan looked round the betting shop as he waited. The race in Hong Kong had finished and the winner was being paraded round the winner's circle.

'Didn't put you down as a gambling man,' said George, who was standing beside Buchanan in the queue, waiting to collect his winnings.

'You come here often?' replied Buchanan. 'I try and stay away, can't afford to lose money.'

'You could try putting a few quid on Turpin, if you know what I mean,' said George, winking.

'I'll remember that, thanks.'

Two minutes later a door that was concealed behind a poster of Northern Dancer at full gallop opened. The clerk signalled with a beckoning hand gesture to Buchanan to follow. 'The manager says he can see you, this way.'

Buchanan turned away from the race that had just started and walked through the door into a long dark corridor. Abandon all hope, all who enter here, he thought, following the clerk to the rear of the building where he stopped and knocked on the door at the end of the passageway. There was an audible sound of an electric lock operating. The clerk pulled the door open and indicated to Buchanan to enter the room.

Buchanan pushed past and entered a well-lit office. The room smelled of cats and long-ago smoked cigars. It contained two desks: one on the right under a heavily-barred window and one to the left of the door he'd just entered, where a young woman sat staring at columns of numbers on a computer screen, her head gently rocking from side to side as she listened to music through her earphones.

Seated at the desk under the barred window was a short, bald-headed man engaged in a phone call. Hanging from the far wall were three large television screens and one smaller in black and white. One of the large screens was tuned to the races in Hong Kong and the other two were showing scenes from racetracks somewhere in the UK. The smaller black and white TV screen displayed a split screen of scenes from the betting shop, one of which was from the inside of the clerk's cage, clearly showing the tills. On the wall to Buchanan's right, there was a dusty chalkboard.

Buchanan waited while the bald-headed man finished his phone call. As he did so, he looked up, smiled and said, 'You must be the chap Olivia mentioned would be round today.'

'That's me.'

'So, you want to understand how betting works?'

Buchanan nodded and reached for a nearby chair. 'Jack Buchanan,' he said, sitting opposite.

'Danny Tomaso. You look familiar – have we banned you from betting here?'

'No, not banned from betting. You might have seen my photo in the *Herald*?'

'You're a policeman! Did you have something to do with, what the papers called the case of the bodies in the Marina?'

'For my sins, yes.'

'There's been a few since, if I remember correctly?'

'Thanks to Mr Miasma. He seems to delight in chronicling my cases.'

'A bit of a Dr Watson. But you didn't come here to talk about that, did you?'

'No. I'm trying to understand the basics of betting odds. I've heard and understand terms such as fifty to one and similar, but never really taken the time to understand the other terms used.'

'There are two ways odds – or prices – are displayed at racecourses in Britain: the traditional fractional system, which most people relate to, or the more recently introduced decimal system. Fractional odds are usually displayed in the format of the fraction, such as four over one. Or you might hear it on television spoken of as "four-to-one", and sometimes this can be written as four dash one.

'Odds are just like simple maths. Here, let me give you some simple examples,' he said, standing and shuffling over to the blackboard. 'So, with the odds of four to one, for every one-pound you stake, you will receive four pounds if you win, plus your stake back. Seven to two odds will pay you seven pounds for each two pounds you bet, plus your stake back. Same with eight to four. Understand?'

'Yep, fairly straightforward.'

'When the fraction is shown the other way round, say one to four, this is called odds-on and means the horse in question is a hot favourite to win the race. You will hear it announced as *four-to-one on*.

'Not a good return if you have to bet four pounds to win just one pound?'

'But don't forget you get your original wager back with your winnings.'

'Suppose someone tries to fix the odds? Olivia said you might have some background information about a race at Plumpton last year when an owner was forced to withdraw two of his runners.'

'Hmm, you are referring to the incident with Turpin and Rambler, am I correct?'

Buchanan nodded. 'What can you tell me about the affair?'

'Nothing was recorded other than the horses were withdrawn at the owner's request.'

'And what was the talk around the paddock?'

'Just a crazy rumour that the horses had been nobbled in some way.'

'Nothing definite?'

'No,' he said shaking his head. 'Nothing definite was ever said.'

'How about the two lads who were looking after the horses?'

'Don't know anything about them. Have your questions anything to do with the Castlewood Cup?'

'Might have.'

'I hear there's money riding on that race.'

'Do you know how much?' asked Buchanan, who'd got up and poured himself a coffee from the jug on the stand.

'It's mostly with the big bookmakers,' said Danny, as he leaned back in his chair and examined the fingernails of his right hand. 'I haven't seen much of it come through here.'

'How much is not much?'

'There's been a few bets in the low hundreds, that's all.'

'Not hundreds of thousands?'

'Not so far,' he said, turning and looking at the office monitor. 'Those two again. I'm going to have to close their accounts.'

'George and Lenny's?'

'Is that what they're calling themselves today? You know them?'

'We've met. Why would you close their accounts?'

'Look at them. Do they look like they can afford to bet five thousand pounds on a horse?'

'No, definitely not. They're a couple of stable hands. Wonder where they could get that sort of money from?'

'Pour us a coffee and I'll tell you what I think they're up to.'

Buchanan put Danny's coffee on the desk in front of him.

'Money laundering is a big problem for bookmakers, more so the smaller independent ones. Like us here at Campsiebet.'

'How does it work?'

'Most of this type of money is derived from all forms of crime, but mainly from the sale of illegal drugs. First, a punter will find an accommodating bookie. Then on a prearranged day the punter will show up with, say, fifty thousand pounds in cash, which he hands over to the bookmaker.

'For the purpose of this example, let's say the race was the two o'clock at Plumpton and Dobbin comes across the finishing line first at odds of five to one. The bookie will issue the punter with a paid betting slip for the sum of five thousand pounds, but it will be timed at somewhere at least one hour before the race started.

'Next the bookie will give the punter a legitimate receipt for thirty thousand pounds for a race timed at two o'clock. A return on a bet of five thousand at five to one is twenty-five thousand, plus he gets his stake of five thousand back.

'You might say that's a poor exchange of funds. But when you consider where the punter's cash came from, giving him a legitimate receipt for thirty thousand pounds was a fair price.'

'What about the twenty thousand the bookie now has? How does he explain that?'

'No problem. He just runs it through the business with fake betting slips.'

'Thanks, I never realised just how easy it is to launder money.'

'It is till you are caught. Recently the high street bookmakers, William Hill, were fined just over six million pounds for money laundering.'

'So, you haven't had any big wagers for the Castlewood Cup?'

'Good heavens no – the Castlewood Cup isn't the Grand National. Do you mind if I ask you a question?'

'No, not at all.'

'The Castlewood Cup, do you suspect it's been fixed?'

'To the best of my knowledge, Danny, it hasn't been fixed. Why would you ask that?'

'When Olivia called and asked if I would talk to you about betting odds, I wondered if something was up. Especially after what happened to Harry.'

'You know Harry?'

'I read something about his accident in the *Herald*.'

'How was that? The paper doesn't come out till tomorrow, Friday.'

'I had a look online.'

'Do you remember what it said?'

'Not much, something about the assistant stable manager at Castlewood getting trampled by a horse. Do you know different? Is there something going on?'

'You know as much as I do, Danny.'

'You will let me know if the situation changes? Fixed races cause the industry millions.'

'I can assure you, Danny, if the race was fixed, you'd be one of the first to know,' replied Buchanan.

'Glad to hear that. Keep me in mind if you discover anything creeping under the rocks.'

'Will do,' said Buchanan, standing and reaching for the door.

◆

14:00

Buchanan peeled the parking ticket from his windshield and climbed into his car. First thing on his mind was he needed to think, and that required coffee. He started the engine and headed for his field office, Starbucks.

◆

14:35

Starbucks had changed, he thought, as he stood in line waiting to order his coffee. He missed Jade with her cheeky welcome and hoped she was still enjoying her new job working in the call centre.

The new manager and staff had brought a change of atmosphere. Buchanan wasn't complaining about the changes; Mike, the new manager, had created a warm and friendly atmosphere, and he'd finally managed to get the internet fixed – now that was a real accomplishment.

Coffee in hand, Buchanan set to work, thinking. He slowly sipped his coffee and came to the conclusion that the first task would be to see what he could find out about the directors of Sovereign Secure Investments, and that would require the assistance of Aaron Silverstein.

Buchanan picked up his phone and called Aaron Silverstein's office. If anyone knew about local accounting firms, he would.

The receptionist answered and said he could see Buchanan in twenty minutes. He could feel the cold clammy hand of urgency tapping him on the shoulder.

Finishing his coffee, Buchanan left to go and see Aaron Silverstein. He took the Pevensey by-pass to the A22 and on into Eastbourne and Kings Drive. He'd forgotten the chaos that the road works in the town centre were causing and was a few minutes late in getting to Aaron Silverstein's office.

♦

15:05

As he did just over a year ago, Buchanan parked on a double yellow line in front of Silverstein's office and noticed there were still no customer parking spaces. The highly polished brass name plaque on the door read: A Silverstein CPA.

'Yes, sir, can I help?' asked the receptionist.

'Detective Chief Inspector Buchanan, to see Mr Silverstein, please.'

'Ah, yes, sorry. I didn't recognise you. I'll buzz him to let him know you're here. Would you like a drink while you wait?'

Buchanan settled for a black coffee and a chocolate biscuit. As he sipped his coffee, he looked at the reception office and thought about the last time he'd been here. What was it Miasma had called the investigation – *The Case of the Bodies in the Marina*. He missed Glasgow; but was quite happy he was here in Eastbourne; crime had no loyalties to location.

Polished mahogany wood-panelled walls, drapes that would look at home in any country house and carpets looking like real wool, business was certainly good for Aaron Silverstein. As Buchanan lingered over his coffee he thought about the present scenario. Was there really a crime in the offing and, if so, what exactly was it going to be? Money was the motivating factor, but whose money and how much?'

'Inspector,' said Silverstein's secretary, interrupting Buchanan's musing, 'Mr Silverstein will see you now.'

Buchanan stood and followed her into the office of A Silverstein CPA.

'Inspector, good afternoon,' said Silverstein, as he stood up. 'My secretary said you'd called; sorry I wasn't able to take your call.' He sat down. 'Please, have a seat. Can I offer you some refreshments?'

'No thank you, your secretary has already offered me a coffee.'

'Angela,' said Silverstein to his secretary, 'no calls please. Now, Inspector, what can I do for you?'

'I've been offered an opportunity to invest some money and I was wondering if you could tell me about the company involved?'

'Is this a personal matter?'

'It was initially, but now I've had to change hats and come at it from another angle.'

'Interesting use of metaphors. What is the name of the company you are interested in?'

'It's not so much about the company, I'm more interested in the individual who's running it.'

'The name?'

'Julian Du Marchon.'

'How about his company name?'

'Sovereign Secure Investments.'

'Let me have a look.'

'I see you have another Osborne,' said Buchanan, as Silverstein opened his laptop and began to type.

Silverstein turned to see which picture Buchanan was looking at. 'Ah yes, he's a wonderful artist. I like fine art, and it's also a good investment. Why don't you come round here and sit beside me? That way you can see the screen.'

Silverstein returned to his laptop and continued to review the on-screen information. As he read, he shook his head.

'What's the matter?' asked Buchanan.

'With figures like these, it's a wonder they are still trading.'

'Why is that?'

'To anyone casually reading the figures, they look fine. But to me they look artificial, contrived even.'

'Does it show the names of the directors?'

Silverstein scrolled down the page.

'There are six directors listed for Sovereign Secure Investments.'

Buchanan wasn't surprised to see Julian Du Marchon mentioned, but the big surprise was Victor Mountjoy's name. He took a note of the other names: Frances Donaldson, Doctor Mary Becker, Sandra Harrison and David Edington

'It looks like Mr Du Marchon is involved in a couple of other businesses,' said Silverstein. 'Fortnoy Accounting, I know that name, but not Echo Taxis. This Julian Du Marchon, do you think he might be doing something illegal?'

'I have no idea; he just seems to be a bit too smooth for my liking.'

'Let's see what the Financial Conduct Authority has to say about him,' said Silverstein, typing. He shook his head again and looked up at Buchanan. 'All it says is he is not allowed to invest client money – do you suspect he is taking money from people?'

'He offered to invest the money I supposedly gained from the sale of a house.'

'I'd stay away from that. Do you want me to report him to the FCA?'

'No, that won't be necessary at this point. I'll do some more investigating first.'

'Fortnoy's,' said Silverstein. 'I know them; they haven't been the same since dear old Samuel passed away.'

'You knew him?'

'We used to meet up at business meetings, despite him being a *goyim*, we got along well.'

'What about his business partner?'

'Jenifer? Samuel's wife was a partner in name only. Samuel was the brains; he ran the company.'

'What is the company doing now?'

'I thought they closed when Samuel died but, according to what I see here, they are still trading.'

'Do you think Jenifer is now running the company?'

'I don't think so, she only played a minor role in it. I might still have a number for her,' he said, pulling out a desk drawer.

He took out a leather card wallet and thumbed through the collection of business cards. 'Ah, here we are,' he said, passing a weathered business card over.

'Thanks,' said Buchanan, as he entered the number into his phone's memory. 'I'll give her a call. What about the other members, do you recognise any of their names?'

Silverstein looked back at the screen and shook his head. 'Sorry, no.'

'Will you be at the dinner on Saturday evening?'

Silverstein looked up at Buchanan. 'Ah, you are referring to the awards dinner at Castlewood.'

Buchanan nodded.

'Yes, we'll all be there.'

'All being yourselves and the Bashirs?'

'Yes. Will you be there, Inspector?'

Buchanan smiled. 'That depends on what happens during the next couple of days. I'm not at Castlewood for the race. I'm just there for a few days' rest, I'll be back at work next Monday.'

'I get the feeling all is not well, Inspector, should I be concerned? My daughter is riding in the race.'

'Your daughter will be fine. I'm looking into a completely unrelated matter.'

'Glad to hear that.'

Buchanan stood. 'Thank you for your help, Mr Silverstein, maybe see you at Castlewood on Saturday?'

'Is that where you are going now?'

'I'll be doing that later, for now it's a trip into the office.'

♦

15:50

The first item on Buchanan's list was the accounting firm of Fortnoy. Companies House had just one director listed: Jenifer Fortnoy. Though their accounts were up to date, the website looked outdated and when he clicked on the *Contact Us* button, he was redirected to a generic email form. The *About Us* page just mentioned the basics of when they started in business and the types of work they handled, but nothing about the current directors. Companies House gave Fortnoy's an address on Commercial Avenue.

Out of curiosity, he googled the name of Jenifer Fortnoy. The name came up in the search showing a listing on Facebook. He clicked on the link and saw a healthy-looking fortyish woman in a pub wearing a Brighton football shirt. She had a pint glass of beer in one hand and a Brighton supporters' flag in the other. Amongst her posts that were available were of a day at Plumpton racecourse and another showing her at a friend's hen party. An interesting profile for an accountant, thought Buchanan.

He looked online for Echo Taxis. All he could find was a banner webpage for the company, a phone number and address. Buchanan smiled to himself when he saw the address - it was the same as for Fortnoy Accounting. He dialled the number and waited; after the sixth ring his call went to an answering machine. The message informed him that they were extremely busy, would the caller please leave their phone number and Echo Taxis would call back as soon as someone was free. Fat chance of that happening, thought Buchanan, as he saw from their entry on the Companies House register that they were three months late with their filing of their last year's tax returns. If Fortnoy Accounting were handling Echo Taxis' accounts, they were being extremely neglectful.

Where would PC49 have got to with his investigations had he access to tools such as the internet, wondered Buchanan, as he googled the first name on his list: Frances Donaldson. The name popped up in several places, Facebook, LinkedIn and the *Herald*. The *Herald* appearance was for that of an advertisement for a hair and bridal salon on Terminus Road. Quite a catchy name he thought: Hair Today, Gown Tomorrow.

He called the salon and asked to speak to Frances Donaldson.

'This is she; how can I help?'

'Ah, yes.' That caught him off guard, he wasn't expecting her to answer. 'Jack Buchanan. I'm trying to find a former work friend, David Edington. I seem to remember he mentioned your name once or twice.'

'I did know a David Edington. Why did you want to talk with him?'

'He'd mentioned he'd met you at an investment evening, that's why I gave you a call, thought you might have his contact details.'

'Really?'

'I was hoping he could give me some advice on investments. I've just come into some money from the sale of a house and I remember him saying something about an IFA he knew and trusted. I know it's a stab in the dark, but these days you can't be too careful when it comes to investing money.'

'Mr Buchanan, I'm sorry to have to tell you this, but your former work friend passed away about a year ago.'

'Oh dear, now what do I do?'

'I could tell you who I use.'

'Oh thanks, that would be so helpful.'

'His name is Julian Du Marchon and his company is called Sovereign Secure Investments. I only have a phone number for him, he's between offices at the moment.'

Buchanan wrote down Julian Du Marchon's phone number and thanked Frances. Just as she was about to hang up, he asked, 'Do you happen to know a Doctor Mary Becker?'

'I'm sorry, Mr Buchanan, I have to go and attend to a customer. Goodbye.'

Bull's eye, thought Buchanan, he'd confirmed he had talked with the correct Frances Donaldson. Next, he googled Sandra Harrison and once again found an entry for LinkedIn, Facebook and mention in the *Herald*, but not the *Eastbourne Herald*. This news item was in the *Sydney Morning Herald*.

Miss Sandra Harrison, formerly from Eastbourne, England, has had her identity as a police informer revealed by a former boyfriend. She is now in police protective custody.

So much for Miss Sandra Harrison. That left Doctor Mary Becker. Once again, a search on Google revealed something interesting. According to Facebook, Doctor Mary Becker, former assistant director of Sanduskey Health Centre on Lismore Road, was currently working with Médecins Sans Frontières in Africa, and had been for the last eleven months.

♦

16:30

He called the number for Jenifer Fortnoy and wasn't surprised to get her voicemail. He left a short message as DCI Buchanan and asked her to return his call as soon as possible.

He was about to drive off when his phone rang. He looked at the display and was surprised to see it was from Jenifer Fortnoy.

He pressed the call button on his phone, 'DCI Buchanan. Jenifer Fortnoy?'

'Yes. I'm responding to your message; how can I help?'

'I would prefer to talk face to face, if possible?'

'Where are you?'

'I'm in Eastbourne.'

'You pay for the coffee and I'll meet you in Patisserie Valerie's in fifteen minutes.'

'Perfect, see you in fifteen.'

'Wait a minute, how will I recognise you?'

'I'm wearing a black fedora.'

'Good, I like men who wear hats.'

10
Thursday Afternoon

16:45

Buchanan found a seat at the rear of the café and waited for the arrival of Jenifer Fortnoy.

'There you are, Mr Fedora,' said Jenifer Fortnoy, easing her way past a busy table and carrying H&M and Next shopping bags. 'Have you ordered?'

'No, I was waiting for you to arrive.'

'Good man,' she said, putting her shopping on the floor and waving at a waitress.

'Yes? Are you ready to order?' asked the waitress.

'I'll have a cappuccino and a strawberry tart,' said Jenifer.

'Sir?'

Buchanan took a glance at the menu. 'Could I have an Americano and a slice of shortbread, please?'

'Whew, shopping is pure madness today,' said Jenifer, as the waitress left to get their order. 'All those special Brexit prices, it's like Black Friday on steroids.'

'My wife is going to like that. We are just about to move into our new house.'

'Where are you moving to?'

'The village of Westham.'

'Nice. I hear it's fast becoming the place to live, pity about the pond.'

'Yes, dead fish doesn't do much for house prices.'

'So, Inspector Fedora, what is it that's so urgent you wish to talk to me about?'

'Julian Du Marchon. What can you tell me about him?'

'That rat. He was the cause of my husband dying at an early age.'

'Can you explain that?'

'Samuel was a dear man, not an evil thought in his body. We had a very successful business offering an excellent service to Eastbourne businesses. Several years ago, Samuel and Julian met at a business dinner. Samuel was not the brightest of men when it came to judging people's characters. Honest he certainly was, but sometimes a bit malleable when pressured to make decisions on the spot. Julian took advantage of that and talked Samuel into working with him and doing tax returns for his clients.'

'That sounds like a good deal. Do you remember when that was?'

She shrugged as she took a sip of her coffee. 'That's what we thought back in 2011.'

'You now think differently?'

'I watched Samuel go from a happy, carefree, outgoing man with a great personality to that of someone who was scared of his own shadow.'

'Why was that?'

'I first noticed he wasn't coping when he came down with a cold, which turned into a bad bout of flu. Medically, he recovered from that, but was never really the same after.'

'When was this?'

'July, about five years ago now.'

Buchanan wrote down the date in his notebook then asked, 'Did you work with Samuel?'

'Not quite. We had just taken on the responsibility of fostering twins, hence Samuel's decision to work with Julian. I had been his secretary up till then.'

'So you became a full-time mother?'

'Yes.'

'Who handled the office work? I mean who answered the phones, took care of correspondence, those sorts of things?'

'Hmm, that was where the rat got in the henhouse. Julian supplied a secretary to take the stress of that away from Samuel.'

'Do you have a name for this person?'

'Sandra Harrison.'

'What happened to her?'

'When Samuel died, she left and moved to New Zealand.'

Buchanan nodded. 'What happened to the business?'

'I thought I was the remaining director but, when I showed up at the office, I found it empty. Julian had emptied the office of all the computers, documents and furniture. All he left was a desk, a chair and a phone with an answering machine.'

'Did you ask him what was going on?'

'He said it was none of my business.'

'But you were a part owner and a director, you were entitled to know.'

'A month before he died, Julian managed to get Samuel to transfer the business to him, though the change was never registered with Companies House. I went from having fifty percent share in the company to a mere twenty percent. At least he sends me a dividend cheque once a quarter.'

'Was that legal?'

'I don't know.'

'How did your customers take to the changes?'

'They never knew.'

'What about Julian? What do you know about him?'

'One evening Samuel told me about his business partner, and how he got started. I suppose you'd like to hear what he said?'

'First, would you like another coffee?'

'Why not?'

Coffee on the table in front of her, she began. 'Julian started in business working legitimately as a junior partner in an accounting company. The company had many wealthy clients, mostly people he met through his charitable work, golf courses etc. They also looked after small companies' pension plans. When the time came for his partner to retire, Julian bought out his share of the business with the promise he would take on another partner. That partner turned out to be my Samuel, along with our company's customer base.'

'A normal business practice these days.'

'Well, let me tell you something, and this is where things really went wrong. One of those customers fell under Julian's spell and, when she passed away, she left Julian a sugar plantation in Columbia. He looked around for a place to invest his new-found wealth and that was when the idea of maximising his investment led him to look at going offshore.'

'That's not illegal, as long as the investments are properly recorded.'

'That is so.'

'If you are no longer involved with the company, how do you know so much about what he did?'

She smiled, took a slow sip of her coffee then said, 'Sandra Harrison. She wasn't happy with the way the company was being run, so she confronted Julian. He said her services were no longer required and let her go.'

'Just like that? She called you out of the blue and told you all this?'

Jenifer shook her head. 'When she first went to work for Julian, she and I would meet once a week at lunch time. Sometimes we'd go for coffee. When the weather was really nice, we'd walk down to the seafront and have lunch at the Beach Deck.'

Buchanan nodded. 'Know it well, please continue.'

'Well, at first she'd ask questions about the accounts and I'd do my best to answer her. Then one day she said she was worried about something. I asked her what was wrong, but she just shrugged and said it was nothing. I persisted and finally she told me. She said Julian had been offered a large sum of cash – he should have questioned its source, but greed took over. From then on, he regularly accepted drug cash. To cover his tracks, he made up a fictitious list of investors.'

'When was this and who has this list?'

'It wasn't long after Samuel died. Julian thinks he's the only one who has the list.'

'I don't understand.'

'When we were in business, I was always worried about fire, our office burning down and us losing all our customer information.'

'Quite a reasonable concern. What did you do about your worries?'

'Samuel purchased a separate computer and had it set up as a backup server.'

'But didn't that go when Julian cleared out the office?'

She smiled. 'The whole purpose of having a backup server was to keep the data secure. It was stored in a cupboard under the stairs at home. We had the two servers connected by the internet; as the information was stored on the office server, it was automatically backed up at home.'

'So, what happened to the backup server?'

'I think it's probably still backing up under the stairs in my house.'

'Even since the business was taken over?'

She shrugged. 'Probably.'

'Do you think it would be possible to have one of our experts have a look at the contents?'

'Shouldn't you have a search warrant to do that?'

'Only if you decide to deny us access.'

'I don't know. I'm not sure who the server really belongs to. But I suppose since it's been in my house, using my electricity and space, and it's never been asked for, you may as well have it.'

'Thank you. If you'll give me your address, I'll arrange for it to be collected.'

'Ok, do you have a pen?'

'Yes, never without one. Oh, we'll probably also need the password for access.'

'No problem. When will the server be collected? I'd like it gone as soon as possible.'

'Within the hour, will that do?'

'How about now? I've got more shopping to do before the shops shut, but I need to get this lot home first. It's not every day the shops go crazy trying to get rid of their over-stock.'

'Do you need a lift home?'

'Are you offering?'

'Certainly.'

'Good, by the time I take the bus home and back the deals will have gone, and a taxi is quite out of the question.'

'That works for me, especially since I'm under the hammer with this issue. I need to resolve it before Saturday.'

'Well, why are we sitting here? I've still got some shopping to do.'

♦

16:45

Once again Buchanan removed the parking ticket from the windshield and stuck it in his inside jacket pocket. He opened the back door and helped Jenifer pile her shopping on the seat.

'Can I have directions to your house?'

'That's easy, I live in Friston. Just head towards Brighton on the A259. Friston is the first town you get to after leaving Eastbourne. You take a second right into the village, it's a gated community. My house is on Peakdean Lane. I'll shout before we get there, I don't have a house number displayed.'

His next order of business was to call Stephen. 'Hi Stephen, are you free to pick up a server? No, not that type of server, this one is a computer – you are? Good. Also, can you get the tech services to come along with you? Who knows what procedures are required in shutting the server down? Here's the address, see you shortly.'

Buchanan turned right on to Cornfield Road and immediately got stuck behind a number 1A bus waiting to pick up passengers.

'Dreadful state of affairs,' said Jenifer, 'why does it take so long to do road works? Look, it's just typical, three men standing watching while a fourth does all the work.'

'Yes, it never seems to change, does it?'

The bus collected its passengers and moved on. Buchanan turned right at the war memorial and made his way through town and on up to the A259, Beachy Head and Friston.

'This is it,' Jenifer said, as they approached a detached chalet-style house with a private driveway. 'Here we are, pull into the driveway.'

Buchanan parked in front of a double garage and got out. He opened the rear door and extracted Jenifer's shopping while she unlocked the front door to the house.

'Would you mind taking it through to the kitchen, please?' she requested, taking off her coat. Having deposited the shopping on the kitchen table Buchanan returned to the hallway.

'The server is in there,' she said, pointing to a cupboard under the staircase. 'There's a light switch on your right as you go in.'

Buchanan pulled the door open and leaned into the cupboard. He felt for the light switch and flicked it on.

'It's at the back, behind the Dyson,' said Jenifer.

Buchanan carefully made his way into the gloom of the under-stair cupboard. The server was indeed hiding behind the Dyson plus three battered suitcases. It consisted of a black, Hewlett Packard tower computer, a twelve-inch CRT screen, a yellowed keyboard and a grimy mouse. A blinking green light on the face of the tower told him it was still powered up and ready to receive data.

He made his way back out of the cupboard and said, 'I think I'll wait for the technicians to arrive and power down the computer. Oh, where did you say the password was located?'

'I seem to remember it's written on a piece of masking tape on the back of the keyboard.'

'Thanks, I'll let them know.'

'While you wait, would you like something to drink?'

He was about to ask for a cup of tea when his phone rang.

'Excuse me,' he said, taking his phone out of his jacket pocket.

'Buchanan. Oh, hello, Karen. How are you? They have? I can't just now – I know I'm supposed to be taking time off but needs must. Can't you take a taxi? They're what – they've all left? I'll see what I can do, call you back in a minute, 'bye.'

'What's up?' asked Jenifer.

'My wife and daughter have just arrived on the ferry at Newhaven and can't get a taxi. She says there are several people desperate to get home.'

'She's tried all the taxi firms?'

'So she says.'

Buchanan's phone rang again. 'Hello – you have? Good. Which firm? They must be new. Ok, wait a minute, why don't I pick you up at the station then we can head up to Castlewood for dinner– yes, just you and me.'

'Your wife found a taxi?'

Buchanan shook his head, 'A limousine service, South Downs Tours, they have an eight-seater, air-conditioned minibus. I said I'd collect them from the station.'

'That's her sorted then, how about me? I need to get back into town, those Brexit bargains won't last forever.'

'My men won't be long. You mentioned something to drink?'

'What do you want? I've got some sixteen-year-old single malt?'

'I'm working – coffee if you have any.'

She returned from the kitchen with Buchanan's coffee as Stephen arrived with Hanbury and a white van with two civilians. Buchanan thanked her for the coffee and went out to talk with Stephen and Hanbury.

'Congratulations,' said Hanbury.

'Congratulations?' said Buchanan.

'The hearing in Glasgow. You do remember what the hearing was all about?'

Buchanan nodded. 'Yes, I do remember, who told you?'

'I heard it from the desk sergeant –'

'And he heard it from the janitor,' said Buchanan, shaking his head. 'The server is under the stairs, I'll show you.' He turned to the two civilians and asked, 'How have you two been keeping?'

'Fine, thank you.'

'You're Palmer?' said Buchanan. 'I remember you from last year when you set up my office on Hammonds Drive.'

'Nice of you to remember. Under the stairs you say?'

'Yes. The password is written on a piece of masking tape under the keyboard.'

'C'mon, Dave,' said Palmer, 'let's go and have a look at the baby.'

Buchanan stood in the hallway while Palmer and Harrison made their way into the rear of the under-stair cupboard. Palmer exited carrying a bulky black HP tower computer followed by Harrison with the screen keyboard and mouse.

'We'll take this back to the station,' said Palmer, 'what do you want done with it?'

'I imagine the NCA will want to have a look at its contents, treat it as evidence.'

'Do you have a case number?'

'There was a young lad called Harry Janski brought in to the DGH a couple of nights ago from Castlewood, a GBH case. Use that number.'

'Will do. Are you coming back to the station?'

'Not yet. I've got to take Mrs Fortnoy into town, then go to collect my wife and daughter from the train station. You two go ahead and have a look at what's on the hard drive, but go easy on it, the National Crime Agency and the Financial Conduct Authority will want to have a look at it as well.

'Do you want us to contact them?'

Buchanan thought for a minute then said, 'No, I'll take care of that. If you two would take it to the station and get it set up, I'll catch up with you later.'

♦

17:20

'You can drop me at the station,' said Jenifer Fortnoy, 'The walk will do me good.'

Buchanan drove into the passenger drop-off area and said goodbye Jenifer Fortnoy. While he waited for South Downs Tours to deliver Karen and Jill, he called the FCA. After being passed around a couple of times he finally got to talk to the person he needed. When he explained the situation, he was told the person who dealt with those types of cases had gone home and would not be back in the office till Monday morning.

He hung up from the call and pondered what to do next. He was sure the answers to what was going on would be found in the details of the files on the server. But even if Palmer and Harrison could get the data printed, who would be able to interpret the information? Then he had a flash of inspiration: he'd ask Aaron Silverstein and Achmed Bashir to have a look. No doubt they would charge for their time.

He looked at his phone and saw it was only five-twenty. He dialled the office number for Aaron Silverstein.

'Yes, it's Detective Chief Inspector Buchanan. I was with Mr Silverstein earlier today and I was wondering if I could have a quick word with him, please, it is very important.' He hummed along with the music-on-hold. 'He can? Fifteen minutes? I'll be there.'

He got out of his car and looked across the road at the back of the Beacon shopping centre. Even though some of the shops had been doing a brisk business since before Christmas, the rear of the building already looked tired. He opened a fresh tube of fruit gums and waited for the arrival of Karen and Jill. He had finished the orange-flavoured sweet and was sucking on a lemon one, when a brightly sign-painted minibus arrived.

Karen waved from the window as the bus came to a halt.

'Welcome home,' he said, hugging her. He saw Jill standing a few feet back, smiling. He took two steps towards her and gave her a welcome home hug as well.

'Been waiting long?' asked Karen.

He shook his head. 'No, but I need to run an errand before I run you home. How about you stick your bags in the car and get yourselves a coffee at Starbucks?'

'Will you be long?' asked Karen.

'I shouldn't think so. I need to run round and ask Aaron Silverstein for some help on a case.'

'I thought you were supposed to be resting from work pending the outcome of the review?' said Jill.

He nodded. 'That's all settled, no further action to be taken.'

'Glad to hear that.'

'Look, go grab your coffees and I'll meet you in Starbucks in twenty minutes.'

He walked with Karen and Jill along Terminus Road till they got to Starbucks.

'Remember, twenty minutes or we come looking for you,' said Karen.

'Don't worry, I'll be there.'

He said goodbye and continued up Cornfield to Lushington Road and Aaron Silverstein's office.

He opened the door and approached the receptionist. She waved at Buchanan indicating she was on the phone and wouldn't be long. He smiled and nodded his understanding.

She hung up from the call and said, 'I've just buzzed Mr Silverstein, he knows you are here.'

The internal office door opened and Aaron Silverstein leaned out. 'Inspector, this way.'

Buchanan smiled at the receptionist and followed Silverstein into his office.

'What can I do for you?' said Silverstein, sitting down at his desk.

'It's a long shot, but I urgently need someone to examine a company's accounts.'

'I could have a look later next week – would that help?'

'This is urgent. I'm hoping to prevent a massive fraud from taking place.'

'What about the FCA, have you tried them?'

'Like you, they are unable to help before next week and I need the information by tomorrow evening at the latest.'

'I'd have to charge you for the service.'

'That's not a problem.'

'Is it just the company accounts that you want me to look at?'

'No. There are investments that I will need advice on whether they are legitimate or not.'

'Sounds like a job for Achmed.'

'Achmed Bashir?'

'Yes, you remember him from that case you were working on last year?'

'Of course, I do. Would you mind calling him and asking if he is available to help?'

'Certainly. Just a minute.'

While Silverstein called his friend, Buchanan went over to the paintings hanging on the office wall and once again marvelled at the skill of the painter.

'What time would you like him to be available?' asked Silverstein, breaking into Buchanan's musings.

Buchanan looked away from the painting. 'Could he meet us at Hammonds Drive police station in an hour?'

Silverstein went back to his phone call. 'How about an hour from now? Yes, at Hammonds Drive. No problem, I'll pick you up.'

'Thank you for arranging that,' said Buchanan

'Glad to be of assistance.'

'Thanks, but I do need to go,' said Buchanan, 'I've left my wife and daughter at Starbucks. I'll drop them off at home and meet you at the police station.'

Buchanan walked back to Starbucks and saw Karen and Jill deep in conversation, half-drunk coffees on the table between them.

'Sorry for leaving you,' said Buchanan. 'Ready to go?'

'Yep,' said Karen.

'I need to go into the office to check on something. I'll drop you at your flat, Jill, then I'll take you home, Karen.'

'I thought you were resting this week?' said Karen, putting on her seatbelt.

'It's a long story. Tell you what, why don't you stay at Castlewood with me till Sunday? I have a double room and we can eat dinner in the bar.'

She looked at him and said, 'That would be lovely. But I'll need a change of clothes. Dinner on a tray in front of the television with mother is one thing, dinner at Castlewood is a whole different matter.'

◆

17:35

Buchanan left Karen at the house in the harbour then drove to the police station at Hammonds Drive.

He stopped at the reception desk. 'Dave,' said Buchanan, 'have you seen Palmer and Harrison?'

'Yes, they've gone up to your office. They were carrying a computer, is that for you?'

'Yes, it's going to be evidence in an ongoing case.'

'Which case is that?' the sergeant said, looking at the incident board.'

Buchanan shook his head. 'The GBH case at Castlewood that happened two nights ago. I haven't processed the paperwork yet.'

'Ok. Do we need to know anything at the moment?'

'I should be able to get the info to you later this evening. Oh, I also have two people coming in to help me with some information on the hard drive of the computer Palmer and Harrison just carried up to my office. They should be here within the hour. Their names are Aaron Silverstein and Achmed Bashir.'

'I'll call you when they arrive.'

'Thanks, I'll head on upstairs.'

As he walked down the corridor, he heard the sounds of excited voices.

'We've borrowed a printer from the next office, hope they don't mind,' said Palmer 'We also borrowed a large screen. The one that came with the server is a bit small to use as a working terminal.'

'No problem.'

'Shall I power it up?' asked Palmer.

'Go ahead.'

Palmer pushed the power switch. The sound of the fan and hard drive powering up broke the stillness of the office.

'So far so good,' said Harrison, as the monitor came to life. The message *To log on, press Control, Alt, Delete*' appeared on the screen. Harrison held down these keys; the screen blinked and the server restarted. When it came back online, they were challenged by the request for a password. Harrison looked at Palmer's note and keyed in the password.

Seconds later the header page for Sovereign Secure Investments appeared.

'Is this what you expected, Inspector?' asked Palmer.

'I have no idea what to expect. I'm going to wait for my experts to arrive.'

'Do you need us for anything else?' asked Harrison.

'How about the internet?' said Buchanan. 'There's a sister to this server somewhere.'

'Hmm,' muttered Palmer. 'We could try connecting through the company network. May not work, but worth a try. Do you have a spare network cable?'

Buchanan opened his desk drawer and took out a blue two-metre-long network cable and handed it to Palmer.

Palmer plugged into a wall outlet and the other end into the back of the server. Immediately the display on the monitor changed as the server logged into the remote terminal.

As they watched the data scroll across the screen, Buchanan's phone rang. 'Buchanan. They are? Good, I'll be right down.' He hung up the call and said, 'That's the chaps who are going to help me understand the contents of the server, I'll be right back.'

♦

17:55

'Thanks for being willing to help,' said Buchanan, to Silverstein and Bashir. 'If you'll follow me, we've just powered up the server.'

Silverstein and Bashir walked over to the monitor and glanced at its display. 'This is your field, Aaron,' said Bashir.

Silverstein pulled Buchanan's chair up to the desk and started typing. Forty minutes later the printer completed printing copies of the files he'd said were the most relevant. He looked up at Buchanan and said, 'Inspector, these records are going to take quite a bit of analysing.'

'I've just had a cursory look at the data,' said Bashir. 'I think you will need to get the Financial Conduct Authority involved.'

'How much time will you require?' asked Buchanan.

'I understand you require the information before Saturday,' said Bashir.

'Tomorrow if possible.'

Bashir looked at Silverstein and grinned. 'Be like old times, eh, Aaron? Working late into the night.'

'How late do you think you will have to work before you come to a conclusion?' asked Buchanan.

'I imagine we should be through by midnight,' said Silverstein.

'I take it you will do it, then?' said Buchanan.

'Be just like the night of the general election when we sat up late into the night counting votes.'

'In that case,' said Palmer, 'if you don't need us for anything else, we'll say goodnight.'

'No, you're free to go, you've done what was needed, thanks,' said Buchanan. He nodded at Silverstein and Bashir. 'If you two are going to be here till midnight, can I get you anything to eat, or drink?'

'If it's all right with you,' said Bashir. 'I'd prefer to work on this at home. How about you, Aaron?'

Silverstein looked up from the reports in front of him. 'Yes, feels weird to be sitting in a police station.'

Buchanan thought for a minute, then said, 'I suppose the documents are just copies of the originals which are still contained on the server. Ok. I will still have to mark them as evidence though.'

'Will you be here?' asked Bashir.

'No, I'll be at Castlewood. There are still some unanswered questions I need to investigate. And I have to collect my wife and take her with me – I've promised her dinner; sorry I didn't realise this would arise.'

'Think nothing of it,' said Silverstein. 'Our wives and daughters are out this evening. I can't think of anything more interesting than to spend the evening with my friend working on this puzzle.'

Bashir smiled and nodded.

'Well, in that case, I'll bid you both a good evening. But, before you go, let me give you my phone number – just in case you find something I need to know right away.'

Buchanan followed Bashir and Silverstein as they walked across the carpark pushing a trolley borrowed from the evidence store laden with A4 sized boxes full of the financial history of Sovereign Secure Investments and Fortnoy's trading figures.

11
Thursday Evening

18:20

Buchanan parked in front of his house, or his sister-in-law's, he reminded himself. If all went well, they'd only be staying here for a few more days. His sister-in-law and husband were due back from working in Paris in three weeks' time, and they would want to get back into their own house.

He opened the front door and almost tripped over an overnight case sitting in the hall. He walked down the hallway and into the kitchen. Karen was talking on the phone.

She smiled at him. 'Jill, I've got to go, Jack's home – yes, I'll give you a call tomorrow.'

'I see you're ready to go.'

'Of course I am. It's not every day I get to stay with such a sophisticated gentleman at such a prestigious establishment as Castlewood.'

'Keep that up and I'll get my cape out for the puddles. Shall we go?'

'Why did you have to go into the station?' asked Karen, as they drove out of the Marina. 'I thought you were supposed to be on administration leave?'

'As I already mentioned, the incident in Glasgow has finally been put to rest. Helen said I had nothing to answer for and it was now a closed matter.'

'About time. And why did you have to go to the police station when you are supposed to be on suspension?'

'Are you sitting comfortably?'

'Get on with it, I don't have all day, I have a dinner date with a handsome gentleman.'

'Late Tuesday evening, the assistant stable manager was severely beaten and dumped in one of the stalls. The perpetrators hoped it would look like he'd been trampled by the horse in the stall.'

'Did he die?'

'No, in fact he should be back sometime today. Unfortunately, he was so severely traumatised he doesn't remember anything about his assault.'

'Could he be lying, trying to get attention? Self-harmers sometimes have that as a motive.'

'No, I definitely believe Harry was assaulted and, what's more, I think I know who his assailants are. But without a witness statement or corroborating evidence, my hands are tied.'

'So, who is out to hurt him?' asked Karen.

'The assistant stable manager's name is Harry. I believe he saw something and was given the option of keeping his mouth shut or suffering the consequences. Harry has a criminal past and is currently on probation. From time to time Nathan helps young offenders get back on their feet. Harry is one of those young offenders. He has a very fine mind and loves horses. He's hoping, when his probation is served, he will be able to work full time for Nathan.'

'That sounds fine, but it doesn't quite explain why someone would want him almost killed,' said Karen, as Buchanan turned off the A22 and onto the road to Arlington.

'Harry getting hurt is the key. Up till now I've been busy looking for the key to the puzzle. What I mean by that is I am sure there is a crime being enacted and it involves a great deal of money. So far, I have discovered the players involved in this little vignette are a financial advisor, an army colonel with two horses, two despicable characters who are looking after the two horses, the wife of the colonel, their jockey and an army major.'

'Sounds like a list of characters for an Agatha Christie story,' said Karen, as they turned onto the Castlewood driveway.

'If only it was a story. Oh, before we go in, as far as anybody is concerned, I'm just plain Jack Buchanan, civil servant. There are a few who know my true identity.'

'For instance?'

'In the hotel, Nathan and one of the staff, Lewis. He's in charge of security. In the stable there is Olivia, the stable manager, and of course her assistant, Harry. There is one other person, she's one of the guests, Poppy; she's Travis and Shelly Grant's daughter and Harry's girlfriend. Poppy's dad doesn't approve of her consorting with a known criminal – bad for his image.'

'My, you have been busy! When does World War Three start?'

'Funny, very funny,' said Buchanan, as they pulled up in front of the entrance. Buchanan collected Karen's case and handed his keys to the valet.

'This way,' he said, starting up the steps to the entrance.

'Remember the last time we were here?' asked Karen.

'Nathan and Susan's wedding? Yes, I remember it well. If two people were ever meant to be together, they were. I'll just let reception know you are staying with me for the next few days.'

'Next few days? I'm glad I brought extra clothes.'

'Absolutely, come on, let's get you signed in.'

Buchanan collected a second door key for Karen then led her over to the lift. As the door opened, Cynthia stepped out.

She smiled at Buchanan and asked, 'Will you be joining us for dinner this evening, Jack? Victor has gone off in one of his moods. Oh, hello.'

'Hello,' said Karen. 'I'm Karen, Jack's wife. You are?'

'Cynthia, Cynthia Mountjoy. Victor's my husband.'

'Nice to meet you, maybe see you at dinner? C'mon Jack, I need to get ready,' said Karen, stepping into the lift. Buchanan joined her as the lift door began to close. 'So that was the Cynthia you mentioned.'

'That is her, quite something, isn't she?'

As the lift rose to the first floor, Karen asked, 'What do you think she meant about her husband, *gone off in one of his moods*?'

'I'm not sure, but if it has anything to do with his relationship with Julian Du Marchon, I might not get much sleep tonight.'

'All right,' said Karen, sitting down on the chair by the dressing table. 'Who is Julian Du Marchon, and are there any other characters in this drama of yours that I should know about?'

'Julian Du Marchon is an independent financial advisor. He intimated he could get a good return when I invest the profits from the recent sale of my house.'

'What sale? I thought we agreed we were going to keep the house in Glasgow and rent it out?'

'Relax, I haven't sold it. I was just fishing. I wanted to see just what sort of advisor he was.'

'And what sort is he?'

'He's as straight as a dog's hind leg type of advisor. You may meet him at dinner this evening.'

'I'm not sure I'm looking forward to that. Are Nathan and Susan going to be there?'

Buchanan shook his head. 'When I last talked with Nathan, he said he was off to Glasgow and wouldn't be back till sometime on Friday.'

'So, you're in charge of security till he gets back?'

'What on earth gives you that idea?'

'Thirty-five years of marriage, that's what. Now, tell me exactly what you are working on?'

Buchanan took in a deep breath then exhaled slowly. 'I believe there's a conspiracy to fix the Castlewood Cup. Whoever is behind the conspiracy stands to make a considerable sum of money. As yet I have only circumstantial evidence and my gut feeling as to who's involved.'

'Who do you suspect?'

'I'm sorry, Karen. If I let on to you the names of who I suspect, you may inadvertently give something away. Besides, if you don't know, you may pick up something that I have missed.'

'So, am I on expenses?'

'My dear, this whole week is on me, let's get ready for dinner.'

♦

18:55

'We will be sitting at table one,' said Buchanan, as he and Karen walked towards the lift. 'I called reception and was told that, since Nathan and Susan are away, we have been given their seats. Should be fun, you'll get to meet some of the people I've been sharing my time with.'

'I hope I'm suitably dressed,' said Karen, catching sight of her reflection in one of the hall mirrors.

'You look fine,' said Buchanan.

'What are the names of the rest?' asked Karen.

'Well, there will probably be Colonel Victor Mountjoy and his wife, Cynthia. He's an army lawyer, Cynthia you've already met. Dean and Angela Branson, and no, they are not related to Richard. Then there will probably be the Americans, Travis and Shelly Grant with their daughter Poppy.'

'Travis Grant? That name sounds familiar. Do you know what he does he do for a living?'

'He said he's a pastor of a church somewhere in America.'

'He's an American pastor?'

'Yes, why?'

'If I'm correct,' said Karen, 'I've seen him on the God channel. And if that's the case, I'm certainly looking forward to meeting him.'

Buchanan led Karen out of the lift, through the ballroom and into the restaurant. One of the servers took them over to their table and seated them. As on other evenings, Buchanan was beside Cynthia.

'Good evening all,' he said, unruffling his napkin. 'I'd like to introduce you to my wife, Karen. She's been in France with our daughter this last week.'

'We've already met,' said Cynthia, glancing up from her menu. Beside her was an empty chair where Victor should have been seated.

Karen gave an acknowledging nod as one by one the guests at the table introduced themselves.

The waiter left with the drinks orders and Karen asked, 'Excuse me, Travis, but have I seen you on television?'

'If you watch TBN, then probably yes.'

'I thought so. As soon as Jack mentioned your name, I said it had to be you. I was discussing your message on Daniel chapter two a couple of weeks ago with the ladies at my afternoon Life Group.'

Travis shook his head and let his breath out slowly. 'I got it in the neck from some of the congregation on that one. I was actually accused of attacking our president. Although there are quite a few of my flock who say they see a resemblance between him and Nebuchadnezzar'

'We didn't see it that way. Our impression was you were saying that it doesn't matter much about what the voters do. God is in charge and it is he who ultimately appoints the leader people deserve.'

'Well, I'm glad someone saw what I was getting at.'

Further discussion about who ruled the world was prevented by the arrival of their drinks.

'Cynthia,' said Buchanan, turning to her. 'Will Victor be joining us this evening?'

'Later,' she replied, turning over her menu to look at the dessert page. 'Victor said he and Julian had something urgent to discuss.'

An alarm bell sounded in Buchanan's mind. He wondered if the shifting of the off-site server had somehow been noticed by Julian and, if so, what would he do if he thought someone was spying on him? Victor and Julian going off to have an urgent pow-wow reinforced in Buchanan's mind that they were definitely both involved in some sort of nefarious scheme. How they reacted would depend a great deal on how the off-site server settled down and how technically savvy either Julian or Victor was.

'Cynthia,' continued Buchanan, 'I was wondering if Victor knows much about computers? My laptop has problems saving files.'

She looked away from her menu. 'Does Victor know anything about computers? That's a laugh. I have to show him how to change channels on the TV.'

'What about his friend, Julian, do you think he knows much about computers?'

'I have no idea,' she said, shaking her head and turning back to the menu, 'you'll just have to ask him yourself.'

'Thanks, I'll catch up with him later.'

Cynthia put her menu down and turned to look at Buchanan. She glanced at Karen, smiled, then looked back at Buchanan and said, 'Jack, could you be a dear and go and find Victor for me? Tell him we're all waiting to order, and we can't till he gets his backside in here.'

'In those actual words?'

'No, just tell him everyone is ready to order.'

'Jack?' said Karen.

'It's all right, Karen,' said Buchanan, winking at her. 'I'll be right back.'

As he pushed his chair back, Cynthia put her hand on his and said, 'You'll probably find him in the mess, as he likes to refer to the bar. Please remind him this isn't an army function.'

Karen smiled and returned to her conversation with Travis.

Buchanan walked through the restaurant on the way to the library. As before, he picked up snippets of conversations:

'They said the horses, all purebreds, were wearing bronze-plated military saddles and were ready to go when Mount Vesuvius erupted and buried them all … '

'She evented in the sixties and competed at Badminton several times. I heard she was a stickler for the rules when stewarding …'

'A retired member of Parliament said that there was a gap between Parliamentarians and equestrians, though horses did like to sniff each other's backsides …'

'You should have heard Audrey moaning about having to swap her wellies for dress shoes. She went on about it all night till someone pointed out she had her shoes on the wrong feet …'

'I ended up with three entered at Hickstead, lucky for me as this was where it all changed, and I realised just how competitive I'd become …'

Buchanan shook his head, dodged round a waiter carrying a tray of drinks and entered the bar. A lone bar-waiter glanced up from wiping a table, looking unsure if he should scuttle back to the bar or keep cleaning.

Buchanan smiled and kept on walking through the bar to the library. He stood at the entrance and looked and listened for Victor Mountjoy. The sound of murmured voices came from the far end and Mountjoy's voice emanated from behind one of the Chesterfield chairs. Buchanan walked slowly across the carpeted floor, trying to catch the conversation between Mountjoy and Du Marchon. He managed to hear, 'I tell you, Victor, it gave me a start.'

'Ah, there you are, Colonel,' said Buchanan. 'Oh, Mr Du Marchon, didn't see you sitting there. Colonel – your wife sent me to let you know that they are ready to order dinner.'

Mountjoy was about to say something, stopped in mid-thought, then said, 'Please tell Cynthia I will be with her presently.'

'Certainly. Oh, just wondering if you know anything about computers? Cynthia said to ask you for your advice, mine is having trouble saving files. I'm afraid I'm a bit of a klutz when it comes to computers.'

'I'm sorry, Jack. I just turn them on and use them.'

'Julian, do you know much about computers?' asked Buchanan, as Mountjoy threw back his drink and stood up.

'I know how to use the programs, mostly financial ones,' said Du Marchon, leaning forward and putting his empty glass on the small coffee table in front of him. 'But when there are issues, I have to rely on getting an engineer in.'

'Does that happen very often?' asked Buchanan, as the three of them walked through the empty bar towards the restaurant.

'Funny you should ask that, Jack. Just this afternoon, our office server had a hiccup. I thought we were about to lose all our data. Then a few minutes later it burped and settled down again,' he said, frowning.

'Sounds like the Russians or maybe the CIA were snooping,' said Buchanan, looking at Du Marchon's face for a reaction.

'Do you think that's possible?'

'Just joking. I've no idea if they can do things like that – unless you are connected to the internet, then maybe it might be possible for someone to hack into your computer.'

'Phew, you had me worried for a moment.'

So, he doesn't know about the wi-fi internet card in his server, thought Buchanan, good.

'We had a lad working in our office who used to say, "every time the office internet goes slow, the CIA are at it again",' said Buchanan, as they entered the restaurant.

Du Marchon smirked at Buchanan's remark.

'I'll catch up with you later, Victor,' said Du Marchon, as he left for his table.

Cynthia looked up as Mountjoy took his seat. 'Nice of you to join us, Victor. I've ordered you soup as a starter; you'll have to catch the waiter for your main.'

Karen looked at Buchanan for a response.

'I'll tell you later,' he whispered, as he sat down. 'Did you order me anything?'

'I ordered you the shrimp cocktail, I presumed you'd want the fillet steak?'

'Perfect, thanks.'

As Buchanan wiped the crumbs of his tiramisu from his lips, he looked around the table and thought; as it was in the days of the Titanic, people were eating and drinking having no thought about what the next moment could bring. He looked to his right and saw Karen deep in conversation with Travis. His wife, Shelly, was chatting to Dean. Victor was telling a barrack-room story to Poppy, who was blushing bright red. When he looked at Cynthia, he saw she looked bored with the evening's proceedings at the table and was busy examining the polish on the nails of her right hand. She looked away from her nails and caught Buchanan regarding her. She smiled at him, held up her empty port glass and nodded towards the bar.

He smiled back and nodded.

She crumpled her napkin, dropped it in front of Victor, then stood. 'Victor, if you can tear yourself away from trying to poison young Poppy's mind for a minute, Jack and I are going through to the bar for a nightcap.

Karen looked away from her conversation with Travis at Buchanan, he smiled and gave her a *I'll explain later* look.

'What? Oh sure, see you later,' said Karen.

'I don't know what I ever saw in him,' said Cynthia, as they worked their way between the tables and into the bar. 'Let's go into the library and sit by the fire,' she said, grabbing Buchanan's hand and leading him towards the two empty armchairs in front of the fire.

She sat down and indicated to Buchanan to sit opposite. The waiter, who had followed them, asked if they wanted anything from the bar.

'I'll have a gin and tonic,' said Cynthia.

'Could I have a whisky and water, please? Lagavulin, if I haven't drunk it all,' said Buchanan.

They sat in silence and stared at the fire while they waited for their drinks. Buchanan, not wanting to interrupt Cynthia's thoughts, closed his eyes and leaned back into the armchair.

'He's up to something,' said Cynthia, as she downed her gin and tonic in one go.

'Sorry, who's up to something?' asked Buchanan.

'Victor, that's who.'

'Oh, I wouldn't worry about him. Travis will sort him out if he tries anything with Poppy.'

'That's not what I'm talking about. Where's the waiter? I need another drink,' she said, leaning round her chair and waving at the waiter while pointing to her empty glass. 'No, Poppy's completely safe with Victor. He may seem a bit of a rogue with the women but that's just the way he is. Outside, a very rough and tumble, aggressive male – inside, a very confused little boy.'

'So, what do you mean by the statement, "he's up to something"?'

'You're not what you seem to be, are you?'

Buchanan took a sip of his whisky as the waiter delivered Cynthia's second gin and tonic.

'I am what you see, nothing more, nothing less,' he replied, shaking his head, slowly.

'Whatever. It still doesn't change the fact Victor is up to something, and I don't think his boss at work would approve of his little scheme.'

Buchanan took another sip of his whisky as Cynthia almost downed her drink in one go again.

'I don't know why, but I feel I can trust you. You are – are something else. Most men I know would have taken advantage of my offers of friendship, but you – you're so old-fashioned and just treat me like a sister. Oh, sorry, I didn't mean that to sound the way it did, please, take my comment as a compliment.'

'I will. You were going to tell me about what Victor was up to?'

'First, I need another drink, this glass has a hole in it.'

Buchanan waved at the waiter for another round of drinks. While they waited, he got up and placed a couple of logs on the fire, Cynthia slouched down into her chair and stared up at the ceiling.

'If I had my say in how my house was decorated, I'd have a room just like this one. A huge fire where I could sit with someone and grow old in peace knowing that someone loved me. You're so lucky, your wife really loves you; I've seen the way she looks at you.'

'Thanks, I know she does. What else would you have in your room?'

'Have you seen this?' she said, holding up a copy of the magazine *Sussex Scene*.

'No, I've been reading the horse magazines.'

'There's an article about Castlewood. in here.'

'What does it say?'

'The bit about the library says: *The room is one of the beautiful rooms created by the architect John Soane for the Duke of Arlington. Here he entertained his guests lavishly, as did his descendants in later years. It was in this room that visitors would have been served their drinks before dinner. The Arlington family were renowned for their hospitality. The house party guest lists, correspondence, and photographs show that over the years many dignitaries have been entertained here.*

That's my kind of house, Jack.'

'Does it give any names of the dignitaries?'

'Several prime ministers and many famous people such as Sir Duncan Fyfe, Winston Churchill, Sir Arthur Conan Doyle, and

George Bernard Shaw, to name a few. Wow, who'd have thought it?'

'Does it say anything else about your perfect room?'

'That's not fair, you're making fun of me.'

'Sorry.'

She continued to read as the waiter placed her gin and tonic on the small coffee table. *When designing and creating this room and, indeed, all the rooms in the house, Soane paid great attention to detail and insisted that his workmen used, as far as possible, the same materials and tools as Tudor and Elizabethan craftsmen. The fine panelling in the drawing room was inspired by the beautiful Elizabethan panelling at Hever Castle in Kent.* She put down the magazine and picked up her drink.

'And your desire is to have a house big enough to have a room just like this?'

She shook her head as she sipped her gin and tonic. 'It wouldn't have to be anywhere this big.'

'How big would it have to be?'

'Just big enough for a fire and two armchairs like the ones we are sitting in and – have wood panelling and a plastered ceiling like the one above us.'

'Have you mentioned to Victor what you'd like?'

She shook her head. 'A complete waste of time, he never listens to me. But he will,' she said, a smile growing on her face.

'Why do you say that?'

'Look, you may as well know, it will be in the papers soon enough. I'm going to divorce Victor.'

'Why would that be newsworthy?'

'I already told you Victor was up to something. I don't know exactly what, but I can tell you it is probably something illegal.'

'What would make you think that?'

'That creepy friend of his, Julian Du Marchon. He and Victor have been working for weeks on a get-rich scheme.'

'If you don't mind me making an observation, to my mind you two are the picture of a very successful couple. By that I mean I've seen the horsebox, your three horses, and I understand you employ a full-time jockey?'

'Pat, yes, he's such a treasure.'

'I think he's more than a treasure to you. Am I right?'

'Is it that obvious?'

'I observed you kissing him under my bedroom window last Sunday evening.'

'Oops! Need to be more careful.'

'What would happen to your divorce case if Victor found out about you and Pat?'

She smiled. 'He'd be in big trouble, that's what would happen. To stay one step ahead of his creditors and the tax man, he put all his assets in my name. Over the last few years Victor has made a lot of bad business deals and owes a lot of money to banks and friends. As a last resort he has borrowed against the value of a farm he inherited, stupid man. On top of that, he has convinced a lot of his friends to put money on Turpin winning the race on Saturday.'

'Who's going to be riding Turpin?'

'He hasn't decided yet but, if it was up to me, I'd have Pat on Turpin. But knowing how Victor likes to be in the limelight it will probably be him who rides Turpin. I just hope his friends are generous and forgiving when Turpin comes in last and they've lost their bets.'

'Why do you say he was a stupid man to have borrowed against the value of the farm?'

'Julian said for tax purposes to put the farm in my name. I doubt if any banks have actually lent him any money. He's probably gone to one of those private lenders you see advertising in the cheap newspapers.'

'Is there a mortgage on the farm?'

'No, it's free and clear, as are all of his other assets I control.'

'Such as?'

'Such as our house, the cars, that lovely horsebox you saw, what cash I've been able to squirrel away in discreet bank accounts, his private pensions, investments and our three lovely horses.'

'So, he has nothing but debts?'

She nodded.

'You said you believe he has borrowed money from private lenders and friends?'

'If his deal with Du Marchon fails, he'll be ruined, both financially and socially.'

'Do you know anything about this deal?'

'All I know is Victor has convinced his friends to bet on Turpin winning the race. He's even taken their money and said he will place them with a bookmaker who will get them better odds than any of the high street betting shops.'

'So, if Turpin wins, he and his friends stand to win a lot of money?'

'Yes.'

'Why can he be so certain Turpin will win?'

'If you've seen Turpin run, you'd know he's the fastest and fittest horse here. And with Pat riding there's no other combination that is faster.'

Buchanan shook his head slowly.

'What's bothering you?' asked Cynthia.

'It's the matter of why Harry was beaten up.'

'Who's Harry?'

'The assistant stable manager.'

'What's happened to him?'

'He was found unconscious in one of the stalls. He'd been severely beaten and left to look like a horse had trampled him. It may be a case of attempted murder.'

'But why would that have anything to do with Victor?'

'I have no proof, but I believe George and Lenny, who both work for Victor, were responsible.'

'Oh, that's horrible. I'll have to tell Victor to get rid of them.'

'No, please don't say anything. I think it was a one-off incident, an argument that went wrong. Besides, Harry will make a full recovery, so no permanent damage has been done.'

'There's more to this, isn't there? Why are you so concerned?'

'I like Harry.'

'You might like Harry, but you're a lousy liar. Are you from army internal affairs? Are you investigating Victor?'

'I'm simply a civil servant here on a week's leave and I'm not from army internal affairs.'

She smiled and yawned. 'Whatever. I'm too tired to figure you out. I'm going to go to bed, see you tomorrow.'

Buchanan stretched out his legs, sipped on the remains of his whisky and thought about the conversation with Cynthia. Victor was definitely in a bad place.

♦

23:45

'I was wondering when you were coming up to bed,' said Karen, as Buchanan shut their bedroom door.

'Sorry, got distracted. Did you enjoy dinner?'

'Yes, thanks. How is she, Cynthia?'

'She appears to be fine, It's her husband who's not.'

'Why is that?'

'She is going to divorce him and move in with their jockey, Pat.'

'Happens all the time. I suppose there's a lot of money involved? The lawyers will like that.'

'I have a story to tell you,' said Buchanan, sitting on one of the chairs in the bay-window.

'Good, I like your bedtime stories. Let me get comfortable first,' she said, pulling back the bedclothes.

'Once upon a time, there was a young woman called Cynthia who met a dashing young army officer ...'

'Whew, that's quite a story, and all the assets are hers, he has nothing but debts?'

'That's what she said.'

'And Major Jackson will handle the divorce and not charge anything?'

'That's what I understand. All Major Jackson wants to do is to wreak revenge on Victor Mountjoy for the death of his nephew.'

'Someone should write an opera about that,' said Karen, as she snuggled down into the blankets.

Buchanan stood, walked over to the bed and kissed his wife.

'Aren't you coming to bed?' she asked.

'I thought I'd just pop down to the stables and see how things are, especially since Harry isn't around to keep an eye on them. I won't be long.'

'You're not having a secret assignation with Cynthia, are you?'

'Absolutely. We're going to discuss running away from our spouses tomorrow night.'

'Well, take your jacket,' said Karen, 'it looks like the mist is setting in.'

He nodded. 'Thanks, good idea, and, for your information, I'm worried about what George and Lenny are getting up to.'

'Still think George and Lenny were responsible for Harry's injuries?'

'Yep. But I think as long as Harry feigns amnesia, he should be safe.'

'Don't be long.'

♦

23:55

Buchanan took the stairs down to reception and walked over to the desk. He had to wait a few minutes before the duty manager came out from the rear office. While he waited, he pocketed an apple from the fruit bowl on the desk.

'Yes, can I help?'

'Do you know when Sir Nathan is expected back from Glasgow?'

'All we've been told is he should be here sometime tomorrow.'

'Do you know if it will be in the morning or afternoon?'

'I'm sorry, I haven't been given that information. Do you wish to leave a message?'

'That's all right, I'll check back in the morning.'

Buchanan entered the library and walked through the bar and the walkway to the stables. The evening air had lost the chill of late winter and had now been replaced by the warm southern air of spring. He nodded to a group of waiters sitting at one of the veranda tables, happily drinking from the leftover bottles of wine.

The stable yard, unlike ten o'clock in the morning, was quiet with wisps of mist floating above the ground like windblown candyfloss. The only sound came from water sprinkling in the fountain in the middle of the yard.

As before, he entered through the stable door closest to Mercury's stall. The main lights were out, and the stables were now illuminated by the night lights. He stood for a minute outside Mercury's stall and listened: he wasn't sleeping. Mercury turned to see who was paying him a visit.

'Hello, boy,' said Buchanan, taking the apple out of his pocket and tearing it in half. He held one of the halves to Mercury, 'Bedtime treat for my favourite horse.'

As Mercury munched on his apple, Buchanan listened to the sounds of the stables. There were occasional sounds of a horse tugging at a hay net, others were lying down and shuffling in the bedding. Occasionally the sound of snoring horses could be heard coming from one of the stalls further along the corridor.

Buchanan gave Mercury's neck an appreciative pat and was about to leave when he heard voices coming from one of the nearby stalls. At five to midnight, there shouldn't be anyone in the stalls with the horses. There was no mistaking the sound of George's voice, but who was he talking to?

'If you know what's good for you, you'll do what you're told.'

Buchanan stepped back behind Mercury's hay net, thankful the dimness of the night lighting provided a welcome shadow. He stood as still as he could, his hearing working overtime.

'I tell you,' said a plaintive voice, 'I've never thrown a race in my life and I don't intend to do it now.'

'What race are you on about? You've been away from racing for years. All the more reason for you to ride Rambler and let Colonel Mountjoy ride Turpin.'

'That fat slob. He'll fall at the first hurdle.'

'He is your boss, he pays your wages and gives you the rides, remember that on Saturday when he tells you he's riding Turpin. And something for you to think about, remember accidents can happen when you are around horses.'

'Was it you and Lenny who did that young lad over?'

'So, what if it was, you want some of the same?'

'Go to hell.'

'Who said it would be you who had an accident, Pat?' sneered George. 'You know you should be more discrete about who you shag.'

'You lay one hand on Cynthia and I'll –'

'You'll do what? Remember, you're just an employee. And for your information, as soon as the race is over, the colonel is going to divorce his wife and leave her with nothing. You two, for all your sneaking about behind the scenes and planning, will end up being penniless.'

'Fuck you.'

There followed the sounds of boots walking on the floor. Buchanan peeked out from behind the hay net in time to see Pat go through the door at the end of the corridor.

So, it was Pat that George had been talking to, thought Buchanan. He saw George go into the Old Coachman's Lodge – so much for keeping an eye on the horses.

'Well, well, what's this, a rough sleeper?' said a voice from behind him.

Buchanan turned and saw it was Lenny who had just addressed him.

'Taking the evening air?' said Lenny. 'George,' he shouted, 'we have a visitor.'

'I told the bugger to go – oh, it's you again,' said George, stepping out of the Lodge. 'What are you doing here at this time of the night?'

'Minding my own business,' Buchanan replied.

'On your own?' said George, walking towards him.

'Of course, I always mind my own business,' said Buchanan, turning his back against the wall and away from Lenny. The phrase out of the frying pan and into the fire came to his mind. No sooner was the incident in Glasgow officially put to rest and here he was again, alone with two miscreants seeking to do him a mischief.

He undid the buttons on his jacket, slipped his arms out and neatly hung it on one of the spare harness hooks beside Mercury's hay net. As he started to roll up his right shirt sleeve, he saw the tell-tale sign he'd hoped to see. Lenny, shoulders forward, was rubbing his open hands on his trouser legs and licking his lips. Buchanan walked closer to George and stopped directly under the lit lightbulb while rolling up his left sleeve. 'Who's first, or do you two fancy a threesome?'

'Are you the guy Victor was talking about?' asked George.

'Taking references, George?' asked Buchanan.

'Victor said you've got nothing to do with horses and you were just another one of Cynthia's gigolos. You do know you're not the only one? She and Pat are having it off, quite regularly Lenny says.'

'Shit, George,' said Lenny. 'He killed two guys in Glasgow. I'm not having any of this. You have a go if you want, but don't expect me to help you.'

'You chicken shit, Lenny,' said George.

'Any time you feel lucky, gentlemen,' said Buchanan, as he rolled his sleeves down and stepped back for his jacket.

He quietly let himself out through the main door and started back towards the club building. He was thankful the mist had thickened; it concealed his walk across the stable yard on shaky legs.

As Buchanan exited the stable yard, he was confronted by a figure backlit by the covered walkway lights. He was holding what looked like a bottle.

'Are you following me?' the figure asked.

'Pat McCall?' said Buchanan. 'Steady on, Pat. It's Jack Buchanan, a friend of Cynthia.'

Pat lowered the bottle. 'What do you want?'

'Nothing. I'd just been down to the stables to check on my horse. Is that where you've been?'

'I couldn't sleep.'

'I ran into George and Lenny. You know them, don't you?'

'They're looking after Colonel Mountjoy's horses.'

'The bar's still open, can I buy you a drink?' asked Buchanan.

'I'm not a guest.'

'I am, and you can be my guest.'

'Ok.'

They walked along the covered walkway in silence and up the steps to the clubhouse. The waiters were still sitting around the veranda table. Buchanan opened the door for Pat, then followed him into the warmth of the bar. Even at this late hour, there were still a few revellers

'Let's go through to the library,' said Buchanan. 'It will be quieter in there.'

He nodded at the barman as they walked over to the chairs that previously had been occupied by himself and Cynthia.

'What would you like to drink?' he asked Pat.

'Lime and soda.'

'I'll have a lemonade,' said Buchanan.

He turned to Pat. 'I had a chat with Cynthia a short while ago. She's quite a lady.'

Pat looked away from the fire and back at Buchanan. 'Oh, you did, did you, and what did she have to say?'

'That after the race on Saturday, she plans to divorce her husband and set up house with you. She even told me what sort of house she wanted; she has quite an imagination.'

Pat McCall smiled and nodded. 'She told me yesterday she would like a small cottage in the country, but with wood panelling and ceilings like the one above us here in the library.'

'Have you known her long?'

'We met at an event at Hickstead. I was there to look at a horse a friend wanted to buy. Cynthia was there with Doxy. She fell off her horse in front of me; I picked her up and that was that.'

'Do you know what her husband is planning to do during the race?'

The smile disappeared from Pat's face. He shook his head. 'If it wasn't for Cynthia, I would withdraw from the race. Cynthia says you're from army internal affairs, are you going to arrest Victor?'

'I'm not from army internal affairs, Pat.'

He nodded. 'So, it's the Jockey Club, then. I was wondering when you lot would get round to investigating what Victor was up to. But why take so long?'

'I was hoping you could shine some light on the subject.'

'As far as I know, I'm booked to ride Turpin and Victor will be riding Rambler, that's all I can tell you.'

'Has anyone tried to coerce you into throwing the race?'

Pat's face momentarily froze. He glanced around the room then back at Buchanan. 'This race is my one chance to re-establish my career as a professional jockey; if I ride, I ride to win. But I'm reluctant to ride this Saturday if by winning I'll be branded a cheat and a race fixer.'

'So, you think the race is fixed?'

He shrugged. 'I don't know, I can't be sure – I suppose you will find out anyway, but I think Victor is going to ride Turpin and make me ride Rambler.'

'Why would he want to do that?'

'Arrogance, perhaps. He certainly can't win, no matter which horse he rides.'

'Do you think you can win?'

'On Turpin, it's a cert.'

'And you don't think Victor has a chance, even if he were to ride Turpin?'

'Not a hope. He's a good jockey, but the horses don't like him and won't respond to him.'

'Suppose you were riding Rambler, how would that be?'

'I'd have a chance, but it would depend on the other horses and riders.'

'Who'd be your main competition?'

'Major Jackson on Warrior.'

'What about Sir Nathan Greyspear on Moonbeam?'

He shook his head. 'The race is between, Turpin, Warrior and Rambler. No one else has a chance.'

'So, the race comes down to which horse you ride?'

Pat smiled. 'Absolutely.'

12
Friday Breakfast

07:30

'What time did you come to bed?' asked Karen.

'Must have been about one o'clock,' said Buchanan, turning on his side to look at the bedside clock. 'Seven thirty, so much for a lay-in.'

'What took you so long? I thought you were just checking the horse?'

'George and Lenny, that was what took so long.'

'I think you need to explain that,' said Karen, turning on her side to look at Buchanan.

He spent the next twenty minutes going over the evening's events.

'You were lucky they didn't call your bluff,' said Karen.

'Don't I know it, though it might have been fun to teach the pair a lesson.'

'Jack,' she said, punching gently on the arm, 'you just got out of one scrape and you're telling me you want to go through that all over again? I've just got used to the idea of living down here in Eastbourne. Where would they send you next?'

'No, I suppose you have a point there. I guess I'll just have to be nice to George and Lenny in the future.'

'You better,' she said, throwing back the bedclothes and getting out of bed. 'What have you planned for the day,' she asked as she walked into the bathroom.

'I was going to check into the background of Victor Mountjoy's jockey, Pat McCall. I thought it would be good to find out if he is what and who he says he is. He knows Cynthia has told me much of what's going on. Then, at some point in the day, I need to catch

221

up with Nathan and fill him in on what's been happening. Later, I hope to hear from Aaron Silverstein and Achmed Bashir about the results of their efforts at understanding what Du Marchon has been up to.'

'Just another quiet day at the office for you,' said Karen, as she dressed. 'Will we get any time together?'

'I'm afraid not, at least not till dinner time. What will you do?'

'Since you are not available, I'll probably go for a walk in the woods then spend the afternoon in the spa.'

♦

08:25

Buchanan turned left out of the lift and walked over to the reception desk.

'Good morning, sir, how may I help?'

'Just wondering if Sir Nathan has returned from Glasgow?'

'Yes, sir. I believe he has. Who shall I say is enquiring?'

'Jack Buchanan.'

'On moment, please.'

The noise of someone dropping a suitcase made him turn to see what had happened. He watched while a rather embarrassed guest quickly stuffed his clothes back into the offending suitcase.

'Mr Buchanan, if you'll come this way,' said the receptionist, lifting the counter flap.

Buchanan was led past the reception desk and into the manager's office. Greyspear was seated behind a desk, a computer spreadsheet in front of him.

'Ah, Jack. You've come to tell me what chaos you've been causing while I've been gone?'

'Is there somewhere we could talk?'

'Had your breakfast yet?'

'No.'

'Good. I was just about to go and get mine. Why don't you join me, and you can tell me what you've been up to? The restaurant is still quiet at this time of the morning.'

222

'Sounds good to me.'

'You'll have to excuse me,' said Greyspear, reaching for a walking stick, 'twisted my ankle jumping down from scaffolding in Greenock yesterday.'

As they entered the restaurant, the head waiter came over.

'Good morning, Sir Nathan. Will it just be two for breakfast?'

'Good morning, André. Yes, just the two of us. We'd like not to be disturbed.'

'The corner table, then. Follow me, please.'

'So, Jack,' said Greyspear, as they walked over to the table,' how is Karen?'

'She's fine. In fact, she's here with me. She and Jill went to see Karen's mother for a few days and, when they returned yesterday, I suggested that Karen join me till Sunday. The new house is not quite ready yet.'

'Good, maybe she'll be a calming influence on you while you're here.'

As André left with their breakfast order, Greyspear said, 'Now we are alone, just what's been going on, Jack? I hear you arrested one of my guests?'

'That's not exactly what happened. It was DI Hanbury who arrested one of your guests, a Travis Grant.'

'So I've since found out, luckily he's being very understanding about the whole affair.'

'Are you aware of the circumstances behind his arrest, and what happened to Harry, your assistant stable manager?'

'Yes, the office said the official story was he'd had an accident, been injured by one of the horses,' said Greyspear, shaking his head. 'Your policeman associate thought that Mr Grant had beaten up Harry over his association with Mr Grant's daughter.'

'It's actually Pastor Grant,' said Buchanan, forking the yolk in his egg.

'You mean he's sort of a church vicar?'

'According to my dear wife, Travis Grant is the senior pastor and an international tele-evangelist. His church owns its own TV station, and he has a congregation of twenty thousand souls to look after.'

'Quite an important person – in his own field.'

'Yep. I left him in the bar and went off to bed. So, you can see DI Hanbury had a reason to arrest Travis Grant. Especially so when he found out that Grant's daughter was having a relationship with Harry, an ex-convict. Can you imagine what Grant may have been thinking when he went to confront Harry over his budding relationship with his daughter?'

'Did Travis Grant actually go to confront Harry?'

'Yes, though he didn't actually see Harry. I talked with Grant and he was very embarrassed about his conduct, especially since he'd long ago given up drinking alcohol.'

'And you believed him when he said he hadn't been responsible for Harry's injuries?'

'Absolutely.'

'I thought Harry would be smart enough to be aware of the dangers when you go into a horse stall late at night.'

'It wasn't a horse,' said Buchanan, spreading marmalade on his toast. 'From what I have been able to put together he witnessed something, or overheard a conversation, he wasn't supposed to.'

'Any idea what?'

Buchanan shook his head. 'I talked with Harry and he says he is unable to remember anything between the start of the evening rounds till when he woke in hospital.'

'Should I be concerned that something evil this way comes to disrupt the race tomorrow?'

'Quoting Ray Bradbury at breakfast, Nathan, I think you have too much time on your hands.'

'If only. So, what do you think is going on?'

'I don't have all the facts yet, but I'd say it involves money, a great deal of money and tomorrow's race.'

'Should I call it off? Reschedule it till you sort out what's going on?'

'I don't think you need to do anything that drastic just yet. I'm waiting for information from two people who, I hope, will shed light on the money angle.'

'Is there anything I should be doing?'

'What have you done about security for tomorrow's race?'

'I have my own staff, and I've got G4s providing backup stewards tomorrow. Do you think that's enough?'

'It's a pity we weren't able to have this conversation a couple of days ago. I would have recommended having G4s stationed in the stables, especially at night.'

'Look, there's a great deal of money and prestige riding on the race. Please tell me what you really think is going on?'

'I wish I could. But at the moment, all I have are vague suspicions.'

'C'mon, you must have some sort of idea?'

'Ok, and this is only my suspicion. I believe that the race is to be fixed. A great deal of money is being bet, some of it is dirty money. Colonel Mountjoy's horse, Turpin, is currently the favourite and should win, especially if its current jockey, Pat McCall, is in the saddle.'

'Go on,' said Greyspear, spreading a thick layer of strawberry jam on his toast.

'Pat McCall and Mrs Mountjoy are having an affair and after the race she is going to seek a divorce from her husband. She has chosen a lawyer to represent her, – Major Jackson, also an army lawyer and one of the competitors here this week. Major Jackson has no love for Colonel Mountjoy.'

'Professional rivalry?'

'No, his dislike for the major runs a lot deeper. It is because Major Jackson blames Colonel Mountjoy for the untimely death of his nephew.'

'And you have found all this out in the last few days? Are you sure you don't want to come and work for me?'

'Thanks for the offer but I'm currently engaged, and besides there's more at stake than who wins the race.'

'What's that? There's more?'

'At this time – and this is only a supposition – I believe Colonel Mountjoy and Julian Du Marchon are working together behind the scenes on a get rich scheme, and I also believe it was Colonel Mountjoy's stable lads who caused the injuries to Harry.'

'But you have no proof it was them?'

'Just an old-fashioned policeman's hunch.'

'How would I recognise George and Lenny?'

'I'd say George is the older of the two. He wears a flat cap, military-green jacket with a fur collar, tight black jeans with black ankle boots that wouldn't look out of place on a building site. Lenny, the taller of the two, usually wears a blue beanie hat, grey hoodie, tight blue jeans and black trainers with mud on the soles that look like it's been there since the flood.'

'Not what you'd expect from stable lads. Should I bar George and Lenny from the grounds? Would that put a stop to what's going on?'

Buchanan shook his head. 'I think things have progressed too far to stop what's going on. With your permission, I'd like to set up a clandestine surveillance on stalls one and two. Harry showed me the existing system the other day; I imagine it shouldn't be a difficult job to connect up two or three more cameras to it?'

'I'll go for that. I'll get Lewis to make the necessary arrangement.'

'It needs to be done when no-one is around.'

'Just a minute,' said Greyspear, as he beckoned one of the waiters.

'Yes, sir?'

'Would you find Lewis and ask him to join us here in the restaurant? Tell him it is urgent.'

226

'Yes, sir.'

'How was Glasgow?' Buchanan asked, as the waiter cleared away their breakfast plates.

'I can't figure out why you'd choose to leave such a vibrant city. Susan and I were guests at a business awards meal in the Kelvin Hall yesterday, and to hear about those people who are making such a difference to the business success of Scotland was exhilarating.'

'You are one of those people with your boat-building enterprise in Greenock.'

'True, but we're just one of the many enterprises.'

Further conversation on the matter was curtailed by the arrival of Lewis.

'You wished to see me, Nathan?'

'Yes, take a chair, we have something we need you to arrange.'

The waiter appeared as Lewis sat. 'Would you like coffee?'

'Yes, please.'

'And leave the jug,' said Greyspear.

Lewis poured the coffees and asked, 'What is it you want me to organise, Nathan?'

'I take it you know Inspector Buchanan?'

'Yes, we chatted on Sunday.'

'Good. You are also aware that young Harry is currently in hospital with injuries suffered by someone giving him a beating?'

'I'd heard he'd been injured by a horse.'

'Inspector Buchanan believes Harry was assaulted by the two stable lads looking after Colonel Mountjoy's horses.'

'George and Lenny,' Lewis said, nodding. 'They do look a bit out of place in the stables. Do you want me to boot them off site?'

'Not quite,' said Buchanan. 'What we'd like you to do is to find out if there is room on the stables CCTV system to add a couple of extra cameras for stalls one and two – and to make sure it is done without anyone realising what is going on.'

'I think that should be doable. If the system is full, we could always relocate a couple of the existing cameras. It's not going to be easy though if you don't want George and Lenny to see what's going on.'

'I think I can solve that issue,' said Buchanan. 'When I went into the betting office earlier this week, George and Lenny were in there. I got the impression it is a regular event for them. They were so busy watching a race they almost didn't notice me. I'll call Constable Hunter and arrange for George and Lenny to be stopped by a patrol car and interviewed about a supposed hit and run incident in the town. I'll make sure he keeps them busy till your people have done the necessary with the security cameras.'

'What about Colonel Mountjoy?' asked Greyspear.

Buchanan thought for a moment, then said, 'Why don't you invite him for a drink in the library? After all, you were in the army once. You could make up a story about raising funds for a drop-in centre catering for ex-servicemen and women suffering from PTSD.'

Greyspear nodded. 'That would work, and to make it look more real I could also invite Major Jackson.'

'Sounds a workable plan. I'll call Constable Hunter and arrange a suitable time to come out and pickup George and Lenny.'

'Great. So, Jack, what do you hope to gain by the installation of these cameras?'

'I'm not sure what the colonel is up to, but just in case they plan to dope the horses, we may have an opportunity to prevent something illegal from taking place.'

'Anything else?' asked Lewis.

'No, not just now.'

'In that case I'll get right on to it,' said Lewis, pushing his chair back and standing up. 'You will let me know when George and Lenny have been taken in for questioning?'

'Yep.'

'Well, Jack. Other than the fact I'm not paying you for this, you could almost say you're working for me.'

'Don't let my boss hear you say that, or she'll find a reason to push me out of the door.'

'Don't you worry about that, especially since I have Lewis working for me. Did you know he was once one of you?'

'Yes, he told me.'

As Lewis left, he was replaced by the head waiter, André, with a message. 'Excuse me, Sir Nathan. There's a Mr Silverstein and a Mr Bashir in reception looking for an Inspector Buchanan. Do you know where I might find him?'

Greyspear looked at Buchanan then back at the waiter. 'I'll come out in a minute. In the meantime, would you show the two gentlemen into the office? Jack, do you want to join us?'

Buchanan smiled at how Greyspear had joined in with his subterfuge of anonymity.

'Yes, of course. Just as long as I'm not going to be in the way.'

♦

08:45

Buchanan followed Greyspear into the office.

'Ah, Inspector, sorry it has taken so long,' said Silverstein.

'That's all right, sorry to have given you such a headache at short notice. Have you been successful?'

'I do believe we have. It took us most of the night, but it was Achmed who finally saw behind the façade of Mr Du Marchon and Sovereign Secure Investments.

'Can I offer you gentlemen some breakfast?' asked Greyspear. 'We can do both kosher and halal breakfasts if you would prefer.'

'That's very kind of you,' said Silverstein. 'Could I just have a small portion of scrambled egg on toast with a cup of tea, please?'

'I'll have the same, if it isn't too much trouble,' said Bashir.

'No trouble at all,' replied Greyspear. 'André, would you take care of that, please, and while you are at it, would you bring a pot of coffee and two cups?'

'Yes, sir.'

'How about we sit round my desk?' said Greyspear. 'I'll get another chair.'

As they waited for the breakfasts to be brought, Silverstein began, 'It was quite a mess to start with. Julian Du Marchon started his financial career working as a junior clerk for a company called Erdis Fund Management. Nine years ago, the senior partner, William Erdis, died. His twin brother, Andrew, then became senior partner, with Julian Du Marchon taking over the role of junior partner.'

'Who is Julian Du Marchon?' asked Greyspear. 'I don't recall his name being on the list of competitors.'

'He's an independent financial advisor. I think he's here as a guest of Colonel Mountjoy and is a late entrant,' said Buchanan.

'Please go on, Mr Silverstein,' said Greyspear.

'It looks like Du Marchon took over the running of the company when Andrew Erdis passed away, changed the company name to Sovereign Secure Investments and bought out the remaining directors of Erdis. To make things look above board he took the company into a partnership with a company called Fortnoy Accounting; the directors were Samuel and Jenifer Fortnoy.'

'You say he bought out the directors of Erdis?' said Greyspear.

'There were only three,' said Silverstein, looking at a sheet of paper. 'Frances Donaldson, Dr Mary Becker and Sandra Harrison. All were paid several thousand to relinquish their directorships.'

'I talked to Frances Donaldson,' said Buchanan. 'She told me there was a fourth director, a David Edington, he passed away the previous year. Was that about the time Du Marchon inherited the sugar plantation?'

'Yes.'

'I had coffee with Jenifer Fortnoy yesterday,' said Buchanan. 'I got the impression she tried to be involved in the running of the company but was rebuffed by Du Marchon. I suppose with all that cash floating about he didn't want anyone poking their nose into his affairs.'

'A valid point, Inspector,' said Silverstein.

'I went through the investment portfolio,' said Bashir, 'and I have to say, I just don't know how he has got away with what he is doing for so long. In the files I found copies of correspondence between Mr Du Marchon and a Miguel Santacruz of Columbia. It detailed the arrangements for the sale of the sugar plantation and the subsequent distribution of funds to an offshore bank account.'

'Miguel Santacruz,' said Buchanan. 'I wonder what the internet has to say about him?'

'I did a cursory look,' said Bashir. 'He's reported as being involved in the production and distribution of cocaine.'

'When the Erdis brothers were running the company,' continued Bashir, 'they offered plans typical of any high street banks, including endowment mortgages.

'Is this what Du Marchon was offering?' asked Greyspear.

'Pretty much so at the beginning and it did work till interest rates went down and the stock market went flat.'

'Because they weren't making money?' asked Buchanan.

'In 2012, the Financial Services Authority did a review and it resulted in a ban on commissions for retail investment advice in the UK. This ban on commissions was applicable to all investment advisors irrespective of whether they gave independent or restricted advice to retail clients. We found a file with one of his brochures,' said Bashir, 'quite a professional-looking piece of fiction. In the brochure Du Marchon advises clients they could put their money in the bank, and with interest, maybe make as much as one to two percent. But he warns them with inflation running at two and a half percent, they are losing money.

'And if they were interested in investing?' said Greyspear.

'In the office they would be invited to fill in a risk aversion questionnaire. Based on their answers he would get his prospective clients to allow him total discretion with the investments,' said

Bashir. 'Unlike the banks, he says he will guarantee a five percent return on their money. But regardless of their grading he invests their money in high-risk offshore investments, making a tidy return for himself. Then he charges them a five percent fee for setting up the account and a five percent fee based on the returns.'

'There is a copy of a letter written in response to an enquiry from an employee, a Sandra Harrison,' said Silverstein. 'In the letter Du Marchon says that the investment of funds from the sale of Mrs Granger's sugar plantation is a company confidential matter, and she should confine her concerns to her position as secretary and leave the decisions about investments to those more qualified than her.'

'So, he's nothing more than a common crook?' said Greyspear.

'In the correspondence files we have found a recent email from the Financial Conduct Authority,' said Bashir. 'In it they are requesting information on his investment portfolio. So, whatever he is up to, I'd say he is about to play one more round, collect his winnings, and go to ground.'

'Do you have any idea what he's up to?' asked Buchanan.

'I'm not trained in forensic accountancy,' said Silverstein, 'but I am trained to follow the money. When I started looking at the overall flow of money through his accounts, it all looked so benign. There were the usual monthly deposits from investors, ranging from between fifty and two hundred at a time.'

'Was there anything odd about the deposits?' asked Buchanan.

'I matched them with the names and addresses of the policy holders, that was when I saw the pattern,' said Silverstein. 'The monthly deposits under one hundred pounds were for random amounts and probably legitimate deposits. Once the smaller deposits were removed from the list, the ones over one hundred formed a pattern. We made a list of deposits by amount and instead of matching customer names, we matched by post code.'

'What did you find?' asked Buchanan.

'That each post code had several names against them, some posting up to two thousand each month.'

'Could it be friends sharing a flat?' asked Greyspear.

'More likely laundered cash from the bookmakers,' said Buchanan. 'How many clients did he have on the books?'

'I counted one thousand and thirty-two active accounts with an average income of seventy-five pounds each per month. Or just over seven hundred thousand a year.'

'But he must have been paying dividends?' said Greyspear.

'Yes, he did, but just the five percent.'

'So, for the last, what, five years, he's been raking in close to three quarters of a million pounds a year?' said Greyspear.

'To my mind,' said Bashir, 'it looks very much like a classic Ponzi scheme.

'Anything else?' asked Greyspear.

Buchanan smiled and said, 'Last Thursday I went into town to a betting shop, but not to bet on anything. Ostensibly I went in to enquire about how betting odds work. While I was there, Colonel Mountjoy's lads were also in the betting shop. The manager said they'd been trying to bet large amounts.'

'How much?' asked Greyspear.

'Five thousand at a time. Danny, that's the manager, told me of how drug dealers will use crooked bookmakers to launder their drug cash. He also said he thought George and Lenny were testing him to see if he was amenable to doing a bit of money laundering.

'Sovereign Secure Investments is totally controlled by Mr Du Marchon.' said Bashir. 'He's been good at hiding the transactions. Recently he's withdrawn a substantial amount of funds from his customer accounts and transferred to SSI's bank account. Then it looks like he's purchased twenty thousand board feet of hardwood from a supplier in Honduras and had it shipped to China. Now, if I was a betting man, which I am not, I'd say the twenty thousand board feet of hardwood is no more than a plank. It's a typical money-laundering trick using false purchase orders and bills of lading.'

'Are there any substantial deposits during the last, say, three weeks?' asked Buchanan.

'I seem to remember one for two hundred thousand,' said Silverstein. 'Would you like me to check it for you?'

'How long will that take?'

'Couple of minutes, I have the information on my laptop.'

'Please, go ahead.'

Buchanan stood and walked over to the window while Silverstein searched for the relevant file on his laptop.

'Here it is,' said Silverstein, 'It just says investment, VM.'

'Got him,' said Buchanan. 'VM, Victor Mountjoy.'

'That's a lot of cash to lay one's hands on,' said Greyspear. 'I wonder where he got it from?'

'His wife said he'd just borrowed against the farm,' said Buchanan. 'He also convinced friends to bet on Turpin winning the race on Saturday. I believe he is holding the bets himself.'

Greyspear shook his head,' Colonel Mountjoy must be quite desperate to take that sort of risk.'

13
Friday Morning

09:15

Buchanan looked at the sky as he walked across to the stables and thought that as long as the weather report was correct, tomorrow was going to be a great day for the race.

As he entered the yard, he saw Harry being helped out of a taxi by Poppy, with Shelly looking on attentively. Buchanan stopped for a moment and watched as Shelly leaned into the taxi and paid the fare while Poppy walked beside Harry, steadying him as they walked arm in arm into the stables.

Buchanan smiled and realised, barring any unfortunate occurrences, Harry was about to become one of the Grant family. Though he wondered how Harry would reconcile his past to that of his impending future within the family.

Buchanan continued with his stroll across the yard and nodded to the driver as the taxi passed him on his way out. He gave Harry time to settle into his flat before he went into the stables. As he entered through the main doors, he caught sight of George and Lenny standing outside the Old Coachman's Lodge.

This was going to be fun, thought Buchanan, as he walked slowly towards them. He partially raised his forearms and started to rub his right fist with his left hand. As he got within six feet of them, George and Lenny eased themselves back into the Lodge.

Buchanan grinned as he climbed the stairs to Harry's flat. The building truly was magnificent. Whoever had the responsibility of turning an old Tudor stable roof space into modern living accommodation had done a superb job. The open network of carved oak beams was set off by the insulated and plastered surfaces in-between. LED spotlights illuminated the corridor running past the doors to the flats.

Buchanan could hear the sounds of an animated conversation coming from Harry's flat. He knocked and entered. Harry, ashen-faced, was seated in one of his chairs, arms dangling, like a boxer who'd just gone ten rounds and been beaten in every round.

'What's the matter, Harry? Are you all right?' asked a worried Buchanan.

Poppy turned to Buchanan and said, 'He's remembered what happened.'

'What do you remember?' he asked.

Harry shook his head slowly. 'Give me a minute. Poppy, can you get me a beer from the fridge?'

'Wouldn't you rather have a cup of tea?' asked Buchanan.

Harry nodded, then slowly let out his breath and said, 'The good doctor policeman suggests a cup of tea. First aid treatment for shock – I suppose I should be a good boy and take my medicine.'

'I'll make it,' said Shelly. 'Where's the tea?'

'He keeps it in the cupboard beside the sink, Mom,' said Poppy. 'A little milk and two spoons of sugar.'

'I won't enquire how you come to know that,' said Shelly, smiling as she opened the cupboard door and extracted the box of PG Tips.'

Harry took in a deep breath and shuffled in his chair.

'Do you feel up to telling us what happened?' asked Buchanan.

Harry nodded. 'It was seeing George and Lenny again when I walked along the corridor past the stalls that has brought it all back.'

'Did they see you?' asked Buchanan.

He nodded. 'They had the cheek to ask me if I remembered what happened. Why would you ask that?'

'Because I'm about to have them both arrested and questioned about what they did to you.'

'You can do that?' said Shelly.

Poppy and Harry both turned and looked first at Shelly, then at Buchanan.

'My full title is Detective Chief Inspector Buchanan of the Sussex CID. I'm supposed to be taking a week's leave here at Castlewood. Till this situation is resolved, I'd appreciate you keeping that a secret.'

'Does Travis know?' asked Shelly.

Buchanan shook his head. 'I haven't told him but, being an intelligent man, he may suspect something along those lines.'

'What's next?' asked Poppy.

'I'd like to hear what Harry has to say about what happened the other night. But first, Poppy, would you mind standing by Harry's door – just in case either George or Lenny come snooping?'

'Ok,' she said, smiling at Harry and caressing his shoulder as she walked past.

'The floor's all yours, Harry,' said Buchanan, as Poppy checked the corridor was still empty.

Harry took a sip of his tea, then commenced with his story.

'I was completing my evening rounds and had got as far as stall three. I'd gone in there to check the water bowl, sometimes the horse pushes the nose tap a bit hard and it doesn't turn off. It was ok and, as I kicked the bedding away from the salt lick, I heard voices coming from the corridor. I would normally not take any notice of them, but since it was after eleven and no-one was supposed to be in the stables that late, I was curious to see who was talking.'

'What about George and Lenny – they were living in the Old Coachman's Lodge?' asked Buchanan.

'I already knew what they sounded like: every second word a swear word. No, these voices were quite educated, definitely not George and Lenny.'

'Do you know who it was?' asked Poppy. 'Were they the people who beat you up?'

'Yes and no. One of them was Colonel Mountjoy, I don't know who the other person was. He spoke like a BBC announcer, but much posher.'

'Then which of them hurt you?' asked Poppy.

'George and Lenny, that's who.'

'Do you know why they did what they did to you?' asked Buchanan.

Harry took a long gulp of his tea. 'As I said, I was in stall three checking the water bowl when I heard voices out in the corridor. I was going to tell them to leave, but when I got to the door of the stall something Colonel Mountjoy said stopped me in my tracks. He was talking to the other man. He was going over his plans to switch horses in the race on Saturday.'

'That's why Mountjoy has George and Lenny watching over Turpin and Rambler and why he has given strict instructions not to let anyone close to either of the horses,' said Buchanan. 'Anything else?'

'Unfortunately, not. I was hit on the head with something and next thing that I knew was George and Lenny had me pinioned to the wall. The other man who was there demanded to know what I'd heard. I said I hadn't heard anything other than the sound of voices.'

'I take it they didn't believe you?'

Harry shook his head. 'Colonel Mountjoy had George and Lenny tie my wrists, then they hung me from a harness hook in the corridor. When he was sure I couldn't get away, he started with the questions. It was like I was being cross examined in court, he just kept at me. When I didn't answer him, he had George and Lenny take turns punching me.'

'Can you tell us what you remember you heard they were talking about?' asked Buchanan.

'I seem to remember one of them saying something about Colonel Mountjoy's plan was to enter both Turpin and Rambler in the Castlewood Cup. His jockey, Pat, would ride Turpin and he,

Mountjoy, would ride the second and slower of the two horses, Rambler. I think I remember one of them said something about them switching horses. That didn't make any sense to me at the time, and it still doesn't. They kept asking questions about what I'd heard and when I didn't give them a sufficient answer, they'd have George and Lenny beat me again. By then I would have said anything to get them to stop the beating.'

'Do you remember being put in the stall?'

Harry shook his head. 'I must have blacked out, because the next thing I remember is waking up in hospital. Which stall was I found in?'

Buchanan smiled. 'Mercury's.'

'That was fortunate. Mercury wouldn't hurt a fly. In fact, he would have been in sheer terror to find an unresponsive human lying on his bedding. The poor chap, huddled all night in a corner of his stall desperately trying to stay awake and not touch the body on the floor.'

'At least it's all over now,' said Poppy, wrapping her arms round Harry's neck and kissing him on the cheek.

'What will you do now?' Harry asked Buchanan.

'I had a chat with Sir Nathan and Lewis. They have agreed to install a couple of CCTV cameras in the stalls one and two area. But to do that, we need to get George and Lenny out of the way while the work is done. In a few minutes I'm going to call Constable Hunter and have him stop George and Lenny when they go into of town for their daily visit to the betting shop. He is going to question them about a supposed traffic accident.'

'But what about Colonel Mountjoy? Suppose he comes down to the stables while the cameras are being installed?'

'Sir Nathan is going to invite him and Major Jackson for a drink in the library to discuss the funding of a drop-in centre for veterans.'

'That should work,' said Harry. 'I think there are a couple of channels spare on the CCTV server, not sure if we have spare cameras, though.'

'I wouldn't worry about that, Lewis will take care of those details,' said Buchanan, as he called Stephen.

'Stephen, it's Jack. Could you be free in about an hour to create a diversion for me? You can? Good. You remember the two cretins who work here at the stables – yes, those two. They have a habit of going to town in the morning to one of the betting shops. How about I watch them as they leave and give you a buzz with their vehicle description and licence number? Then you can choose your moment when to pull them over. I'd suggest you say the imaginary accident happened sometime yesterday morning, when they would have been on the road, that way it shouldn't cause them to be suspicious. Yes, ok, talk to you later.'

'All fixed?' asked Harry.

'Yes. Sergeant Hunter will lay in wait on the A22. When George and Lenny go past on their way into town, he'll pull them over and ask if they saw anything of an imaginary accident on the road yesterday morning. He knows how to keep them busy.'

'Good morning,' said Olivia, knocking on the open door. 'Sorry to disturb. Just stopped by to see if Harry needed anything. But it looks like he is getting all the attention he needs. Hi, I'm Olivia. I'm the stable manager,' she said to Shelly.

'Shelly Grant, I'm Poppy's mom. Poppy's been looking after Harry,' she said, glancing at Poppy, who at that moment was standing behind Harry, massaging his shoulders.

'Harry,' said Buchanan. 'I'll tell Lewis, then check back with you when George and Lenny leave.'

'Ok, see you later.'

Buchanan closed Harry's door behind him as he walked slowly along the corridor. He stopped at the top of the stairs and listened. George was talking to someone.

'I saw him come back from hospital this morning.'

'Where is he?' said Mountjoy.

'Upstairs with his girlfriend and her mother.'

'Not good,' said Mountjoy. 'If he tells them what happened it will mean the police and an end to our little subterfuge.'

'Look,' said George. 'It's fine, he can't remember a thing.'

'How do you know?'

'I asked him. I said, *How are you, do you remember what happened* He replied he was fine, and couldn't understand why the horse kicked him so hard.'

'Good, and lucky for you we don't have a corpse on our hands. What possessed you to hit him so hard? All you had to do was put the fear of death in him, not nearly kill him.'

'The little shit kicked me in the nuts, nobody does that to me.'

'Still,' said another voice that Buchanan recognised as Du Marchon's, 'we have been most fortunate. Even if he remembers, by the time the race is over, it will all be too late.'

'Where are you going to be after the race?' asked George.

'Far away from here, that's all you need to know. And don't worry, you'll get your share,' replied Mountjoy.

'Are you taking her with you?' asked George.

'You mean Cynthia? Not a chance, she and that jockey can go shag themselves silly for all I care. I'm going to divorce her. Stupid woman, thinks she can get the better of me.'

'Victor,' said Du Marchon, 'we need to have a talk. If that lad remembers what happened to him before the race, we need to be ready to act. It may be necessary to arrange another *accident*, this time a more permanent one.'

Not good, thought Buchanan. If Mountjoy and Du Marchon decided not to wait to see if Harry recovered and to arrange a more permanent accident for him, well, that just would not do. He crept quietly away from the top of the stairs and retraced his steps.

Knocking gently on Harry's door, he went in. Olivia was drying the dishes, Shelly and Poppy were sitting on the small sofa chatting with Harry.

'Oh, hello, Inspector,' said Olivia. 'Forget something?'

'No, nothing like that. I've just overheard a rather disturbing conversation, and it concerns Harry.'

'Oh, no!' said Poppy.

'Don't worry,' said Buchanan. 'Nothing is going to happen to Harry, as long as he continues to stay dumb about what happened to him.'

'What should I do?' asked Harry.

'Just continue to act as though you remember nothing. It will require you to be nice to George and Lenny when you see them, but don't act out of normal. They'll smell a rat if you do that.'

'I can help there,' said Olivia. 'There are some fences that need to be mended. Unfortunately, one of the riders ploughed right through the Long Run jump yesterday and it will need to be completely rebuilt. I'll make it known that I've sent Harry and one of the other lads out to repair it, also to spruce up several others and they will probably not be back till late this afternoon. That should be reason enough for his absence from the stables during the day.'

Buchanan nodded. 'That's perfect.'

'And I could help him,' suggested Poppy.

Buchanan looked at Shelly's face and thought that Harry was already part of the Grant family. All that was needed was a proposal, ring and ceremony.

'I'm still not settled about what Mountjoy meant when he said something about switching horses,' said Buchanan.

'If it would be of any help,' said Olivia, 'I could call a few friends and see if there are any skeletons in Colonel Mountjoy's cupboard.'

'What a good idea,' said Poppy.

'I agree,' said Buchanan. 'That might be the key that unlocks the puzzle. I'll check back with you later on today to see if you have been successful.'

Buchanan went down the stairs and was pleased to see that Mountjoy and Du Marchon had left. He could also hear George and Lenny swearing at each other as they went about their morning duties.

He left the stables and wandered back to the clubhouse and the library. From his favourite chair he would be able to see when George and Lenny left for their morning visit to the betting shop.

It was an hour later when he saw the unwashed transit van containing George and Lenny rumble past the window of the library. He picked up his phone and called Stephen.

'Hi, it's Jack. George and Lenny just left Castlewood. You're in an unmarked car? Good planning, should make it easier for you to follow them before pulling them over. I hadn't thought of them using the back roads – let me know what happens. The staff here at the stables think they should be done with setting up the cameras in about an hour – ok, talk to you later.'

With the issue of George and Lenny temporarily resolved, Buchanan returned to the clubhouse reception to let Lewis know the coast was clear.

◆

11:45

Buchanan looked at the time on his phone and decided eleven forty-five was as a good time as any for lunch. He entered the bar and ordered a sandwich and a beer. He took a sip of his beer as his phone dinged to say he had a message. It was from Stephen,

Apprehended the subjects in question. Inspected vehicle, found two non-roadworthy tyres. Subjects currently sitting in lay-by awaiting breakdown service to come out and replace said tyres. Estimated time for return to Castlewood, about two and a half hours.

That was just what Buchanan needed to hear. Now so long as Greyspear could keep Mountjoy and Du Marchon busy, Lewis and Harry had a free run of the stables. He reached over and picked up a newspaper that someone had left behind. He was deep in an article on the effects of Brexit when Cynthia sat down at his table.

'Why didn't you tell me you were from the Jockey Club?' she asked.

'You never asked me if I was from the Jockey Club.'

'Well, are you?'

'No, I'm not. Whatever gave you that idea?' replied Buchanan, knowing full well that was the impression he had given Pat McCall.

'You really are an enigma. Part of me wants to punch you in the nose –'

'And the other part?'

She smiled. 'You know full well what the other part wants.'

'What about Pat? I hear you two are going to get married when your divorce from Victor happens.'

'See, that's just what really gets up my nose about you. You show up not knowing anything about any of us, yet here we are five days later, and you know more about us that we do ourselves. You say you're just a civil servant, but if you expect me to believe that, I've got a bridge to sell you. You don't work for HM Customs and Excise, you're not working for any insurance company, the Jockey Club, or Army Internal Affairs, are you with the Gambling Commission?'

Buchanan smiled and shook his head.

'Oh, you – you're so frustrating! Who do you work for and what are you doing here at Castlewood?'

Buchanan thought for a moment. 'If you answer two of three questions for me, truthfully, I will answer your questions.'

'It's a bargain, ask away, but first, buy me a drink.'

Buchanan signalled the waiter who'd been clearing away one of the nearby tables.

'Yes, sir?'

'Could I have a whisky, and for you, Cynthia?' he nodded at Cynthia.

'I'll have a margarita, make it a large one.

'Two of the questions I don't know the answers to, the third I do. If you give me the wrong answer to the one I do know, I won't reveal who I am.'

'I wish we'd met years ago, before I'd ever set eyes on Victor,' she said, lifting her drink to her lips.

'Question one. What is so special about Rambler and Turpin that they require nets over their doors? Second question, who gave you that necklace you are wearing, and where did they give it to you? And third and last, what are Victor and Julius Du Marchon planning?'

'That's cheating, you've asked four questions.'

Buchanan sipped his whisky, enjoying the banter with Cynthia.

'All right. Your first question about the nets over the doors of Rambler and Turpin. I asked Victor the same question because they don't have them at home. He said it was to keep people away from the horses so they wouldn't get spooked. I said it was a stupid idea, horses like to talk to each other, well, not talk like us, but they do like to know what is going on around them.'

'Next question.'

'I don't know why you want to know about my necklace. It was given me by Pat.'

'And the where?'

'It was three days ago. We were in the woods by the mill pond.'

'And the third question?'

'I don't have an answer to that. All I know is Victor and Du Marchon are putting together a scheme to make a great deal of money. There, do I pass? Do I get to know what you are really up to?'

'Tell me about Pat.'

'That's five, you're cheating. You owe me another drink for that.'

Buchanan signalled the waiter for a repeat of their drink order.

Glass in hand, Cynthia began, 'When Pat was about nineteen, his parents became very sick. Being the only child, Pat gave up his jockey apprenticeship ambitions to look after them. Ten years later his parents had both passed away, so he left Ireland and came over to England looking for work with horses. Being such a natural with them he soon found employment riding out for various stables. I met him while I was at a Nick Gauntlet training day.'

'Who is Nick Gauntlet?'

'He teaches eventing. I was on Doxy and managed to fall off my horse right in front of Pat. He climbed over the railings and picked me up in his arms. It sounds a bit silly when I say it, but it was love at first sight. Over the next few months we met at other events. In the end it was Victor who unwittingly presented the perfect solution.'

'What was that?'

'A few months after the incident of me falling off Doxy, I went with him to look at a mare he wanted to buy for stud. It had a good pedigree, so Victor purchased it. At the sale he asked the auctioneer for a recommendation for someone to look after the horse and train its progeny. He suggested Pat, and that was that. Pat started working for us the following week.'

'That's a neat and tidy arrangement.'

She smiled. 'It was.'

'So, you put the mare out to stud?'

'Yes. It was all Victor's idea. As soon as the mare became pregnant, he got all broody. He wouldn't even let me near the mare till after she foaled.'

'Did that seem odd to you?'

'No, nothing is odd when Victor is involved. I was away during the final weeks of gestation and when I got home Turpin was in the stall.'

'Where was Pat?' asked Buchanan.

She blushed. 'I told Victor I was going away with a girlfriend for a week at a spa. I neglected to say the friend was Pat.'

'What did Pat tell Victor about where he was going?'

'He said he was going back home to a funeral of one of his uncles.'

'Did Victor believe the stories?'

'Who knows? Victor is a closed book. But yes, I think he did. A few days later he bought another colt from a local farmer who had changed his mind about owning a horse. That's how we came to have Rambler.'

'Is Victor trying to get even with Pat?'

A tear came to her eye. 'Victor is so spiteful.'

'Because he knows about you and Pat?'

She nodded. 'Pat so desperately wants to ride on Saturday, but —'

'But?' said Buchanan, waving at the waiter for another round of drinks.

'Pat is reluctant to ride if it means by winning he gets branded a cheat. It breaks my heart to watch him tear himself apart as he tries to justify taking the risk that Victor isn't cheating in some fashion. Don't you see, this is Pat's big and probable only chance to get back into horse racing?'

'Once again I ask you, what do you think Victor is up to?'

'I have no idea. Every time I try to get him to talk, he just laughs and says, *You'll see, you'll see.*'

We'll see indeed, thought Buchanan, as he left the bar. He still had six hours before dinner, so he decided to have lunch then pay a quick visit to the stables to see if Olivia had found out anything.

◆

13:00

He entered the main stable door and turned left to head to the stable office when he heard a familiar voice.

'I'm telling you,' said Pat, 'something is wrong. I'm sure I was riding Rambler, not Turpin.'

'That's nonsense,' said Du Marchon. 'It's just your nerves, especially since this is your first competitive ride since coming out of retirement.'

'What do you know about riding? I'll bet you've never been on a horse in your life.'

'I'll have you know I do have a horse entered, maybe not quite as fast as Turpin, but it'll still give a good show.'

'That'll be the day,' replied Pat.

Du Marchon's reply was drowned out by the sound of a door being slammed. Buchanan smiled and continued towards the stable office.

'What have you managed to find out, Olivia?' asked Buchanan, as he closed the s door behind him.

'It took a bit of digging, but I ended up talking with a chap called Danny O'Dwyer. He's a farmer near to where the Mountjoys live. When I mentioned the name Mountjoy, he almost hung up on me.'

'Sounds like he isn't a fan of the colonel,' said Buchanan.

'Definitely not. Apparently Mountjoy owes him quite a bit of money for destroying the transmission on the tractor he borrowed, amongst other things.'

'Was he able to tell you much?'

'He told me that about a year and a half ago Mountjoy sent him a new-born foal to look after for a couple of months.'

'Cynthia said he bought in the second foal from a farmer who no longer wanted to be involved with horses,' said Buchanan.

'That was a ruse; his mare had twins. The foal that he kept, Turpin, has a white blaze, the other twin, Rambler, has none.

Mountjoy told the vet later the next day that one of the twins died during the night and that only Turpin survived. A couple of months later he brought the twin back telling everyone he'd bought it from a farmer who couldn't afford to raise it.'

'Sounds like an on the spot decision,' said Buchanan. 'He must have seen the possibilities when the mare gave birth to healthy twins.'

'Yes, it does. So, now he had, other than the white blaze on Turpin, two identical horses with Turpin turning out to be the faster of the two.'

'But just how does he intend to make money out of swapping horses?'

'You're the policeman, that's your job. Mine is to look after the horses, and if you're finished with questions, I have my rounds to do,' said Olivia.

'Yes, thanks. I think I'll go back to the club and catch up with my wife. I believe she thinks I'm avoiding her and having an affair with Cynthia Mountjoy.'

'You're not, are you?'

'No. Of course not. Cynthia Mountjoy is having an affair with someone else, definitely not me.'

'I knew that. I've seen her with their jockey, Pat McCall.'

'Yeah, they do make an interesting couple. Anyway, I'll catch up with you later.'

Buchanan wandered slowly back to the club house and the bar. He needed something to help him think.

He ordered a whisky and walked towards the library and his now-favourite armchair. As he entered, he saw Karen sitting in the corner talking with Shelly Grant. Shelly looked like she had been crying.

'Oh, hello Jack, we were just chatting.'

'I was going join you, but maybe you two would rather be alone?'

'No, it's all right,' said Shelly, sniffing while reaching for a tissue. 'I've done my crying for now.'

'Ok, as long as you're sure I'm not intruding?'

'Jack, sit down,' said Karen. 'You might actually be able to help.'

'How?' he asked, pulling a chair over.

'Shelly has been talking about Travis and his issues with stress.'

'Oh.'

'I was just telling her about how your job can affect you from time to time.'

He nodded.

'You remember your recent car accident and how you saw the driver's face of the car that ran you off the road everywhere?'

'But I did recognise him.'

'Yes, I know you did. But it didn't stop you suffering from nightmares, did it?'

Buchanan let out his breath slowly at the memory. 'That wasn't pleasant. Dreaming that I was about to hit the tree at sixty miles an hour.'

'Travis has flashbacks about his time in Afghanistan,' said Shelly. 'He keeps reliving the moment his platoon was almost wiped out by an IED.'

'He told me about that a couple of evenings ago.'

'Really?' said Shelly. 'It's not that he's ashamed about what happened, it's just – he tried to forget, kept his feelings bottled up inside himself. He's only recently been able to talk openly about it.'

'I tried to keep it in,' said Buchanan. 'It just made matters worse. Over the years I've learned to talk things through with Karen; she's been an angel. I've seen some terrible things in my career as a policeman.'

'The first time Travis left for a tour of duty I wasn't prepared for what to expect,' said Shelly. 'For weeks before he deployed, he'd bring home bits of kit till the living room looked like the airport baggage hall. Poppy was only eighteen months old; life was a whirlwind of activity.

'When a soldier deploys, Jack, it's not just the soldier who is involved, the functionality of the whole family goes on hold. When they return the whole family is impacted. I had no idea what the pressure of being a military wife meant, I had no idea who I was anymore. When I tried to get help, I was just told to, *suck it up, you're not the one risking your life.*'

'Then Travis was gone, and it was just me and Poppy. It didn't take long for me to create a routine for us both. The days weren't so bad, Poppy kept me busy, it was the nights that were the worst,' she said, sniffing. 'Waking in the dark wondering what Travis was doing. Was he all right, had he been injured? Every time the phone rang, I'd go into a panic.

Karen nodded. 'I know what you mean. Glasgow was just getting over the worst of the razor-gang problems when Jack joined the police force. I dreaded when he was out on patrol on Saturday nights.'

'When Travis came home. I thought it would be better, but we kept bumping heads and ended up arguing. He became distant, and when I tried to get him to talk, he'd just say I didn't understand. It wasn't long before he was staying out late at night, coming home drunk in the early hours.'

'What changed him?' asked Karen.

'Church. Travis was so desperate to get off the merry-go-round in his mind, so when I told him one of the local churches was running an Alpha course he grudgingly went along.'

'We have those at out church,' said Karen. 'It always changes people's lives for the good.'

'Did it sort out Travis's PTSD?' asked Buchanan.

'Not directly. While there he met several other veterans in similar position. They started meeting for breakfast on Saturday mornings. Since they all had something in common, they realised that their issues were real and could be treated. Once Travis understood he wasn't alone in his frustration he sought professional help.'

'All this from going on an Alpha course – did he complete it?' asked Buchanan.

'Yes, and we are so grateful he did. At the end they had what they call a Holy Spirit weekend. He came home a changed man.'

'What happened to change him?'

'He said he saw Jesus and heard him speak.'

'Really? What did Jesus say?' asked Buchanan.

'That Travis was loved and had a purpose in life.'

'That was it?'

'Yes, that was it,' she said, looking at the smile on Buchanan's face. 'It made a difference to Travis. The week after the course ended, he started attending the weekly Bible study sessions and it wasn't long before he enrolled in a seminary. Also, at church he had emotional support.'

'He mentioned that,' said Buchanan.

'Now you know,' said Shelly. 'He's not cured, but is a great deal better. One day he'll be free from the struggles of his past memories.'

'I hope so,' said Karen, as Shelly rose from her chair.

'I've got to go now, see you all at dinner,' she said.

♦

15:30

'This week's been like a bit of a jigsaw puzzle, Karen,' said Buchanan. 'I have the box with the picture and inside are all the pieces, except the box has pieces of more than one puzzle.'

'You always tell me your knower knows. What's it telling you this time?'

He shook his head. 'It's gone on holiday, that's what it's telling me.'

'How about we go for a walk? The fresh air will help you think. It's only two-thirty and dinner isn't till seven o'clock.'

'Where shall we go?'

'You decide, you know the grounds better than I do.'

18:00

'Your tie is crooked,' said Karen, as she watched Buchanan struggle with the knot in his bowtie. 'Here, let me help.'

'Thanks.'

'Are you a bit nervous?'

'About what?'

'Talking about the charity you want people to support?'

'I've spoken in public before.'

'There, that looks better.'

'Thanks,' said Buchanan, looking in the mirror. 'I'm just going to raise funds for a charity, I'll figure out what to say when the time comes.'

'Good, but you'll have to think of something fairly quick, dinner is in thirty minutes.'

♦

18:45

Buchanan listened to the table banter as he followed Karen between the tables. He looked around the room and saw that just about every table was full.

> 'Emily said if you are injured in a fall, they will give you a £100 voucher …'
>
> 'It's all changed now since they set up the new committee to stamp out cheating …'
>
> 'Our broker said it was getting more difficult to sell insurance as people are opting to self-insure …'
>
> 'It's getting bad, two ponies were killed last week, and nobody saw a thing …'
>
> 'The trainer said if I was out of shape it would put my horse off its stride, took me a few minutes to translate what he said…'

Buchanan pushed the chair in for Karen then sat. Once more he was beside Cynthia.

'Good evening, Jack,' she said. 'Have you had a nice day?'

'Yes, thank you. Karen and I went for a long quiet walk in the woods.'

As Greyspear stood, he tapped his teaspoon against his empty water glass. 'Ladies and gentlemen, may I have your attention for a moment? I won't keep you long as I realise you will all want to be off to bed early for a good night's sleep. As you know, tomorrow is race day. The day will kick off with a pony gymkhana for our younger visitors at eleven o'clock, followed at one o'clock by the main event, the Castlewood Cup.'

'Bring it on!' shouted someone from the far end of the restaurant.

'Now, as some of you may have noticed, I'm wearing the latest fashion in the NHS: a medical boot on my right foot,' said Greyspear. 'This is due to my exuberance when jumping from scaffolding at my factory in Greenock a few days ago. As a result of this incident, I will not now be riding in the race tomorrow.'

'*Aww*, too bad, maybe I'll stand a chance of winning,' said the same individual, at the back of the restaurant.

'But not all is lost,' continued Greyspear. 'Riding in my place and representing Castlewood will be my friend, Jack Buchanan. Jack will not be competing for the Castlewood Cup, but will be riding to raise funds for his charity, which I will let him tell you about. Jack,' said Greyspear, offering him the opportunity to speak.

Buchanan pushed his chair back, stood and collected his thoughts. As he did so he noticed Shelly excuse herself from the table and leave through the ballroom doors.

'Good evening and thank you for that introduction, Nathan. I have been here at Castlewood this week resting. I grew up in Glasgow and saw the deprivation that followed the collapse of the steel, shipbuilding, automobile and coal industries. But thanks to people such as Sir Nathan and his inspired idea to start a yacht-building yard on the Clyde, things have begun to turn around.'

There were sounds of applause for Greyspear.

'According to a recent study, post-traumatic stress disorder in the UK is at crisis level and far more common than was ever thought. Most sufferers of PTSD don't see things building up, or the problems that are going to affect them.

'Some have doubts about whether they can do their job properly and feel everyone is out to get them. Some become a nightmare to live with at home. Unfortunately, some sufferers just put their thoughts away in a box in their brain, leave them there, and never get a chance to go back. Two-thirds of those with PTSD are unaware they are suffering from it.

'As important a fact as that is, there is another group of people, many consigned to the shadows of society. Often their plight is ignored by those they served. I am talking about our servicemen and servicewomen. They, too, often suffer from traumatic incidents in their careers while serving their country. The charity I am raising funds for is called the Blue Van Drop-In Centre. Money raised will go to the cost of running the drop-in centre for veterans. This will be a pilot programme based here in Eastbourne. I envisage it will provide hot drinks, a safe place to chat, or somewhere to offer advice with referrals.'

'Count me in,' said Travis.

'Thanks for that vote of approval, Travis. If anyone wishes to sponsor me tomorrow, Sir Nathan has the details on how you can give.'

Buchanan sat to a spirited round of applause.

'Ladies and gentlemen,' said Greyspear, standing once more. 'I hope Jack has caught your imagination, dig deep into your pockets and give our veterans a chance to get their lives back on track.'

As Greyspear finished speaking, Andrew Jackson walked over to their table and said, 'Jack, brilliant idea, can you take a cheque?'

'Certainly.'

Colonel Mountjoy, flushed by a third glass of after-dinner brandy, and not wanting to be outdone by Major Jackson, added his voice as one of Buchanan's financial donors. Buchanan smiled and wondered just how much the colonel would have available to donate after tomorrow.

♦

23:15

'Is that what you've been thinking about while I've been away?' asked Karen, as they walked along the corridor to their room. 'When did you think of it?'

'It didn't become a reality until two days ago. That was when I saw just how much of a chasm there is between people like us and those less fortunate.'

'Like the veterans you've been talking about?'

'Yes,' replied Buchanan, as Karen got ready for bed.

She climbed in under the covers, turning on the reading light, and when she saw Buchanan standing by the window said, 'Aren't you coming to bed?'

'Not just yet. I think I need to check that all is well at the stables. Don't worry, I won't be long.'

'I didn't till you said not to worry. You're not going to do anything silly, are you?'

'No, I'll stay away from George and Lenny if that's what is worrying you.'

'Don't be long.'

'I won't,' said Buchanan, as he closed the door.

As he exited the lift, he saw Lewis standing beside the reception desk talking with Greyspear. He thought about the lateness of the evening and the friendly welcome he was likely to get from George and Lenny if he showed up alone. He hoped that Lewis didn't have any plans for an early night.

'Can't sleep, Jack?' asked Greyspear.

'No, just thought I'd check up on Harry, and …'

'Good evening, Mrs Mountjoy,' said Greyspear, as Cynthia came from the ballroom and stood at the lift door. 'All ready for tomorrow?'

She shook her head and squinted at Greyspear.

'As I'll ever be. Have you seen that rotten husband of mine anywhere?'

'No, sorry.'

'Not to worry,' she replied, stepping into the open lift, 'maybe he's got stuck up ...' the remainder of her reply was lost as the lift door closed.

'I think we would be better chatting in the office,' said Greyspear, as more revellers exited from the ballroom. 'I'm glad you're both here. Unless you can convince me otherwise, I am going to cancel tomorrow's race. I can't in good conscience run such a public event when one of my employees is almost murdered and the instigator of that violence seeks to defraud my guests and the public. Jack, you are convinced that Colonel Mountjoy intends to fix the race?'

'Absolutely. From what I have been able to find out, he's at a near bankrupt situation and is desperate to make a last-ditch attempt to extricate himself from his financial hole. As to fixing the race, I'd say it's a definitive yes. The how involves swapping horses and riders, which on the surface doesn't make any sense at all.'

'Do you have any suggestions before I make my decision?'

'The way I see the situation is, if you cancel the race, you will have to refund everyone's fees. A plausible reason will have to be given, and as much as he irritates me, Miasma, the crime reporter for the *Eastbourne Herald*, will sniff out the fact that someone tried to kill Harry in the stables. Then, in one fell swoop, Castlewood will become anathema to anyone looking for a quiet weekend golfing or riding.

'So, what do I do? I just can't let Colonel Mountjoy get away with robbing my guests.'

'Can you hold on till breakfast?'

'If I have to, yes.'

'Another thing to consider is,' said Buchanan, 'the colonel might try and make sure Harry can't remember anything.'

'You think he would go that far?' asked Greyspear.

'He's a desperate man, and desperate men have been known to do desperate things. I still can't quite figure out what he's up to, though. I'm still positive the key to the problem lies in stalls one and two in the stables.'

'Was that where you were headed?' asked Greyspear.

'Yes. I was going to see what I could find. Maybe George or Lenny will say something that will give away the plot.'

'Need company?' asked Lewis.

'Yes, please. I don't fancy running into George or Lenny at this time of night. I scared them off the last time, but maybe by now they have regained their confidence.'

◆

23:55

'Do you miss the police force, Lewis?' asked Buchanan as they made their way across to the stables.

'When I was in the force, I had a purpose in life. No matter what came at me I just put up with it, realising those I was working with felt the same. When I left, I struggled to settle to anything and, having a leg that I couldn't trust to hold me up, well, that was a bit too much.'

'You're walking fine now.'

'Yeah, thanks to the surgeon who replaced my knee.'

Buchanan led Lewis to the main stable door, opened it and beckoned him to follow. As on the previous occasion, all was quiet. He listened at the door to the Old Coachman's Lodge for any sounds of activity; there was nothing but the sounds of gentle snoring.

Buchanan tried the door and found it unlocked. He smiled at Lewis and gently pushed it open. He crept in and was surprised to see George and Lenny, fully dressed, fast asleep in their chairs. Two empty dinner plates with a half-eaten chunk of bread lay on the table between them. Empty wine glasses lay on the floor directly under empty hands.

'They must have had one too many,' said Lewis, pointing to the empty wine bottles.

'Let's hope when they wake they have suitable headaches. Fourteen percent alcohol,' Buchanan said, holding up one of the bottles, 'pretty strong wine, no wonder they're well out of it.'

'While we're here, let's have a look around,' said Lewis.

'Have a look in the bathroom and at their wash bags. There wasn't much when I last looked.'

While Lewis rummaged around in the bathroom, Buchanan noticed something on Lenny's forearm, several three-inch scars running up his left arm like a ladder. Poor sod, thought Buchanan, for all his bravado Lenny was a self-harmer.'

'You're right, not much to see in there,' said Lewis, as he came out of the bathroom. 'No drugs. I was hoping there would have been some, then we could have had them pinched for possession. I don't mind telling you,' he continued, 'I'll be glad when these two are off the estate. Shall we go?'

'Yes,' replied Buchanan. 'They won't be getting up to any trouble tonight.'

As he closed the door, Buchanan was disturbed by someone coming down the stairs.

'Are they asleep?' asked Harry.

'Yes,' replied Buchanan. 'What's been happening? Have you, George and Lenny become friends?'

'No, certainly not. I just came down to see if they were asleep.'

'Did you feed them?'

'Just part of the plan to keep them guessing. A large meal, a bottle of fine wine, they should sleep till late in the morning.'

'They were not suspicious when you offered them dinner?'

'I didn't do the offering, that was Poppy's mother.'

So that's where Shelly went, thought Buchanan, remembering it odd that she would get up from the table and not return.

'Something wrong, Bob?' asked Harry. 'Haven't seen you down here before at this time of night.'

'Jack asked me to come with him to check out the stables. He's been worried about what Colonel Mountjoy is up to with his horses,' explained Lewis.

'It's been all quiet tonight. Poppy and I have been watching the CCTV most of the time.'

'Did you notice anything out of the ordinary?' asked Buchanan.

'There was a bit of a ruckus earlier in the day when Colonel Mountjoy's jockey had an argument with the colonel's friend.'

'Do you know what it was about?'

Harry shook his head. 'The voices weren't very clear. But you were there, Jack, I saw you on the screen.'

'Pat was saying something about being on the wrong horse,' said Buchanan. 'Didn't make sense then, and still doesn't make sense now.'

'What shall we do?' asked Lewis.

'With George and Lenny fast asleep we have time to think about that,' said Harry.

'Harry,' said Buchanan, 'can you keep a real close watch on Hansel and Gretel tomorrow? I'll see what I can do to stop the colonel and his plan.'

'Will do. See you tomorrow, oops, it's past midnight, so I guess it's now today. I'll collect my dishes and try to get some sleep before the race. It's going to be quite a day.'

'Good night, Harry,' said Buchanan, as Harry went in to retrieve his dinner dishes.

'Hansel and Gretel – quite apt names for those two,' said Lewis, as they made their way back to the house. 'Did you see the evening dress in Lenny's bag?'

'I had noticed,' said Buchanan, as they entered the bar. 'Let's meet early in the morning. We need a strategy to thwart the colonel.

'I'll meet you in reception, about six. Ok for you?'

'Fine, see you at six.'

14
Early Saturday

05:35

'You're up really early,' said a sleepy-eyed Karen. 'Your side of the bed doesn't look like it's been slept in. You did come to bed, didn't you?'

'Yes.'

'Where did you go?'

'After I left you last night, I went down to the stables with Lewis to make sure George and Lenny were behaving themselves.'

'And were they?'

'Sleeping like bugs in a rug when we got there.'

'But why are you up so early?'

'To prevent a great travesty. Look, I need to go out right away, I'll explain it all later.'

'Can't I come with you? I'm wide awake now.'

Buchanan looked at the display on his phone. 'Hmm, five-forty. Ok, but you need to be quick, hopefully there will be some breakfast waiting.'

'Ok, I will. All I need to do is my hair and makeup. I showered last night.'

'And get dressed?'

'Yes, of course I need to dress. But it won't happen if you keep interrupting me.'

◆

05:55

'Why are we going down to the restaurant for breakfast so early? It won't be open yet,' asked Karen, trying to keep up with Buchanan as they approached the lift.

'We're not having breakfast in the restaurant.'

'We're not? Then where are we having breakfast?'

'I think it's in the manager's office. 'We must hurry before it's too late.'

'Too late for what?' Karen asked, as they exited the lift and walked into an empty reception.

'Patience, my dear, Nathan and Lewis will be waiting for us.'

'Good morning, Mr Buchanan,' said the duty manager. 'Sir Nathan and Lewis are ready for you in the manager's office. If you'll follow me, I'll show you through.'

Buchanan and Karen followed the duty manager down the corridor.

'Sorry we're a bit late,' said Buchanan, as he and Karen entered the office.

'No problem,' said Greyspear. 'Help yourself to breakfast from the buffet bar. I've given strict instructions we're not to be interrupted.'

'Are you hungry, Karen?' asked Buchanan.

'Not very. It's a bit early for me.'

'Coffee?'

She nodded and shrugged. 'Well, if you're eating, I suppose some scrambled eggs with a couple of tomatoes sounds good. Also, a slice of brown toast, please.'

'Good morning, Karen,' said Greyspear.

'Good morning, Nathan. How's the ankle?'

'Still a bit sore, especially when I go to turn over in bed.'

'I know what that's like. Sometimes I get a backache and need to be careful about sleeping on my side.'

'I've invited Olivia to be with us this morning,' said Greyspear. 'Being the stable manager, I thought it prudent to keep her up to date on what we decide to do. Lewis was just about to fill me in on what you discovered last night, Jack.'

Buchanan turned from piling scrambled eggs onto a plate and nodded at Lewis.

'Not a great deal, unfortunately. We found George and Lenny fast asleep; apparently Harry fed them dinner, complete with a couple of bottles of wine.'

'Has he been able to find out much about what is going on?' asked Greyspear.

'He and Poppy overheard a conversation between Du Marchon and Pat McCall,' said Buchanan. 'I was there at the time and heard Pat McCall complain that he felt he had been riding Rambler yesterday and not Turpin.'

'I don't understand,' said Greyspear. 'Surely a jockey as professional as Pat would know which horse he was riding?'

'That is the mystery we need to fathom,' said Buchanan.

'What would Colonel Mountjoy gain from carrying out his plan of deception?' asked Karen.

'Becoming extremely rich,' said Greyspear.

'But he won't.' said Poppy, who'd just come into the room along with Shelly, both with huge smiles on their faces.

'He won't?' said Buchanan, looking at Poppy. 'I take it something has happened to change the circumstances?'

'Yep, George and Lenny are still fast asleep,' said Poppy.

'You've managed to neutralise George and Lenny?' said Greyspear. 'How did you manage that, and should we be expecting a visit from the police when they wake up?'

'Actually, it was me who did the deed,' said Shelly, 'and no to any visits from the police.'

'How were you able to manage it without running them over with a truck?' asked Greyspear.

'Last night I noticed Poppy wasn't at dinner, so I went to see how she was doing. She had been very agitated earlier in the day,' said Shelly. 'She wasn't in her room when I checked, so I went to the only other place I figured she'd be.'

'The stables?' said Karen.

'Exactly.'

'I was about to make Harry dinner, his favourite, spaghetti Bolognese,' said Poppy. 'Since we had spent most of the day watching the CCTV camera feeds from stalls one and two, I thought it would be nice to finish the day having a quiet, romantic meal together. That was my plan till Mom showed up and spoilt the whole thing.'

'It wasn't only a meal together,' said Shelly, 'she'd been cheeky and charged two bottles of wine to her dad's room. If her dad found out he would not have been pleased.'

'So, what did you do?' asked Karen.

'She joined us for dinner,' said Poppy. 'Ruined my whole evening.'

'You'll have time for many more, my dear.'

'Does that mean…?' said Karen

'Harry hasn't actually asked me, yet,' said Poppy. 'But he will.'

'So, what actually happened?' asked Buchanan.

'I've seen how well they work together,' said Shelly. 'But it took a mother to sort things out. Jack, I believe you told Harry not to say anything in front of George and Lenny if he remembered what had happened to him?'

Buchanan nodded. 'Yes, I said to say nothing if his memory came back.'

'Well, he and Poppy were talking about how to find out what George and Lenny were up to without them getting suspicious. It was Poppy who came up with a plan. She said she'd heard someone on Facebook talking about a prank that went drastically wrong and it had given her an idea.'

'So, what was this wonderful idea?' asked Karen.

'About putting laxative in their dinner. Worked at uni,' said Poppy.

'Did you do that?' asked Karen.

'No, we didn't,' said Shelly.'

'Oh, that sounded like a good idea, especially after what they did to Harry,' said Buchanan.

'I had a better idea,' said Shelly.

'Oh, and what was that?'

'I asked Poppy to make an extra-large pot of spaghetti. Then, when the stables were quiet, I went down and asked George and Lenny if they were hungry. I explained I was Poppy's mother and was quite angry when I found my daughter in Harry's room making dinner for him. I laid it on a bit for George and Lenny. I said my spoilt and ungrateful daughter – sorry, Poppy – wasn't going to get away with it and would they like to have the dinner instead, including some wine I'd found them getting ready to drink.'

'I presume they jumped at the chance?' said Karen.

'I explained that we were a Christian family and didn't allow our daughter to be alone with a man till after she was married, or to consume alcoholic beverages when under age.'

'What did they say?' asked Karen.

'The one called George put on a worried expression and said, *quite so, we don't think it's right either*. So, I said that since my daughter was making such a wonderful meal of spaghetti Bolognese and would not now be eating it, would they like it instead?'

'What did George say?' asked Karen.

'The cheeky so and so actually wanted to know if the wine was part of the dinner! Of course, I said yes, especially since my daughter was underage to be drinking.'

'No, I'm not,' interrupted Poppy. 'In this country I can drink at eighteen.'

'That may be so, my dear. But just don't let your dad see you doing it. It took a few minutes for George to believe I was being serious. I said to give me thirty minutes and I'd be back with their dinner; the rest was easy.'

'Why was that?'

'I brought down the spaghetti in a large bowl, complete with hot French bread right out of the oven and the two bottles of red wine, unopened. I told them the bottles of wine were a special gift given to Harry by a well-wisher, but since he was trying to get Poppy drunk, and since she was underage, he didn't deserve to have them. So, I said they may as well drink it themselves. But what I neglected to tell George and Lenny was that I had laced the spaghetti with a high dose of temazepam.'

'What? Where did you get the drug from?' asked Karen.

'It's quite handy to have a husband who is a walking pharmacy,' said Shelly. 'As part of his treatment for PTSD, Travis carries a substantial collection of medication with him, including temazepam. While they were waiting for their dinner, I dashed up to our bedroom and helped myself to a double dose for George and Lenny. They should sleep till just before lunchtime.'

'So, the stage is set to thwart Victor Mountjoy's plan of cheating all those people out of their money?' said Greyspear. 'I like this.'

'Have you or Poppy had breakfast?' asked Buchanan.

'No, not yet.'

'Good, there's plenty to eat, just help yourself.'

'Thanks.'

'But I still don't see how Colonel Mountjoy was going to make any money out of his plan?' said Karen.

'Neither did we,' said Poppy. 'So, after we had dinner, Harry and I did the only thing we could, we went back over the CCTV recordings – beginning at six o'clock yesterday morning.'

'And this is where we discovered what the colonel's plan was,' said Harry, yawning. 'It took us till just about a half an hour ago to see what was going on.'

'We watched as George and Lenny painted a white blaze on Rambler, identical to Turpin's' said Poppy, 'and coloured Turpin's blaze black.'

'So, anyone looking at them would just assume Rambler was Turpin, and Turpin was Rambler,' said Greyspear, limping his way back to the breakfast table. 'It's a wonder it's never been done before.'

'But it has,' said Olivia. 'The couple I know about took place in 1920 and 1844. In the 1920 incident, Peter Barrie dyed the white face of a mare called Shining More, dark brown, then ran her under the name of Silver Badge. She won by six lengths. The scam was found out and in October 1920 Peter Barrie was sentenced to three years hard labour.

'The other case was of a horse entered by Goodman Levy called Running Rein. It ran in and won the 1844 Derby. The real name of the horse was Maccabeus. The win was disallowed, and Levy left the country to avoid the law and those who had backed the horse.'

'So, this is the colonel's plan?' said Greyspear.

'Exactly,' said Buchanan. 'Now it all makes sense. Colonel Mountjoy's plan was on the day of the race to take the ride away from Pat, who would at that moment actually be riding Rambler disguised as Turpin and put him back on Turpin disguised as Rambler. In doing so, he would ensure the fastest horse would win.'

'But how would the colonel make any money out of that?' asked Lewis.

'According to what Aaron Silverstein and Achmed Bashir found while trawling through Du Marchon's server,' said Buchanan, 'it looks like Colonel Mountjoy has taken substantial cash bets from friends saying he will lay the bet on Turpin with a syndicate that will give them a higher return than betting at the local betting offices. Instead he has put the money on Turpin disguised as Rambler, that way when Rambler, disguised as Turpin, comes in anywhere but first, he won't have to pay out to his punters. Likewise, Du Marchon has taken twenty-five percent of his customers' investments and placed them on Turpin, disguised as Rambler.'

'But that would look weird to those watching and betting on the race,' said Greyspear. 'I had Lewis keeping an eye on who was watching the practise sessions.

'That's correct,' said Lewis. 'During the week I've seen several touts with binoculars following the progress of the horses. When I confronted them about why they were there and asked them for their opinions as to which horse they thought would win, they all said Turpin.'

'Were they observing yesterday morning when Pat McCall said he thought he was on the wrong horse?' asked Buchanan.

'No. He went out early, they didn't show up till afterwards.'

'So, the punters didn't see the change in performance of the colonel's horse?' said Greyspear.

'But I still have problems understanding why Colonel Mountjoy would choose to ride Turpin disguised as Rambler,' said Karen. 'It doesn't make sense to do that.'

'My thoughts as well, till I read the *Eastbourne Herald* sports page this morning,' said Buchanan.

'What does it say?' asked Poppy.

'There's an interview with Victor Mountjoy done on Thursday afternoon where he says he will be riding Turpin, not Pat McCall.'

'I'm sorry, I still don't understand.'

'With Victor Mountjoy now riding the horse called Turpin, we know is really Rambler, and Pat McCall riding Turpin disguised as Rambler, the horse no-one expects to win will actually win. That is exactly what Victor Mountjoy wants.'

'Because that's the horse he and Du Marchon have put all their bets on,' said Greyspear. 'What a brilliant idea if it works, and you're criminally inclined. Is he going to get away with it?'

Buchanan smiled as he poured himself another coffee. 'Not now.'

'Early this morning,' said Poppy, 'while George and Lenny were sleeping off their over-indulgence of last night, Harry and I changed Turpin back to being Turpin by washing off the painted-on hair colouring.'

'All this while George and Lenny slept. Brilliant!' said Olivia.

'So now Rambler is Rambler and Turpin is Turpin?' asked Greyspear.

'Not quite. Turpin is definitely Turpin, but we left Rambler still disguised as Turpin as we didn't get time to wash the white blaze off.'

'But how will you deal with Victor Mountjoy? Especially when he sees there are two Turpins?'

'We figured if Harry walked the real Turpin up to the parade ring before Colonel Mountjoy arrives for his horse he wouldn't notice. The real problem is we just need to get Pat McCall to go along with the ruse.'

'That could be a problem,' said Greyspear.

'I have an idea,' said Buchanan. 'I need to have a chat with someone first, but I don't foresee any problems.'

'What about Colonel Mountjoy?' said Poppy.

'Ah, now that's where you have a part to play, Nathan,' said Buchanan. 'Do you think you could keep Colonel Mountjoy busy while Pat gets saddled-up and led up to the parade ring?'

'No problem. I'll say I was giving his suggestion about the veterans drop-in centre some serious thought and needed to have a quick word.'

'Great, that should give Harry plenty of time to lead Pat up. to the parade ring.'

'So, what's the plan when the colonel gets down to the stable?' asked Greyspear.

'You've seen how ungainly he is,' said Poppy. 'Well, Harry is going to suggest he mounts his horse, which he will still think is Rambler disguised as Turpin, in the yard. Then when he is ready, Harry and I will lead him out of the stable yard and up to the start-finish line.'

'And how will that make a difference?'

'On the way out of the yard, I will keep the colonel deep in conversation while Harry sponges off the white blaze on Rambler's forehead,' said Poppy.

'So, when Victor Mountjoy arrives at the start-finish line, he won't realise he's not on Rambler disguised as Turpin, and since he knows he's riding Rambler, he won't notice while riding either?' said Karen.

'Got it in one,' said Poppy.

'But couldn't we just tell the colonel we have discovered his plan and make him withdraw from the race? That would surely simplify the situation?' said Shelly.

'We could,' said Buchanan. 'But my gut instinct is that even if we warned the colonel off from this race, he is likely, and desperate enough, to try it somewhere else where there might not be the same scrutiny. No, I believe the best way is to let him think he has succeeded with his plan, and when he realises that he has been found out, his guns will truly be spiked, and he will be finished with plans to cheat at horseracing forever.'

'But that could ruin him financially,' said Shelly.

'From what I understand, he is already ruined financially. This, I believe, is his last-ditch effort to recover from many years of a profligate lifestyle,' said Buchanan.

'His poor wife, what will happen to her?' asked Shelly.

'I believe Cynthia will be all right, no matter what the outcome of the race is.'

'Brilliant,' said Greyspear. 'The reputation of Castlewood, the race, and may I say it, my good name has been preserved.'

'You look washed out, Jack,' said Karen, 'are you OK to ride?'

'I'll be fine, I'll go back to the room and take a quick nap. But first, I've got someone that I must have a chat with.'

07:35

On his way to his room, Buchanan stopped at the reception desk.

'Yes, Mr Buchanan, can I help?'

'I hope so, can you tell me which room Pat McCall is in, please?'

'Certainly, one moment.

'Why are you wanting to talk to Pat?' asked Karen.

271

'Because he's vital to the plan.'

'Ok, all this cloak and dagger stuff has me wondering if you've strayed away from who you are.'

'Excuse me, Mr Buchanan. Mr McCall is in room twenty. Shall I call him for you?'

'No thanks, that won't be necessary. I'll catch up with him later.'

Buchanan walked up the stairs, Karen walking behind trying to keep up. He turned left at the top and waited for Karen to catch up with him.

'What's the hurry, Jack?'

'Don't want to miss them.'

'Them?'

'You'll see. C'mon follow me and get a big surprise.'

He walked down the corridor and continued walking till he reached room twenty. He listened at the door for the sounds of activity. Not hearing any he knocked on the door. 'Room service, personal message for Mrs Mountjoy.'

Karen looked at him and smiled. 'Now I see.'

There was no sound, so Buchanan knocked louder, 'Room service, personal message for Mrs McCall.'

Karen gave Buchanan a gentle punch in the arm.

Moments after saying he had a message for Mrs McCall, there came the sound of shuffling feet from the bedroom.

'You've got the wrong person, there's no Mrs McCall here.'

'Good morning Pat. It's Jack Buchanan. Be a good lad and let us in.'

'Go away, it's too early to talk.'

'Well, let me have a word with Cynthia, I know she's there with you.'

The door opened and revealed an angry Pat McCall. 'Look, I don't give a shit if you're from the Jockey Club. What I get up to in my own time is my business, now bugger off.'

Before he could completely shut the door, Buchanan had his foot in the opening and barged into the room, followed by Karen.

Cynthia, bleary-eyed, propped herself up on one elbow, shook her head and said, 'Who's that? Oh, Jack, what are you doing here?'

'I'm your guardian angel, Cynthia. Today is the first day of the rest of your life.'

'What are you blabbering about?' said Pat.

'Let me introduce myself,' said Buchanan, shutting the bedroom door after Karen.

'I know who you are, you're a meddling sod from the Jockey Club.'

'No, he's not,' said Cynthia. 'He's one of those newspaper jerks. Is she the photographer? Do you work for the *Sun,* looking to get rich writing a big exposé?'

Buchanan put his hand up. 'Wait, wait a moment, before this affair turns into a plot for a Gilbert and Sullivan play. We don't work for any newspaper, and neither am I from the Jockey Club. Karen is my wife and has put up with me being a policeman for the last thirty-five years. I am Detective Chief Inspector Jack Buchanan of the Sussex CID. I am here at Castlewood on a week's furlough while the matter of the two men under a police car in Glasgow is put to rest.'

'You are?' said Cynthia. 'Then what are you doing in our bedroom?'

'It's about the race today,' said Karen. 'We want to help.'

'You're too late for that,' said Pat, 'I'm not riding.'

'Why on earth not?' asked Buchanan.

'I'm reluctant to get Cynthia involved and I do not want to be branded a cheat.'

'You mean you were threatened if you didn't ride Rambler, Victor would have George and Lenny do something unmentionable to Cynthia?'

'That bastard. He knows she intends to divorce him and marry me.'

'Well, what's stopping you?'

'He's got some sort of plan to swap horses. Don't you see, this was to be my one chance of getting back in the saddle. I know this is a race for amateurs, but the publicity would open the stable door for me to get into professional racing.'

'Pat, Cynthia. I know I said I was a policeman, but please believe me when I say I really am here on furlough. The only reason I got involved was because of what George and Lenny did to Harry.'

'So, it was them,' said Pat, shaking his head. 'I didn't believe a horse would do that, especially Mercury. I've seen him, he'd be frightened if a mouse got under his hooves, he'd never do that to a human.'

'We have a plan, Pat, but it all depends on you riding Turpin.'

'He'll never win, not the Turpin Victor wants me to ride.'

'I know all about that, and we've arranged a small surprise for Victor, but you must ride.'

'Go on, Pat,' said Cynthia. 'I trust Jack and whatever plan he's got up his sleeve.'

Pat looked away from Cynthia and back at Buchanan. 'How can I trust you? How do I know you're not in this with Victor?'

'We know all about Victor's scheme to run Turpin as Rambler and Rambler as Turpin.'

Pat shrugged. 'So what? I already know that. He'll never win on Turpin and I doubt if I could coax enough out of Rambler to win. Where's the sense in any of that?'

'You obviously haven't read the sports section of yesterday's *Eastbourne Herald.*'

'Of course not, why would I want to read the local rag?'

'If you had you would have learned that Victor is planning on swapping rides with you. He's going to ride Turpin and put you on Rambler.'

'That's what you just said, and I told you I know that.'

'But what you don't know is Turpin and Rambler are twins. Victor has swapped Turpin and Rambler by painting a white blaze on Rambler and dyeing Turpin's forehead with black hair dye.'

274

'So,' interrupted Cynthia, 'when Pat rides the horse called Rambler, he will actually be riding Turpin. I never thought Victor could be that devious.'

'Then I'm definitely not going to ride. No way am I going to be party to such a scam.'

'Not so quick, Pat. As I said, we are wise to Victor's scam, as you call it. Please go ahead and ride Turpin, but we need you to get to the stable before Victor or Julian gets there. As soon as you get saddled up, Harry will lead you up to the parade ring. When he has delivered you and Turpin to the ring, he and Poppy will get back to the stable in time to help Victor saddle up. Sir Nathan will keep Victor busy until we give him the all clear.'

'But won't Victor realise he's been found out?'

'No. When the colonel gets to the stables, he'll be told that you've gone ahead on Rambler, and Turpin is waiting for him in his stall. He'll look at the forehead on his horse and seeing that it has the white blaze will assume it is Rambler dressed to look like Turpin. When Harry and Poppy lead him up to the parade ring, Poppy will distract Victor and, while he's not looking, Harry will quickly sponge off the white dye revealing the plain forehead of Rambler. Of course, by the time Victor realises what has happened it will be too late. What do you think about riding now?'

'Where's my silks?'

15
Race Day

08:30

Buchanan lay on his back staring at the ceiling. He could do a lot more of this he thought if he gave in and retired, but not today, especially not today. He was going for a ride, the ride of his life. His daydream was interrupted by the bedroom door being opened by Karen.

'Are you going to get up? It's almost nine.'

'Yes. Just been remembering something.'

'What was it?' she said, pulling back the curtains.

'Oh – just something Nathan said. I think I'll have a shower to wake up,' he said, throwing back the bedclothes.

'Fine, I'll lay out your riding clothes.'

Buchanan turned on the shower and stepped under the hot spray. He closed his eyes and let the hot water flow over his body, waiting for the involuntary shivering to cease.

He'd been shocked, to say the least, when Nathan had asked him to represent him in the Castlewood Cup by taking his place in the event. 'Don't try and win, Jack. Just go out there and enjoy yourself,' Nathan had said.

'Have you gone back to sleep?' Karen shouted from the bedroom. 'You'll miss the race if you don't hurry.'

'No, just thinking about yesterday.'

Buchanan had looked at his friend, then down at the foot encapsulated in a medical boot, and remembered Nathan saying he had twisted his ankle during the week when he jumped down from a scaffold tower in his boatyard in Greenock. Buchanan had wondered why Greyspear had picked him and not one of his stable hands, such as Olivia.

'Because you are my friend,' Nathan had said, as if he'd read Buchanan's mind. 'Besides, you can use it to raise funds for a charity of your choice. You could have it as a sponsored ride if you'd like. Tell you what, I'll make an announcement at dinner, you could tell us all about your charity. How about that?'

Buchanan had thought about the proposal for a moment then agreed. 'So long as I can just canter round the course.'

'Of course, my friend, whatever you like, just make sure you wave the flag for Castlewood.'

Buchanan would have normally refused to do something he hadn't had time to contemplate, but Nathan's suggestion had formalised an idea that had been gestating in the recesses of his mind ever since he'd arrived in Eastbourne.

The first night he'd been out on the Eastbourne precinct with Jill he'd seen the sad sight of people, some of them veterans, living rough. Of course, he'd said to himself, many towns the world over had their share of rough sleepers and there was no way he could help them all, but if he could only make a difference to one veteran's life, it would be worth it. With this proposal from Greyspear, Buchanan had been presented with an opportunity to do a little towards helping those he could.

'You'll be late for your big day!' shouted Karen again.

Buchanan shook himself out of his daydream and stepped out of the shower.

'I've laid out your clothes on the bed for you,' said Karen, 'and there's a cup of fresh coffee on the dresser.'

'Thanks.'

'Are you nervous?'

He thought for a moment. 'Yes, just a bit. I think I'd be more relaxed being cross-examined by the defending barrister in a murder case.'

'You've done that often enough. What's the matter? You've gone quiet.'

'George and Lenny, that's what. If they wake up early, they could put two and two together and warn the colonel.'

'What can you do? You can't very well wait till they wake and get them to take another dose of temazepam.'

Buchanan smiled. 'Got it. I'll call Stephen and Jill and have them come out to Castlewood and arrest George and Lenny for the assault on Harry. As long as it is timed correctly, they should be gone before the colonel knows what has happened.'

'That's my Jack. Can I get you anything else?'

'No, thanks.'

'In that case, I want to catch up with Shelly, I'll see you at the start.'

♦

09:15

Spring was definitely in the air thought Buchanan as he walked across the walkway to the stable yard. Wisps of mist floated in front of the hedges where the early sun had yet to penetrate. As he entered the yard, he was confronted by at least a dozen ponies, all being attended to by their riders or grooms. Competitors for the pony gymkhana, he mused.

He walked past the Old Coachman's Lodge listening for the sound of voices as he walked: nothing, total silence. He wasn't sure if that was good or bad. He hoped that what Shelly, Harry and Poppy had got up to had worked and, at that moment, George and Lenny were still sleeping like logs.

He opened the stable door, entered and stood still. There wasn't any activity from stalls one and two, a good sign. The top door to Mercury's stall was open and his friendly face looked out as Buchanan walked towards it.

'Morning, lad,' said Buchanan, offering up a chunk of apple. 'How are you today? Ready like I am? I hope you are, lad. I'm relying on you to keep me from making a fool of myself.' He patted Mercury on the neck. 'Be back later to get you ready.'

He looked to his left and saw two horses tied to hitching posts. They were being groomed in readiness for the race later in the day, the two young grooms busy with their brushing and chattering to each other.

Reassured that all was still as it had been earlier in the morning, he walked down to the Old Coachman's Lodge and listened at the partially-open door. No sound. Did that mean that George and Lenny were still asleep, or had they woken from their drug-induced slumbers and gone off in search of the colonel? Buchanan pushed the door open and listened, still no sound. It was at that moment a thought came to him. Suppose the double dose of temazepam combined with the wine that Shelly had given George and Lenny was too much for their systems? Now he would be faced with calling Dr Mansell to inform him he was needed at Castlewood. Concerned that the quietness of the Lodge was not a good sign.

He needn't have worried though. He found George was slumped over the arm of the chair mumbling something about a blue chair in a tree, while Lenny lay snoring on the settee, his right arm and leg dangling off the side. Buchanan looked at the wall clock and decided it was time to call Jill and interrupt George and Lenny's dreams.

'Jill, good morning. It's Jack – yes it's today and that's why I called. You remember the young lad, Harry – yes, that's the one – well, I would like you and Stephen to come out and arrest the culprits. No, I'll be keeping out of the way – except for a few people here, no one knows I'm a policeman. When? The race is due to start at one, can you get here within the hour? Great, that should give you time to haul them off before too many of the competitors come down for their horses. Oh, another thing, can you use an unmarked car? That way you shouldn't attract too much attention. Good, I'll wait for you in the stable block. Call me when you arrive, and I'll come down.'

Buchanan left George and Lenny to their dreams and walked quietly up the stairs to Harry's flat. He knocked and waited.

'Hello, Inspector, come in,' said Harry, opening the door and stepping aside for Buchanan to enter. 'I've been asleep, not long up, we had a very late night.'

'So, I heard,' Buchanan said, looking round the room, his eyes alighting on the blanket and pillow on the floor by the armchair.

Harry saw where Buchanan's gaze had settled. 'Yes, Poppy was here. I slept alone, in my own bed. Poppy's mum made sure of that.'

'I'm not surprised. Poppy seems to know her own mind.'

'I'm glad Shelly stayed,' said Harry. 'I like Poppy very much and wouldn't want anything to happen that would spoil what we have going. They left a couple of hours ago. Have you seen them this morning?'

'They came into the meeting room and told us what you all got up to last night.'

'Would you like a coffee? I've just put the kettle on.'

'Please, one more won't do any harm and may help me to keep my wits about me as I ride.'

Coffee cup in hand, Buchanan asked, 'How were things last night?'

'The bit about George and Lenny was fine, Poppy's mum took care of that. She said that by the time they woke, it would be too late for Colonel Mountjoy's plan to work. She said they should wake about lunchtime by themselves, just before the race starts.'

'You look a bit puzzled?' said Buchanan, as he sipped on his coffee.

'I am. After we had fed George and Lenny, the three of us had our own dinner. Shelly and Poppy made the spaghetti,' Harry said, grinning. 'It was the best I've ever eaten, and the company couldn't have been better.'

'So, what happened to make you puzzled?'

'It was a very relaxed dinner, spaghetti Bolognese, salad, French bread and as a surprise for Poppy, a very expensive bottle of red wine. I don't care for wine, I usually prefer beer with dinner, but the wine that Shelly brought has given me a whole new appreciation for the taste of the stuff.'

'Yes, fine wine does that to the pallet. So, what happened to make you puzzled?'

'It's really cosy in here and, after the big meal and a couple of glasses of wine, Poppy fell asleep in the chair,' he said, pointing to the armchair with the blanket on the floor. 'Well, after Poppy fell asleep, Shelly and I started talking, though it was more like a question and answer session with Shelly asking the questions.'

'What sort of questions?'

'She wanted to know if I currently had a girlfriend, what sort of girls did I like and where did I see myself in ten years.'

'What did you tell her?'

'I said that being on probation was making it difficult to get about and socialise, so I didn't currently have a girlfriend. She pressed me on what sort of girl I was attracted to. I shrugged and nodded towards Poppy. I think that pleased her because she then wanted to know about my ambitions workwise. I told her about going back to university to get my BSc in accounting and wanting to be involved in finance management of some sort.'

'How did you feel about all that?'

'Felt like I was being interviewed for a job.'

Buchanan chuckled. 'You were, Harry. You were being interviewed for the position of future son-in-law.'

'Oh, now it makes sense!'

'Does it bother you?'

'No, sort of makes me feel happy inside.'

'Glad to hear that. How will you do with being the son-in-law to a church pastor?'

'I don't know, ask me again in ten years.'

'I will.'

'Now about the race, are you ready?'

'Yes.'

'Do you want help getting Mercury ready?'

'Thanks. But first we have the matter of George and Lenny to take care of.'

'Oh yes, I've been wondering if they'll realise what happened to them when they wake up?'

'It won't matter if they do. I have Detective Sergeant Hunter and Constable Hunter on their way to arrest them for what they did to you. You are willing to testify that they assaulted you?'

'Oh, yes, but won't it be just my word against theirs?'

'I haven't talked to the doctor who examined you yet, but I'm sure there will be DNA evidence taken from your injuries that will be more than enough to convict them,' he said, reaching for his phone.

'Buchanan. That was quick. You are? Great. I'll meet you in the yard.'

'Was that your police officers who are coming for George and Lenny?' asked Harry.

'The very same.'

'Good, I'll enjoy watching this.'

'Maybe better if you watch from the shadows. I don't want them to create a fuss when they realise you have been playing them for fools.'

'Fine by me, I'll watch from the end of the corridor.'

Harry followed Buchanan down the stairs and wandered off to the far end of the stables so he could watch the impending spectacle. Buchanan walked out into the yard to meet Jill and Stephen.

'Good morning, Jack,' said Jill.

'And a good morning it is. Morning, Stephen.'

'How's the holiday?'

'Very funny. Shall we get on with it? I've got a race to ride and I need to get my horse ready.'

'Where are they?' asked Jill.

'Sleeping in the Old Coachman's Lodge. Follow me and I will direct you.'

Harry watched from the end of the stables as Buchanan, followed by Jill and Stephen, entered the Old Coachman's Lodge. Buchanan walked over to the slumbering George and shook him vigorously.

'Wakey-wakey, George!' he shouted. 'The scales of justice have swung against you.'

George opened his eyes and tried to focus. When he realised who it was, he tried to punch Buchanan, but, before he could connect, Stephen grabbed his wrist and attached one link of his handcuffs and before he could resist further, both wrists secured.

'What the –?' shouted George, trying to make sense of what was happening.

'George Reilly, I am arresting you for the assault on Harry Janski You do not have to say anything. But it may harm your defence if you do not mention when questioned something which you later rely on in court. Anything you do say maybe given in evidence,' said Buchanan, as Stephen put a set of handcuffs on the prostrate Lenny.

'Who the hell are you to arrest me?' said George, as Stephen pulled him up onto his feet.

'You don't know him?' said Stephen.

'How the hell should I?' replied George.

'George Reilly, let me introduce you to Detective Chief Inspector Buchanan of Sussex CID.'

'What? I thought you were a reporter from the *Sun* trying to dig up a scandal about Mrs Mountjoy.'

'Your mistake, George.'

'Doesn't matter,' he replied. 'The colonel will sort it out, you'll see.'

'Not if he's in jail with you, he won't.'

'What?'

'We know all about the colonel's plans for swapping Rambler and Turpin, George.'

'You do?'

'I told you it wouldn't work,' said Lenny, who'd just woken and understood what was going on. 'I said it was a stupid idea.'

'C'mon,' said Stephen. 'There'll be plenty of time to discuss the colonel's plan when we have you booked in.'

Harry came out of shadows of stall three as George and Lenny were driven off to the police station.

'So that's it then, justice is done. When do you want me to give my statement?'

'One day next week, there's plenty of time for that, but right now I have a horse to get ready for a race.'

'Will they stay in jail until they go to court?'

'That's a good question that I cannot answer. Usually in these situations they would be charged then released on police bail, pending a court date. I don't think a judge would keep them in custody till they come to trial. With what evidence there is against them, I imagine they'll be back on the streets by Monday.'

'They better not try anything.'

'I shouldn't worry about that. I imagine they'll get an order banning them from coming anywhere near Castlewood.'

'Glad to hear that. Still want me to help?'

'Please, but if Pat McCall shows up for Turpin, I'd like you to help him first.'

'Ah, yes. You said he has to be saddled and on his way to the parade ring before the colonel shows up.'

Buchanan nodded as he took a sip of his coffee.

Harry waited for him to finish it, then helped with saddling up Mercury.

From the peace of a stable just waking to a new day, the scene that greeted Buchanan and Harry was that of well-orchestrated chaos. Most of the horses were out of their stalls and tied to hitching rails as their riders or grooms prepared them. Buchanan walked over to the open stable doors and looked out. The last of the ponies were being ridden out of the yard towards their event in the field in front of the house. He was about to go back in when

Pat and Cynthia walked into the yard; he waved at them to be quick.

'What's the hurry?' asked Cynthia, as she and Pat entered the stables.

'You do remember what I said earlier – Pat needs to be gone before Victor gets here.'

'Of course we do, but why should it matter now? We've stopped him from cheating.'

'Yes, we've certainly done that. I suppose I could go tell him that his plan to cheat has been discovered and is no longer viable. Is that what you want me to do?'

'What do you think, Pat?' Cynthia asked.

'If it was up to me I'd let the bastard rot in hell and throw away the key, especially for how he's treated you over the years. I'm going to see how Turpin is.'

'Then that settles it, Jack. Let him race thinking he's got away with his plan. But I want you to promise I get to be there when he realises he's been screwed by someone much cleverer than himself.'

'So be it,' said Buchanan. 'To this point he hasn't actually committed any crime, other than to orchestrate the beating of Harry.'

'How much time do we have?' asked Cynthia.

'There's more than enough,' said Harry. 'The children's gymkhana has just started and by the time the prizes have been awarded they won't be back here for at least another forty minutes.'

'Hi, Harry,' said Poppy, who'd just entered the stables with Travis and Shelly.

'Hello, how are you?'

'Bit sleepy.'

'That's your own fault,' said Shelly. 'Early bed for you tonight.'

'Oh, that's not fair. It's the awards dinner dance this evening and Harry has promised to show me how well he can dance.'

'Life's not fair, my dear. But since it is our last weekend before we go home, I suppose one more late night can't hurt.'

'When do you go home?' asked Harry, with a startled look on his face.

'Thursday morning,' said Travis. 'Our flight leaves at nine-thirty, gets into Dallas at two-thirty-five in the afternoon, just in time to beat the rush hour.'

Buchanan looked away from Harry's face to that of Poppy's; it was a toss-up between the two of them who looked the most distraught. To Buchanan it was obvious that this was the first time either of them had given thought to the inevitable moment of parting.

'I don't want to go home,' said Poppy.

'I'm afraid that is not an option,' said Shelly. 'You have to study for your exams. You know we have your name down for SMU and getting admitted isn't a walk in the park.'

'But Mom – *please*.'

'Poppy, this is neither the time nor the place to discuss this, your dad and I have to get ready for the race.'

Buchanan looked at Cynthia. She was about to say something, then changed her mind and walked over to Doxy's stall.

'Can I help, Pat?' asked Harry. 'I can get Turpin out of his stall for you.'

'Thanks. But I think George and Lenny might object to you doing their job for them.'

'I doubt it, they've been arrested for beating me up.'

'So, who fed Turpin and Rambler if George and Lenny aren't around?'

'I did, first thing this morning. Their hay nets have been kept full for them as well.'

'I wish all stables took such good care of the horses as you do here.'

'I'll let the management know you appreciate it.'

'So those two shites are finally getting their come-uppance,' said Pat. 'Hope they get put away for years.' He nodded, agreeing with his own statement, then said, 'Let's get to work, I've got a race to win.'

As Harry got busy undoing the netting from the front of Rambler's stall containing Turpin, Buchanan watched as Poppy walked over to a bale of straw and sat down to think. A noise from behind the bale caught her attention. She leaned over and picked up the source of the noise, it was one of the kittens apparently separated from the mother.

It wasn't difficult for Buchanan to imagine what was going through Poppy's mind as she held the tiny lost kitten close to her chest. Buchanan looked over to where Shelly was talking earnestly with Travis. He thought they would be better off talking with Poppy, otherwise she might do something really silly. Harry was her first love, her Romeo, and like the classic pair, their romance was doomed to failure before the flames of passion could be fully fanned into a blaze. He looked back at Poppy and had an idea, but first he needed to talk with Karen.

The sound of horses' hooves clattering on the cobbles brought him back to the present. He followed Harry as he led Turpin out into the yard and tied him to a large metal ring set into the stable wall. They were followed by Cynthia and Pat leading Doxy.

'Can I help?' asked Poppy, who had found the mother cat and returned the lost kitten.

'You really love him?' said Buchanan.

Poppy nodded. 'I don't know what to do, Jack. What would you do if you were in my situation?'

'I'm sorry, Poppy. I can't answer that question. What would your mother do?'

Poppy smiled. 'My mom would pray about it and wait for an answer from God.'

'Does that work for her?'

'Most times.'

'What about when it doesn't work?'

'She just says it's God's will and goes back to praying.'

'Maybe you should try it.'

'I have. I haven't stopped since I heard Dad call the airline to confirm our reservation to fly home.'

'My wife prays a lot as well.'

'What about?'

'Me staying safe at work. It makes her happy, so I just let her get on with it.'

'It obviously works, you look quite healthy to me,' said Poppy, smiling.

'Maybe. But in the meantime, I need to get Mercury saddled up.'

'Thanks.'

'For what?'

'Listening.'

'My pleasure.'

'Can I walk up to the parade ring with you?'

'Certainly,' said Buchanan, as he checked Mercury's girth strap. 'But aren't you and Harry supposed to be walking back up with the colonel?'

'Oops, I forgot. I'll hang on till Harry gets back.'

As he mounted Mercury, Buchanan saw Major Jackson approach the stables accompanied by Colonel Mountjoy. He motioned to Poppy to wait a moment while he adjusted his stirrup strap. He continued to fiddle with the strap till the colonel and major got close enough for him to hear what was being said.

'I don't give a damn, Andrew. She's not getting a penny from me; in fact, she can whistle till the cows come home if she thinks I'm going to make it easy for her to get a divorce. I want you to tell the scheming bitch I want her out of my house by this time next week. If she's not, I'll throw her out myself. And another thing –'

'Good morning, Colonel,' interrupted Buchanan. 'Lovely day for a race?'

Colonel Mountjoy looked up at Buchanan and thought for a moment, then remembered today was the day he was to become exceptionally rich.

'Yes, it is, Jack,' he said, as his face lit up with a million-pound smile. 'In fact, today's race is a race in a million.'

'I'll have a word with your wife,' said Jackson. She has an appointment in my office next Wednesday.'

'You do that, and make sure she realises she's not getting a penny from me.'

For someone it probably is a million-pound race thought Buchanan as he dismounted, but it wasn't destined to be the colonel.

'Is something wrong?' asked Poppy, as Buchanan passed her the reins.

He shook his head, pointed to Harry walking across the yard, then spoke loudly. 'I think I've dropped my gloves in the stall, Poppy. Will you hold Mercury for me? I'll be right back.'

Buchanan returned to Mercury's stall and waited for the inevitable outburst of anger from Colonel Mountjoy. He didn't have to wait long; the first indicator was the colonel shouting for George and Lenny. Buchanan counted to ten then walked out of Mercury's stall.

'Are you looking for your grooms, Colonel?' asked Buchanan.

'Of course I am. Have you seen them?'

'I believe they went off in a police car about an hour ago.'

'What? How – how, what happened? If they've been fighting again, I'll kick their arses from here to – how do you know it was a police car?'

'Because it had two policemen in it,' replied Buchanan, remembering Lonnie Donegan singing about the fact his dustbin was full of toadstools because *there was not mushroom inside.*

'It's not a laughing matter, Jack. This is a very special day for Sir Nathan. Any signs of a scandal would be dreadful. What are you doing back in here? I thought you were off up to the start?'

'I left my gloves in Mercury's stall,' said Buchanan, waving them in the Colonel's face. 'And I'm sure it was just a mix-up with your grooms, probably a case of mistaken identity. I wouldn't let it spoil your day. I'll see you at the start.'

Buchanan walked back out of the stables and over to Poppy. She was in deep conversation with Harry while still holding on to Mercury.

'All set, Harry?'

'Yep. I walked Pat McCall up to the ring on Turpin, and you should have seen the heads turn as he did a lap of the parade ring. Definitely a winner if ever there was one.'

'The colonel is in the stables; he seems to be missing his two grooms. Maybe you and Poppy could go give him a hand to get ready?'

'Certainly, we can,' said Poppy, passing Mercury's reins back to Buchanan. 'Come on, Harry, we have work to do, we can't let the colonel be late for his big race.'

'Ok, see you later, Jack,' said Harry.

16
The Race

11:45

'You look like a general getting ready to ride his charger into battle,' Buchanan said to Travis, as he caught up with him on the way to the parade ring.

'I wish I felt it,' Travis replied. 'Maybe I should have entered the pony gymkhana instead.'

'Nonsense, you'll do fine. Your horse certainly looks ready,' said Buchanan.

'Yes, he does, doesn't he?' replied Travis, patting his horse's neck. 'It's just, I'm not really cut out for this sort of competitive-style riding. Back home we usually get on our horses and head out onto the open trails. I much prefer being out in the country where you can just meander along and get lost in your own thoughts.'

'Surely you have competitive events?'

'Yes, we do. The Stockyards on Friday and Saturday evenings, fantastic family entertainment. But that's rodeo stuff, done in an arena by professional riders.'

'Do you and the family go to the rodeo very often?'

Travis nodded. 'Yes. In our state it's a big family outing. The Saturday night rodeos run from March through to the last weekend in November. After the rodeo there is live music and dancing if you have a mind for it. If you get hungry there are many vendors selling food and drink, especially BBQ ribs and burgers.'

'Sounds like fun.'

'It is. But we do also have dressage events, and horse jumping, though nothing as big as the rodeo. Of course, horse racing is very big in the States, like it is here in England.' He shrugged as they entered the parade ring, then added, 'And there are also quarter horse events, but nothing like what you have here at Castlewood.'

As they entered the parade ring Buchanan could see some of the horses with jockeys on-board milling around, sometimes stopping for a jockey to lean down for a quick word with a family member.

Standing on the platform that had been specially constructed as a start-finish podium, Buchanan could see Greyspear leaning on his crutches deep in conversation with Susan. Also on the podium was Susan's sister and several others including, much to Buchanan's surprise, his boss, the present ACC, and also Gillian Atkins, the former ACC.

Now why was she here, he wondered? Then the obvious answer presented itself. She had taken early retirement and gone to work for G4S. Since they were looking after the security at the race, it was quite reasonable to find her here.

Buchanan took off his hat and waved at Gillian. She stared at him for a moment, then realised who it was and waved back. Buchanan grinned as he saw his former boss immediately get involved in a conversation with Helen Markham, his present boss.

He looked around at the gathered contestants and saw that Greyspear had done his job in delaying Colonel Mountjoy well. Walking up to the parade ring were the last three competitors, including the colonel led by Harry and Poppy. Buchanan smiled as he looked at Rambler and saw that Harry had managed to sponge off the offending white blaze from the horse's forehead, while Poppy was doing an excellent job of keeping the colonel busy chatting.

Further conversation amongst the gathered crowd was curtailed by the sound of someone tapping a microphone on the PA system.

'Ladies and gentlemen,' began Greyspear, 'to paraphrase a great American actor – all things considered, I'd rather be riding, and not here on the podium. I'd rather be out there with you in the parade ring. But be that as it may, I'm sure you would want to join me in wishing all competitors success with their ride today in the Castlewood Cup.

'In my place, representing Castlewood, is my good friend Jack Buchanan. He has graciously agreed to take my place in the race, and for those of you who weren't present at the dinner last evening, Jack is being sponsored to raise money for the charity, the Blue Van Veterans Drop-in Centre in town. Please dig deep and give generously.

'Now, it is my delight to make way for my wife, who will do the honours and start the race. Riders, would you please assemble at the start-finish line?'

Pat McCall on Turpin, followed by Major Jackson on Warrior, led the pack out of the parade ring to the start-finish line. Buchanan worked his way alongside Colonel Mountjoy and engaged him in conversation to keep him from noticing that Rambler had been unfrocked.

As they walked, Buchanan saw Du Marchon trying to work his way across to get Colonel Mountjoy's attention. It was obvious to Buchanan that Du Marchon had noticed the missing blaze on Rambler and was now probably wondering if the colonel had either made a mistake or had changed strategy about who was riding which horse.

Buchanan was enjoying Du Marchon's confusion and said to the colonel, 'Looks like your friend, Mr Du Marchon, is trying to get to the start before you. If I am not mistaken, I'd say he's out to beat you in the race.'

'Not bloody likely!' shouted the colonel, and with that kicked Rambler into a quick canter up to the start-finish line, well away from Du Marchon who continued to attempt to get his attention.

'Riders, are you ready?' shouted Susan Greyspear over the PA system.

Heads all looked towards the podium and Susan Greyspear, who at that moment was holding up a huge Greyspear Yachts company flag. 'On your marks – GO!'

Too late now, thought Buchanan as he saw Du Marchon try and gather his reins and go after the colonel.

Karen and Helen waved as he passed the start-finish line. Regardless of Buchanan's plans to take it easy, Mercury had other ideas and charged ahead trying to catch up with the leaders, who were now several lengths ahead.

Buchanan struggled as he settled into Mercury's rhythm and had moments to prepare for the upcoming jump, *Badgers Bend*. He recalled Olivia had said the start-finish straight went in a gentle curve to the left and to be correctly lined up for the landing on the far side of the jump, to take *Badgers Bend* at a slight angle from the middle of the course, but to watch out for other horses overcooking the run-up to the jump.

Looking over his left shoulder, he saw he had at least four lengths on the closest horses and prepared to turn sharply to the left on landing. 'Here we go, lad,' he whispered into Mercury's ear.

Buchanan pushed himself slightly out of the saddle, leaned forward and tensed for the inevitable momentary feeling of being out of control. He took a deep breath just as Mercury prepared to jump; two of the horses behind him underestimated their speed, overtook him on his left and arrived at the jump two lengths ahead. One horse swerved away to the left from the jump unseating its jockey, while the other just managed to clear the jump, but due to the horse's speed, over-ran the landing allowing Buchanan to pass.

He breathed out and prepared for the run up the hill to *Quarry Drop*. That leaves nineteen riders Buchanan said to himself, as he remembered Olivia's advice to drift to the middle of the course on the way up the hill.

Within fifty yards from landing after *Badgers Bend*, he noticed that the pack had split into two groups, and he was pleased to see he was at least only last in the first group; there were seven riders plus a lone horse behind him. Buchanan let out his breath and relaxed as he positioned himself for the run up to *Quarry Drop*, a sprint he remembered well from last year when he and Greyspear had gone for an impromptu ride.

As he approached *Quarry Drop*, he positioned himself to jump so that he would be on the left side on landing, well away from the fenced off quarry edge on the right. Olivia had suggested this as the sheer drop into the quarry unsettled some horses. That fence alongside the quarry wouldn't do much to stop a rider going over and down into the quarry below, he thought, as he settled for the run up to *Old Oak*.

The *Old Oak* jump was named after the oldest oak tree on the estate. Greyspear had had it dated back to when the estate had originally been created. This was where the trail turned sharply to the left and on down to *Widow Maker*. Although the horses ahead bunched up as they approached the jump, they all manage to clear it without mishap. This allowed Mercury to catch the leading group. To Buchanan's amazement he saw he was lying a close eleventh out of twenty starters and could clearly make out the lead horse, Turpin, about a hundred yards ahead.

Widow Maker, being a downhill jump with the landing in water, had caused issues during the week with some of the less experienced riders, but not for Mercury. He managed to clear the jump with feet to spare. Unfortunately, one of the riders ahead lost their stirrup on landing and after a few strides came off their horse, ending up in the ditch. That put Buchanan into tenth place with now only eighteen riders left.

The next jump was *Long Run*, situated at the bottom of the slope. Upon landing horses had to change pace for the long uphill run to *Shooters Aim*. This jump, Harry had warned Buchanan, should be taken as far on the left as possible, otherwise he would be too far on the right-hand side of the course when landing, making the run down to *Vicar's Leap* more work for the horse than was necessary.

As they approached *Vicar's Leap* the stray horse from an earlier dismounting ran diagonally across the path of two of the horses ahead of Buchanan unseating both riders. Buchanan was now in ninth place and closing fast on the horse ahead of him.

The next section of the circuit Buchanan remembered from his ride earlier in the week. He steadied Mercury on the approach to *Longford*, the ford where the stream ran into the lake. The water in the ford wasn't deep but did create quite a splash when more than one horse crossed at the same time. Buchanan followed three horses through, grateful for the cooling mist left in the air.

There was only one jump left on the first time round the course and that was one that would test the horses to their limit, especially on the final lap. It was *Uphill*, at the top of a steep climb that led up to the entrance road. One of the jockeys ahead misjudged the timing and his horse stopped dead, throwing its rider over its head and right into the top bar of the fence. Buchanan was now eighth, though not any closer to those of the front seven which included Colonel Mountjoy, Pat McCall, Major Jackson, Travis Grant and Cynthia. As he crossed the road that led up to the club house, he realised he was closing fast on Cynthia on Doxy.

It surprised Buchanan just how competitive he'd become since the start. He urged Mercury on and as he moved up on Cynthia, he decided he wanted to win. He remonstrated with himself and realised that unless everyone in front of him fell off, there was no chance of that. In any case, he decided to put on a show and urged Mercury on.

As he passed Cynthia, he looked at her and smiled, she grinned back, shook her head and shouted, 'You cheat – I thought you didn't know how to ride?'

'I don't. I'm just sitting here while Mercury does all the work. See you,' he shouted back, tapping his helmet with his riding crop hand and thinking to himself he was now in seventh place.

Buchanan leaned forward, attempting to emulate what he had seen professional riders do, Mercury sensed Buchanan's desire to make a good show and imperceptibly increased his pace. Buchanan glanced to his left as they flew past the start-finish line. He was sure he saw Karen jumping up and down urging him on.

The next jump was number ten, *Badgers Bend,* or number one on the first-time round. The difference this time was the horses were now thoroughly warmed up and in their stride. Even though he'd already cleared the jump, he remembered to position Mercury for the landing and the run up to *Quarry Drop.* Mercury landed clear of any of the other horses and forged ahead.

He was about to jump *Old Oak* when one of the more ambitious riders from the second group caught up on his left just as one of the loose horses from an earlier rider unseating came alongside on his right, squeezing Buchanan and forcing him to pull back and give room to the other horses to jump ahead of him. The loose horse on the right, now not having Mercury to his left, cut right across in front of the horse to Buchanan's left, unseating its rider. There were now only fourteen riders left, and he was still in seventh position with only a further six fences to jump.

One issue with the *Widow Maker* jump wasn't just the fact it was a downhill jump with water on the landing area, if the rider took it too far to the left, they stood a chance of landing in the stream leading out of it. Buchanan watched the rider in front of him do just that. He swerved to the right to avoid landing on top of the jockey standing knee deep in the stream. He was now in fifth place.

All the riders managed to clear *Long Run* and settled for the charge up the hill to *Shooters Aim.* The excitement was getting to be too much for one of the riders ahead of Buchanan. He kept coming alongside Travis and bumping him. Buchanan watched as Travis was struck with the rider's whip, a very big mistake. Instead of striking back, Travis pulled back half a length allowing the miscreant rider to go ahead on their approach to *Shooters Aim.*

The incident of using the whip to force Travis out of the way had momentarily distracted the jockey and he misjudged the approach to the jump. Buchanan smiled at the case of poetic justice as the horse refused to take the jump. Buchanan nodded to the rider who was trying to turn his horse in an attempt to have another go at the jump, and realised it was Du Marchon. Buchanan was now in fourth place and was steadily catching up to the familiar profile of Victor Mountjoy.

Buchanan looked back to see how Travis was doing and was pleased to see him on Pilar bearing down from behind. Buchanan and Victor Mountjoy jumped *Vicars Leap* side by side, with Travis only one horse-length behind. As they accelerated away from the jump Buchanan looked at Victor Mountjoy, smiled and nodded.

From the look on Victor Mountjoy's face Buchanan could see he was having trouble figuring out why he was still back in third place behind Major Jackson and Pat McCall.

Buchanan urged Mercury on and was soon running side by side with the colonel down to *Longford*. Halfway down the hill they were overtaken by Travis. Buchanan was now back in fourth or fifth place, depending how he and the colonel were able to urge their respective horses on. It was obvious to Buchanan that the colonel was having trouble controlling Rambler. Every time Mercury came alongside Rambler, he tried to shy away.

Buchanan reasoned, as far as the colonel was concerned, he was riding Rambler disguised as Turpin, and all he had to do was finish the race and he would have succeeded in making himself a considerably rich man. He'd probably hoped to have made a better showing of his ride. Coming a close second would have made a better impression on those watching and betting.

Buchanan could see the colonel was losing concentration, probably thinking about his impending wealth, and just when he should have been focussed on the charge through *Longford*, he turned sideways to Buchanan, grinned, and tried to take a swipe at him with his whip. The sudden change in position of the colonel's body weight caused Rambler to falter, lose his footing and tip himself and his rider into the water.

Buchanan glanced over his shoulder at the colonel and saw him standing knee-deep in *Longford* water, desperately trying to calm his horse. Two other riders passed him as they charged up the hill towards the final fence.

All the leading horses cleared the *Uphill* jump and made the dash for the finish line. It was quite an experience for Buchanan. A considerable number of the spectators had made their way back alongside the finish straight and were madly cheering the lead horses, including Mercury. Buchanan waved at the cheering crowd, especially at Karen who had joined Shelly and Poppy to cheer on the winner.

Mercury did his best to keep the two late challengers at bay and came in fourth behind Travis in third place on Pilar, Major Jackson in second place on Warrior, and Pat McCall in first place on Turpin.

17
Final Act

14:55

Once they had passed the start-finish line, the jockeys slowed their horses to a walk, then at a leisurely pace circled back to the parade ring, now transformed into a winners' enclosure.

As soon as Pat, still seated on Turpin, arrived, Cynthia Mountjoy, who'd just got to the enclosure, ran over, reached up and gave Pat a kiss then draped a garland of flowers over Turpin's neck. She was well prepared, thought Buchanan, wondering where and when Cynthia had got the flowers. With a huge smile on her face, Cynthia stood beside Turpin while a photographer from the *Sporting Life* took a photo of the jubilant winning team of Cynthia, Turpin and Pat.

This was definitely an unusual situation for Buchanan. Normally he would just drift out of the limelight and let others take the adulations. Today, there was no escaping the attention of the crowds.

'Well done, Jack,' said Stephen.

'Thanks. Thought you'd be babysitting our friends George and Lenny?'

'Not today, it's one of my few days off. Jill and I thought we'd stop by and watch the race.'

'Where is Jill?'

'She went to find Karen.'

'What about George and Lenny?'

'Hopefully still banged up. They should be in custody till midday tomorrow at the least.'

'Glad to hear that.'

'Glad to hear what?' asked Karen.

'Been wondering where you were,' said Buchanan.

'I was talking to Shelly about Poppy. Then when Jill showed up, I introduced her to Shelly.'

'I presume Poppy has gone to be with Harry?'

'Most likely,' said Karen. 'When the excitement of today has quietened down a bit, I'd like to have a chat with you about Poppy and Harry.'

Buchanan smiled. 'Great minds think alike.'

'How do you feel?' asked Karen, as Buchanan steadied Mercury.

'Not sure. It's bit of a shock to the system. I never would have thought I'd come in fourth in a horse race,' he said.

'Glad to see you survived,' said Jill.

'Thanks for coming along to watch. Are you staying?'

'No. Stephen wants to go and see football. Brighton are playing at the Amex.'

'Of course, it's Saturday,' said Buchanan, as he gathered the reins. 'I'm afraid I must take my leave; Mercury has worked very hard and needs to return to his stall.'

'Mind if I come with you?' asked Karen.

'Of course you can.'

'You rode well, Jack,' said Karen, patting Mercury on the neck as they made their way back to the stables.

'It was Mercury who did most of the work.'

'A successful outcome of the event, nonetheless,' said Karen, smiling. 'You know, you really do surprise me. We've been married thirty-five years and there are still things I don't know about you.'

'That's to keep you on your toes, my dear.'

'I took a picture of you coming across the finish line. I'll send a copy to your parents; your dad will be surprised.'

'I bet he will. The last time he saw me on a horse was at a pony club event in Busby. That was before you and I met.'

'What's going to happen to Harry, especially if the colonel decides to get even?'

'I'm not sure, there's still the incident of him being assaulted to be resolved.'

'I thought Stephen arrested the culprits for that?'

'He did. It's those behind the beating I'm interested in bringing to justice.'

'You said something about the colonel,' said Karen, looking around to see if anyone was in earshot. 'Do you think he's figured out that his plan has been discovered?'

'Although he hadn't noticed prior to the race,' said Buchanan, as he dismounted, 'as soon as he stood up from his fall the colonel must have seen that the white blaze that should have been on Rambler's forehead was definitely gone, and it would be clear for all to see that he'd actually been riding Rambler.'

'But at that point he'd be thinking that Pat's horse would still have the white blaze blacked out,' said Karen. 'That must have really confused and worried him.'

'Yes, but he'd only think that till he got back to the finish,' said Buchanan, while feeling between Mercury's forelegs to see if he was sweating. 'Good, he's cooled down. Did you see the colonel's face when he entered the enclosure at the end of the race?'

'No, I was looking at someone else's face.'

Buchanan smiled. 'If you had, I'm sure you would have seen a look of confusion. He'd have looked at Turpin's forehead, seen the white blaze and realised that Pat McCall had been actually riding Turpin.'

'But wouldn't he realise at that moment the evidence of his subterfuge was gone?'

'No, I don't think so. His real confusion would come when he'd try and work out if his plan to swap horses had been discovered and if George and Lenny had undone the disguises on Turpin and Rambler. Then he would really get angry when he thought of all those bets he'd backed, the money he'd borrowed, and the fact he was now worse off than when he first thought about his plan.'

'I almost feel sorry for George and Lenny,' said Karen. 'Being arrested for beating Harry, then being blamed for the undoing of the colonel's plans.'

'The real problem will be for Harry. When the colonel talks to George and Lenny, he will soon figure out that Harry was responsible for removing the disguises from Turpin and Rambler.'

'What can we do to protect him?'

'I have a plan for that, just need to have a chat with a couple of people first. I'll let you know what they say.'

'Good. I wouldn't want to have anything happen to him, not now since it looks like he and Poppy are so close.'

'You think he'll propose?' said Buchanan, as he replaced Mercury's bridle with a rope halter then tied it to a hitching rail.

'I'd be more surprised if he hasn't already popped the question. What is it, what did I say?'

'I was just thinking about Travis and how he'll react to the news of his daughter's engagement to someone who, just six days ago, he was calling a criminal,' said Buchanan, putting down a pail of water for Mercury to drink. 'That, and what his congregation will think of him.'

'I talked to Shelly about that.'

'What did she have to say?'

'I think she likes Harry and wouldn't be opposed to him as a son-in-law. Can I help with the brushing?'

'Sure, just brush with the direction of the hair.'

'We've never groomed a horse together before. Would you like to own one?'

Buchanan stood up from cleaning Mercury's hooves. 'Not really. It was fun to be here at Castlewood this week, and I will admit I really did enjoy racing today, but – I don't think I would enjoy doing it all the time.'

'Pity.'

'When it is time for me to retire, I will find something suitable to do with my time, but that time is not yet.'

'Fine. What time is dinner this evening?'

'Eight o'clock, it's –' Buchanan's reply was interrupted by the arrival of Turpin, led by Cynthia and Pat.

'Well done, Pat,' said Buchanan, as they passed.

'Thanks, and well done to you coming fourth. Also, thanks for your help and advice.'

'My pleasure.'

'Have you seen Victor?' asked Cynthia.

'Not since his arrival in the winner's enclosure.'

'Thanks, I'll check Rambler's stall.'

'Maybe we'll get lucky and find Rambler here, and Victor long gone,' said Pat.

'Will she be all right?' Karen asked, as Cynthia and Pat led Turpin down to stall one.

'I think once the storm of her husband's nefarious activities has blown over, she and Pat will be just fine.'

'Good, they look like a really nice couple.'

'Let's get Mercury into his box,' said Buchanan. 'He needs a good feed and a rest.'

'That shit,' said Cynthia, stopping at the door to Mercury's stall.

'I presume you are referring to Victor?' said Buchanan.

'You know what he did, or should I say didn't do?'

Buchanan looked at Karen then back at Cynthia. 'No, sorry, I don't know what he didn't do.'

'He's only gone and left Rambler in his stall, still with his saddle and bridle on. That I cannot forgive. He should be stripped naked, hung from a harness hook, and horsewhipped for that.'

Buchanan had a Reggie Perrin moment, an imaginary glimpse of the colonel stripped naked and being whipped by Cynthia; not a pleasant picture he said to himself.

'Can I help?' asked Karen.

Cynthia shook her head. 'Thanks, but Pat will take care of Rambler. I'm looking for the assistant stable manager, Harry, have you seen him?'

'He's probably helping with some of the other horses,' said Buchanan. 'You could try the stall for the Grants' horse.'

'I will, this is just not on, leaving a horse like that.'

♦

17:15

As they waited for the lift, one of the receptionists motioned to Buchanan that there was a message waiting for him.

'You go ahead, Karen, I'll go and see what the message is.'

'Ok, don't be long.'

Buchanan waited for the lift door to close then walked over to the reception desk.

'Yes, what is the message?'

The receptionist passed Buchanan a small envelope. He opened it and saw it was a message from Hanbury to call him asap. Buchanan dialled Hanbury's number and as he waited for him to answer he watched as one of the guests tried and coax a timid puppy into the lift.

'Your geese have flown the coop,' said Hanbury. 'They've been released on police bail. Someone came and picked them up.'

'Who collected them?'

'Someone called Julian Du Marchon.'

'Do you know when this happened?'

'About thirty minutes ago, I thought you'd like to know.'

'They were quick off the mark, wonder what's got them so worried?'

'Who were?'

'The colonel and his partner in crime, Julian Du Marchon. Other than the actual case of a GBH charge against George and Lenny, there isn't much for them to worry about. Of course, thanks to our efforts to thwart their plan to fix the race, there is no evidence to charge them with conspiracy.'

'What about the lad who was beaten? You said he heard them conspire. His testimony coupled with yours should be enough to bring a charge.'

'True, but a bit nebulous.'

'Maybe not. I heard about a case in the States where a veterinarian switched horses in a race, ended up going to jail for his crime. The details are probably still online if you've time to look them up.'

'Thanks, I'll give that some thought, but in the meantime, I need to get over to the stable and warn Harry to keep a low profile.'

♦

17:30

Buchanan went straight to the stable office.

'Olivia, have you seen Harry?'

'No. Not since he led the colonel up to the race, why?'

'What about the two who were staying in the Old Coachman's Lodge?'

'Last time I saw them was when they were hauled off to the police station.'

'How about the colonel and Julian Du Marchon?'

She shook her head. 'No. Not in the last half hour.'

Buchanan returned to the clubhouse and rode the lift to the first floor. He knocked on the door to Poppy's room but got no answer.

He then went to Travis's room and tried again by knocking on the door. It was answered by Shelly.

'Oh, good afternoon, Jack, looking for Travis?'

'No. I'm actually trying to find Harry and wondered if Poppy had any idea where he might be?'

'I'm sorry, I can't help you there. Poppy said she was just going for a walk after the race and we haven't seen her since. Why?'

'The two men who attacked Harry have been released from prison and no one seems to know where they are.'

'She's probably with Harry,' said Travis, who'd just come into the bedroom from the bathroom.

'Ah, that's not so good. Harry hasn't been seen since just after he brought Turpin up to the parade ring.'

'Should I ask the obvious, did you try calling him?'

Buchanan nodded. 'Just goes to voicemail.'

'Oh, Jack,' said Shelly. 'You don't think she's in danger, do you?'

He shook his head. 'I'm sorry, I can't give you a definite answer to that.

'Oh – you don't think,' said Shelly, turning to Travis, 'that she's done something silly, do you?'

'Like what?'

'Like running off to get married.'

'Excuse me for butting in,' said Buchanan. 'This isn't Las Vegas. You can't just run off and get married that quickly in the UK.'

'You can't,' said Shelly, slumping down into a chair. 'Poppy can be so headstrong when she can't get her own way,' she continued, with tears welling up in her eyes.

'Would you like me to get Karen?' asked Buchanan.

'What could she do?'

'Company – a sympathetic ear?'

'Ok,' she said, smiling. 'We're just going down to the library.'

'I'll let Karen know.'

◆

17:55

When he entered their room, Karen was sitting in front of the mirror brushing her hair.

'It must have been a long message?" she said, while looking at his reflection in the mirror.

'George and Lenny have been released on bail and are currently missing. Nobody knows where Victor Mountjoy and Julian Du Marchon are, and finally to add to the missing register, so are Harry and Poppy.'

Karen stopped brushing her hair, put down the brush and turned to look at Buchanan. 'You don't think they've run off to get married, do you?'

'Who, George and Lenny? Or do you mean Victor and Du Marchon?'

'Harry and Poppy, you ninny!'

'Not likely, it takes a minimum of sixteen days from registering before you can get married in the UK. I'll bet they're taking advantage of the fuss about the race this afternoon and have gone off for afternoon tea somewhere. You know how many tea rooms there are around Eastbourne.'

'I suppose you're right. Oh, what did you come back to the room for?'

'I offered your services to talk to Shelly. For some reason she's really shaken by Poppy's disappearance.'

'She's worried about losing her daughter.'

'She shouldn't, we'll soon find her.'

'That's not what I mean. Poppy is becoming a woman, soon to leave home and start her own family. Shelly is sad about losing that intimacy mothers and daughters have before their daughter finds a mate.'

'Ah, I didn't think about that. Can you go and see Shelly?'

'Ok, let me finish my hair, then I'll pop along to their room.'

'Shelly said they were just going down to the library.'

'Where will you be?'

'It looks like my holiday is prematurely ended. With George and Lenny having been let out on bail and Victor Mountjoy and Du Marchon missing, I think I need to go and have another word with Nathan.'

Buchanan said goodbye to Karen and continued along the corridor to the lift. The lift door opened, and Pat and Cynthia stepped out..

'Found that shit of a husband of mine yet, Jack?' Cynthia asked, in passing.

'No, not yet,' replied Buchanan, as he let the lift go without entering. 'Cynthia, before you go, I have a question.'

'Sorry, I'm taken,' she said, smiling at Pat.

Buchanan shook his head. 'This is a serious question.'

'I was being serious.'

'I'm just curious, is Victor capable of violence, or is it all show?'

Cynthia walked over to Buchanan, stood two feet from him and pulled her hair away from the right side of her face revealing a three-inch scar. 'He did this, does that satisfy your curiosity?'

'Thank you.'

Buchanan walked down the stairs and over to the reception desk.

'Yes, Mr Buchanan, can I help?'

'I hope so. I'm looking for Colonel Mountjoy and his friend, Mr Du Marchon.'

'I believe they have left.'

'Did you see what car they were driving?'

'I think the colonel flew out with Mr Du Marchon in his private plane about forty minutes ago.'

'May I use the phone? My mobile battery is flat.'

Buchanan called Hanbury. 'Hi, I've got some bad news, looks like our birds have done a runner – I know it's a crap metaphor. I'm worried that the colonel may have made good on his threat to silence the only witness to their crime – yes, Harry, he hasn't been seen all afternoon – no, not in a car, they apparently left in Du Marchon's plane – yes, it must be nice to afford one. Can you call Air Traffic Control and see if they can see them? Here's the registration: G-YMMM. I'll try the local airfields, see if they've landed somewhere – oh, that's ok, I'm fine working on my own right now; if things get bad, I'll call for help. Talk to you later.'

'Is there anything else?' asked the receptionist.

'Yes. Is Sir Nathan about?'

'I'll check for you,' she said, picking up the desk phone. 'Sir Nathan, Mr Buchanan would like to talk to you – ok, I'll tell him. He said to go through to his office, shall I show you the way?'

'That's all right, I know my way.'

Buchanan knocked on the door and entered.

'Ah, Jack. What can I do for you?'

'Can you tell me what arrangements were made for the light aircraft that are here this week?'

'Thinking of going flying?'

Buchanan shook his head.

'All pilots were advised to arrive with just enough fuel to get them on to a nearby airfield for refuelling.'

'Why can't they refuel here at Castlewood? Gardners helicopter refuels at the back of the warehouse.'

'The strip here at Castlewood is on the golf course and quite short. With full tanks it might make some planes too heavy to get off the ground in time.'

'So, they will need to land somewhere soon and refuel?'

'Looks that way.'

♦

18:05

Buchanan returned to reception and saw a very quiet area. Which wasn't so surprising, he reasoned. The great race was over, all horses had been groomed, fed and watered and their riders were probably now resting and dreaming of what they might have done differently and the ensuing result.

The sound of music drew his attention to the entrance to the ballroom. He wandered over and saw that it was being prepared for the evening's celebrations. The wall dividing the ballroom from the restaurant had been folded back and the tables had been arranged in a large circle round the dance floor. To his right, the band that would be providing the evening's music were going through the playlist.

He was about to leave them to it when the band started playing Marlow's tune. Buchanan leaned against the doorframe, closed his eyes and once again imagined hearing the voice-over from Robert Mitchum as PI Philip Marlow. He was staring out of the hotel window and saying he was getting old, words that were becoming too familiar in Buchanan's life. He left Marlow to his ruminations.

Buchanan walked into the library and saw that Karen, Shelly and Travis were sitting by the window drinking coffee.

'Any news about Harry?' asked Karen.

'No, but don't worry, he and Poppy are probably wandering about the grounds.'

His thoughts were interrupted by the arrival of Cynthia and Pat.

'You know where Victor is?' she said.

'No, I've been told he and Mr Du Marchon flew out about forty minutes ago,' replied Buchanan. 'Do you have any idea where they might have gone to?'

'Yes,' said Cynthia. 'He's just called from Headcorn. He's with Julian, they stopped for a meal and to top up the tanks. But before they could refuel, they had to show proof that they could pay. Apparently Du Marchon couldn't find his wallet, and Victor says his cards won't work.'

'Probably mixed up the pin number once too often,' said Shelly. 'It's easy to do when you are in a hurry.'

'That's not what happened,' said Cynthia. 'As soon as I heard he'd done a runner, I called the bank and said my purse, with all my cards, had been stolen. They put an immediate freeze on all of them.'

'Where exactly is Headcorn?' asked Buchanan.

'Not far from Ashford.'

'What did you tell him?'

She smiled. 'I said what a bother. I told him to wait there and I would call the bank and get back to him.'

'What did he say to that?'

'What he said is unsuitable for repeating in present company.'

'When was this?'

'Three or four minutes ago.'

'Excellent. I'll call Ashford Control and have someone drive over to your husband and arrest him.'

'Really? That's the second-best thing I've heard all day.'

'That's sorted,' said Buchanan, hanging up from his phone call. 'Ashford Control said it's a cross-country drive, but they should have someone there within the next half an hour. I've asked them to return him to the club. I have some questions for him. Cynthia, when you call Victor back, tell him the bank is working on unfreezing the bank cards and they should be useable within the hour.'

'I like you,' she said, taking her mobile out of her pocket.

Buchanan went back over the day's events in his mind as Cynthia called Victor to give him the news about his bank cards.

She breathed out slowly and hung up from the call. 'You know what the rat said when I told him the bank would unfreeze his cards within the hour?'

'I could make a few guesses,' said Buchanan. 'I'll bet he's pissed because now he can't fly to Lucanland?'

'Where's that?'

'My joke. Lucanland is my name for where Lord Lucan disappeared to after he was suspected of killing the children's nanny. What did he say?'

'He said he'd had enough of me and as soon he got the plane fuelled up he was leaving. I said the sooner the better. That really pissed him off.'

'So, they've left George and Lenny in the lurch.'

'They deserve that, especially after what they did to Harry.'

Buchanan smiled as he thought about the cheeky colonel's wife he'd only met a week ago. 'You know something, Cynthia? I really like you. I hope you and Pat get the happiness you both deserve.'

'What does that mean?'

'Make sure Karen and I get an invitation to your wedding.'

'Invitation? I want you to give me away!' replied Cynthia.

'I'd be honoured. I suspect your husband hopes to leave the country, trying to avoid all those people he has cheated. I just hope you and Pat aren't stuck with his debts.'

'Not a chance. I told you the silly fool put everything in my name to avoid paying taxes and having his toys repossessed by the bailiff. I suppose we might end up losing the farm though. But that doesn't matter, it's a bit of a ruin anyway.'

As the waiter arrived to see if they wanted more coffee, Poppy walked across the library to the table.

'Where have you been?' demanded Travis.

'Mom,' said Poppy, tears in her eyes, 'I can't find Harry. I've been to the stables, up to his flat, he's nowhere.'

'You should have called us; we've been worried frantic.'

'Didn't you hear?'

'Hear what?' said Travis.

'Poppy,' said Shelly, 'why don't you come sit by me and tell us from the beginning what happened?'

'After the race was over, I went looking for Harry,' said Poppy. 'I looked in the hospitality tent but, when I couldn't see him, I wandered over to the stables and that was where it happened.'

'What happened?' asked Travis.

'That was when I heard the colonel talking about what they were going to do to Harry.'

'Can you remember when this was and exactly what they said?'

'The colonel was livid, he said he'd lost a fortune and is ruined because of what Harry did to the horses. The other man was egging him on, he said they'd lost everything, and Harry was going to have to pay for it. The colonel said to the short one – I think his name is George – he said no matter what, when they got hold of Harry, they had to silence him. Without his testimony there wouldn't be anything to convict them of fixing the race.'

'Did they say where or when they were going to do this?' asked Buchanan.

'The colonel said as soon as they had Harry, they were to silence him permanently and take him where no-one would find the body. The one they called George shook his head and said no way was he going to do the kid in without proper compensation.'

'I knew they were a bad pair,' said Pat, 'but I had no idea just how bad they were. We've got to do something for the lad before it's too late.'

'What was the colonel's response?' asked Buchanan.

'He said he would take care of the money. He said he was about to go back to his stables and get the cash he'd hidden away for a rainy day, and not to worry as there was more than enough for all of them – but to make sure they got rid of Harry now.'

'That shit,' said Cynthia. 'I knew he was desperate, but not that desperate.'

'Would it be enough for him to take the risk he has?' asked Buchanan.

'Probably, if he was just looking out for himself.'

'So, his cash pot is the money he's taken from friends and what he's raised from borrowing against the value of the farm?'

'Precisely.'

'Poppy, where were you when you heard what the colonel was planning?' asked Buchanan.

'I was halfway up the steps. I was going up to Harry's flat to see if he was there.'

'So, what did you do?' asked Shelly.

'I crept up the stairs to his flat. Part of me wanted Harry not to come back, to just stay away till the colonel and his friends left. The other part wanted to be close to Harry and protect him. I quietly opened the door to his flat, but when I went in all I could see was the mess. It looked like someone had gone in there and ransacked it. I was so worried that Harry might come back any moment and be caught.'

'Did you stay long?' asked Cynthia.

'I was going to wait for him but changed my mind and went next door and waited till it got quiet downstairs.'

'You took a big risk doing that,' said Karen.

'Please, Jack, can't we do something? Standing around here – we can't just leave Harry to be beaten to death,' pleaded Poppy.

'We're not going to do nothing,' said Pat. 'I for one am going out to look for Harry – anyone going to join me?'

'I need to wait here,' said Buchanan. 'I have a patrol car bringing the colonel back to the club.'

'I'll wait with Jack,' said Travis. 'If George and Lenny are involved, Jack might need a backup.'

'Fine by me,' said Pat.

'I'll join you,' said Cynthia. 'Harry deserves at least that.'

'Where will you look?' asked Shelly.

'Everywhere,' said Cynthia, linking her arm through Pat's.

'Castlewood grounds are very large, and it will be getting dark soon,' said Shelly. 'How will you do your search?'

'On horseback. Pat and I will be the Castlewood posse,' said Cynthia.

'Well, if you two are going, so am I,' said Poppy.

'Mind if I join in the search?' added Shelly.

'Time's wasting,' said Pat. 'Let's get on with the search. It will be dinner soon.'

18

Curtain Down

17:55

'Wish you'd gone with them, Jack?' asked Travis.

'I didn't want to dampen their enthusiasm, but I think they're wasting their time if they think they'll find Harry out in the grounds somewhere.'

'Where do you think he might be?'

'I have an idea, but I won't be sure till I have a chat with Lewis.'

'Who's he?'

'He's in charge of security at Castlewood. I'm hoping he can run through the security camera feeds. There might be something there that will help.'

'Do you need my help?'

'Yes, I like to have a backup in these situations. Though it's quite possible Harry's gone into town for something and will show up without a scratch.'

'Well, if you two have the situation in hand, I'll sit here in case Harry or Poppy shows up,' said Karen. 'Jack, make sure you take your phone with you.'

'Will do.'

Buchanan and Travis left the library and walked through to reception and waited while the receptionist took a phone call.

'Yes, Mr Buchanan, how can I help?'

'Have you seen Lewis anywhere?'

'Not in the last hour. Would you like me to call him for you?'

'Yes, please.'

'One minute,' she said, picking up the phone and dialling. 'Hi Lewis, Jackie in reception. There's a Mr Buchanan and a Mr Grant here looking for you. Mr Buchanan would like to talk to you – ok, I'll tell him, 'bye.' She hung up and turned back to Buchanan. 'He said he will be right out.'

'Thanks.'

Buchanan was looking at one of the taxi brochures lying on the counter when Lewis appeared. 'Looking for me, Jack?'

'Yes. I was wondering what sort of CCTV coverage you have here at Castlewood?'

'Pretty much the whole estate. Anything in particular?'

'How about the main entrance for a start?'

'That can be done. Let's go to my office.'

Buchanan and Travis followed Lewis behind the reception desk, past the door to the manager's office, and into the office next door.

'Welcome to my domain,' said Lewis, sitting down on his swivel chair and turning on his monitor. 'Any particular time?'

'Could we start with just after the race ends?'

'Certainly.'

Buchanan and Travis watched the screen as Lewis scrolled through the different camera shots.

'This is the main gate at 15:00, just after the race ended. No gate traffic, but we'd expect that. I'll run the video forward.'

At 15:45 a car exited the gate and turned right.

'Do you know whose car that is?' asked Buchanan.

'That's Harry's car,' said Lewis, looking up at a list of staff car registrations. 'The guest car register is on the right. Want me to keep looking?'

'Yes, now we know Harry left the estate, it would be good to see when he returns.'

It was at 16:00 before there was any further vehicle movement. A bright blue Mercedes exited the gate. Lewis looked up at the list and said, 'That's Cynthia Mountjoy's car.'

Next vehicle to leave was one of the caterer's vans at 16:15. It wasn't till 17:23 that Cynthia's car reappeared on the screen.

'That must be when Du Marchon returned from collecting George and Lenny from Hammonds Drive,' said Buchanan.

Thirty minutes later Harry returned. 'I wonder where he went?' said Buchanan.

'Could he have gone to see where Du Marchon went?' asked Travis.

'Don't think so,' said Buchanan. 'Can we get a close-up of the driver and passengers in Mrs Mountjoy's car?'

'Not from this angle, I'll switch to the main entrance camera.' With a couple of clicks on the mouse, the display on the screen showed Cynthia's Mercedes stopping in front of the entrance to the club. The valet opened the driver's door for Du Marchon while the rear doors opened and disgorged George and Lenny. While the valet drove off to park the car, the colonel came out of the club and the four of them walked out of camera shot.

'Looks like they are headed for the stables,' said Lewis, changing the camera shot to a long view from the stables looking back along the covered walkway.

'Wish we could hear what they are saying,' said Buchanan.

'We could if we were to look in the stables,' said Lewis.

'How?'

'The stable cameras all have microphones fitted,' said Lewis, seeing the puzzled look on Travis's face. 'The microphones are for night security in case a horse gets sick. Or in the unlikely case of a break-in.'

'Makes good sense,' said Travis.

'Do you record sound as well?'

'Yes.'

'How about the night Harry was assaulted?' asked Buchanan.

'I could have a look – that was on what day?' Lewis asked, as he scrolled back through the video files for the stables.

'Late Tuesday evening,' replied Buchanan.

'Just a moment.'

'Looks clear,' said Travis.

'What time should I be looking for?'

'Harry told me he usually does his rounds at about eleven.'

They watched and listened as the sounds of an occasional snort of a sleeping horse disturbed the silence of the night-time stable. The stillness was broken at eleven-fifteen by the appearance of Harry exiting from one of the far end stalls. They watched as he stopped at each stall. At Mercury's stall he opened the door and went in. While he was in the stall the far end door opened and colonel Mountjoy, followed by Du Marchon entered. Du Marchon pulled the door closed behind him then followed the colonel over to the door to the Old Coachman's Lodge.

It took several minutes of banging on the door before it was opened by George.

'What the hell is this?' shouted the colonel. 'I'm paying you to keep an eye on my horses, not spend it sleeping.'

'It's Lenny's turn,' whined George. 'I did my shift earlier.'

'Well, where is Lenny?'

'On the shitter, he's got the trots.'

'Stupid idiot! Go get him out here now, I'm not paying him to sit on his arse.'

Buchanan, Travis and Lewis watched and listened as the colonel and Du Marchon chatted in low voices while they waited for George and Lenny to reappear.

A few minutes later George and Lenny came out of the Lodge, Lenny doing up the belt on his trousers.

'Are you two sure you know what you have to do?' demanded the colonel.

'Sure, we do,' said George, as he tried to recover his composure. 'We do just as we did at Plumpton last year. We paint the white patch on Rambler's forehead and black-out the white patch on

Turpin's forehead, then swap stalls so you can cheat all those stupid punters you've taken money from.'

'That statement is enough to get a conviction and jail term for fraud,' said Buchanan.

'And when do you do this?' demanded the colonel.

'Thursday evening, just after the stable shuts for the night,' said Lenny, looking like he was about to explode.

The colonel looked at him and said, 'Go on, before you shit yourself.'

As they continued to watch, Buchanan said, 'I think this is where Harry gets caught.'

As if on cue, they watched as Harry came out of Mercury's stall and tried to make his way back up the stables while keeping to the shadows. He managed to get four stalls along the stable block before he was seen by the colonel.

'Grab him!' he shouted.

Harry turned to run but was hit on the head with a bucket by George.

'Bring him here,' said Du Marchon. 'Douse him with water, he's no good unconscious.'

'What did you hear?' asked the colonel, as Harry shook his head to stop the water running down his face.

Harry shrugged. 'Nothing, I was looking at the horse's hooves.'

The door to the Lodge slammed as Lenny came out. He looked a bit surprised to see Harry being held by George, but before he could ask what was going on the colonel pre-empted his question.

'Ah, Lenny. You're just in time to help George. Tie the lad's hands, then string him up to that harness hook,' he said, pointing to the hook outside stall two.

Buchanan watched Travis's face as Harry had his wrists bound with bailing string in front of him. He was clenching his teeth; little beads of sweat appearing on his face and his huge fists were balled like a fighter getting ready to enter the boxing ring.

As George grabbed Harry from behind to walk him over to the harness hook, Lenny got a little too close. In a move that would make any centre forward proud, Harry swung his right foot up and hit Lenny in the crotch, sending him convulsing in pain onto the ground.

'You'll regret that piece of stupidity!' said Lenny, getting to his feet as George forced Harry's bound wrists over the harness hook.

Travis gave a groan as Lenny picked up a rope halter and began to whip Harry across the face with the end of it.

The colonel smiled and said, 'Now you know we mean business, maybe you'll be a good boy and answer my question. What did you hear?'

Harry shook his head.

The colonel nodded to George. 'You know what to do.'

Buchanan, Lewis and Travis watched as the colonel kept asking the same question. Harry stolidly refused to answer and was beaten alternately by George then Lenny. After half an hour of severe beating, Harry passed out and when two pails of water refused to waken him the colonel gave the order for him to be thrown into Mercury's stall.

'The horse will finish him off,' said the colonel, as George bolted the stall door leaving an unconscious Harry lying on the floor beside a startled Mercury.

'Now there's a young man I'd be proud to have in my platoon,' said Travis.

Buchanan looked at Travis's face: they were wet with tears.

'Lewis,' said Buchanan, 'I will need a copy of that recording for evidence in the colonel's trial.

'No problem, I'll do a copy right now.'

'What about the stables this afternoon?' said Buchanan. 'We know Harry came back, but he hasn't been seen since.'

Lewis flicked through the screens till he got to the camera that showed the end of the stable block outside the Old Coachman's

Lodge. George and Lenny were standing just outside the door talking to Harry, who'd just come out of stall three.

'They've got balls,' said Travis. 'For all they know, Harry could have remembered who put him in hospital.'

'Right,' said Lewis, 'let's hear what was said.'

'Harry,' began George, 'just had a message from the front desk, your girlfriend is looking for you.'

'What was the message?'

'Something about going for a walk and would like you to join her?'

'Did the desk say where she is?' asked Harry.

George shrugged. 'Something about waiting for you at the end of the car park?'

'Thanks, I'll go and look for her.'

'Do you have a camera for the carpark, Lewis?' asked Buchanan.

'Most of it, let me have a look. Yes, got him, but where is he going?'

'That doesn't make sense,' said Lewis. 'That's going away from the house towards the woods.'

'How long ago was this recorded?' asked Buchanan.

'Fifteen minutes,' replied Lewis.

'What are we waiting for?' said Travis.

Buchanan was a competent walker, but he had to up his pace to keep up with Travis. It took them a further five minutes to arrive at the spot where they'd last seen Harry.

Travis bent down and looked at the ground.

'What are you looking at?' asked Buchanan.

'Footprints, this one is Harry's, and the rest are probably from guests.'

'You can tell that by just looking at the ground?'

Travis nodded. 'My grandfather was a Comanche, he taught me how to track.'

322

'Out on the reservation maybe, but this is a gravel carpark, you won't be able to track here,' said Buchanan.

Travis smiled at Buchanan and said, 'Watch, ye of little faith.' He bent down and beckoned Buchanan to follow his lead.

'These are Harry's, see how they show him walking purposefully across the car park? And these beside the tyre marks? These are the footprints of someone getting out of a car, opening the trunk and taking out a suitcase.'

Buchanan shook his head. 'I see nothing.'

'Look closer,' Travis said, pointing. 'See the pattern of how some of the gravel has been pushed aside? That's the footprints. Those over there that are a bit deeper are the tyre marks.'

Buchanan looked at where Travis was pointing and nodded. 'I do see now that you point them out. Can you tell anything else?'

'Yes. Harry was worried. See the outline of his feet? I'd say he was wondering where Poppy was. Let's follow the tracks and see where they go.'

Buchanan followed Travis as he walked hunched over, reading the trail in the gravel as easily as Buchanan could read a charge sheet. Travis stopped at the edge of the car park and shook his head.

'What's wrong?' asked Buchanan.

'He was indecisive,' said Travis, crouching down to look at the grass. 'By looking at the way the grass has been disturbed, I'd say he was trying to figure out which way to go. Then he took a couple of steps, stopped and bent down to pick something up.'

'How can you tell that?'

'By the way his feet have disturbed the grass. See these prints where he stopped? Then they change as he bends down and his body weight shifts to his toes.'

'I'll take your word for that.'

'I'd say when he got here, there was no sign of Poppy. He looked about and saw something lying on the grass verge –

possibly something of Poppy's. Look, he's stood up and headed off into the woods.'

'I think I can make a reasonable guess of where he might have gone,' said Buchanan. 'When I was out riding on Monday, I came across an old mill building beside a pond. It is currently used by the maintenance staff to store their tractor and other equipment. I had a look round and it didn't look like anyone lived there. Do you want me to show you the way?'

'How about I lead, and you tell me if I'm on the wrong track?'

'Fine by me, but whatever we do we need to hurry, they've got at least a twenty-minute head start on us.'

Travis took a moment to confirm the direction in which the tracks led, then looked at Buchanan, who nodded in agreement. Where was Travis in his head wondered Buchanan, as he followed directly behind. Back in Helmand province looking for a lost soldier? What drove him? Here was a man who had the spiritual responsibility for thousands of church members yet could cry over just one single person he'd only just met.

'If we head straight into the forest,' said Buchanan, 'we should reach Douglas.'

Travis looked at the trail and nodded.

'When we get to Douglas,' said Buchanan, 'we turn left and follow the boulevard up to Ash.'

They had gone fifty yards when Travis stopped and looked down at the tell-tale marks in the grass.

'What's the matter?' asked Buchanan.

'My guess is he heard something – see how his pace shortens? Notice the distance between his feet as he makes a half-turn, most likely looking over his shoulder to see who was behind him. Then – he decides to make a run for it. Look, over there, two sets of footprints emerging from the bushes. They catch up with Harry and a struggle ensues.'

'You can read all that from looking at the grass?'

Travis nodded. 'It probably was those two cretins from the stables, George and Lenny.' He once more consulted the trail. 'Let's go, we may be only twenty minutes behind them, but let's not give them anymore.'

'At the end of Ash, there's a cross track that leads up Oak,' said Buchanan. 'That's where the track goes into the old mill and pond. We go left there, it's about fifty yards ahead.'

'That makes sense,' said Travis, as they turned onto Oak. 'See here,' he said, pointing, 'Harry was struggling to break free, see how the grass is torn up?'

Buchanan followed Travis along the track, nodding his assent each time Travis pointed to the trail ahead.

They stopped where the trail ran off Oak and onto a barely visible track. 'Does this lead to the old mill?' asked Travis.

'Yes, it curves round to the right and ends beside the pond. The old mill is about twenty yards further on. There are trees both sides till you get to the pond.'

'Can we get to the old mill if we stay in the trees?'

'Yes.'

'Good. Here's what I propose. I want you to walk towards the old mill, make it look like you are looking for somewhere to relieve yourself. That should keep them guessing if they see you. Give me two minutes to reconnoitre the place, then come and knock at the door'

'Where will you be?'

'If all goes well, I'll meet you at the front door with Harry.'

'Not sure I think it's a good idea you going in there on your own. But I assume you've done this sort of thing before?'

Travis smiled and said, 'Just what an old soldier needs, bit of rough and tumble to get the juices flowing before dinner.'

'That's not what I had in mind when I set out to find Harry.'

'You want to go knock on the door and ask them to hand Harry over?'

'No,' said Buchanan, shaking his head, 'not quite. I usually call for backup before I kick the doors in, but since backup is still on the way, let's go and see what we can do to rescue Harry.'

'I like you Brits, you've got balls.'

'I'm Scottish.'

'Whatever. Times a-wasting, let's go get Harry.'

Buchanan took three steps away from the cover of the trees, strolled over to the pond and glanced behind him; Travis was nowhere in sight.

◆

18:30

'I just loved the look on Poppy's face when she saw Harry,' said Karen, as she sat in front of the mirror doing her makeup. 'Will Travis get in trouble for what he did to George and Lenny?'

'No. I'll just say, as Travis will in his statement, that George tripped over Lenny and fell down the stairs. A simple case of them being injured while trying to escape.'

'What really happened?'

'I wandered over to the pond like we'd agreed while Travis went round the back of the old mill and in through the door. I meandered around, giving him the time to get in, then I went over to the front door. I was about to try the handle when Travis opened the door and motioned to me not to say a word. He pointed up the stairs, so I assumed that was where George and Lenny were keeping Harry. For someone as big as Travis, he didn't make a sound as I followed him up.'

'How did you feel about that?'

'What?'

'Following someone – you usually lead the charge.'

'I didn't give it a thought – you know something, I bet the men under his command would have followed Travis anywhere, he's such a natural leader.'

326

'Here, let me help you with your tie,' said Karen. getting up from her chair. 'So, what happened? How did you get Harry away from George and Lenny?'

'I tried as best as I could to creep up the stairs behind Travis. Though it wasn't all that necessary because George and Lenny were arguing whether they should wait for the colonel to bring the money before dispatching Harry.'

'What a pair of creeps! There, that should do it,' Karen said, standing back to look at her handiwork. 'So, tell me, how did you two rescue Harry?'

'It was Travis who took care of that. While I was weighing up our options, he just stepped into the room and grabbed them from behind by the necks and threw them into the corner, just like they were a couple of dirty rags. I guess we'll never know what would have happened had I not been there to stop him from doing some real damage.'

'Where was Harry while this happened?'

'Tied to a chair in the corner of the room. You should have seen the look of relief on his face when Travis grabbed George and Lenny.'

'What did you do?'

'I went over to Harry and started untying him, while Travis checked on George and Lenny. When he was satisfied they wouldn't be bothering us, he came over to check on Harry and that was when it happened.'

'What happened?'

'George and Lenny tried to make a dash for freedom. George managed to reach the top of the stairs first but didn't get any further as Travis grabbed Lenny and threw him like a bowling ball at George. They both ended up in a heap at the bottom of the stairs.'

'Are they all right? You don't need to go through another investigation like the one in Glasgow.'

'No permanent injuries. George has a dislocated shoulder and possible fractured leg, while Lenny will never look good in a dress again.'

'What about Harry?'

'He will need some time off work to recover. He was quite shaken to have twice been the subject of George and Lenny's aggression.'

'And Travis?'

'If you listen closely, you'll hear him whistling *Dixie*.'

'Anything on the colonel and Mr Du Marchon?'

'By now they should be on their way back from Headcorn. First thing Monday morning they'll be charged with conspiracy to murder, amongst other things,' Buchanan said, while sliding his arm into his dinner jacket. 'Shall we go down for dinner?'

♦

18:55

Buchanan pulled the door closed behind him and, as he walked along the corridor with Karen, he thought just how fortunate he was to be married to her. As if reading his mind, she turned to him and said, 'C'mon Jack, get a move on, it's not every evening I get to show you off.'

As they turned the corner, they met Pat and Cynthia waiting for the lift. Cynthia was looking resplendent in a figure-hugging shimmering green evening dress while Pat, who Buchanan had never seen in anything other than jockey clothes, looked extremely smart in his tuxedo.

'Good evening Jack – Karen,' said Cynthia, pointing to a notice outside the lift door.

'What does it say?' asked Karen.

'It asks guests to go the main staircase for photographs prior to going in for dinner'.

As the lift descended, Buchanan watched as Cynthia linked arms with Pat then laid her head on his shoulder. Buchanan glanced at Karen, who smiled.

'I just talked to Victor,' said Cynthia.

'Oh, how is he doing?' asked Buchanan.

'Fuming. I told him there was a hiccup at the bank and it might be another hour before the bank cards were reactivated.'

'I imagine he wasn't pleased about that.'

'No. he wasn't. But who cares? I'm going to dinner with my friends, what could be better?'

They exited the lift and joined the queue to have their photographs taken.

'I never realised just how tall Travis is,' said Karen, as they watched Shelly saying something to her husband, irritating the photographer who was trying to set up their photo.

'Two guesses as to who she's looking for,' said Buchanan.

'She's probably looking for Poppy. I expect Poppy's somewhere with Harry,' said Karen. 'Remember the Grants return to the States on Thursday.'

Their photo successfully taken, Buchanan and Karen followed the other guests over to the ballroom.

As they were being led to their table, Buchanan listened to the table talk:

'Isn't that Pat McCall cuddling the colonel's wife? Wonder if he knows …'

'I could have won if I hadn't got thrown at the first jump …'

'I never realised how many falls there have been on the flat this year, and I've heard some courses are now insisting on the jockeys walking the course first …'

'I don't see how they've got time to review hunting with Brexit taking up so much of their time …'

'We were just wondering if Castlewood will be expanding the exercise facilities, it's such a wonderful place to ride …'

'It scared the daylights out of me and Darcy, something should be done about those electric cars and how quiet they are …'

Pat and Cynthia were already seated when Buchanan and Karen arrived at their table.

'Good evening,' said Greyspear to Karen, as Buchanan pushed her chair in.

'Good evening, Nathan. I must say your team have made quite a transformation to the ballroom.'

'Ah yes, thanks. I'm glad you like it.'

As Buchanan reached for his wine glass, his phone rang. He listened for a moment then hung up from his call.

'That was Ashford Control Centre.'

'What is it, what did they say?' asked Cynthia.

'They said that when the patrol car arrived at Headcorn airfield, Victor and Julian jumped back into the aircraft and, before the police could stop them, they took off.

'If they're heading to the farm, they should be landing in about twenty minutes,' said Cynthia.

'Good, if you'll give me the address, I'll call the control centre and ask them to contact the local station and have a patrol car meet them as they land.'

'Suppose they aren't going there?' said Pat.

'I'll call Headcorn tower and see if they know which direction they are heading,' said Buchanan.

He hung up from the call and shook his head.

'What's the matter?' asked Cynthia.

'It doesn't make sense,' said Buchanan. 'Cynthia, you said Victor's farm is near Maidstone, that's due east of Headcorn. So why are they flying south?'

'They must be heading across the channel; Julian's cousin owns a small farm just outside Abbeville,' said Cynthia.

Buchanan shook his head. 'That's not good. Headcorn control said they did not have time to take on fuel.'

'Can the control tower track them?' asked Travis.

'Not as far as the coast – I asked,' said Buchanan. 'I'll call control and ask them to contact Air Traffic and see if they have sight of them.'

Twenty minutes later Buchanan's phone rang. 'They did? How for out were they? Has the coastguard been informed? Good, maybe they made a soft landing. Thanks.'

Seven pairs of eyes looked at him. 'That was my control centre, southern Air Traffic said they lost contact with the plane that Julian and Victor were flying about thirty miles south-west of Brighton. The coastguard has dispatched a search and rescue mission. They also said the weather in the channel is bad and visibility is down to a hundred metres.

♦

19:55

Just as the entrées were being served, Poppy rushed over to the table and exclaimed, 'Look, Mom, look at what Harry has just given me.'

Travis turned and looked at Harry, who was standing back not sure quite what sort of reception he would get at Poppy's announcement.

Nothing was said at the table as Travis got up from his chair and stepped forward in front of Harry. 'Welcome to the family, son,' he said, wrapping his arms around a rather nervous Harry in a bear hug. 'I'm really looking forward to getting to know you better.'

It took Harry a few moments to absorb the news of his acceptance about joining the Grant family.'

'This calls for a toast,' said Greyspear. 'Not only are we celebrating a wonderful outcome of the inaugural Castlewood Cup, but the engagement of Harry and Poppy.' Turning to the ever-present waiter, Greyspear said, 'André, could we have two bottles of the Pol Roger?'

While they waited for the champagne to be brought to the table, Poppy made the rounds, followed by Harry, showing off her engagement ring.

'How do you feel, Harry?' asked Greyspear, when they got back.

'Still a bit shaken.'

'What did the doctor say?'

Harry shrugged. 'He said I should take a couple of weeks off work and rest.'

'Sensible man.'

'I can't. I don't have enough holiday time.'

'Nonsense,' said Greyspear. 'If the doctor says take two weeks off, then take it. Your injuries are work-related, but don't worry, I'll sort it out with Alice in HR.'

'Then, in that case,' said Poppy, 'if Harry is not working, he could come home with us and meet the rest of the family.'

'Perfect,' said Travis. 'We'll get you out on the range and there you'll experience some of the best trail riding ever.'

'If you'll excuse me,' said Greyspear,' I wish to make a short announcement.'

A hush descended on the assembled diners as Greyspear walked through the ballroom, stepped up onto the bandstand and removed the blue velvet cover from the Castlewood Cup.

'Ladies and gentlemen, I would like to thank you all for being here this evening. Now, for the moment all of us have been waiting for, the official presentation of the Castlewood Cup. It is my great pleasure to present this magnificent trophy to the winning jockey,

Mr Pat McCall, who I hope you will agree with me rode a magnificent race on Turpin.'

Pat, all the worse for consuming a little too much champagne, accompanied by resounding applause almost made a straight line over to the bandstand to receive his well-deserved trophy. He was met on his return by Cynthia on her way to collect the owner's and winning trainer's cup plus cheque for fifty thousand pounds.

Buchanan leaned back in his chair and watched as Andrew Jackson went up for his second-place trophy and cheque, followed by Travis Grant for his third-place trophy and cheque. What Buchanan didn't expect was to be called forward to receive a fourth-place trophy and a cheque.

Several of the guests came over to the table to congratulate Pat on his win and also for enlarging the contents of their wallets.

While everyone at the table was dancing, Andrew Jackson invited himself over and sat down beside Buchanan.

'Excuse me, Inspector, while there's no one about I was just wondering what will become of Colonel Mountjoy if he's ever found? What charges would you bring against him?'

'Concerned for your comrade in arms?'

'You might say that. Do you intend to charge him with anything?'

'The main charge will be conspiracy to murder, other charges will follow. Now, let me ask you a question, will he be court martialed?'

'I'd say without a doubt.'

'In that case, would you be defending him?'

'If you bring charges and he is court martialed, it will be my pleasure to provide him with the defence he deserves,' said Jackson, rising as Karen returned from powdering her nose.

'What did Andrew want?' asked Karen, as she sat down.

'Just wanted to know what would happen to the colonel if he was ever found alive.'

'There's not much chance of that, is there?

Buchanan shook his head. 'Recently a young footballer died when the plane he was being flown in, crashed in the channel. The pilot was never found but the body of the footballer was recovered from the aircraft on the bottom of the sea. According to what I read, there was high levels of carbon monoxide in his bloodstream. He probably never knew what happened. He was probably unconscious long before the plane crashed into the sea.'

'How sad. What's in the envelope?'

'Before I tell you, I have a question for you. A couple of days ago, you had something you wanted to say about Harry and Poppy?'

'Oh, that. You remember when we were dating?'

He smiled at the memory. 'Do I well! I used to ride my bicycle all the way over to Rutherglen to see you. What's that go to do with Harry and Poppy?'

'I just thought Harry can't earn much working here at the club and if he goes back to university, he won't have any income at all. How will he be able to afford to fly to Dallas to see Poppy?'

Buchanan smiled and handed Karen the envelope. 'We could give them this.'

She looked inside and pulled out the cheque. 'All of this?'

'Less a donation to the Blue van drop-in centre.'

'Jack, you old romantic, I love you.'

The End

Printed in Poland
by Amazon Fulfillment
Poland Sp. z o.o., Wrocław